DEBAUCHERY
PART I

Debauchery: Part I is a work of fiction.

All names and identifying details are from the author's imagination or are used fictitiously. Any resulting resemblance to any persons living or dead, is coincidental.

Every effort has been made to reference any copyrighted material within this book.

Paperback ISBN: 978-1-7384024-0-3
Hardback ISBN: 978-1-7384024-1-0
Large Print ISBN: 978-1-7384024-2-7
E-Book ISBN: 978-1-7384024-3-4

A *Related Irrelevance Collection*™ publication

Copyright © 2024 by Andy Bramley

Copyright © 2024 *Related Irrelevance Collection*™ by Andy Bramley

All rights reserved.

No portion of this book may be reproduced in any form without explicit permission from the publisher or author, except as permitted by the copyright law.

PART I

ANDY BRAMLEY

Dedicated to everyone who isn't a Tory.

Never forget how much of an embarrassment they made us to the world.

Fuck the Tories.

PART I

ANDY BRAMLEY

dih-baw-chuh-ree (*noun*).

Seduction from allegiance, duty and morality.

PROLOGUE
CONFESSIONAL

The Church of Saint Augustus had always been known for its colourful back catalogue of tragedy. In 1571, Reverend Alastair Gillespie accidentally preached a completely Catholic diary entry to commemorate the birthday of Pope Pius V to a perfectly Protestant congregation. Because of a new order the previous year to persecute all Catholics, as ordered by Queen Elizabeth I, they butchered the good reverend in God's name that same day.

In 1630, the witch trials graced its presence, with twelve members of the church congregation hanged for 'bewitchment'– seventeenth-century code for being female and outspoken.

Thirty years later, in 1666, the Black Death made its way across Europe, killing millions. A well-meaning Reverend Claude Wolf took to hanging the bodies of butchered rats around the chapel to ward off the 'demonic spirits', only to bring the contagion to the entirety of his congregation.

DEBAUCHERY: PART I

In 1704, wood-cutter Cyril Bennett had what is now known as a psychotic episode, killing three people with his axe and barricading himself within the safety of the church.

In 1943, at the height of the Blitz, Liam Garland was fixing damage to the roof during a storm. A freak bolt of lightning struck, ending both his list of chores and his life on Earth.

And most recently, Wanda Sullivan, grandmother of five, slipped on disinfectant she had been using to wash the nave floor in 1968 and broke her hip. The family sued, given that a loose paving stone had contributed to the fall, leaving the church in a state of almost bankruptcy.

The Church of Saint Augustus thus existed as an infamous building for centuries, and as Reverend Peter Stephenson ran down the aisle of his beloved church, little did he know he would be a part of its final, sorry chapter.

The startled reverend focused solely on the small vestry door that lay a stone's throw from the altar ahead of him. The breaking of wood, gushing of blood, and clanging of metal filled the poor man's ears, all encased in a chaotic blanket of demonic sounds and biblical verse. A war was taking place in the reverend's beloved church, and as his frantic mind raced to grasp the situation, a sudden bang tore through the building, and his body immediately fell to the floor.

    He lay for a few seconds, ears ringing and heart pounding. Shaken, he sat up and wiped the sweat from his brow, his face splattered with blood. A thick cloud of dust obscured everything.

The sound of rubble and breaking glass added to the surrounding chaos. The reverend brought forth trembling, blood-soaked hands. He panicked and crawled through debris to seek a moment of sanctuary behind a pew. The harrowing noises around him were unforgiving. As he stared cautiously through a dissipating fog toward the vestry, a lifeless body fell in front of him. The reverend's tired eyes widened in horror as he stared into the cold, faded pupils of the poor soul in front of him. Brushing his grey hair aside, he shuffled further into the chaos, performing a hurried scope of his surroundings as he moved.

Bodies filled the pews from every angle, a blur of people and disarray. Debris from his beloved building had fallen, broken remnants of stained glass laying abstract at his feet. Despite this biblical carnage, something inside urged him to keep going. Whether it was divine instruction or an in-built human urge to survive, he listened to the voice.

The petrified reverend pulled himself up, inhaled, and moved as swiftly as possible through the graveyard of his fallen passion. He stumbled up to the altar, past a huge crucifix which had fallen from its domineering perch above. The figure of Jesus lay in a pool of blood. This macabre reminder to keep faith did little to motivate him. His saviour had fallen once more, and he was truly alone within a mass of sin. *Keep going*. The reverend exhaled and ignored everything his senses showed him: every blasphemous image, every haunting sound, every gut-wrenching smell. He pushed into the final hurdle. A wrinkled hand clung to the iron handle of the vestry door as he fell to his knees.

With his last ounce of strength, he dragged his weakened body through and slammed it shut. He placed any remaining faith in the idea that his body weight alone would keep everything at

DEBAUCHERY: PART I

bay. The reverend rested his head against the door, body covered in dirt and panting for breath. Staring toward a cold stone ceiling, he closed his eyes and whispered The Lord's Prayer. Fumbling through pockets, a small silver crucifix was cradled in shaking hands. His calloused fingers clasped the cross as blood ran down his arms. An abrupt noise hit the other side of the door, causing the reverend to jolt forward in shock. He closed his eyes tighter as whispered prayers turned to panicked cries to the heavens.

An incessant mumbling came within earshot, forcing the reverend back into reality.

"The game is rigged. The game is rigged. It's rigged. The game is rigged..."

He knew the voice immediately, and as his eyes focused on the figure, the reverend saw an old family friend.

"Nicholas? What's going on?" said the reverend, still fragile on the floor.

A man of twenty-nine stood in a leather jacket and jeans. Underneath, the reverend noticed a t-shirt, ripped and sodden with blood. His long hair, usually styled, was messy, falling in front of a blood-splattered face. Devoid of dust and dirt, the reverend could only deduce that his faithless friend had been there for quite some time.

Nicholas' teary eyes were red as he stared blankly at the floor with each step. The reverend felt that Nicholas was only somewhat present as he continued to whisper, "The game is rigged... It's rigged..."

"My boy, are you okay?" the reverend called out cautiously.

"We did everything..." he mumbled, trailing off with every sentence. The reverend could feel stress emanating from Nicholas and listened for any semblance of sanity within his broken friend's ramblings.

"They're everywhere. They're fucking everywhere. I can't even sleep. I can't let my guard down, and they're gone. They'll get me. Fuck!"

"Who will get you, Nicholas?" the reverend whispered.

Nicholas suddenly snapped back into the room and, as he locked eyes with the reverend, blurting out, "Peter!"

Relieved to have his friend's attention, Peter smiled as warmly as possible, considering the circumstances. His friend didn't return the gesture and instead slumped into a chair behind the vestry's desk. Pushing every bit of emotion back, Nicholas said weakly, "Forgive me, Father, for I have sinned..."

Peter had always known Nicholas as a confident and well-put-together man, but now a family friend sat before him, wounded and broken.

"Nicholas, this isn't a Catholic church. I don't offer confessional here, you know this," said Peter gently as he got to his feet, trying to grasp the situation.

Nicholas groaned in pain or exasperation. "Well, can I please *talk* to you? It's all the fucking same, isn't it? Bullshit words for self-satisfaction?"

A second bang against the door came shortly after, as though the entire building shared his frustration. Peter jumped and nodded quickly. "Y-Yes, of course."

Peter's entire body shook. A dilemma of wanting to console a friend but also contain the carnage outside lay in front of him. He took a step towards Nicholas but was interrupted.

"NO! This... This won't take long."

Nicholas looked up at Peter, pressed against the door, and said forlornly, "I'd like to confess the sin of... everything. I've done... everything."

DEBAUCHERY: PART I

"What are you talking about, Nicholas? You can tell me what's going on. Why has this hell entered my church? Is this you? This *can't* be you, surely?" Peter stopped shaking and stood transfixed by Nicholas, who struggled even to sit up. Blood fell from his fingers, dripping down the arm of the chair and to the floor.

"I'm so tired..." said Nicholas, his eyes watering.

"Nichol—"

"No! Don't make this harder than it already is! The truth is... I brought this here. Everything out there is exactly where it needs to be, not that it would matter, anyway. It'd just happen somewhere else..." His voice tapered off into a sigh, soon broken by yet another bang against the old wooden door.

Peter's caring nature took hold as he attempted to disregard the havoc outside. He surrendered the dog collar and became the friend Nicholas had always known. He slowly took a step towards Nicholas and then another, desperately trying to reach out and comfort the wreck of a young man who he had known for so long.

"Nicholas, we all have trials at some point, and some are worse than others. Today we got pretty unlucky, my boy." Peter smiled nervously. Nicholas returned the favour, albeit out of politeness.

"Do you remember when I was little and I saw you at the beach?" Nicholas whispered, causing nostalgia to sweep over Peter.

"I had an ice cream cone. I don't even like fucking ice cream," he said. Peter smiled, warmed by the memory, as Nicholas continued.

"We were on that beach all day. Then I saw you. You were with your wife in a t-shirt and swim shorts, walking through my field of shit sandcastles."

A metallic bang threw them back into reality. Peter's heartbeat quickened as the scream of a woman came from behind the door. It was a gut-wrenching and visceral sound, but Nicholas simply kept staring at the floor, immune from anything outside this tiny pocket of calm.

"Do you remember what you said to me that day?" Nicholas said, looking up at Peter. His eyes shone green and hopeful beneath all the pain.

Peter smiled and put a shaking hand on the desk next to Nicholas. "You asked me if I could make you like ice cream because all the other kids thought you were weird."

Nicholas laughed, the creases in his face forcing out a tear. It was the first time he'd laughed truly and genuinely for so long.

"I believed that if you helped people in church, you could do something as simple as make me like ice cream... It was a kind of faith, I guess... But a faith in you. It was what you said that stuck with me. You said, *'Being weird is one of the best things you can be. You can only be yourself'*."

He paused for a moment and, with a shaky voice, said quietly, "I just want to say thank you. Thank you for telling me that. I mean... There's just so much of me which doesn't seem to fit..."

Peter smiled. "Then don't fit."

This gentle reassurance brought Nicholas to tears. Peter held his hand, ready to comfort him, but stood and let him drain the emotion that had been building in his soul for so long. A minute or two passed with a young man crying in front of an old friend. A strange bubble of therapy and solace encased the tiny room. However, calamity was calling, trying harder and harder to break through. After some time, Nicholas composed himself as best he could and stood up from behind the desk to look directly at Peter.

"Thank you for letting me know I am accepted. It's the best

DEBAUCHERY: PART I

gift any person can give another. Invaluable..." He trailed off before continuing. "You're the purest, nicest person I've ever met. Which is why..."

Nicholas fell silent as he reached into his coat pocket. A scratched handgun appeared, and immediately any feeling of comfort and serenity dissipated. Nicholas shakily aimed the gun at near point-blank range towards Peter's forehead.

"N-Now Nicholas! This isn't the way! This is the wrong thing to do! Please, my boy! You know I have a family!" Peter put his hands up and went as far back against the door as he could, choosing to risk sinking into chaos than be in this scenario.

Nicholas stammered to speak under the weight of his emotion and replied, "I'm so... fucking... sorry." He removed the safety, took a deep breath and whispered, "The Devil made me do it."

Peter looked straight into Nicholas' red raw eyes and said softly, "I'll pray for you."

Nicholas lowered the gun for a second, only to adjust his grip with both hands and raise it once more. Shaking, he choked out the words, "Please do," before pulling the trigger to give Reverend Peter Stephenson the silence he had so desperately prayed for just moments ago.

The reverend's body slumped to the floor, a pool of blood forming around his head like a gruesome halo. Nicholas' face cracked and his bottom eyelid flickered, trying desperately to fathom the reality he had created in front of him. It was too much, and as a frantic knocking on the vestry door became more frequent, Nicholas raised the gun to his head. The chaos had found him, and it was calling his name.

He choked on the tears, struggling to breathe from the weight of the emotion escaping his fractured soul. His body could not function, and his mind had broken. He simply found reality unbearable.

Nicholas turned to a small window, and through the frosted glass, he saw the postcard image of a normal sunny day. Cold metal rested delicately against his skull as he whispered, "Praise Satan," before pulling the trigger once more.

Seven months earlier…

STEPHANIE SHAW stared at a reflection of greatness in her vanity table mirror. Platinum blonde hair cascaded down her neck, flawless and lush, to rest gently on her shoulders. The bright glow of a ring light illuminated an image of perfection. Here sat an influencer radiating beauty, confidence and a fiery passion. Destiny had so many special things planned for her; she knew it. An unfortunate phone call was only twenty minutes away. She smirked, ready to burn another bridge. It was never his fault; she had simply grown bored with him. Her blue eyes shone bright, flickering with glee as she saw the only person she needed right in front of her. She was divine – an authentic example of a goddess on Earth who could change the world if she wanted.

Now just wasn't the time…

Stephanie had always felt it deep within her heart, but she never questioned what this feeling was.

It had only ever been

1
PRIDE COMES BEFORE A FALL

The opening of '99 Red Balloons' by Nena filled the world alongside a blanket of rain. A September gloom had lingered for the past few days, and as Stephanie Shaw lowered neon pink headphones from her ears, she whispered, "Fuck." A single unfortunate task bounced around a peroxide-blonde brain.

She was a thin woman of twenty-nine, wearing a white tank top and denim shorts. Her bright blue eyes were tired, and mascara ran down her cheeks into an ever-growing puddle of rain at her feet.

Steph sighed and dialled a number on her phone like the chore it had become. With the phone to her ear, a man picked up almost immediately.

"Hey Steph, what's up?"

"Everything," She sighed as she inspected her manicure.

"Okay, so what's everything? And why are you outside? Isn't it raining?"

"A guy… and yeah, I don't want my family to hear this. You know what they're like."

"Well, that's only one thing, so I don't think you need to worry too much about one guy. What's he done this time?"

"He's neglecting me. I need to end it, but it's soooo difficult." Steph's voice shook. "He's just so hot and ginger."

There was a pause as she sighed again, moving damp hair from in front of her eyes.

"Steph, if you don't think it's right for whatever reason, you need to do what's best for you. You can't stay with someone just because they're hot. If you don't feel you're getting enough from this relationship, you need to end it. Now stop using me to stall. I've booked today off to play a new game, so make the call and I'll speak soon, okay?"

"Okay. Thanks Isaac, I'll see you soon." Steph smiled right until she hung up. A frown and an eye roll ensued as she mumbled, "Selfish knobhead, leaving me for a game. I wasn't stalling."

With the call over, Steph was alone again. She moped in the rain, feeling both grossly hard done by and over everything. It was all just so unfair. The rain was unforgiving, and every second she stood out there meant her hair got worse, yet she secretly relished the melodrama.

Huffing to herself, she dialled a second number on her phone, one that she had memorised. It had to be done so she could finally end the injustice she was suffering. The phone rang three times before a familiar voice picked up. His voice felt like home, but Steph was ready to move out.

"Hey babe, you okay?" said the voice.

"Hey Noah, not really. I need to talk to you."

"Oh, okay… Well, me too."

Confused, Steph's mind raced. *What could he possibly want to talk about?* She pushed for an answer, replying, "Okay, you go first."

"No, you go first," said Noah, standing his ground.

DEBAUCHERY: PART I

"No, *you*," Steph hissed.

"Okay, well…"

"Yes?"

"You're too much, Steph. I can't do this anymore. To be honest, I'm tired of your selfishness."

Both parties fell deathly silent, with rainfall quickly becoming an unwelcome soundtrack. As she seethed, a shadow descended over Steph's eyes, focusing her rage on a soggy cat opposite, hoping it would spontaneously combust. Noah's voice returned as he attempted to save himself from the meteor of rage hurtling towards him.

"Look, I know this must be hard to hear, and I don't want to hurt you. This wasn't how I wanted it to end, but this was the best time to do it. I have so much going on, and you're too much. The money, the parties, the amount of attention you need. I knew that a relationship with an influencer would be a lot of effort, but I didn't realise you needed so much attention. I feel like I'm only here to help you edit your videos and be a trophy."

Steph somehow inhaled and erupted in the same breath. "I'm too much? What does that even mean? I was only ringing to ask if we could meet up more!" She knew the latter was a lie, but wanted to shiv this garbage person with guilt. "I have been sitting here, waiting for you for FOUR DAYS! FOUR! How can I deal with this type of long-distance relationship? I know you want time to yourself, but this is just ridiculous. What about me? I only have my fans, but they're not even people! They're just numbers! NUMBERS, NOAH!"

The voice on the other end groaned. "Look, I need time for me. I spend all my money on you and I've put up with your shit for *way* too long. I've tried for so long to explain this and fix us, but honestly, you're a bully and you just won't listen—"

"I'M NOT A BULLY, YOU LITTLE CUNT! I never get anything I want, and I do so much for you! YOU can't break up with ME! Who will edit my videos?"

She started pacing back and forth, clothes sodden from the continual rainfall, yet warmed by white-hot fury burning within her chest.

"But Steph—"

"Don't you 'But Steph' me!" she shouted, making several curtains at the bottom of the street open ever so slightly. Steph caught the eye of one unfortunate onlooker, who promptly retreated out of view. Huffing, she stomped over to the house and opened a small squeaky gate, shouting, "Oh, you want a show? I'll give you a fucking show!" With one hand holding her phone, Steph began slapping a small bush with her free hand. The only thing she accomplished was giving her new-found ex a window of time to hang up. She realised this a few seconds later and screamed.

Six minutes passed with Steph trying to strangle an innocent circular shrub before she withdrew from the stranger's garden. Back in the middle of the street, she shook with anger. Her lip quivered as she looked at her phone; it read 5:46 pm.

How has my life come to this? What made me sink so low? Why the hell is my phone not as waterproof as first advertised? These were the thoughts sitting under sodden blonde hair. There was, however, one grim fact which came to mind, taking precedence over them all: *I'm single.*

Steph hated that word. It suggested lack of attention, loneliness and dying alone. It was too much. She opened the floodgates and cried, releasing every bit of hurt and woe that had built up inside for the last few minutes. Steph's sadness drenched Coultas Close

DEBAUCHERY: PART I

more than the rainfall ever could and gave quite a show to the brave souls who dared peer through their curtains a second time.

Ignoring them, Steph thought, *I need Adrian*. She started a journey to her best friend and the only man left on Earth she knew who wasn't total scum.

As Steph made her way out of the street, she noticed several kids playing on a football field opposite the road. She walked over and remembered what it was like to be young. To have no interest in men, no bills, and no pressure from six million adoring fans. She smiled, reminiscing fondly and failing to notice that she'd stepped out onto the road.

A vision of an oncoming car threw Steph back into adulthood and almost into hospital as a driver with good reflexes slammed down his break. She stared at the young man who wound down his window and shouted, "I know you're probably doing a walk of shame right now, sweetheart, but can you not plaster it over the fucking road?"

"FUCK YOU!" Steph barked as she walked across the road, shaken and embarrassed. The man aimed a middle finger in her direction and sped off.

Her heartbeat returning to a normal pace, Steph continued her pilgrimage across the football field and through a seemingly endless array of streets. She drifted in and out of daydreams, balancing on the kerb edge and jumping into puddles, trying to reclaim her youth with little success. She merely felt stupid and single.

The abrupt noise of a horn caused Steph to spin around and see a lorry tearing through the rain. A cascade of water splashed up the kerb, forming a wave which now pursued her. She panicked, body flailing as she ran directly ahead instead of simply stepping to the side.

She stopped and turned around to face her fate. She shouted some incoherent sound, only to be slapped in the face by a harsh torrent of rainwater in return.

Steph waved her hands in front of her to prevent herself from crying and, by some miracle, it worked as she gained the confidence to show a weak smile, thinking to herself, *It literally can't get any worse.* At that moment, a football came hurtling towards the back of her head. As it physically smacked the smile from Steph's face, her hair exploded into a blonde matted mess.

"Sorry, lady!" came the voice of a child in a tracksuit. He smiled sheepishly as he grabbed the football before returning to his friends. Steph didn't even bother to turn around, instead standing silent for a moment before taking a deep breath and screaming. The sound echoed, spooking several birds in nearby trees. Feeling somewhat cleansed, she continued her journey.

After what seemed like forever, Steph finally turned the corner of Walker Road. She'd known her friend since college, and the sight of his bright red car was always a welcome one.

A white cat emerged from under the car when she opened the gate to number 66. He was Sylvester. This short-haired furball remained the largest, most masculine cat Steph had ever known. He meowed proudly as he strolled toward Steph, giving no thought to the rain. Sylvester had a penchant for trying to crawl up her skirt every time she was around, and today was no exception.

"Ohh, hello. No, no… All right, that's enough…" Steph said as she picked up the furry hornball and, to his dismay, put him to one side.

Despite being mentally drained and cold, Steph still found

DEBAUCHERY: PART I

the energy to fling the front door open dramatically.

"Okay, I'm here!" Steph announced, almost knocking out her friend's housemate, Harry.

Harry was a socially awkward nerd with greasy brown hair. He stood in sweatpants and a grey hoodie, and had several bracelets around his wrist in varying shades of grey and turquoise. His origin was unknown to Steph. He'd been around for so long that she assumed he was a feature of the house, like a conservatory or a bidet. The only thing Steph really knew about Harry was that he had a wealth of emotion towards her, yet was penniless when it came to expressing it.

"Hello. Where's Adrian?" said Steph.

"You're wet," Harry replied immediately.

She looked at him blankly. "Yes? It's raining."

"Oh."

The two stood for a moment without speaking, before Steph eventually broke the silence. "So… Where's Adrian?"

Harry merely pointed toward the stairs.

She smiled feebly and stepped forward, but found that whichever direction she moved, Harry moved too. They exchanged apologetic glances and unnecessary bodily contact before Steph finally broke free and headed upstairs.

She entered a total pigsty. Crisp packets, empty plates, dirty cups, and several half-eaten bars of chocolate lay strewn across the carpet, a monument to quiet nights in. Within this, her best friend sat on a large plum-coloured beanbag, lost within an even larger TV.

Adrian Hader was the lead singer of Acid Lobotomy Demonic Lacerations, aka the greatest death metal band this side of Yorkshire. A tall, black, slightly muscular man, Adrian's body was adorned with tattoos, two of which were sleeves running right down to ringed fingers. An adventurous snake slithered upward, from a chest tattoo and up to his throat. Band sigils, skulls, snakes and flames tore their way across an inked canvas; a declaration of love for all things loud. Black, twisted dreads fell over his shoulders. By day, a clean, tied-back unit; by night, a sweaty, thrash metal mess. Amongst this cacophony of the alternative, Adrian had kind hazel eyes and a warm heart, which was all Steph had ever seen. She smiled at the sight of him.

After a moment, Adrian's deep voice finally acknowledged her with a simple, "Hey, you alright?"

"Hey, how have you been?" Steph asked out of politeness, but it fell on deaf ears. She moved over to his bed, frowning at every bit of rubbish as she moved. Sinking into a pile of empty pizza boxes, Steph salvaged a section of the duvet. Sodden, she slumped against the wall, drained and drowned out by noise.

Adrian extended a tatted arm to grab a remote, turning down the volume of the TV without looking.

"Check out my new TV. This thing's awesome; the picture quality and sound are quality, mate! Have you seen this, Steph?... Steph?"

Adrian finally unplugged himself from the TV and turned to see his friend sitting with matted hair, tears in her eyes and a pouty lip. He put down the controller and sprung to his feet to join Steph. He hugged her, only to pull back with a frown. "You're wet."

"Ugh, I've been through this with Harry," Steph groaned.

"Sorry, tell me what's up." He put his arm around her, and she held one of several rings on his fingers gently.

With attention finally on her, Steph took a deep breath and began.

DEBAUCHERY: PART I

"Noah's cancelled. He dumped me! My own boyfriend! HE dumped ME! This is literally the worst thing I've ever had to deal with in my entire life. Everything is literally so unfair right now! He broke up with me in the street like I was a whore! He wasn't even there! I was in the street, Adrian! I was in the street being rained on like a stupid whore, and he was sitting on his phone inside and not being rained on!

He said that I was selfish and dramatic! Me? He said that I've become too much effort and that I'm self-absorbed and it was getting in the way of his life. I hate him! I hate him so much! Who's gonna edit my videos now?" She sobbed for a moment before talking through tears, "A-And there was this lorry that splashed me a-and these boys threw their balls at me a-and you wanna know the worst part?" She looked at him with shining blue eyes and whispered, "I had to do all this in flats..." She covered her mouth, ashamed of the wicked confession that had just left her lips.

Adrian smiled as he hugged her. "It'll be okay."

"FLATS, Adrian! I could've worn any other shoe!" Steph wailed.

"Fuck's sake, Steph! I don't mean the bloody flats, I mean life! You're gorgeous, and guys are always falling over themselves to get with you."

"You really think so?" Steph said in the most artificially coy tone he'd heard yet.

Adrian smiled. "I really think so. Do you wanna stay over? We can get pizza."

Steph exhaled and stared at the pizza boxes for a moment. "Yeah, now that I've seen those, I kinda want one. I need to change. Can I wear one of your t-shirts?"

"Sure, and which pizza do you want?"

Steph jumped up and turned around to get changed. She had always had very little issue with flaunting herself in front of people, and Adrian was no exception.

"Oh, I dunno, I'm still a vegetarian…" She pulled the wet top over her head and a muffled voice continued, "So like chicken, or I dunno?"

Adrian got up off the bed. "Steph, you know chicken isn't what veggies eat, right?"

"I know," she said as she threw one of his many band t-shirts over her head. "But chicken doesn't count."

She lifted her hair from within the t-shirt and beamed at him. Her smudged makeup and messy hair made Adrian smile.

"Chicken it is, mate," he said before making the call.

Steph removed her skirt, grabbed some boxers from his drawer and put them on, praying they were clean before slumping into the giant beanbag. It was warm and fluffy; she was dry and happy. As she sank into the floofy goodness, she stared around his room.

Three of the four walls were covered in band posters from obscure stoner-rock bands and Adrian's metal idols. The entire space echoed the sentiments inked onto her friend's skin. The remaining wall paid homage to his band, which remained the crowning glory of his life to this day.

Steph threw her head back and stared at the ceiling, musing over how dedicated Adrian was to his singing and how similar she felt about her social media presence. One day she would be the world's most popular makeup artist; she was sure of it. She smiled and returned her focus to Adrian, who had conveniently finished the call.

"Right, they'll be half an hour. Do you want a brew? Milky tea, right?"

DEBAUCHERY: PART I

"Yes, please," Steph said softly.

"Okay, go on a game if you want," Adrian said as he left the room.

Now alone, Steph stretched as she sat up and looked at the TV. She ejected his current game disc before placing it on the top of the console in an act of gaming blasphemy. Wobbling up from the comfort of the beanbag, Steph stared at his games collection.

She reached for a racing game, and a wire caught her eye. Intrigued, she followed it to discover it was connected to a small camera housed between the mess of the bottom shelf. "Meh," she said and grabbed her game of choice. Slumping into the beanbag once more, Steph watched the TV with feigned enthusiasm. The door slowly creaked open, and a familiar miaow came from behind it. Sylvester strolled in, and Steph exhaled as the damp white cat sat cleaning himself beside her. With a vague knowledge of how to play, Steph picked up the controller and hoped this would be one of the rare games she actually enjoyed.

The title screen blasted from the TV speakers, making Sylvester jump abruptly into the air. Steph fumbled for the remote, turned it down and proceeded to pick the only pink car as Adrian returned holding two mugs.

"Here you go," he said as he put the mug down next to her. He plonked himself on the floor next to Sylvester and smirked. Steph grinned as WRONG WAY! filled the TV screen.

Adrian watched her for a race or two before joining her, and they wasted the night playing games, eating pizza and pushing a damp cat away from Steph's groin.

The two friends chatted into the early hours, discussing life, relationships and everything in between. Steph was elated. No longer feeling painful heartache, Adrian's friendship was the therapy she needed.

No longer did Steph feel single. She felt free.

DIET LIFE

An alarm taking the form of "Fuck Me Pumps" by Amy Winehouse filled Lily Finley's room at 4:30 pm. A brown pixie cut emerged from under a duvet, followed by a pair of hazel eyes, which opened reluctantly. She caught sight of her work clothes, which waited for her on a chair opposite. An evening shift beckoned, taking the form of sensible black trousers, a white shirt and a garish lemon-yellow fleece with a name tag on it. She groaned into her pillow, raised an arm to her phone and set it to snooze.

The sound of "Fuck Me Pumps" by Amy Winehouse filled Lily Finley's room at 4:45 pm. Her eyes opened a little less reluctantly as they caught sight of her work clothes, which called for her to fall into adult life. The evening shift taunted her. She felt annoyed, stuck an arm out of bed and set her phone to snooze for a second time.

"Fuck Me Pumps" once again filled the room at 5:00 pm. Her work clothes looked at her impatiently. She sighed and stuck an arm out from under the sheets, this time to turn off her alarm. She then tilted the screen towards her, declaring, "Shit, I'm late!"

DEBAUCHERY: PART I

before leaping out of bed.

Lily threw work clothes over her skinny body, covering up a tattoo of a string of butterflies on her leg, and ran to the bathroom. She scrambled to the mirror above the sink as a mess stared back at her. Still slightly dazed, she picked up a hairbrush and attempted to tame a rebellious pixie cut into something approaching presentable.

Running back into her bedroom, Lily frantically searched for her work shoes. She salvaged one from the war zone under her bed, but the other was missing in action.

Much like its inhabitant, Lily's room existed in a constant state of fatigue. Fallen posters rested gently against the skirting board. A calming dreamscape of pastel blue walls contrasted the floor, which could barely be seen. A defeated wardrobe sat sadly in the room's corner, spilling its guts in a cascade of clean clothes. This pattern continued across the floor with a graveyard of dresses, jeans, tops, and underwear. A lone unworn/unwanted floor-length black gown was on a hanger clinging desperately to the edge of a mirror. Her clothes coexisted in harmony alongside a micro-kingdom of week-old plates and cups.

Lily traversed the bombsite for ten minutes looking for her shoe, to no avail. Emerging from a mountain of unwashed t-shirts, she cast her eyes to a wonky clock above. She had forty-five minutes to get to work with one shoe and a hastily brushed pixie cut.

"Shit!" she said, springing to her feet and throwing on the garish yellow fleece.

Lily bolted from her room and down the small hallway adorned with photos of better times. Her long-suffering housemate Heather sat eating cereal in pyjamas whilst watching cooking programmes.

Heather knew her housemate had lost her shoe because she had been passing occasional glances at it between mouthfuls of cereal. It had been upgraded to the position of doorstop for most of the day before, and gone unnoticed by Lily since she had put it there after her last shift. Heather sighed, moving bright blue hair from her face. If it wasn't a shoe, it was a sock, a bra or sometimes even her trousers. Regardless, it was the same frantic ballet of bad timekeeping as always. Apathetic to her friend's cause, Heather's attention stayed fixed on the TV.

"Heather! Heatheerrr!" came Lily's usual pleas as she desperately looked in drawers, under the coffee table and on top of a small piano demoted to a bookshelf. From within her self-made chaos, she turned and ran face-first into the door, the sudden bang making Heather's bowl shake. As she fell to the floor, Heather said with a mouth full of cereal, "Door."

"Gee, thanks," Lily said, clambering to her feet and moving to the kitchen.

Both she and Heather had loved the open plan area of their apartment so much because they saw it as an overblown book nook. A creative space for ideas to flourish. However, Lily quickly realised after the fourth day of slamming bread into the toaster while half-dressed, simultaneously trying to boil the kettle and brush her teeth, that she wasn't as disciplined as the building made her out to be. She merely stood tense, staring at the toaster, hoping she could toast the bread via willpower alone. She hated being busy because it made her stressed, but she was only ever stressed because her version of being busy just meant being late.

After three painfully slow minutes, Lily gave up and cancelled her dreams of toast, instead choosing to chow down on warmed

DEBAUCHERY: PART I

bread. She grabbed a knife, buttered it, and made her way to the sofa, leaving a trail of crumbs as she walked.

Lily parked herself next to Heather on an old grey sofa, moving a pile of books penned by the great Gertrude Perkins. The two sat silently for a moment as Heather blindly put spoonfuls of cereal in her mouth, still fixated on the TV.

"You late again?" she said, not breaking eye contact from the screen.

"Yeah," Lily replied, more or less inhaling her toast.

"Did you tidy up in the kitchen?"

"Yeah…"

There was a flicker of calm in the room until Lily looked at her phone and saw it was 5:30 pm.

"Shit!" Lily said, jumping up and covering her friend with crumbs. She ran through to grab her phone from her room and slammed the apartment door shut. Glorious silence filled the air as Heather stood up. It lasted for an entire minute before Heather saw the mess in the kitchen, exclaiming, "FOR GOD'S SAKE, LILY!"

At least she's cleaned her room for once, Heather thought, comforting herself. She left the kitchen and made her way towards her bedroom, making the mistake of catching a glance inside Lily's bedroom door. "OH FOR GOD'S SAKE, LILY!"

Lily leapt down the stairs of her apartment and out the front door to be greeted by the prospect of the same miserable journey to work she'd taken for the last six years of her life. She sighed before making her way down the front path and up Scaife Street. Her dull neighbourhood comprised a football field and a line of shops with strips of concrete in between. She made her usual monotonous journey, staring up at the usual tired bus shelter.

The same slanted red bar attempting to be a seat beckoned her inside. Resting her rear on her usual spot, Lily was grateful to be out of the seemingly endless rain.

She stared at the world around her. It was Sunday teatime, and the roads were quiet. Her frantic need to arrive at work was dulled by the sight of calm. The few cars which drove by caught her eye occasionally, and she stared at the small worlds within. A white car passed by, housing a woman with pink hair applying lipstick in the rear-view mirror. A blue car adorned with several red 'L' plates had a seventeen-year-old driver who slowly learnt he could change gears without stopping to look at them. Moments later, a bright yellow car crawled by, driven by an elderly man and a parade of angry drivers tailgating behind.

Then, from the corner of her eye, she noticed a young woman with blonde hair on the opposite side of the road. She looked wet and upset. Lily watched the girl suddenly break into a sprint as a lorry and a large torrent of water eventually came into view. The girl ran as fast as she could, but it was in vain. She got splashed by this massive wave of water, leaving her standing there drenched and still.

The pure theatre of it all made Lily laugh, just as a red double-decker bus pulled up in front of her, signalling a premature curtain down on her show. A group of teenagers got off the bus as she stepped on. She asked for her ticket from a disgruntled driver and walked down the near-empty bus to take a seat near the back. She slumped into it, getting as comfortable as she could before pulling out some earphones and plugging herself into some music via her phone.

Lily's fellow bus dwellers were a mum trying to prize a tablet from her son, a large child covered in chocolate, a woman with

DEBAUCHERY: PART I

seemingly insane spending habits and a teenager whose entire personality seemed to revolve around chewing gum. The bus took its usual route past houses and takeaways. Every so often, it would stop for more dampened passengers to shuffle aboard.

As the bus filled up, people walked towards the seat next to Lily, only to sit on the opposite side, leaving her both relieved and insulted that no one had joined her. Lily's attention eventually waned once again as the bus continued its route. Five minutes later and without warning, the driver hit the brakes. She peered down the aisle to see what had happened, only to hear the driver screaming obscenities out of his tiny window to a person she couldn't see. The offending car sped off and the slam of the tiny window could be heard. The drama slowly settled, and business as usual resumed. After what seemed like an age, Lily finally pushed the button to leave the bus. It was nearly 6:45 pm as she stepped back into the rain. She removed her earphones and stuffed them into her fleece pocket as she headed towards a supermarket where she knew a storm was brewing inside.

Giant letters on the front of the building spelt HUGE in the same garish yellow as Lily's fleece. She looked to the floor as she walked. The words became intimidating, as though they knew she was a completely unreliable employee. She hurried through the entrance, smiling timidly at the staff at the kiosk, and went through a *Staff Only* door. Running up the stairs to a locker room, Lily threw her phone inside the locker and grabbed a bright yellow name badge with her name spelt *Liily*. In an instant, she went from human woman to retail drone. Rushing downstairs, Lily tried to switch her mindset as fast as possible, ready to engage with the general public.

The warm air of the shop floor hit her alongside cold, hard

capitalism, which echoed from the speakers above.

"Now on at HUGE, a crate of ten-thousand tea bags is reduced from £160 to £159.90! Thank you valued customers of Earth and always remember; a HUGE customer is a happy customer!"

Promotional deals rattled in her skull with a metallic monotony as she journeyed to the chilled section. Fake-smiling her way through the aisles, Lily's face reset to a forlorn retail gaze which could only ever be translated as, *how am I here yet again?* Her job didn't quite sink to the depths of labour camps in North Korea, but the constant addressing of supermarket patrons via loudspeaker did little to inflame Lily's lust for life.

Lily finally arrived at 'Designated Area A' and sighed as her eyes met with a tall trolley cage filled with an array of refrigerated goods. She stood next to it and stared through the bars, knowing that this was her supervisor's psychological warfare in action. Lily pulled the cage door open and began unloading tubs of coleslaw unenthusiastically.

Twenty minutes of uninterrupted replenishment allowed Lily's mood to lift. *Perhaps I'm not in* THAT *much trouble.* She turned to the fridges, happy at the potential of a quiet, solitary shift.

Her dreams of retail mundanity were cut short moments later as a stern "Hello Ms Finley," sounded out. Lily's lukewarm attitude manifested as a singular, chilled sigh.

"Hello," Lily said blankly as she turned to face the six-foot-five behemoth manager of the chilled aisles, Mark Barker. He stood with tired eyes and greasy-looking hair in a pink shirt. A name tag was proudly clipped at eye level so everybody knew exactly who he was. A black pen poked out from its snug within his breast pocket. Hairy arms folded, Mark tilted his watch to face her. His lips released a thin smile. Red tape, bureaucracy and black coffee

DEBAUCHERY: PART I

were his lifeblood, and as Lily locked eyes with him, he broke into one of his infamous speeches, pacing as he spoke.

"Lillian, I see this shop as an anthill. Simple on the outside, but very complex and busy on the inside. We are all the worker ants and every one of these ants have a simple, inescapable choice of stability and strength over chaos. They are needed to build a strong and stable business which will continue functioning with precision and remain oven-ready for the future. HUGE must be trusted to deliver. We need a clear plan and bold action to secure our future. Do you understand what I'm saying, Lillian?" He stopped pacing and looked at her.

"Yes," replied Lily quietly, staring at the last box in the cage.

"Well, it would seem, Lillian, that you are nearly one hour late, doesn't it? I run a tight ship here, this is not a fun house, and we can't go on like this. Do you understand what I'm saying, Lillian?"

"This is definitely not a fun house," said Lily flatly.

Mark frowned but continued. "Look, I don't want to be the bad guy. We're definitely all friends here, but you have to think of the implications of the business if you continue to be late. You're not just letting yourself down, you're letting the team down."

Lily remained silent.

"Improve your work ethic, Lillian. It's very important that you do. I think it's quite a reasonable thing to ask, considering that this is the job you're paid to do. Do you understand what I'm saying?"

"Yes," Lily whispered.

"I'm going to need to hear that again, Lillian. We all need to have a team spirit or this ship will sink."

"YES!" Lily barked, making Mark's eyes widen. Her body ached to ask whether they were in an ant colony, a funhouse or a boat, but she chose silence.

"Well then, please continue. You have four more cages after that one," he said before confidently strolling away, hands behind his back, his silver watch shining under strip lighting.

Lily's mood had fallen through the shop floor. She returned to the cage, knowing that four more lay in wait. Groaning to herself, Lily was exasperated at how her life had ended up. She was twenty-nine and six years into a job she hated. Her lateness was almost as though her body was repelled by the building. Lily didn't want to be late; she was just so tired of mundanity that even her introverted soul cried out for excitement. She was tired of this diet life, and as she looked at her misspelt name badge in the reflection of the cold metal shelving, she whispered to herself, "Is this it?"

BEFORE + AFTER

Kent Row was a singular long road connecting seven large houses. Rain fell over a well-maintained lawn in front of a grand building. A cool breeze blew through trees which gave the house some privacy. The *SOLD* sign at the gates of number six had garnered attention from the few neighbours in this wealthy area, and the new owner relished it. A removal van had pulled up several hours previously, and all had been quiet until an abrupt smash of plates brought unwelcome noise pollution into the neighbourhood.

A bald and buff removal man wearing grey sweatpants and a vest blurted out, "Shit! Sorry mate, sweaty hands." He threw several awkwardly apologetic looks towards the new owner of the house.

"It doesn't matter. I can buy more," came the apathetic voice of Nicholas Faust. He was a slim guy with jet-black hair, pale skin and sunglasses. Painted fingernails held a cigarette gently and a chest tattoo could be seen peeking out from a V-neck t-shirt. Dressed head to toe in black with one boot up against the wall, his long funnel neck jacket blew as he took a drag of his cigarette, a nose ring shimmering.

The removal man blurted out, "Er, standard. I'll grab another box, mate, and we'll get the rest in as quickly as we can," before shuffling back up the path to a removal van parked on the road.

The new homeowner stared at the mess on his pavement and began sweeping the broken crockery aside with his boot. A second chubbier removal man with a sort of mullet emerged from within the house to stare at the mess, look toward his partner and then continue to shuffle off towards the van, pulling his sweatpants up from his rear.

Returning to his place against the wall, the new homeowner continued his cigarette and watched the men jump into the back of the van. A few clunking sounds could be heard before they emerged into the rain, holding boxes and smirking.

"Where do you want these, Nicholas?" asked the bald buff guy.

"The kitchen… and it's Nicky," said Nicky, unimpressed.

"So where do you want this box then, Nicholas?" said the chubby guy a moment later.

"Also the kitchen… and it's still Nicky," he replied, deadpan.

The men walked in together, whispering quietly before laughing loudly. Nicky turned his head to listen as they went upstairs, overhearing one man smugly declaring, "Dumb emo fuck!"

Nicky had spent the entire morning listening to them going through his new house and offering varying critical comments about his aesthetic behind his back, and he was over it.

They passed him with yet another load of boxes. Nicky took a final drag of his cigarette, holding in a mouthful of smoke before saying, "Careful, that's fragile."

The men looked at each other and smirked. "We'll be fine, mate."

DEBAUCHERY: PART I

"I wasn't talking about the box..." said Nicky, blowing smoke into their faces and flicking the cigarette butt on the floor.

The two men looked blank and simply carried on.

Nicky was done and called out after them, "Oi you two, Before & After! I have errands. I'll be about an hour, okay?"

Envisioning the prospect of being left alone to gossip, they smirked at each other, with the chubby guy saying, "Okay, mate."

Already halfway down the path, Nicky walked over to a green vintage Rolls Royce parked next to the van and got inside. Putting the key in the ignition, he thought, *How did I get such inferior quality removal men for the price I paid?* before driving away.

He sang badly to loud music blasting from his phone, which sat in a holder on the dashboard. Passing rows of shops, a church, and a group of teenagers laughing obnoxiously loudly, he continued along the road. Engulfed in his own thoughts, he suddenly caught a view of a young woman stepping out into the road in front of him.

Nicky slammed his foot onto the brakes, his seatbelt choking him slightly. Lifting his head up, he moved his hair from in front of his face before winding his window down and shouting, "I know you're probably doing a walk of shame right now, sweetheart, but can you not plaster it along the fucking road?"

"FUCK YOU!" replied the girl, who just carried on walking as though nothing had happened. He brandished a middle finger and drove away.

"Moron," he mumbled as he carried on with his journey to the store, heartbeat at double speed.

He drove for a further ten minutes before turning into the car park. He parked at the back where there was the most space, got out and made his way through the rain to the entrance. The words HUGE were stamped on the front of the store in a garish yellow, and he joined a flow of people in a near-constant rush to either enter or leave.

Receiving the usual generic greeting from a security guard as he entered, Nicky grabbed a basket and made his way to the chilled aisle. His basket eventually filled with a few basics, he meandered around the store and dodged a constant sea of people. Turning down the electronics section, a man dressed in a devil costume leapt in front of Nicky, making him jump and hurl his fist at the figure.

"Shit! What the hell? I'm so sorry, but what the hell?" said Nicky, his heart racing once again. "What's the offer today, then? Free heart attacks for the unprepared?"

A shaky devil replied, "Yeah… We, er, do some script about products being devilishly good. The offers change each week, but this week it's butter."

Nicky looked as concerned as his face could manage, saying, "Well, your nose isn't bleeding, and if it makes you feel any better, I've already got the butter. If you don't scare me to death next time, I'll let you know if it's as good as you claim. Take this as an apology." Nicky looked around and quickly pushed £1000 into the man's top.

"Shit dude, are you serious? I can't accept this on shift!"

"Say nothing, just take it," Nicky said, walking away with a clear conscience.

His dance with the devil was quickly replaced with a battle against clueless trolley jockeys as Nicky fought his way to the electronics aisle. He grabbed two pairs of earphones and put one in his basket. Turning to leave the aisle, he stuffed the other in his pocket with expert precision. A security guard turned the corner and Nicky smiled directly at him, knowing he'd gotten away with

DEBAUCHERY: PART I

it once again. *It's always about the rush...*

Nicky promptly made his way to the self-checkout and clipped onto the end of a queue that was far too long. He stared at the harsh strip lighting above him and swept his damp hair back, reminding himself that he'd forgotten to buy hairspray. After several minutes of staring at customers doing everything in their power to check out at a glacial pace, Nicky stepped towards a free machine. He scanned his items with only one item messing up the entire time. Nicky eagerly left the realm of the general public. He threw a quick smile at a cardboard cut-out of a security guard on his way out.

Content, Nicky drove towards the exit of the car park, musing over how much of his stuff Before & After had gone through while he had been gone. *Am I even allowed to leave these people alone?* he thought to himself as he pulled out onto the road, only for a bus horn to snap him back to reality.

Nicky's foot slammed onto his brakes.

"WHAT THE FUCK ARE YOU DOING JUST DRIVING INTO THE ROAD, YOU FUCKING IDIOT?" screamed the driver, making several cars on the road slow down to witness the drama.

Feeling stupid and defensive, Nicky wound down his window shouting, "FUCK YOU!" which only seemed to make the driver's face redder. He stuck his finger up at Nicky as they drove around each other to go their separate ways.

He wondered what else could shock him on the drive home, but as he turned into the small parking space at his second errand, he became calmer.

The Church of Saint Augustus wasn't a grand building, but it stood proud regardless as Nicky gazed up at a weather vane. The building looked solemn, yet beckoned Nicky in with a silent welcome. As he entered the small foyer, he was instantly blasted with a dusty sense of history exclusive to churches. The building reeked of childhood obligation, being forced to sing and using the word 'Christingle'. Nicky associated the place with so much positivity, despite never feeling warm physically or spiritually.

He made his way into the nave of the church, looking up at the familiar pictures on stained glass. One depicted Noah's Ark, another The Crucifixion, and one that he could never understand, which featured the Devil. All three scenes had faded over time, but scaffolding housing a toolbox and several blankets promised revival.

Nicky saw a familiar face ahead and ambled down the central aisle. He smiled and took a seat halfway. The church was mostly empty, but Reverend Peter Stephenson had always kept the place ticking over, considering the building's age. Nicky pulled up a pew, sinking into the atmosphere. He wished he could stay in this orthodox time capsule forever.

"You know, if you clean that any harder, you'll whittle it down to a toothpick," Nicky said, his voice echoing upward.

Peter jumped and spun around. "What have I told you about sneaking up on me like that? You'll be the death of me one day!"

"I've got your butter and milk. The butter's *devilishly* good, apparently, so I'd be careful about having it around here," Nicky said as he walked up to Peter.

Peter took the bag and smiled. "Time for a cuppa?"

"Go on then. I'm only paying some removal douches to break all my stuff by the hour."

Peter smiled. "You know, one day you'll get in a lot of trouble for speaking your mind. Oh, and watch your step. This place is a mess since those builders came in," he said, leading Nicky through to the vestry.

DEBAUCHERY: PART I

The two friends spent the next hour lost in conversation. They spoke about family, friends, and Nicky even spoke about his love life, which he was notoriously secretive about. The tiny room had housed so many conversations over time, and Nicky had always enjoyed putting one more into the pot with every visit. It was at 8:30 pm when he put down his cup. "I should probably be off. My fan club awaits," he said, eyes rolling.

"You mean your new house awaits…" Peter said.

"That too! Seven bedrooms, four bathrooms and a heated pool! Sixteen rooms altogether, I think! A lot of room for so few fucks to give!" Nicky said as he left the vestry. He was halfway down the aisle when he heard Peter call after him. Nicky turned around. "What's wrong?"

Peter remained silent, walking up slowly towards him. He stopped in front of Nicky and sighed before saying warmly, "I just wanted to say thank you. It means a lot that you came to chat with me. Look, I know it's probably somewhere 'uncool' that all your friends would steer clear of, but—"

"Hey, listen, I don't give a shit who thinks it's uncool. I barely give a shit about anyone. I've known you for years, and I'm happy to help whenever. You've… You've listened when there has been no one around. If anything, I owe you."

Peter put both hands on Nicky's shoulders. "You owe me nothing, my boy. I mean, look at you. All grown up with your own thoughts and opinions. It makes me proud to know that I know three generations of a family who are the tops."

Nicky grinned. "Well, I have broken that tradition occasionally…"

Peter smiled awkwardly. "What do you mean?"

"Never mind!"

They reached the entrance, and Peter paused. "Nicky, I just

wanted you to know how much your company means, that's all. Since Alice died, I sometimes feel so alone, even with all my family around. Seeing that extra face means everything. I associate you with so much good, so thank you for making this old man happy."

Nicky smiled. "I'm glad I can be there for you."

They hugged, and Nicky left to return to his new house.

He pulled up in front of the removal van and emerged from the car, looking into the back of the van to see that it stood empty. "Praise Satan," he said under his breath.

Walking into what would soon be his living room, he saw the two men on the sofa looking at a sea of boxes with pride. They saw him and immediately sprang to their feet.

"There you are, mate! Wondered where you've been?" said Before.

"I just bumped into a friend, that's all," replied Nicky nonchalantly. The two men looked at each other, smirking.

"Oh, aye? Sounds good, mate, so, err, looks like we're done here. Anything else you want us to do for you?" They looked at each other and grinned as they made their way out of the house. Nicky followed, and as they reached the front door, a smirk appeared on his face before he piped up, "Well, there's something you can do if you want?"

The two men turned around cautiously. "Oh aye, mate?"

Lighting a cigarette and finally removing his sunglasses, Nicky grinned. "Yeah, so I'm just gonna pay you to both fuck off my property. Five grand each should do it. It's bad enough I've had to hire two idiots turning up in a tired-ass wagon looking ready to steal a bunch of dalmatians, but to hear you judge my stuff? That's something I take personally. Now do one."

DEBAUCHERY: PART I

The two men, drained of all colour, stared at him in stunned silence before promptly taking the wad of cash in Nicky's outstretched hand. As they rushed away, Nicky laughed and blew smoke into the air.

The sun set on his first day at a new home as he pulled a phone from his pocket. Clicking on the removal company's social media page, he left a review.

"Devilishly good service. A+."

iv
I JUST WOKE UP LIKE THIS

A shaggy pile of blonde hair taking the form of Steph sprung up in Adrian's bed. She felt rough after a busy evening of binge eating and complaining. A bowl of what was once ice cream fell from the bed as Steph stretched. She frowned at the sticky blob before manoeuvring herself as gracefully as possible over her friend.

She shuffled to the bathroom and checked herself out in the mirror. *I look like shit,* she thought, moulding her hair into a better shape with her fingers. An unopened toothbrush caught her eye as the bathroom door opened slightly. Harry stepped into the bathroom, only to see Steph and back away.

"Oh, er, hi. I-I didn't think anyone was in here," he said, staring directly at the floor.

"Well… I am," Steph replied blankly, focusing her energy on opening the toothbrush.

"Okay…"

They stood in awkward silence before Steph threw one of her 'looks' at him, loudly declaring, "OKAY BYE!"

He fled, closing the door behind him, leaving Steph to start

DEBAUCHERY: PART I

her inflated version of 'presentable'. This involved brushing her teeth, using mouthwash, flossing, scrubbing her face (twice), moisturising, styling her hair with volumising hairspray, making sure her eyebrows looked on point and putting on 'emergency makeup' that Adrian kept for her in a small pink basket. As she dabbed gold glitter under her eyes, she heard an electronic buzz from behind a bottle of shampoo. Curiosity piqued, Steph moved it to find a small camera pointing towards her. "Ugh," she remarked, abandoning the beautification process.

As she stepped out of the bathroom she bumped into Harry, saying, "You really are a fucking creep, you know," as she walked by. He merely looked confused before shuffling into the bathroom and promptly closing the door.

Adrian was still asleep as Steph returned. His breathing was heavy, and a small sliver of drool fell from the corner of his mouth onto the pillow. Steph clambered back into bed, sighing loudly in the hopes of waking him to relive her traumas. It didn't work, so she resorted to her backup plan of laying with her arms folded.

"Ahem!" she said, trying to rouse her unconscious friend, who simply turned over. Irritated, Steph decided that the only logical course of action was to punch her best friend in the face, but lightly.

Adrian sprang up in a panic as she slammed herself back into a lying position. "W-What? Steph, what's wrong, Steph?"

He stared at her, confused as she gave an award-worthy performance of pretending to wake up, "Hmm? Sorry, you woke me up. What's the matter?"

"Something hit my face... Didn't it?"

"Well, I don't know. I've just been here sleeping," Steph said coyly, stretching her arms.

"Never mind. Wait, why do you look so… awake?"

Her blue eyes shone in a patch of sunlight, glitter sparkling gently as she said, "I don't know what you mean, Adrian. I just woke up like this."

She calmly sat up, rummaging for her phone underneath the bedding. The words *10% BATTERY REMAINING* flashed over the screen, causing Steph to break character. She skimmed the notifications and gazed upon a stream of parental concern.

"ARGH!" she said, making a dazed Adrian jump. "I have to go!"

"Oh, okay. Parents?"

Steph leapt over him and put on her somewhat dry clothes from yesterday, nodding quickly.

"Well, ring a taxi and I'll transfer the money later. I'm too tired to drive," Adrian said with a yawn as he reluctantly got out of bed.

Steph huffed before hurriedly dialling the taxi firm as Adrian wobbled forward in his boxers. She stared at his six-pack as the phone rang. Adrian was never anyone she'd seen in any kind of way, but Steph was constantly alerted to the fact that he was attractive to so many. From his broad shoulders to his tatted body and 'V' lines, he really was the gold-standard friend Steph knew she deserved. She smiled at this reminder as they made their way downstairs. Sylvester cleaned himself on the most awkward step, unbothered, as Steph nearly fell down the stairs trying to get past him.

"Will you be okay?" said Adrian, sweeping back a head of wild hair.

Steph absorbed the concern and pulled the fakest strained expression, biting her lip and sighing, "I *think* I'll be okay. It's just so… difficult."

"I know it is, but it'll be alright." Adrian had taken the bait,

DEBAUCHERY: PART I

so Steph had the chance to spend the five-minute wait for the taxi milking her bad day for all it was worth. A car horn rudely interrupted them, with Adrian immediately stepping in to hug. She embraced him tight, whispering, "Thank you for last night."

"Any time. Now get going, I need to get to the rehearsal before the gig tonight. You know how eager Eric gets!"

"Okay, I'll see you soon!" she said, opening the door to an autumn breeze and waving frantically.

"Where we goin' to luv?" came a strong Yorkshire accent attached to a bald head.

"6 Coultas Close, please," said Steph, exchanging awkward eye contact with the driver in the rear-view mirror as she stepped in. She watched his eyes take the familiar route down her body before starting the actual journey. *It's difficult being beautiful.*

Steph soon ended up back on her home turf. She unbuckled her seatbelt before presenting the bald head a damp ten-pound note. His eyes appeared once more. "You tek care now, luv."

"Thanks, keep the change," she said, promptly leaving the taxi to stand in the exact spot as the day before. Watching the taxi leave caused a breezy despair to come upon her, as her new-found singledom seemed to be taunting her. The voice was cruel and held an 'L' shape to its forehead, mocking her tearful eyes as it reminded her she had been dumped. *You'll be miserable and alone in this tired outfit you've worn for two days now.*

The glitter dimmed as Steph walked up the garden path. A faded wooden door was the only thing between Steph and one of her stepdad's lectures. Mum's incessant worrying would follow soon after, causing a double whammy of smothering love. Her parents had always been overly protective of her, but at twenty-nine, their concern had become acrylics across a chalkboard. She inhaled, stepping through an 'always open' front door.

"Steph? That you?" came a booming voice immediately.

"Yeah," she replied wearily, clicking the door shut. The moment to creep upstairs came and went immediately as her mother burst forth from the living room, a glass of rosé in hand.

"Oh Steph, where have you been? I was worried sick, you know! You could at least text me when you're doing those all-nighters!"

Sally Shaw was a small woman with bleached blonde hair, similar to her daughter's. She had given birth to Steph at a very young age, so had always opted to think of herself as more of a big sister than a mother. She had made damn sure that fake tan, false eyelashes and a strong contour were hereditary. Sally clung to a youthful mindset, but Steph's behaviour always dragged her back to motherhood.

"I just stayed at Adrian's," Steph mumbled eventually.

"Oh Adrian, he's a love! Out of all those young men you gallivant around with, you have one right under your nose who's such a sweet boy! Why, if I was ten years younger—"

"MUM! He's my friend! We've always just been friends."

Steph's mum frowned. "Such a waste…"

The deep voice of her stepfather joined the conversation, and Steph stared longingly towards the stairs, praying she could just teleport into her room there and then.

"Gotta wonder where he's from originally though, haven't yer? Don't want the wrong kinda guy getting with my princess… and where d'ya think you're creepin' off to, young lady?"

Steph sighed, turning around unenthusiastically to face him. Callum Shaw strode into view, tall and proud. He had always been a wrecking ball of testosterone with a 'reputation' to uphold in the local area. He stared, offering his best version of a quizzical

DEBAUCHERY: PART I

look, a bottle of beer clasped between calloused fingers.

"Adrian's British, and he wants to be a singer, I'll have you know," Steph said defensively.

"Ahh, but that's a sign, princess! Probably a poof! What kind of man wants to stand there singin' about what he's feelin' all day? No *real* man has time for that shit. People are too sensitive nowadays, and every Tom, Dick and 'arry got to tell everyone everything they're feelin'. In my day, men were men and women were–"

"—Okay, can I go now?" Steph interrupted.

"Now just hold on, sweetie, how are things with Noah?" asked her mum, softly taking Steph's hand. It was always the soft voice.

Lulled into a false sense of security, Steph whispered fast, "We-broke-up."

"What?" said her parents in unison. "Why?"

"Differences."

Neither bought this simple explanation as truth. Callum strode towards her, saying firmly, "If 'e hurt you… If 'e did anything–"

"–Now Callum, don't get yourself worked up," said Sally, gently holding his hand too. "She'll tell us when she's ready."

"Thanks Mum!" Steph said, making a quick escape. Her hand had no sooner touched her bedroom door before her mum called, "As long as in your own time means later, dear!"

Steph groaned, promptly shutting herself away. Safe at last.

Unsurprisingly, Steph loved the colour pink, and it showed in her room. The space comprised a bed with fairy lights around it, an overworked wardrobe filled to the brim with clothes, and a white sheepskin rug with a lipstick stain. Her centrepiece was a huge vanity table adorned with fluffy things and instant photos of happier times, stuck slapdash on the mirror's edge. The table housed perfumes and hair products, creams and lotions alongside the biggest makeup box one could own. A mirror covered in fingerprints stood proudly over this vast kingdom of self-care. Further fairy lights danced around the mirror, casting a warm glow, silently welcoming Steph to the table every time she entered the room.

A ring light and an expensive camera setup pointed at her, reminding her she had makeup tutorials to record. Her lucrative career as a famous beauty vlogger aside, the camera offered just the right amount of slightly voyeuristic attention Steph craved within her candy-coloured kingdom.

Posters filled every wall, her music taste exploding around the room in a cascade of eighties and nineties pop coexisting with various other megastars, creating a perfect video backdrop wherever she sat.

Steph's room was her hot pink pride and joy. She had finessed it to aesthetic perfection, mixed with fluffy goodness and chrome clichés. There was nowhere on Earth as intrinsically 'Steph' as here.

Slumping onto a throne-shaped chair, Steph saw her reflection and stared. She looked good but saw creases in her face. It hurt that she didn't have the same perfect skin she did when she was twenty-one. Emotion poured out of her, tears falling once more. She was painfully aware that she was only creating more lines. Steph mulled over all that had happened and everything she'd become. She was single and was going to die alone. What happened to the Steph she knew and loved? The towering pile of confidence with a honeyed voice and boobs like a porn star? How could this now-obsolete man bring her to her knees when she was the superior one? Steph was arm candy, so how and why was she rotting?

Steph screamed with frustration, lashing out at the mirror and

DEBAUCHERY: PART I

cracking it. She looked at herself and saw a pathetic mess. There was only one solution for one feeling so weak. *I need surgery.*

"Maybe collagen?" she mused aloud before jumping as her pocket vibrated. She removed her nearly dead phone and promptly plugged it into a charger. In the bright glow of the screen, Steph saw a notification from Adrian.

Free entry to Snakes Nightclub in this link. Keep your mind off things :) xxxx

Through newly ruined makeup, a fragmented smile appeared as Steph whispered, "Gold standard."

POLLY

A plus-size woman of just over six feet stood up, her hair a mess of black with purple stripes. She stumbled her way through a labyrinth of nightclub corridors in the least graceful way possible. Once at the other end, she straightened a band t-shirt and rearranged her tartan skirt (for the third time). The air within Snakes nightclub was rife with booze, sweat, and good vibes. As the woman proceeded to the bar, she looked around and smiled to herself at the completion of another successful night out.

Snakes Nightclub had thrived for decades as a sanctuary for the alternative, and was the loudest place an introvert would willingly visit. Its darkened walls and sticky floor had granted many a generation of goths, metal-heads, geeks, punks, emo kids, and anyone within the LGBTQ+ community a temporary shield from the shittiness of the outside world.

White painted snakes wrapped their way around blackened walls, illuminated by bright red lighting. A sea of people filtered between several rooms of music. The maze-like structure of the building created bizarre acoustics of being able to hear everything or nothing at all. Several tables and chairs were scattered

DEBAUCHERY: PART I

throughout, all cordoned off by metal bars that wouldn't look out of place in a BDSM dungeon. Teenage angst congregated alongside the adults who knew that said angst was merely early-onset mental health issues. Whatever problems the world threw at them mattered little when armed with the knowledge that you could get blitzed for under thirty pounds.

Within this clusterfuck of post-hardcore punk, at one of the barred tables, Nicky sat impatiently waiting for his friend to return. He had been invited to see her favourite black metal band, playing the part of the one guy who didn't really care for them. Nicky's hair-sprayed locks slowly turned into a mess befitting any head-banging alternative. He stared through blurred vision at his drunken friend struggling with basic social interaction at the bar and smiled.

Amy Duncan was his best friend, an iconic partner-in-crime, even if she couldn't walk properly at this moment.

"Yeah, so I'll have two, no FOUR double screwdriver orangey vodka things and shots. TWO OF THEM... The ones with the energy drink in them!" Amy screamed over the counter at an attractive bartender with a mohawk.

Nodding wearily, he turned to make the order while Amy perched on a bar stool as best she could. Her alternative appearance made her incognito, and she smiled. Leaning forward, she attempted to make herself comfier, though merely ended up with her elbows in the remnants of previously spilt drinks.

Turning to her left, Amy saw a guy making out with a girl and clumsily trying to stick his hand up her skirt. She grimaced at this blatant heterosexuality and turned to her right to see a pretty girl with blonde hair slumped over the bar. She looked so out of place that Amy risked a potentially disastrous conversation with her while she waited.

"Hello woman. Why do you cry?"

The girl turned and shouted over the music, "What? No, I'm not okay! My boyfriend dumped me yesterday, and I'm not who I used to be. I came to see my friend play in his band, but he hasn't come on yet, so I might as well just sit at this bar and just fucking die."

"Oh... Okay!" Amy said, turning back to be presented with a tray full of drinks. "Ooh, excellent— wait, so... You know the guys in the band playing?"

She nodded.

"*You* know Acid Lobotomy Demonic Lacerations?"

She nodded once more.

"No offence, but you don't look the type."

She fake-smiled. "I don't like this music, but it reminds me of Adrian. This is like his happy place, and I want to be in it."

"Fair... Wait, Adrian? *YOU* know the lead singer of ALDL? Fuck my life! I gotta tell Nicky!" With that, Amy grabbed her precious cargo and made her way quickly through the sea of alternatives back to the safety of the table with the news of the century.

"Nicky! Nicky! Nicky!"

"Yes? Yes? Yes?"

"Hold on to your titties because I've just made a direct connection with someone who's friends with the lead singer of ALDL!" Amy declared, a fiery excitement in her eyes.

Nicky stared at Amy and then his drinks. "The mind boggles. Now, can we just carry on with the drinking?"

"You're a twat, and yes. Yes, we can!" Amy yelled, grabbing a shot. "Come on! Together! Down it one, two, three!"

Nicky swallowed the lukewarm concoction, declaring

DEBAUCHERY: PART I

afterwards, "You know these really aren't *that* strong?"

"Yeah, I know, but at this point we're on like our twenth drink and I'm fucking wired!"

"Twenth?" Nicky grinned.

"Exactly," slurred Amy. She paused for a moment before abruptly shouting, "OH MY GOD! Nicky!" and grabbing his arm.

"Jesus! Are you trying to scare me to death, woman? What?"

"You see that girl over there at the bar? She was miserable, and she's probably going to do a suicide."

Nicky laughed. "'Do a suicide!' Oh my God! Maybe we should join her. God knows our lives are shit enough."

"You're right, but finish our drinks first, yeah?"

"Obviously!"

┿

Steph had been at the club for two hours now, and there had been no sign of Adrian or his musical screamings. She had been drowning her sorrows over the bar with the bartender, occasionally asking if she needed water. What made matters worse was that a couple opposite had the nerve to make out so close to her when she was clearly single. Everyone was in lust except for her, and she was definitely going to die alone because of it.

Woefully downing yet another drink, Steph heard a noise behind her. She turned with her glass still to her mouth to see a man and woman, both dressed in black, adorned with drunken smiles.

"Hello there! I'm Nicky," said the man, a nose piercing glistening under red lighting.

"Hi… I'm Steph," she replied, giving a weary smile.

"And I'm drunk!" declared the woman cheerfully.

Steph stared silently, and Nicky grinned. "She's Amy."

Steph looked blankly before turning to the overworked barman. "Can I just have the same as last time, please? The rum one that's pink?"

"You got it, Steph," replied the barman, who immediately whizzed away.

"See!" Amy hissed, grabbing Nicky's arm. "He knoowssss!"

Nicky ignored this as he was far more interested in being a bar-side agony aunt. "So, what's up? I heard you weren't doing so well, so come, let us be an ear!"

"We are ears!" proclaimed Amy, proudly raising her arms.

Steph received her drink and turned to look at Nicky. His eyes were glazed, and his speech was slurred, but he looked genuinely interested in her woes.

"My boyfriend left me, and it's really hard to cope with, and I don't feel special at all anymore, and he was an arsehole, but I miss him so much, and I just don't feel myself."

"Well..." said Nicky thoughtfully. "Have you tried cutting your life into pieces?"

"Oh, I don't know, Nicky. That seems like a last resort," grinned Amy as the two of them looked at Steph, only for her to burst into tears.

A pang of guilt hit Nicky, and he extended his arms for a hug saying, "I'm sorry, come here!"

Amy rolled her eyes, putting two fingers to her lips and mouthing the word, "Fag?"

Nicky frowned mid-hug. "Oh, well fuck you too!"

"No, dipshit! I meant do you want to go for a cig or do I have to say it correctly, *like the kiiing?* Dearest Nicholas, dost thou wanteth to goeth for a fagerette on this, our final Saturday of the montheth of September…eth?"

"Fuck off. Hey Steph! Do you smoke? You're welcome to join us?" Nicky said, releasing her with a kind smile.

"I don't."

"Oh, okay, we'll be like ten minutes! Don't move, and then we'll buddy up until you see your friend again."

"Yes, please," Steph said through ruined mascara.

Nicky smiled as Amy took the lead past a small collective of goths towards the smoking area.

The atmosphere changed instantly from organised chaos to unbridled conversation. The smoking area was under a canopy and debate was rife. No mere rainfall could extinguish the ramblings of thirty-something anime senpais, pothead philosophers, metal elitists and gothic Lolita girls. As Amy and Nicky added themselves to the mishmash of misfits, a welcome blast of cool air came over them.

Nicky looked down at his phone as Amy moved to the metal stairs to roll their cigarettes.

"It's nearly midnight," said Nicky, swaying. "We should go soon. I'm so fucked and I can't rest against the fire exit, thinking about life anymore. It takes me like three days to recover!"

"It's the air," Amy said, rolling paper between her lips. "When you go outside, you always realise how drunk you are."

"Mate, I'm twatted."

The two remained silent for a moment, hoping that the fresh air would somehow cleanse at least a little of the alcohol from their system. Amy handed her friend a dampened cigarette before standing up and staring at the sky. As they exhaled the first glorious puff of smoke, time seemed to stop. It was then that a beam of light hit them from a floodlight above. Shielding their eyes with clumsy hands, a voice snapped them back to reality.

"Once upon a time, there was a frankly *brilliant* woman who waited *eighty-four* damn years to *finally* grace you with her wonderous presence!" the figure declared playfully. "Imagine keeping *me* of all people confined to a fire escape! Shall we begin?"

They stared up at the silhouette of a woman standing on the fire exit of the upper floor. Boots hit metal stairs as she descended, illuminated by the floodlight. A strangely stitched patchwork leather trench coat came into view. A cigarette delicately placed between her fingers sent a thin line of smoke drifting up to a grin.

The midnight air blew her jacket open slightly, revealing a simple black dress. Strips of barbed wire clung to her body as though an accessory. It started as a choker, ran down her body, past her cleavage, with another piece winding around her arm. Her facial features were still obscured by the bright glow behind her, but Amy and Nicky stared regardless, transfixed, at the most physically gorgeous woman they'd ever seen.

"Can I ask you a question?" the woman said as she stepped delicately onto the concrete.

"Er..." said Nicky, confused.

The woman smiled, face coming into view. Her eyes were a deep hazel in the bright light, and her lips a luscious shade of red. She revealed a gloved hand, which tossed voluminous jet-black hair over her shoulder. Amy stared, noticing that the gloves had the same stitched brown pattern as her jacket. A sense of unease swept over the two friends, but Amy nodded. "Ask away."

The woman exhaled the cigarette and with smoke in her breath smiled. "You stand on the pinnacle of something that is so deeply important. Ask yourself, what is evil, what is good, and

DEBAUCHERY: PART I

how far will you go to survive? You will be tested. The pieces are in position and the game has begun once again. This game, however, will be the most important…"

They stared at the woman, then at each other. Amy shook her head at Nicky, who merely shrugged before saying sheepishly, "I honestly just thought you were going to ask us for a lighter or something."

The woman laughed, clapping her hands together gleefully, exclaiming, "Oh sweetheart, you have no idea! I can't wait for you all to find out!" Without warning, she blew an unnatural amount of cigarette smoke into their faces.

"What the hell?" shouted Amy.

When the fog cleared, they stared at an empty wall.

"Where did she go?" said Nicky, flummoxed.

"Up here, of course! Keep up or check out!" called the woman, now back at the top of the stairs.

"Wait!" Nicky shouted. "What were you talking about? What's your name?"

The woman skipped along the metal walkway, declaring, "Good grief, I just have so many! What's in a name? I could be anyone, really! Call me Polly! I think it's best for this universe, don't you? We'll all be BFFs in no time, darling!" And with that, she skipped out of view.

Nicky and Amy exchanged glances, immediately breaking into a sprint after the enigmatic woman, sobering up by the second. Darting up the stairs and along the walkway, they ran through the fire escape into the upper level of the club.

"Hey, stop!" Amy called, but they were only to be greeted by the rock 'n' roll floor of the club, packed to capacity as usual. A 1965 live performance of 'Have I The Right?' by The Honeycombs in glorious black and white blasted from TVs and several speakers above. Amy and Nicky fought their way through people, joyously clapping their hands and stomping their feet on the dancefloor.

"I can't see anything!" shouted Nicky, his voice dulled by televised teenage screams of yesteryear.

They proceeded on, deeper into the crowd, clumsily nudging the drinks in people's hands as they moved.

"Fuck this!" declared Amy, grabbing her friend's arm and yanking him through a clump of misplaced indie kids. They returned downstairs to the bar where their buddy Steph once sat, but the seat was now occupied by a man with a split tongue and dermal implants.

"Excuse me, have you seen a blonde, about yay high, miserable as all hell?" asked Amy.

The man shook his head.

"Bugger."

"Can we just go? That Polly woman kinda killed the mood," said Nicky.

"But… But ALDL! I want to enjoy their cool menthol shriekings!"

"If we go now, I'll buy you front-row tickets for their next show?" grinned Nicky.

"Well, now that you mention it," said Amy, feigning a yawn, "it is getting late. The night is dead, so we should really get going…"

They left the club with the second blast of fresh air feeling far less cruel. Released into the night, they wobbled across the road, ready to book a taxi home.

Nicky sat on a small wall close to a lone burger van, lying in wait for drunkards looking for junk food. Amy joined him as he dialled his usual taxi firm.

"Hi yeah, can I have a taxi as soon as possible, please? Yeah, Kent Row please… Yeah, okay. Thank you!"

DEBAUCHERY: PART I

Time passed with the friends talking nonsense and discussing the oddities they had encountered. Any sense of urgency or intrigue was quelled by inebriation, and they found that the more they discussed their meeting with Polly, the more they doubted whether it had even happened. Their brains replayed it and, over time, the thought of their beds became more important as the cool breeze turned cold.

Nicky called the company and in his least irritated voice said, "Hi, so I ordered a taxi about an hour ago and it hasn't turned up. Am I okay to get an update on where it is, please?"

Amy, who had demoted herself to the damp pavement, slumped against the wall to ease her newly acquired lower back pain.

"Yeah, okay, I can wait…"

Amy removed her shoes and placed her hands inside them, declaring, "I… Made… *THESE!*" She put her hands together proudly, shouting, "Hand! Shoes!"

Nicky laughed just as the woman replied before saying, "Sorry, yeah, five minutes is fine. Thank you."

"Hand… Shoes Nicky! This is very important—wait, is that the blonde?" Amy sat up and pointed the hand shoes towards a head of blonde hair poking out from a door at the rear of the burger van. Crawling to her feet, both Amy and Nicky moved to the mysterious mop to find a nauseous Steph. Head between her legs, a kindly burger man balanced caring for her with selling burgers. Her head swayed over a neglected tray of chips, a single loose boob resting gently in warm ketchup. Within a gust of wind she mumbled, "But Lobotomy Lacerations Demonic Acid…"

"Oh, it's my fast pass to the VIP! What do you think we should do with her?" said Amy.

"Well, we could put her tit away for one thing."

"I'm guessing she's with you guys, then?" came the voice of a chipper burger man.

"Yeah, she's ours. Well, we said we'd look after her at least. We can make sure she gets home," said Nicky, taking Steph's hand.

Steph rose to her feet, slurring, "Must stay for Demonic Lobotomy Acid Lacerations," as the burger man looked them up and down suspiciously.

Nicky snapped, "Oh, come on, mate! We can't leave her boob-out at the burger van, can we?"

"Okay, okay! You best take care of her! She's not in a good place by the sound of it!"

Amy scoffed, "In this miserable country, is anyone? Everything is fucking terrible! The best thing we could do is launch her into the sea—"

"—Which we obviously won't do!" interjected Nicky.

A car horn sounded, making them jump.

"THANK YOU, JESUS!" Amy shouted, raising her hand shoes to the sky.

Nicky shuffled Steph onwards, putting her breast back in her top before guiding her towards the taxi. The driver, who sported a bright blue turban and a luscious beard, wound down his window to look at Steph and shake his head.

"Not you too! You have our address. We're hardly inbound for Saddleworth Moor, are we?" spat Nicky.

"The doubt we have endured on this night..." said Amy, shaking her head in disappointment.

"Fine," huffed the driver as he unlocked the car.

Nicky pushed Steph gracelessly into the back seat before clambering in himself.

"Acid Demonic Lacerations Lobotomy..." Steph whispered

DEBAUCHERY: PART I

into the window, her chemical breath steaming the window as Amy entered from the other side.

She slammed the door shut and said to the driver, "I promise this person is not a shifty man, he is just a gay…" as the car drove off.

"Thank you for outing me everywhere you go," replied Nicky as an unconscious Steph fell onto his shoulder.

"You are most welcome, MY DARLING!" beamed Amy as the taxi drove away from one of the weirdest nights out they'd had so far.

VI
THE ENIGMA CARD: PART I

Steph's shaggy blonde form sprung up in a different bed from her own. Her head throbbed following a busy evening of binge drinking and complaining. 'Ugh, where am I?' she thought, suffering headaches and a strong sense of déjà vu. Steph grimaced as she sat up, her memory a mess of badly edited noise laced with sporadic cranberry burps.

She looked around and saw patches of sunlight fighting its way through. Sliding out of bed to throw them open, Steph shielded her eyes like a hungover vampire at the sudden blast of brightness. She turned to see her phone charging on a table opposite and her clothes from the night before neatly folded on a chair.

As she picked up her phone, Steph noticed several boxes marked 'Spare Room'. Using her own brand of expert knowledge, she deduced that because of the lack of furniture, she was probably the first person to stay in this room. A strange sense of accomplishment came from this as she left the room.

Gracing the landing with her presence, Steph followed a grey carpet leading to several doors. She had never seen a house like it. Despite being almost empty, just one area of the house felt bigger

DEBAUCHERY: PART I

and more expensive than anywhere she'd ever stayed. Natural light from a second bedroom opposite caught her eye. Choosing to ignore it, Steph saw staircases to both her left and right. She peered cautiously up one set to see an attic room. "Nope!" she declared as she grabbed an ornate bannister and descended further into the unknown instead.

A confident foot hit the carpet of the ground floor as Steph called out, "Hello? I'm here!" She saw the front door and stared into a huge room on her right boasting photography equipment and further boxes. The mere fact she was somewhere unfamiliar did little to spur Steph's confidence. Turning to her left, a voice suddenly called out to her.

"Hello, uh, girl-whose-name-I-can't-remember! Are you alright? I've made you breakfast! Or lunch… Either or!"

A promise of food quickened her step as Steph passed several rooms, guided purely by wafts of bacon in the air. She stopped, inhaled and pushed the door open, ready to bless another new soul with her company.

A man in a black dressing gown stood in a bright red kitchen. His hair was messy, and a familiar nose ring shimmered. He was preparing a fry up, surrounded by boxes marked 'Kitchen'.

"Sorry about the mess. I haven't been here long. Did you sleep well? I've made you bacon, eggs, sausage and toast. Is that okay?"

Steph stared in silence. She recognised the voice but could not place who he was.

"Ohh, you're not vegan, are you? Do you want me to make something else—oh, and I'm Nicky, by the way." A tattooed arm plated precious cargo that formed a hangover breakfast.

"I'm Steph. Thanks for cooking for me," she said, taking a seat. "Oh, and I'm not a vegan, but I'm a vegetarian. Thanks for asking."

"Ah okay, well I've got plenty of food in, I'll make you something—"

"—Oh, it's okay, I'll eat it," said Steph, tearing the plate from his hand.

"Not a diehard veggie, then?"

"Bacon doesn't count," said Steph, with a mouthful of food.

Nicky laughed and grabbed a second plate, taking a seat opposite.

"So, Nicky. Can I ask something?" Steph said as she dipped her toast into the egg yolk.

"Sure."

"Did we have sex?"

Nicky choked on a mouthful of fresh orange juice, immediately holding his finger up to pause the conversation. He caught his breath, saying as calmly as possible, "I think I'd definitely remember something like that…"

"Well, I woke up, and I didn't know where I was, and I don't really remember anything from last night. I broke up with my boyfriend, you see, and now my life is just a mess, and I'm going to die alone because I'm so single," Steph explained.

Nicky stared blankly. "Right… Well, me and my friend saw you at Snakes last night. You were at the bar waiting for your mate and looked like some kind of hot mess, so we looked after you. Well, we did until we lost you, but then found you again, so it's okay!"

Steph paused, attempting to absorb what had just been said, before vacantly smiling. "Oh, okay! So… this is your house?"

Nicky smirked. "Nah, this is my backup house. I only cook strangers' breakfasts in house number two so they don't find out where I really live."

"Ah… that makes sense," said Steph.

Nicky stared. "That was sarcasm. This is my house. Despite

DEBAUCHERY: PART I

moving in recently, I brought you back here last night because it was that or you'd be knee-deep in vomit on the street."

"So, we didn't hook up?"

Nicky rolled his eyes. "No, Steph, why would we hook up and then sleep in separate beds? Haven't you figured it out yet?"

"Figured what out?"

"Well, what kind of guy would pull you from a vulnerable situation, put you in a guest bedroom of his own house, fold your clothes, put your phone on charge and cook you a fry-up?"

"Um," Steph pondered, "a nice one?"

Nicky paused. "Touché… But no, I mean, I'm gay."

Steph's eyes glowed. "Oh my God, I *love* the LBGTs!"

Nicky sighed. "Right… Shall we take you home now?"

"Ooh yes, please!"

The two stood up, leaving the plates on the table, and proceeded upstairs.

"Right, I'll just get dressed and we'll be off. You wanna grab your things?" said Nicky.

Steph nodded eagerly, and they went to their separate rooms. Steph looked around the bedroom to find her bag before going back downstairs. Nicky descended moments later and grabbed a leather jacket. Steph noticed a chest tattoo poking out from under his vest as he grabbed car keys from a hook on the wall.

"Right, ready to go?" said Nicky.

Steph nodded promptly. "What is the tattoo on your chest?" she asked as he locked up.

"It means Live, Laugh, Love," he said, his deadpan wit out in full force.

"Oh my God, really?"

"No, of course not! I just wanted something badass and

vaguely geeky."

"Oh, then you'd love my friend Adrian. He loves games too!" Steph beamed as she turned to the sunlight. Nicky whipped out a pair of designer sunglasses, unlocking a vintage green Rolls-Royce resting proudly on a huge gravel path. Steph gasped.

"Your car is amazing! Oh my God! Your garden is amazing! It's so big!"

Nicky smiled. "Yeah, I bought the car a while back and I upgraded my house to something a little better. My old place was some four-bedroomed hovel, can you believe it? I really think seven bedrooms work better."

"Seven? What will you put in all that space?"

"Well, I'm gonna be here forever, aren't I? There's plenty of time to fill it."

They got into the pristine car and buckled their seatbelts. As Nicky turned the ignition, he grinned. "You know, you're going to have to tell me where we're going at some point."

"Oh! Sorry! It's Coultas Close, number 6."

"Awesome. I'll stick it in the app on my phone. We're house number twins!" Nicky started the car, and the journey back to Steph's began.

Five minutes passed in complete silence until Steph whispered, "Thank you."

Nicky smiled, eyes focused on the road.

"I've enjoyed this morning. It was nice to talk to someone new because I enjoy seeing how happy I make them. Making people happy is all that matters."

Nicky turned, grinning at Steph. "Well, you're definitely an experience."

"Oh definitely. It's just... I've felt really alone lately, and it sucks."

DEBAUCHERY: PART I

"Ah yes, the dying thing… Do you have much family?"

"Yeah, but only like a mum and a dad, and several cousins."

"Fuck's sake, I thought you were an orphan or something!" Nicky laughed.

Steph frowned. "Well, they don't really understand me. They treat me like I'm still young. I have a lot of friends too, but I don't really feel like they're my actual friends. I get drunk with them and we text a lot, but I don't really feel like they'll be there forever, if you know what I mean?"

"True," said Nicky, his eyes going back to the road.

"Look at this! My parents have both texted me three times each asking where I am. I'm twenty-nine! I just wish they'd leave me alone!"

"Yeah, but they're your parents. If they stopped texting you, it'd hit you hard. They just care, even if it's a bit grating. I mean my mum—"

Nicky stopped to slam his foot on the brake. Heart in his throat, he checked his rear-view mirror, immediately thankful for an empty road. Turning his attention forward, Nicky was presented with an erratic-looking man dressed in a tattered black suit. The torn trousers had one leg, and the frayed parts that remained were battered. An ill-fitting blazer sat limply over a dirty shirt that Nicky could only assume had been white in a previous life. With his insane brown hair, unkempt beard, and widened eyes, he offered an expression of shock and awe at the sight of them. A cardboard sign was bolted into flailing hands with the words 'The EnD IS NEEЯ' drawn in what looked like charcoal.

"You there! FOLKS! I know you!" shouted the bizarre man, seemingly unable to control the volume of his voice. He moved to Nicky's window, tapping on it, doing a spinning motion with his hand. No longer able to disregard the man's existence, Nicky groaned and reluctantly lowered his window.

The man smiled, revealing perfect white teeth, contrasting everything else about him.

Nicky rolled his eyes and mumbled as the man leapt headfirst through the open window.

"Ugh! Personal fucking space! You ever heard of it?" said Nicky, pushing the man away and putting the window up. "What do you want and how much?"

The man beamed, slamming the cardboard sign against Nicky's windscreen. Steph, who had been stunned into silence, gazed at the sign. She turned to Nicky, who wore the same confused expression. Further inspection revealed that the sign was adorned with various symbols, all of which made very little sense to them. Each symbol was sketchily drawn in charcoal, giving it a sinister edge.

"Street art from the great unwashed, lovely," Nicky said flatly.

"Ah, but you folks haven't seen it yet!" shouted the man, his voice muffled behind the safety of the car. "The end is near and I'm the messenger to tell you about THE PROPHECY! There's something coming your way, an adventure! It's the end of this life and the beginning of your new life and—"

"—Enough!" said Nicky, foot slamming against the accelerator, throwing Steph back in her seat. The card flew over the top of the car as the man's frantic rants quickly faded into nothing.

Both Nicky and Steph fell into silence for the rest of the journey. Nicky mused about what the man had said, and Steph merely wondered how a tramp could have better teeth than her.

A robotic confirmation of arrival came from Nicky's phone, pulling them from their thoughts. Nicky parked the car, but

DEBAUCHERY: PART I

neither of them moved nor spoke.

"What was that?" Steph eventually whispered, breaking the silence.

"I... don't know," said Nicky.

"Well, if you figure it out, here's my number," Steph said, showing Nicky her phone. He quickly recorded it as she opened the door, saying one final "Thank you" before slamming it shut. Nicky watched Steph go into her house from his car before dialling an all-too-familiar number on his phone.

"Hey, are you alive?"

"No, I'm dead," Amy replied, her voice croaky.

"Good, well, listen. I nearly ran over that homeless guy you text about earlier. Sorry I didn't reply, I've just dropped off Steph, and that man stepped out in front of my car."

"Badly spelled cardboard sign and Hollywood teeth?"

"Yeah, that's him. He's been weird with us, too. Did you end up researching any of it?"

"Nicky, I'm dying. I'm literally dying of death right now... but yeah, I may have found something. Bring food."

$$\dagger$$

Amy yawned, leaning over her apartment balcony in her underwear, an aura of cigarettes and shame circling her. Taking a drag of a joint, she heard a buzz at the door and went to answer it.

The moment between letting people into the building and waiting for them to arrive existed as sacred time. These precious flickers of calm were usually spent reminiscing about happier, drunker times, or a reminder that she needed to wash the dishes. She cast her eyes up towards a tired ceiling fan, which had unsuccessfully hidden her smoking habits from the landlord for over a year. Her small apartment wasn't perfect, but it would do for now.

A duvet resting on the sofa beckoned. Amy promptly scooped it up and sank into the squishy goodness. A headache throbbed against her skull, and she groaned. A lone arm emerged from its haven and aimlessly searched for the TV remote. After shifting two days' worth of empty cans across a small wooden coffee table, Amy turned on the TV. She was greeted by daytime programming taking the form of the show, Six In A Bed.

"We decided to give an eight for cleanliness because, after pulling up the floor, we found a stray pube and an active bomb. Simply unacceptable for the price they were charging per night."

A sudden knock at the door made Amy jump. She wobbled to her feet and shuffled along laminate flooring, refusing to leave her duvet cocoon.

Nicky stared at his phone as she opened the door. He looked up at the six-foot-tall duvet standing before him, grimacing. "Oh God, you're not nude, are you?"

"No, I'm not nude! I'm hanging like fuck!" Amy protested, stray bits of black hair falling over her face. Ignoring her groans, Nicky moved immediately to the kettle. Amy retreated to her squishy hideaway on the sofa.

"I've brought food," Nicky said, dropping a fast-food bag on the counter and throwing his jacket next to it.

"Uhhh thank you, uhhh," came a voice from within the duvet.

"So how long have you been awake, then? Did you sleep on the sofa? You've got a fucking bed literally right above me!" said Nicky over the increasing sound of the kettle.

"UNHhhh…"

DEBAUCHERY: PART I

The kettle became a harbinger of an unwelcome return to normality. Nicky brought his friend offerings of junk food, which was swiftly pulled into the duvet to be consumed.

"So…" he said, sitting next to her, "let's discuss."

Amy whinged, but soon accepted defeat. Emerging from her cocoon, she pushed it down to her waist, and with a mouthful of fries, began.

"Right, so you know this tramp that pestered you?"

"I'm familiar," Nicky said, sipping his tea.

"Well, he's pestered me too. He followed me home after I left yours the other day, waving this weird cardboard sign at me. I obviously shouted at him and asked what the hell he was playing at."

"Sure."

"Well, he just smiled at me and said something about a 'prophecy' being fulfilled. I got so annoyed I snatched the sign from him and walked off with it."

"Wait a minute, you took the sign? That means we can actually see what was on it! When he stepped in front of my car, he had a sign too. I thought he was insane, so I just drove off."

"I just put it in that sideboard because I've never had anything to put in a sideboard," Amy said. "So obviously when I came home, I was like, 'oh my God, I finally have something to put in my sideboard!'"

"Well, praise the sideboard!" Nicky declared, as Amy shuffled over to grab the vaguely familiar sign.

"Ooh, gimme!" said Nicky, holding out his arms. Amy threw the cardboard in his direction as though it were some cursed frisbee, only for it to hit him in the face and bounce out of the balcony doors.

They froze and looked at each other in unison, eyes wide and mouths agape. Nicky raced outside, one arm half-stuck in his coat sleeve and the other frantically beckoning Amy to join him. They leapt down the stairwell, and Amy's duvet was promoted to an unwilling cape in the process.

They burst out of the apartment building, and Amy caught a glimpse of the sign blowing down the pavement. She sighed into the warm rainfall and waddled forward, with Nicky blindly running ahead next to her so fast he ran face-first into someone.

"Shit! I'm sorry. Me and my mate were just running after… something," Nicky said as Amy scuttled ahead, laughing.

"Oh, it's alright mate, I know you liked my service last time…" came the familiar but unwelcome voice of one of his removal men. Nicky's face soured.

The bald man stood a little higher than Nicky, wearing the same grey sweatpants and vest combo as before – only this time, he donned a turquoise eye patch with a strange symbol on it.

"Oh, it's you… After. What's with the eyepatch? You look like a villain from a kid's cartoon," said Nicky with a frown.

"My name is Chace."

"Amazing. Well, this has been an experience, but I have to 'chase' a vastly more interesting piece of cardboar—"

Then, Chace grabbed Nicky's arm tightly, pulling him in and holding his gaze intensely.

"You're going to die, you know? Surrender to New Truth… mate."

Stunned into silence, Nicky pulled his arm free. "Y-You what?"

Chace squared up to him and whispered, "You heard. The Community knows all about you. You have been found and you will be destroyed as soon as I get permission! You are scum and a cancer that infests the Earth."

DEBAUCHERY: PART I

"...I've told you before, it's Nicky."

Chace merely smiled, "Your days are numbered."

Nicky frowned, masking his anxiousness with flippancy. "No shit, Sherlock! We call it a calendar 'round these parts."

Unnerved, Nicky walked away at an ever-increasing speed, occasionally throwing a glance behind him. Chace stood silent, a greasy smile plastered on his face. Nicky moved to the first turnoff he saw to escape the bizarre interaction.

A discarded duvet and two Amy-shaped legs were dangling from a skip. He ran up to them, still looking back. "You wouldn't fucking believe what I've just—oh, never mind. Did you find anything?"

"No, nothing, but you won't let this slide until we find it, so let's just get on with it."

"What happened to the duvet?" grinned Nicky.

"The universe ate it," echoed Amy's voice from within the damp metal.

"Well, if you're looking here, I guess I'll look elsewhere."

Nicky backtracked. Chace was nowhere to be seen, so he ventured to a row of bushes opposite. He got onto all fours, mumbling through the shrubs, "Typical, just typical."

He eventually caught sight of the sign resting within a small pile of twigs. With scratches and dirt as his battle scars, Nicky eagerly grabbed the sign and left the bush. As he made his return, picking leaves from his hair, he stared down the alleyway for Amy. An abrupt voice called out behind him, making him jump.

"Nicky, darling!"

He froze, turning around to see Polly smiling at him a small distance away.

"Hello uh... Polly, was it?"

Polly smiled softly as she gently bowed and waved. She stood in the same bizarre outfit as before, barbed wire dancing over a perfect figure. Seeing her in daylight, Nicky noticed her boots shone with a strange iridescence.

Transfixed, he watched as Polly skipped closer, light and whimsical. As she moved, her long jet-black hair bounced, but Nicky noticed only one thing – her eyes shone. They were a deep hazel as before, but now he noticed an almost fiery orange centre. Even at a slight distance, her eyes flickered in the daylight, making her even more beautiful. She reeked of a sexuality and intrigue Nicky felt he couldn't ignore.

"Be not afraid or whatever," said Polly as she applied scarlet lipstick. "I heard what that horrible man said to you back there, and it made me sad."

Her voice was ethereal and warm, yet filled him with caution as she came uncomfortably close.

"You did? How? I didn't see you. Who *are* you?" spluttered Nicky.

Polly smiled gently and closed her eyes. "Questions are fun, but answers are much more interesting." With a playful candour, she grinned. "Especially when you can make them up! I have a suggestion that would render your situation with Chace terminated. Best of all, it'd be *super* fun!"

"Tell me! Who even is he? Why did he say that? What should I do?"

"It's simple, really," Polly said, a twinkle in her eye. She leaned close to Nicky, a hand to the side of her mouth and whispered, "You kill him first."

Nicky paused and stared at her smile widening maniacally before a hand landed on his shoulder.

"Oh, you found it!"

Startled, Nicky spun around, blurting out, "What?"

DEBAUCHERY: PART I

"The sign, you found the sign!" Amy said.

Confused, she watched him turn back, but there was no one to be seen.

"D-Did you see her?"

"What are you talking about?" said Amy, looking over his shoulder to an empty path.

"Did you see her?"

"There's no one there!" Amy said, irritated. "What's up with you? Shall we go back now? I'm kinda in my underwear…"

Nicky stared into the distance, his eyes glazed. Amy pulled him forward, and the two friends walked back to familiar territory. Nicky's mind was abuzz with questions.

Amy put her key into the apartment door as Nicky finally spoke. "Am I mad?"

Amy frowned and felt his forehead, pausing for a moment before softly saying, "Yes, you have crippling mental health issues and need to be put down."

Nicky laughed, and as he shut the door of apartment 222, he said to himself, "Meh, let the universe eat it…"

VII
THINKING STRAIGHT

Two weeks had passed since Nicky had delivered Steph back to her house, and in that time, she had accomplished an extraordinary amount of nothing. Her first week was spent texting friends to sort out meetings she never intended to turn up to, plus a good deal of wallowing in self-pity over the recently deceased relationship. Week two was a chance to gain any sympathy she could whilst simultaneously being over the relationship altogether. Steph had always been aware that her parents would forever take the bait, but as a third week beckoned, they grew weary of her sorrow. The corpse of Steph's relationship was festering, and her mother put it upon herself to be the one to bury it once and for all.

"Steph, sweetie, can I come in?" came the muffled concern of Sally Shaw. Her request was met with silence, so she took it upon herself to enter. Sally found her daughter sat face down at her vanity table, blonde hair sprawled over a mass of beauty products.

"Steph, you need to come out of your room. I can't keep

DEBAUCHERY: PART I

coming up here and catering for you. You need to stretch your legs. The fresh air will do you good."

"Oh, so you don't even care enough to look after me now?" wailed Steph, springing up dramatically, causing makeup to fly in every direction.

"You know I care about you, darling," Sally said calmly, seeing through the act immediately. *Like mother, like daughter.* "You know as well as I do you can't live among dirty plates and old clothes forever. You're better than this."

Steph looked at her through the cracked mirror, then at herself. Her eyeliner was running, her clothes were crumpled, and she had bags under her eyes. She cried at the sight of herself, and Sally immediately ran over to throw her arms around her child.

"It'll be okay, gorgeous."

"W-Why is it so h-hard?" blubbed Steph into her mother's jumper, beauty products still falling from the table.

"Because all men are the same. They play this really big game, then can't deal with what they end up with. You are worth a million of him, you hear?"

The two embraced for a moment before Steph's mother released her from an iron grip, saying softly, "Now come on, Callum is waiting for you downstairs. He has some news for you."

Steph baulked in terror at the prospect of a conversation about men with her stepfather.

"Don't worry, gorgeous, it's not bad. We'll be waiting for you when you're ready to come down. Take your time." She walked to the door, adding, "But don't be too long, okay? Leanne is on her way in the next hour or two," as she closed it.

Steph sighed as she sat alone, a mountain of makeup at her feet and emotionally blackmailed into leaving her room. She racked her brains for everything her stepdad could want to say to her and everything else he'd say if she didn't move from her room. Coming downstairs, as she turned into the living room, her mother breezed in behind her from the kitchen.

"Here you go," she said, handing Steph a cup of tea and breezing past to stop at a wobbly coffee table at the opposite end of the room.

"Aaand here you go," she said, placing a second cup in front of the bald behemoth that was her stepfather.

"Thanks, babe," he mumbled. He sat in his usual groove on a cream leather sofa, staring blankly at a huge TV which blasted football near-constantly.

Steph took to the sofa to his left and sat next to their pet Rottweiler, Bruce. The fifteen-year-old, arthritic and too-old-for-this-shit pooch rarely left the living room, existing on a strict diet of second-hand smoke, casual racism and occasional dog food.

Bruce yawned, causing Steph to yawn, too. She turned to face Callum and said over the roar of the TV, "You have something to tell me?"

"Aye I do, Steph," he said, turning his attention to her.

Steph had always kept her distance from her stepdad, despite his undying love for her. As shallow as Steph could be, she found his visceral hatred of anyone different to himself repugnant. She always wondered how he could be the acceptable but also the exceptional. Even now, seeing him in a simple polo shirt and tracksuit bottoms repelled her. *Deeply average,* she thought, frowning.

"So, ya know yer my princess? Always have been since I first laid eyes on yer and always will be 'til that horrible day when you have to leave. But 'til that day comes, I can still do my best to make sure yer have the best life I can give yer."

DEBAUCHERY: PART I

"What do you want to tell me?"

"I've got some news that'll make yer day for sure. Princesses like you need a prince, init? I've got yer a date! Might've found yer a new bloke, and this one isn't some fairy cake who will up sticks 'n' leave yer!"

"Oh my God, Callum, why?" Steph shouted as the spectators on the TV cheered.

"Fuck's sake! Yer useless overpaid nonce! Can't even deflect a penalty! Fuckin' bellend!" Callum bellowed, making Bruce jump. Sally joined her husband on the three-seater, deliberately sitting between the two of them in case things became too heated.

"Indoor voice, Callum! You know what the neighbours will say."

"Fuck the neighbours," he mumbled, scratching a tattoo of a bulldog on his arm. "Game o' kings right 'ere! Where were we, anyway? Oh yeah, now I know you'll probably have something to say about this, but it'll be good for yer. Found you a proper man this time. He'll look after you."

"But you can't!" shouted Steph, standing up in protest.

"And why not? I don't just pick anyone yer know! This guy's from good stock!"

"Ugh, you can't just hook me up! I'm twenty-nine! I'm not a horse! YOU CAN'T BREED ME!"

"Yeah, but while yer living under my roof, young lady, yer follow my rules, you hear? Give this guy a chance!"

"And less of the 'breeding' Stephanie, thank you," added her mother, sipping her tea and becoming strangely regal for all of three seconds.

"I can't see this man," Steph replied, slumping back onto the sofa, arms folded.

"Give me one good reason, missy," hissed Callum.

"Because…" Steph paused and racked her brain for anything she could think of before blurting out, "because I'm already dating someone new!"

Both parents sat up in unison.

"Oh?" said her mum, feigning indifference but immediately on a mission to get every shred of intel possible.

"Who is he?" said Callum, ready to swing into action.

"He's just someone I've known for a bit, but I really like him and we just hit it off."

"What's his name?"

Steph paused and turned to Bruce. He stared directly at her through sleep-deprived eyes, as though curious himself to see how this one would play out.

"Nicky, his name is Nicky."

Several miles away, Nicky was unpacking boxes with Amy and shuddered.

"What's wrong with you?" said Amy, clasping a pasta dish.

"I don't know. I just sense… a disturbance."

Amy stared at him for a second then resumed unboxing, barking, "Whatever, come on! You have way more shit than I thought!"

Back at Steph's house, her mum and stepdad were sitting bolt upright, staring at their daughter. Steph looked back, hoping the sofa would just swallow her and be done with it.

"Oh," said Callum. "Well, I'll let this guy know you've already got someone then, but you cudda let me know! This one better be alright! You can invite him over! Gotta meet the guy who makes my princess happy!"

"I'll go call him now," Steph replied calmly as she stood up

DEBAUCHERY: PART I

and left the room. As soon as she entered the hall, she broke into a sprint up the stairs, saying, "Shit!" with every step she took. Closing her bedroom door, Steph frantically pulled Nicky's number up onto her phone and called him.

"Hey Steph, what's up?" came the apathetic tone of Nicky's voice.

"Oh, nothing," Steph said as she walked into her room.

"Oh God, not nothing. What's wrong? Tell me."

"Well, I've spent the last two weeks being upset and hurting over my ex, and I went downstairs today because my parents said that they had news, and now I know that the news was that they had set me up on a date like a horse, but I don't want to be a horse so I told them I had a date already and that date is you."

There was silence on the other end for a moment before Nicky replied, "Okay, learn to split up sentences, and also, what the hell? These two weeks were supposed to be uneventful. You can't just sign me up for dates!"

Amy's laugh could be heard in the background.

"I know, I'm sorry! Can you please come over and pretend to be dating me? Please! I'll make it up to you, I promise! It'll just keep my parents off my back," Steph pleaded.

The desperation and naïve hope in her voice made Nicky groan and begrudgingly mumble, "Okay, fine, but just for tonight, okay? When do you want me?"

"Oh my God, thank you, thank you, thank you! Um, if you can come over in like an hour, that'd be good."

"AN HOUR? For God's sake, Steph… Fine, I'll see you then."

He hung up, and Steph breathed a sigh of relief. Making her way back down to the living room, her parents and Bruce stared at her expectantly.

"He'll be here in about an hour. He's really excited to meet you!" she beamed. "I'll go and get ready."

"Oh, that's great! He can meet Leanne! She's due around the same time!" Sally smiled.

Steph's soul left the room at the news of a very much unwanted guest in the form of her aunt. She merely smiled, ready to leave the room and find a hole to crawl into and die.

Whipping her phone out once more, Steph fumbled a quick message to Nicky about her aunt's visit, frustrated at herself for forgetting. Rushing into her room, Steph looked at the time and slammed her phone down on the vanity table. Only an hour to make herself look presentable. Makeup fell to the floor as the path to perfection began anew.

In no time at all, a knock at the door caused Steph to leap from her chair and get as far as the landing, before her parents beat her to answer it.

It can't have been an hour already. I was only doing a little makeup… she thought as she wobbled, slowing her pace to appear casual as she descended. Steph quickly saw that Nicky was already surrounded by a wall of parental concern.

"So, you must be Nicky," said her mum, throwing a polite smile into the fray.

"Yes, it's nice to meet you both… at last," Nicky said through a fake smile he'd perfected over the years.

"Isn't Nicky a bit of a girl's name?" Callum said snarkily.

"Callum!"

"It's okay, it's short for Nicholas. Nicky just stuck with friends, so everyone just calls me that. Only my family really calls me Nicholas."

"That's fine petal, please come in and make yourself at home."

DEBAUCHERY: PART I

Steph heard the word petal and made her way down the rest of the stairs to join them. *Mum accepts him!* she thought, smiling.

Steph grabbed Nicky's hand and yanked him into the living room. As she looked at him, she noticed he had removed his nose ring and blasted his messy hair back with hairspray. She saw for the first time that he had a half-decent jawline and big green eyes. He wore blue jeans and a white long sleeve t-shirt to cover up his tattoos. She'd never seen him wear anything other than black, so admired his attempt at a neutral first encounter.

They were promptly greeted by an extra guest who had seemingly appeared from nowhere. Steph had spent the hour being so absorbed in her own reflection that she'd missed the arrival of her aunt Leanne.

Leanne Shaw was a woman with proud curves and brightly dyed red hair. She had a primal need to flirt when in the presence of any human male. Infamous for bad timing and alcoholism disguised as a celebratory attitude towards the weekend, Leanne sat with a smile. As Steph walked towards her, she put a large pink mood board onto the rickety coffee table and burst into action.

"Stephanie! It's been too long! And who is this hottie you've brought with you?"

"This is Nicholas… but everyone calls him Nicky," said Steph.

"Nicholas! I've never known one of those before. Perhaps you can park yourself next to me and we can get to know each other a little better. I'm here to discuss weddings."

Nicky's eyes widened at the lack of context, but before he could speak, Steph piped up, "Nicky is my boyfriend, and it's very important he sits next to me," pushing him down on the sofa opposite.

Callum, who had disregarded the whole conversation,

slumped into his groove next to Leanne. Steph quickly sat next to Nicky, with Bruce squashed between them.

"This is Bruce," Steph said proudly as the dog moved and slumped itself over Nicky's legs, trapping him indefinitely.

"Hello Bruce," said Nicky, struggling to mask his disdain. They sat there not saying a word, the garish pink wedding mood board on Leanne's lap an ominous presence. Nicky and Steph forced themselves to ignore the mass of frills and tassels screaming for attention and watched the TV instead. The evening news was on with another breaking story. A woman sat in a news studio with a sober look on her face, ready to give out the daily news.

"Good evening. Here is the news for today. As the humanitarian crisis on the English Channel increases, charities around the United Kingdom call upon the government to provide further aid."

"Bahh!" barked Callum, making every jump. "Charity begins at home, init. Don't you agree, Nicholas?"

Nicky's eyes narrowed, "Sure... So which charities do you donate t—"

"—Oh, Nicky, I've missed you!" interjected Steph, whose only defence from further conversation was to hug him tightly. Sally breezed into the room, finally ending the awkwardness.

"Here we go. I've got a teapot, milk and sugar. If you don't like tea, Nicky, I can make you a coffee."

"Oh, no that's great, I actually prefer tea," said Nicky, leaning over the dog and attempting to pour a cup. The Shaw family followed suit, with everyone making their respective brews. Drink in hand, Callum started his line of questioning.

"So, where yer from then, lad? How old are you?"

"I'm from the other side of the city, but not too far really, and

DEBAUCHERY: PART I

I'm twenty-nine."

"Ah, the same age as Steph then!" exclaimed Sally, taking the role of moderator.

"Aye, so what do yer do?"

"I'm a photographer, self-employed."

"Yer take photos? Self-employed is good though. Gotta love a self-made man even if what yer do ain't a proper job. None of this artsy shit will lead anywhere. See these? These are workers hands, from graft. I tell Steph that all the time. Not that I'm not proud, yer know? It's just that your generation is soft."

Nicky merely nodded blankly in his direction.

"So do yer play any sports?"

"Er, I like swimming. I actually have a pool... near me."

"Hm, don't like the footy, eh? I guess that's how it is now, though, really. Back in my day, it was standard. Now everyone's just prancing around talking about their gender. I'll never understand why they have to go on about it. You're born a boy or a girl, and it's as simple as that. People just let it take over their lives when regular guys like me never even bring it up."

Nicky stared ahead, simply saying, "Okay..."

"So, is this handsome man going to be the plus-one at my wedding, Stephanie?" Leanne asked, who had given up trying to hint and opted to dump wedding talk into the conversation.

"Um, well, I was going to invite Adrian, but if Nicky can come too, that'd be great!"

Nicky flung his head round in her direction and tried to scream at her through sheer willpower.

The mood board quivered as Leanne curbed her fury with a single, intense smile. "Well, it is meant to be strictly a plus-one event, but I'm sure I can change it. I'll just have to let the rest of the family I turned down know there'll be one extra…"

"Great!" beamed Steph, oblivious to the ever-growing bridezilla.

"The dress code will be pink," said Leanne, as blush acrylics gripped the mood board.

"I don't really like pink," Nicky said bluntly. "But I'll try to find something that isn't black."

Leanne's eyelid twitched, and her smile fell south. "Black is for funerals, Nicholas. You can come, but you *will* wear pink."

Nicky frowned and opened his mouth to reply, but Steph blurted out, "So Nicky, let's go up to my room! I've got so much to tell you since I saw you, uh, very recently." She stood up, put her cup down and shoved Bruce onto the now vacant spot, to his disgust.

Nicky sprang up awkwardly. "Well, it was… um. Well, I met you all. Steph, can I just use your bathroom before we go up?"

"Anything, my love. Literally *anything*," she replied through gritted teeth, yanking him away as quickly as possible to avoid further questioning.

Steph showed Nicky the toilet, pushed him in and said, "I'll be upstairs waiting. I'm so sorry."

Nicky shut the door to the bathroom and went over to the toilet. *What even is today?* He sighed and, as he went to wash his hands, heard a knock at the door.

"I won't be a second," he called out as he reached for a towel, but Callum barged in regardless, striding uncomfortably close. Nicky stood his ground and continued drying his hands. The two stood in silence, with Callum staring intensely at Nicky's face before growling, "What's yer game?"

"Game?" said Nicky, sliding around him and putting the towel back on the hook. "I don't have a game."

"You had any girlfriends before?"

DEBAUCHERY: PART I

"Oh, yeah. I've been with a few…" Nicky said, unsure whether he should brag or feign celibacy.

"What is your ex called?"

"Chris… tine."

"You better be good to her, yer know; I'm watching you," he said, backing away slowly, two fingers pointing to widened eyes and then towards Nicky as he moved. As the bathroom door closed he understood why Steph had called him to assemble such a farce.

Nicky had no longer gone through the bathroom door when 'Without You' by Mariah Carey echoed from Steph's room. Nicky sighed and went upstairs. As he stood outside her door, he whispered "Enough" and quickly planned to liven her up.

The first half of the chorus was playing, and he could hear her crying. As the second half came on, he grabbed the door handle and burst into the sanctuary of her bedroom, lip-syncing the words into a microphone-shaped hand and scaring Steph to death. She let out a frightened yelp but quickly realised what he was doing, grabbing a hairbrush from the table to duet with him. The two of them lip-synced to the rest of the song, and the forced tears slowly vanished from Steph's face. She felt far less alone, far less upset and exceptionally relieved that there was someone else who could, like her, break into impromptu lip-syncing.

As the song finished, they smiled at each other. Nicky had noticed immediately that Steph was wearing a tiara. Mixed with her running mascara and room aesthetic, he could only smile.

"Why are you smiling?"

"It's like your inner child is on the outside."

"Is that a good thing?" Steph asked in a slightly panicked tone.

"It's endearing."

"Well, I've had them both pierced since I was fifteen, but

thanks for noticing."

Nicky laughed and finally bit the bullet. "So, what's the deal with the tiara?"

"I dunno. It just makes me feel good, that's all. You should buy one sometime."

Nicky grinned. "Maybe I will."

"Why did you sing at me, by the way? You scared me!"

"You needed help," said Nicky. "And you just needed to transform your sad night in."

"Transform it to what?"

"A sad karaoke night with a guy who knows too many pop songs," he grinned.

Steph smiled and flung her arms around him. Nicky had never known anyone wear so much heart on so little sleeve. He remained quiet, simply wrapping his arms around her to embrace.

"I'm sorry about my stepdad… and aunt, by the way. I completely forgot she was coming over," she continued, staying in Nicky's embrace.

"It's okay. There are plenty of guys like that around. You just get used to it," Nicky said, trying to break away as Steph's tiara began pressing into his throat. "You don't have to worry about me. I'm a tough cookie."

Steph smiled and stared into his eyes, "You know, you're so much like Adrian. Your hair is different, your clothes are different, and you have piercings and tattoos but… you're one of the nicest people I've met. All the people who look like my stepdad have said really horrible things. They've only ever wanted me for my looks, but at least with you I can just be myself."

"You know we're not actually going out, right?" Nicky smiled nervously.

DEBAUCHERY: PART I

"Yeah, I know… er, do you have a boyfriend, though?"

"I do."

"Oh my God, really? What's his name?"

Nicky smiled. "His name is Ethan. He's away on holiday at the moment, but I'm sure you'll meet eventually."

"I'd love that so much! Shall we watch a movie?" Steph said, making any excuse to drag the conversation back to her room. She moved over to a small collection of movies hidden behind her bedroom door.

"Well, sure, but why don't you tell me all about this job in the beauty community, oh famous one? Don't think I didn't do my research before coming here today."

Steph glowed, relishing the chance to talk about herself. "Well, I'm a beauty vlogger and I have like a few million subscribers, and I tell them how to apply makeup properly and how to go shopping and dress properly, and I think that it's really important that people look good because you never know what'll happen and OH MY GOD! You should be in one of my videos sometime!"

Nicky blinked several times as he processed the unbroken torrent of information. A moment passed before he smiled and said, "Sure, okay."

"Oh my God, like now?" Steph said, immediately flicking several switches near her. The main light went off as coloured disco lights flashed, a ring light beamed on and a fog machine whirred into life simultaneously – Steph's near-psychotic eagerness illustrated in dazzling primary colours.

"Err, maybe we watch a movie tonight and do the video another time, eh?"

Steph sighed and went to turn the lights back, but Nicky put his hand over hers to stop her.

"Before the movie, maybe one more power ballad? Now that we have the concert setup and all?" he grinned.

Steph's eyes welled with excitement as she slammed her hand against her music player and grabbed a hairbrush microphone.

The next five minutes and twenty seconds were spent performing an almost live rendition of 'It's All Coming Back to Me Now' by Céline Dion to a camera. From the moment the song built, they clasped their hairbrush microphones, created more fog, more intensely coloured lights, and discovered Steph's fan still worked as the fog blew around them.

Steph felt the sadness over her failed relationship fade. The feeling of loss and the worries for the future fell away, replaced by a fresh excitement for things to come. The song finished, and they both fell onto the bed, laughing.

There was a moment of silence before Steph whispered, "Thank you."

Nicky smiled, sitting up and declaring, "Well, that was the gayest thing I've done in a while."

"You're different to Adrian in that way, you know. It's nice. I didn't think I could have both."

"What do you mean?"

Steph looked away. "Well, Adrian would NEVER do things like that with me. Like, he's so funny, but... not like that."

Nicky smiled. "Well, now you have both. It's just being stupid. I just figured you needed it dealing with your dad."

"*Step*dad!" Steph protested.

"Fair... Do you wanna watch the movie now?"

"Well," she said, leaping back up and flicking through a modest movie collection, "What kinda films do you like?"

"Love horrors, don't mind the others and partial to a chick

DEBAUCHERY: PART I

flick. Pick whatever," Nicky took his trainers off and slumped back onto her bed. "You know I had virtually no preparation time for this charade, right?"

"Oh no, they normally do that at Christmas. It's fine," Steph replied, not looking up from her search.

"Wait, what?"

Steph rooted through her movies before screaming, "Eee!" making Nicky jump. "Have you seen *The Notebook*? It's so sad!"

"Er, yeah, I've seen it. Is that the one about property development and dementia?" Nicky said, making himself comfortable on her bed.

"You wanna watch it? I LOVE CHICK FLICKS!"

"Sure, and we can make sure this ex-boyfriend is dead and buried too in the process."

"Oh, I don't want to kill him. I just want to get over him," she said, putting the disc in the player.

Steph flicked the disco lights off and butterfly-shaped fairy lights on before joining him on the bed. They watched the film as time flickered away. Between the on-screen crying and intermittent noises from their smartphones, Steph had not felt so relaxed since she had been with Adrian the night she became single. Halfway through the film, she put Nicky's arm around her and they cuddled.

Nicky noticed but kept quiet. *She needs this.*

By the end of the film, Nicky was fast asleep. Steph sat up as the credits rolled and stared at him. She smiled and thought about how thoughtful he'd been in her time of need. They hadn't known each other very long, yet here he was hugging her in her room, under the warm glow of her fairy lights. She turned to face Nicky before leaning over and gently pressing her lips against his. At that moment, Nicky floated back into consciousness and sprang backwards, banging his head on the wall.

Steph leapt up, spluttering, "Oh my God, I'm so sorry. I got carried away. I'm so sorry, Nicky!"

"I-It's fine, it's just… Not something I was expecting, that's all. It's fine. It's like a punch in the face. Everyone gets one. I should go anyway. It's really late."

"Okay, but yeah, I'm sorry. I really am." Their eyes met for a second. Through her tears, Steph prayed they could just forget everything and be transported away. As Nicky made his way to the door, she felt a sinking feeling.

"Look, try not to feel so bad, okay? It's nothing, really," Nicky said as they went downstairs. "I'm going shopping with Amy tomorrow. Do you want to tag along?"

Steph looked at him with a smile and said, "Yes, please!"

"Okay cool, I'll pick you up tomorrow afternoon, about one o'clock?"

"Definitely!"

Steph turned the keys to unlock the front door, and no sooner had she opened it, her parents came barging out of the living room to see him off. Steph pushed Nicky forward, shouting, "GO! RUN! I'LL SEE YOU TOMORROW!" before slamming the door shut, throwing him both into the street and a friend-zone somehow created by both parties.

viii
CAN'T EVEN

"You know you could've told her you meant food shopping and not material possessions shopping, right?" whispered Amy as Nicky placed a loaf of bread into a trolley.

"I know, but it was so awkward. I couldn't have just left."

"Sure you could."

Nicky put a few cans in the trolley as they slowly made their way down aisle eight of the supermarket. Steph drifted behind them, fixated on the previous evening. She felt horrible for ending such a good time without properly saying goodbye to Nicky, but was incredibly thankful that she could at least see him today. She caught up to them both and jumped in between them, putting her hands on their shoulders.

"Hey you guys! I'm going to go look for pretty things!"

Amy grimaced. "Okay then."

Steph beamed at them and skipped away.

"Now I definitely need pasta at some point..." Nicky said to himself.

"Why do you hang around with her?" Amy probed, adjusting her leather jacket over a red dress. "You barely know her, and she's so toxic. She's like a child, and she's so painfully white!"

Nicky frowned. "Maybe gays just have an affinity for free-spirited women who make men's lives difficult. Anyway, I think you're judging too quickly and also, we're pale as fuck, so stop hating on your own kind."

"Wash your mouth out! She's dumb, and besides, you told me she has a tiara! *A fucking tiara!*"

"Well, she's obviously just a princess, isn't she?" grinned Nicky.

Amy turned around, declaring, *"DESPAIIRRR,"* as they turned to the next aisle.

Meanwhile, Steph stared at rows of chocolate and fizzy sweets.

"What to buy…" she said, putting her fingers over her lips thoughtfully. She opted for a box of fancy chocolates, but as she reached out to take one, a hand grabbed her arm, making her shout a startled, incoherent noise.

"Steph! Oh my God!"

She spun around and saw her friend Isaac. Standing six feet tall, he was a Persian guy in his thirties, with messy black hair and a heart-shaped birthmark on his neck.

"Listen to me!" he said, grabbing her arm. Her eyes widened as she noticed his appearance. Her friend stood in a burlap-type sack with a simple piece of rope wrapped around the waist. He was barefoot, his skin was grubby, and he looked freezing.

"Isaac, what on earth are you wearing? It's definitely not a vibe…"

"Look, Steph, I know this might sound crazy, but I've been somewhere. Somewhere amazing! I don't know how to explain it, but I was at home and then I wasn't, and there were these people. They look just like people I know! There's this castle, and

DEBAUCHERY: PART I

he put me in prison! I managed to escape, but there's stuff... stuff you wouldn't believe, it's incredible!"

Isaac's lip was cut and a trickle of blood fell from his hair past desperate eyes.

"Isaac, I... don't understand."

"You need to come back to Volataris with me to see it! You'd love it so much! We need to go now! Just so I know it's real!"

Steph frowned, "Well, I suppose so. Let me put these back and I'll go let my new friends know I'm coming with you."

"There isn't any time. We need to go NOW!" he shouted, gripping her tighter.

"Isaac, you're hurting me!"

He looked around toward the security cameras and quickly let go. Steph backed away before returning the chocolates to the shelf. "Look, Isaac, just come with me and we can go to my friends to get all of this sorted out, okay?" Determined to help, she turned around only to see that he had gone. The entire aisle was empty. She stood for a moment in complete confusion, trying to process what had just happened.

Amy and Nicky were greeted by a wall of colour and flavour as they turned into the World Foods section.

"Look, all I'm saying is there are so many random characters popping up it'd be hard for anyone to follow," Amy mused. "I feel that there is so much more to this than we think."

"Honestly, I have no idea what's going on, especially with that Polly woman. She literally just appeared and disappeared. It was like magic," said Nicky, finding his pasta at last. "Anyway, can we change the subject? What are we doing for Halloween?"

Amy sighed. "I haven't thought about it 'til now. Maybe we can just stay in, watch gross shit and get pizza?"

"Sounds like a plan."

"Oh, and don't invite Steph," Amy said firmly.

"That's not nice."

"Look, I just don't like her."

"Give her a chance. You're just suspicious of other women, that's all. She's harmless."

"Nicky, she's a plank!" Amy protested.

"Okay, okay, we won't invite her, but don't let her know we're doing this. It can be just us two."

"Deal," Amy said as they turned to the next aisle.

Steph made her way down aisle six, feeling completely over what she had just seen. Having quickly grown bored with trying to find her friends, she decided that the best course of action would be to expand her makeup collection.

She pored over lines of foundation, blush and lipstick, transfixed by the idea that each item would make her even more beautiful.

"Should I be bad?" she whispered to herself.

"Oh sweetheart, I thought you'd never ask," came a voice which pulled her from her thoughts.

Steph spun around. "Who's there?"

"And here she comes, making her grand appearance down the aisles of a supermarket of all places! How utterly tragic! We see here that I am wearing a *gorgeous* patchwork jacket adorned with *stunning* avant-garde metalwork to *die* for!" came Polly's sultry voice, confidently pushing a trolley towards Steph. "Watch as I transcend all things *fabulous* with ease! Have we seen an iconic

DEBAUCHERY: PART I

fashion moment quite like this? Don't be ridiculous, darling! It's unheard of!"

Steph gawked as Polly stopped in front of her. Twirling hair between gloved fingers, she smirked, "Life is just *soo* difficult, isn't it?"

"Oh my God! You're so gorgeous! I love your boots!" Steph squealed as she noticed their iridescent sheen.

"Thanks, gorgeous!"

Polly's voice was the coolest voice Steph had ever heard. She wanted to know everything about this woman and be best friends with her forever.

"Who are you?" Steph whispered, hypnotised by her beauty.

"I'm kind of a big deal around here," she said, dropping a single red lipstick into the deep trolley, only for it to fall through to the floor.

"Oh, me too," beamed Steph.

Polly laughed. "It's all just so confusing, isn't it? The stuff with Isaac and that crazy homeless guy… and what's the deal with that guy trying to kill Nicky? Totes spooky!"

"How do you—"

"—know these things? Oh munchkin, I know *all* sorts!"

Steph found Polly's genuine happiness uneasy, and as she turned to look down the aisle, she was met with nothing. The checkouts were empty, and all customers had seemingly vanished. Any regular hustle and bustle had drained away, cloaking the aisle in deafening silence. Spooked, Steph cast her eyes to a motionless clock above her, panicking as Polly grinned.

"So, I spoke to Nicky the other day, and he was as confused as you. It was really quite boring! He wanted *all* the answers to *all* of his questions immediately. Whatever happened to just enjoying the ride? I can, however, answer one question for you. That's always fun!"

Steph's mouth hung open with her brain in overload as Polly skipped away, hands behind her back.

"Come on, gorgeous, the clocks might've stopped, but time's still a tickin'! It's not all about you, unfortunately!"

"Wait! Er… who are you?" shouted Steph as the woman reached the end of the aisle.

"How *vastly* basic!" Polly scoffed as she waved and skipped around the corner. Sound resumed abruptly, making Steph jump.

"There you are! We thought we'd lost you… again," came Nicky's voice. Steph looked at them, throwing confused glances between the clock and the checkouts.

"What's wrong?" said Amy, caring very little.

Steph's phone vibrated, and she quickly yanked it from her pocket. A notification came up on her screen that said NO DATA REMAINING.

Between Polly, Isaac, no data and being called basic, Steph lost herself to confusion. Her shallow thoughts were buried under valid questions and she felt simply overwhelmed. Instead of talking, a sociopathic moment took hold. A knee-jerk reaction to garner sympathy en masse. A theatre of pride beckoned, and it stirred her soul. It was at this moment that Stephanie Shaw fell to the floor of aisle six, uttering the immortal words, "I can't even."

Nicky lunged forward and dropped to his knees in a swiftly failed attempt to catch her. Amy merely stood befuddled.

"Oh my God, are you okay?" Nicky said frantically.

"I can't even."

"Oh, fucking hell!"

"What's wrong with her?" frowned Amy.

DEBAUCHERY: PART I

"She can't even!" replied Nicky.

"You're kidding? snapped Amy, patience immediately falling short. "What in the 'Just Girly Things' is this shit? Do we *really* have this much free time in our lives?"

"White girl can't even!" shouted Nicky up the empty aisle. "Grab her phone!"

Amy walked around the trolley slowly, with as little urgency as possible, before taking Steph's phone. Delicately holding the baby pink case, she sighed, "Now what?"

Nicky had Steph's arm over his shoulders and had somewhat successfully yanked her up to a sitting position. "Call the white people! Go into her contacts and call the whitest name on the list! NOW!"

Amy jumped, becoming strangely embroiled in the chaotic yet pointless production taking place.

"Are you calling the white people?"

"They're all bloody white!" shouted Amy, briefly locking eyes with a bewildered elderly woman clasping a bottle of jojoba extract shampoo.

"Hello? Is this Claire?"

"Excellent!" said Nicky, cradling a limp Steph in his arms.

"Hello, I'm with Steph and she..." Amy exhaled. "She can't even."

Steph's head bobbed side to side as though nauseous, quietly repeating over and over, "Can't even. Can't even. Can't... even." Every moment was theatre, and she was the star.

"Look, I don't understand either, but she 'can't even' and you're the lucky recipient of that information, so can we just get this over with? I have to be literally anywhere else right now."

"Ask her if she's wearing yoga pants! Does she have a tan?" said Nicky.

"Okay, could you say some white stuff?" There was a pause before Amy put her hand over the speaker to face Nicky. "I'm getting 'shabby chic' from Claire. Is this any good?"

"DREAMS OF PARIS!" bellowed Nicky.

Amy turned the phone away, shouting, "ANY MARILYN MONROE QUOTE EVER!" at the top of her voice.

"LINEN-SCENTED WAX MELTS!"

Steph slumped to the floor, and Nicky backed away.

Amy merely hung up on Claire, whispering, "Did it work?"

"I think she's rebooting," Nicky said, approaching her as though she were a robotic fawn in a woodland clearing. "Steph, are you okay?"

"I-I'm fine," she mumbled. "There was just… a lot and I have… no data."

Steph sat for a minute with Nicky, and Amy stood next to her.

"This whole time, it was about mobile data? Are you actually shitting me?" Amy seethed. "The fucking caucacity of this woman, Nicky! Why do we have anything to do with her?"

Meanwhile, the entire shop had ground to a total standstill. A mass of hushed whispers and judgemental stares tore their way down the aisle. Steph rose to her feet, absorbing every bit of attention. It didn't matter whether it was positive or negative – she was being seen.

They shuffled to the checkouts and started placing items on the conveyor belt as quickly as possible.

"Here Steph, I'll pay for your stuff, it's fine," said Nicky.

Steph smiled, put her items on the conveyor belt and helped load the rest of the shopping as Amy packed and glared at Steph. The cashier scanned the items quickly, and after the fifth packet of noodles caught Nicky's eye. "You two got kids?"

"No, just depression," replied Nicky, who continued to pack. The woman smiled nervously and returned to her job.

When the order was put through, the checkout assistant became brave enough to speak again. "Would you like any extra bags?"

"Yes, please, just the one," said Amy calmly. "I'd like to put it over my fucking head so I can end this awful situation as fast as possible."

IX
THE ENIGMA CARD: PART II

Steph left her house that afternoon in a long white dressing gown she had stolen from a spa, with a matching towel wrapped around her head and pink headphones poking out. 'Spice Up Your Life' by the Spice Girls instantly became the soundtrack to her journey. Lip-syncing the words as she skipped up the street, her goal of acquiring face packs was the single most important thing in life at that moment. She broke out a few dance moves, twirling as the entire world became a dancefloor.

Eventually, she arrived at a line of shops. Steph danced by two takeaways who were frantically trying to out-market each other with offers plastered over the windows. She glided past a pet shop known for housing a crude-mouthed Macaw and even ruder staff. Casting her eyes ahead, she saw a small corner shop sign, *Mahmood's*, in back-lit letters. It was her final destination.

The antiquated corner shop had stayed afloat for years through a mixture of Steph's regular custom and the public's endless need for milk, bread, and casual discussions about waning mental health. Steph had remained faithful to the small shop, and as she walked through the door, a familiar bell announced her as a

DEBAUCHERY: PART I

customer. The smells of unknown foods had become a familiar scent to her, paired with the crackle of an Arabic radio station.

The counter on her left sold jars of Victorian-style sweets with cigarettes locked away behind something resembling a Soviet bunker. The shop boasted only two aisles, but the shelves were crammed floor to ceiling with everything a person could ever want.

Steph peered down the dimly lit aisle before smiling at a friendly face coming cheerily towards her at break-neck speed.

Mahmood rushed over to greet her, remarking, "Ah hello!" in a strong Lebanese accent. He had greying black hair and the warmest smile of anyone she knew. Despite years of struggling, Mahmood's demeanour stayed colourful and bright. A friendship with his customers was the bedrock of his service.

"Hi Mahmood, I've come for—"

"—ah yes, Gorgeous Beauty face pack? How are you?" he interrupted, spinning around and vanishing down the left aisle immediately.

"I'm good, thank you. I'm having a 'me' day!" Steph shouted after him. She could hear mumbling from within the aisle as he searched for the pack. He returned moments later, clasping a small pouch labelled 'Gorgeous Beauty' above an Arabic woman with a purple face.

"Still no pink?" Steph said, taking it from him.

"Wha— er no, no. No pink just yet! Soon though, I've ordered in! Two pounds sixty!"

Steph handed over her money, and Mahmood beamed. His fragmented English and smiling face had been there throughout most of her life. This shop was where she felt safe and warm. It was a simple sanctuary and a lifeline when she needed it. Steph smiled as he rang the item through and the till drawer flew open.

He put the money in and it snapped shut, nearly taking his hand with him.

"This register! It's stupid. Like that show on the TV, yes? That is funny! Anyway, two pounds forty change," he said, placing the money in her hand and patting it.

After enthusiastic goodbyes, Steph left the shop and reached into her dressing gown pocket for her headphones. As she did, she noticed a familiar man in a tattered suit, frantically waving a sign with one hand and gripping a woman in a bus shelter with the other. Steph immediately realised that it was the same man who had jumped in front of Nicky's car. His appearance was identical to when Steph had seen him previously, but his abstract interest was now aimed towards a woman in a bright yellow work fleece. Steph marched up to the bus shelter, determined to look like a heroine and perhaps even help the woman.

"Hey you! Leave her alone, she hasn't done anyth—"

"—Oh you! Hey you!" interrupted the man. His eyes grew so wide they looked ready to burst from their sockets.

"Can you just leave me alone, please?" the woman pleaded desperately as she tried to release herself from his grip.

"Leave her alone, you freak!" barked Steph, taking a confident step forward in solidarity, arms spread open and towel wrap coming loose and flopping over her face.

"They are *together!* THE END IS NEAR!" the man screamed, throwing his hands into the air and shaking them.

Steph looked horrified as onlookers stared at the bizarre scene before them. The woman poked her head out from behind her beautiful saviour timidly.

The man walked up close to Steph and stared directly into her eyes. She retreated but he simply moved closer. After a painful

DEBAUCHERY: PART I

thirty seconds of silent staring, Steph extended a robed hand and whispered, "You really need to sort those pores out."

He merely smiled, bearing perfectly white teeth and saying proudly, "You two will know! You two will join with more and YOU TWO WILL SUFFER! Things are coming to you folks, oh yes! Ol' D has to tell you all the things! It's all just SO IMPORTANT!" He brandished the cardboard at the two women, who just stared in a befuddled silence.

Without warning, he turned and broke into a sprint, waving his arms in the air once more and shouting, "Ol' D will be back! The battle between good and evil has already begun, sister women! Speakables soon but 'til then… THE END IS NEAR!"

Steph turned to the girl at the bus stop, who looked unnerved.

"Thank you," she whispered.

"Are you okay?"

"I'm fine. I was just on my way to work and this weird guy came up to me and started shouting and waving that sign at me. He was quite aggressive, so I'm a bit shaken, that's all."

"I've seen him before, so that's why I came over. He's a freak and I sensed such a negative aura from him. Definitely not good vibes! I'm Steph, by the way."

"Lily," replied Lily, offering a nervous smile. "And I suppose that man is Ol' D. Very peculiar."

An awkward silence followed before Steph piped up, adjusting her towel wrap in the process, "So, what were you doing here? It's like such a random place to be."

Lily stared, saying plainly, "Well, it's a bus stop. So, I was waiting for a bus… but I'm going to be late again. It's bad because I'm so close to losing my job and—"

"—That's nice. I'm having a 'me' day! I've just been so stressed lately because this guy dumped me and it hit me really hard, and he's probably already looking for another girl. I mean, I've never known anyone so selfish!"

Steph sighed, pulling a sad face toward the sky. "Life's just so unfair for us, Lily, and now we have this Ol' D to deal with. I'm gonna be thinking about this forever, ugh."

Lily gazed up at the road for any sign of her bus before saying quietly, "Well yes, it definitely is strange, especially because his sign had all those Baphomet symbols on them…"

Steph spun around, her towel wrap coming undone again, slapping a shocked expression onto her face. "What did you say?"

Lily glimpsed her bus in the distance and was relieved. "Well, the sign he was holding. They were symbols of Baphomet. You know, like, the Devil?"

Steph kept her stunned expression underneath a now flat towel, frozen on the spot.

"Well, I've got to get this bus. It was nice meeting you," said Lily.

Steph grabbed her new acquaintance's arm as the bus signalled to stop, stammering, "No! You can't go! Come with me to my friend's house and tell him what you've just told me! The thing! The thing about Bathmat!"

"Baphomet," said Lily. "I can't. I'm already in so much trouble with work. If I don't turn up, I'll probably—"

"—but this is so important I can feel it! Please come with me! Please! This horrible man will keep following you unless we all get together and figure this out!" pleaded Steph.

As the bus pulled up to the curb, Lily looked towards Steph. There was a desperation in her big blue eyes which belied a previously unnoticed passion. Even though Lily didn't know this woman, an intense curiosity burned within her. Her life had

DEBAUCHERY: PART I

become mundane, and this was the first time in an age where intrigue and excitement beckoned.

"Okay," said Lily as she sheepishly waved the driver on. He mouthed obscenities in her direction, but she didn't care. The slight rebellion of deviating from a daily path filled her with feelings rendered alien over time. Concerns over tardiness vanished behind the glow of alternate adventures.

"Ooh yay! I'll get this guy to pick us up! I've only known him a few weeks, but I've got a really good feeling about this…"

Lily scratched her head. "Okay, but can I ask something? I kind of wanted to ask when I saw you, to be honest."

"Sure, what's up?" said Steph, her expression switching from joyful to deeply concerned in a second.

"Well, I just wanted to know why on earth you're wearing a dressing gown and have your hair in a towel when you're outside?"

Steph's joy returned. "Oh, that! I'm having a 'me' day because my boyfriend dumped me and I'm going to be single forever—oOoh, Nicky's replied! He's on his way!"

"Right. I don't know about this," Lily said anxiously. "You've told me that this man waving cardboard at me is mad, but I'm following you into a guy's car who you barely know, all while you're dressed in a bathrobe?" She sat back down, unsure of whether Steph represented adventure or a chore.

Steph plonked herself down beside her and held her hand, saying perkily, "Oh, well, I'm obviously not mad, am I? I have this face pack. Who in their right mind wouldn't have a fabulous skincare routine, duh?"

☩

"Okay," said Nicky, starting a fresh journey home. "Why did I drive all the way out here to pick you up when your friend could've just picked you up?"

"Because this girl has really important information about the crazy man we saw the other day and mentioned something on his card. He's called Ol' D, by the way, and just has, like, this… freaky aura," said Steph from the back seat, applying her purple face mask as she spoke.

"Right… So who is this yellow woman?"

"I'm Lily," came a quiet voice from the backseat.

"Okay, and why are you wearing a dressing gown, Steph?" Nicky continued, throwing a confused look into his rear-view mirror.

Steph caught his eyes on her, stopped rubbing her face and said flatly, "Well, I'm having a 'me' day, obviously! Also, I've rung Adrian and told him to come to your house. I can't do anything without Adrian."

Nicky looked at her blankly. "Right. So, who's Adrian again, sorry?"

"Oh, he's my best friend, and he's a sin—"

Amy's voice burst through the car from the front seat, "—THE LEAD FUCKING SINGER OF ALDL IS COMING TO YOUR HOUSE, NICKY? OH MY GOD!"

Nicky frowned. "And why the hell are you here?"

Amy sat in a grey hoodie, clasping a half-eaten sausage roll. "Oh, well, I don't know. A little thing called *adventure!*" she spat.

"Oh, stop it! You're getting crumbs everywhere!"

The car fell into silence. Everyone watched Amy consume a further sausage roll before wiping her mouth with her sleeve and saying, "Hi, I'm Amy, and I'm just here for the laughs," to the back of the car.

DEBAUCHERY: PART I

"Hi Amy," replied Steph immediately. Lily sat quietly; her hands tucked into the sleeves of her work fleece. "I'm Steph. I was with Nicky when that weird tramp jumped in front of the car and I met you in the supermarket the other day when we went shopping, and also the nightclub."

Amy narrowed her eyes at Nicky, saying, "Is she having a fucking stroke?"

"Oh, and I met Lily at the bus stop near me and she knows a lot about this piece of card with symbols of Maphobet on it."

"Baphomet," said Lily.

"Wait, did you say Baphomet?" Nicky said, throwing a look towards Lily in his rear-view mirror. "Baphomet, as in the Devil, Baphomet?"

"Yes, that one. I did philosophy at university and we studied the varying facets of belief and spirituality."

"Oh, you studied philosophy at uni?" said Amy as she turned around, sweeping black hair from her face. "I guess that's why you're dressed as a lemon, then? You're fully trained up for life to not give you any?"

Nicky and Amy grinned as Steph merely sat with a purple face. Lily wrapped her arms around herself defensively.

"Hey, just know that the front of the car is full of arseholes," Amy said in her own apologetic way. "I'm glad you have the know-how for this kinda stuff because I only have what I found online. Haven't had the chance to mention it to Nicky."

"Haven't had the chance?" exclaimed Nicky. "If there's some aggressive Satanist following us, then it probably would've been best to have mentioned it at least once!"

"You had mental health issues!" Amy snapped.

"I had mental health issues because my removal man randomly

called me the scum of the earth. Then that Polly woman appeared and said I could stop this idiot by just killing him myself!"

"Wait, what? A reference to the Devil on some mad tramp's cardboard isn't as important as what you've just said!" Amy yelled, grabbing a third sausage roll.

"Can I have one?" said Steph, taking a risky lean forward.

Amy threw the bag in her face without looking and continued, "Why was your removal guy threatening you, and why did that Polly woman appear only to you?"

"Look, I don't know, okay?" Nicky said, exasperated. "Can we just get back to mine so I can at least put the kettle on?"

"Yes, please!" piped up Steph, resting her chin on the front seat and getting purple on Nicky's cheek.

"Ugh, thanks Steph!"

"Don't worry. It's berries!" she beamed.

"Are you always like this?" asked Amy as she turned round to face her for the first time.

"Like what?"

"Different..."

"I'm very uncomfortable," stated Lily, a little overwhelmed by the three large personalities.

"Do you want to borrow my towel wrap?" Steph asked as Lily immediately shook her head.

Nicky practically punched the radio on and the four of them listened to the cheery tone of the presenter.

"*Naturewatch* comes to your screens this Monday evening to discuss the subject of birds. We've received a gorgeous video from Maureen in Lincoln of tree sparrows hurling their bodies against the frosted glass of her conservatory. It's really this breed of inspirational content that keeps us up to date with their

DEBAUCHERY: PART I

migratory path and why their numbers are falling in the UK."

"We're here!" said Nicky, pulling up to his large front gate. Lily craned her neck upwards to look.

"You really live here?" said Lily.

"Yeah, I've only recently moved in, though, so you'll have to excuse the clutter."

Upon opening the black iron gate, Nicky drove down a long gravel path as the passengers gawked. Clusters of chrysanthemums sat at the base of conifer trees with varying earthworks in view. Autumn crept into the vast garden, throwing visions of orange, yellow, and brown amongst the evergreens. A gentle breeze rustled the trees, sending delicate leaves to fall gently across the path. There were ponds with lilies alongside contrasting geometric sculptures, and wherever she faced, Lily could hardly believe her eyes. They pulled up to the house, driving around a domineering yet inactive fountain.

Steph and Lily got out, staring back at a gorgeous image of October.

"You've really outdone yourself this time," remarked Amy as she joined them.

"Cheers. I really feel that I can accomplish everything I want to do in my career with this space... and obviously, it gives me and Ethan space."

Nicky left his car and led the way.

"Don't mind the fountain. I haven't got it working just yet, it needs maintenance. Make yourselves at home, anyway, once you're inside."

Everyone shuffled through the front door and Lily's jaw fell to the floor once more.

"What on earth is your job? I've never seen a house like this in my life!" exclaimed Lily.

"I'm a photographer. My mum is too, but she lives abroad in Italy. I'm carrying on the family business, I suppose, but a lot of my clients come from her. I get recommended as a 'younger eye' so I've made a moderate dent in the industry already."

"A fucking dent, he says, with his Gatsby car!" scoffed Amy as she removed her shoes. She was used to her friend's lavish lifestyle and had learnt to become part of the furniture wherever she ended up with him.

With both Lily and Steph following suit, Nicky ushered everyone into the living room, remarking, "Well guys, like I said, my home is your home, unless you're murderers or some shit."

"I'm gonna wash my face!" declared Steph, breaking away from the group. "The purple is hurting."

Amy glared as Steph bounced up the stairs cheerily. "I can't believe you're letting that run free."

"Well, I let you and my bloke run free, so what's one more idiot? We might lose her anyway."

They grinned as Steph's voice tore down the stairs. "Oh, and Adrian's on his way, Nicky! I can't wait for you to meet him!"

She hadn't even finished her sentence, and Amy's eyes ignited. "ALDL?"

They entered the room and were immediately blasted with a strong smell of fresh paint. A huge television, a games console, a coffee table and two chocolate-coloured sofas were the only pieces of furniture there so far and sat directly in the middle of the room. Clumps of boxes marked 'Reception Room' sat in piles scattered around the large room. Nicky and Amy shuffled through the small sea of boxes to take a seat on the two-seater. Lily stood glued to the carpet near the door as an awkward silence ensued.

DEBAUCHERY: PART I

"It's okay, you can come over. Be not afraid, likely introvert."

"Look, babe!" said Amy, grabbing Nicky's arm. "She's coming closer! Oh, I wish we'd brought a camera!"

Lily shuffled over to take a seat, leaving space for Steph who burst in seconds later, releasing her towel wrap and declaring, "I AM FRESH!" Her long blonde hair fell gracefully down her shoulders as she took a seat on the sofa.

"Okay, so where shall we start?" Nicky said to get the conversation started.

"Ooh, can we shut the curtains?" said Steph excitedly.

Nicky and Amy looked confused, saying in unison, "Why?"

"Well, it'll be more mysterious if you put the lights on and shut the curtains."

"Okay," said Nicky, getting up and shutting the curtains.

Darkness fell over the room, and as Nicky walked over to the light switch, Steph abruptly screamed, "ADRIAN'S HERE!" causing the entire room to jump.

"What the fuck? Are you trying to kill me, you fucking dingbat!" Amy seethed after her as she raced back outside.

$$\dagger$$

Adrian stood at the gate of Nicky's house, fresh from band practice and dressed in his tour merch. Ringed fingers pressed a buzzer and curious eyes peered through the gate.

This can't be the right place...

He went back to his little red car, sat amongst empty crisp packets and pulled up his phone screen. He looked through Steph's frantic texting just to double-check. As he found the address she'd sent, the gates opened, making his heart rate quicken.

A soft breeze wafted through his tied hair. It was a peaceful place with a smell of damp foliage in the air. Without warning, he saw a small, yet flailing, figure running towards him. He squinted as the surrounding trees rustled to see a woman in a bathrobe now breaking into a sprint. She was shouting something but was so far away it was inaudible.

As the figure came closer, wild blonde hair billowed, and the unmistakable sound of Steph's voice emerged. Breathing a quick sigh of relief, he smiled as she ran, still unable to hear a single word. It didn't stop her, and eventually, the distant incoherence rose to become a loud wall of speech.

"OH MY GOD ADRIAN YOU HAVE TO SEE THIS HOUSE IT'S AMAZING AND I'VE MET THE MOST AMAZING PEOPLE AND I ALSO MET THAT WEIRD MAN I TOLD YOU ABOUT HE'S CALLED OL' D AND I GOT ANOTHER FACE PACK BUT THE PURPLE BURNT MY FACE BUT I WASHED IT OFF AND NOW IT'S ALL TINGLY BUT AMY IS SO EXCITED TO MEET YOU AND I'M SO GLAD YOU CAME!"

Adrian smiled as Steph ran into his arms and embraced him. The force almost made him lose his footing.

"So, you've had an eventful day then?" he grinned.

"Adrian, these new people are so amazing! I can't wait for you to meet them!"

"They're not posh, are they? I feel so underdressed," said Adrian, staring around the vast grounds of the house.

"Oh no! They're amazingly different and interesting! In fact, Amy is one of your biggest fans, behind me obviously," Steph said with a smile.

"Really? I didn't think I had the reach to places like this…"

DEBAUCHERY: PART I

"Oh yeah! She was at the nightclub with Nicky the other day when I got drunk. They were there to see you play."

"Ah, standard," said Adrian. "Shall we drive up... Wait..." He held Steph's arm as she started to move forward. He smiled. "Well, maybe if she's such a fan, I could sing for her?"

Steph beamed. "Oh my God! That would make her so happy, I'm super positive!"

"I mean, what better way to introduce myself, eh?" He grinned, untying his hair to enter work mode.

"Do you think she'll hear from all the way over here?" said Steph, opening the door to the passenger seat, ready to observe.

"I reckon it'll test the strength of my projection, but I'm sure the sweet sound of metal will reel her in. Amy, was it?"

Steph nodded as she watched her friend grab his phone from his pocket. Tatted fingers tinkered away on a sound-amplifying app, his rings tapping against the screen as he turned every setting to max. He turned the microphone on, gripped the phone and threw himself forward to release a deep metal growl tearing from his vocal cords. Hair fell over his face as a passing car swerved at the sheer wall of sound coming from Nicky's black metal gate.

He started to sing a song, switching the name of a girl to 'Amy' for a custom gig for his biggest fan. Steph merely smiled through the chaos, watching Adrian do what he did best.

After a minute or so he stopped as, without warning, he saw a small, flailing figure running towards him. He squinted as the surrounding trees rustled to see a woman in a leather jacket and big black boots now breaking into a sprint. She was shouting something but was so far away it was inaudible.

As the figure came closer, wild black hair billowed and Amy's voice emerged, the distant incoherence rose to become a loud wall of speech.

"OH MY GOD NICKY IT'S THE LEAD SINGER OF ALDL YOU HAVE TO SEE HIM HE'S AMAZING AND WE CAN FORGET EVERYTHING FOR A MOMENT BECAUSE OF THIS ICON AND HOLY FUCK I'M GONNA PEE MYSELF I'M SO GLAD YOU CAME!"

Adrian threw an awkward smile into the mix as his number one fan lunged forward, locking him in a tight embrace. He laughed and put his arms around her.

"You alright, mate?" he said, noticing Steph's frown and promptly stepping back. Amy stood silent. He could feel her eyes taking in every detail of his soul and he didn't know whether to be flattered or deeply uncomfortable. With a little of both, he spoke up once more. "You okay? You're Amy, right?"

"I. Fucking. Love. You," breathed Amy into his vest top. "You are a GOD."

A new-found shyness came over him as he fiddled with the rings on his fingers, laughing. "Thanks. You know Steph already, I'm guessing?"

The fan service died as Amy looked behind God to see Steph throwing a cheery wave towards her. Her face fell as she mumbled, "We've met."

"Great stuff," said Adrian, oblivious. "You wanna hop in my car with us and we can drive up together? Don't fancy walking this one, to be honest…"

Amy nodded eagerly and they all got into the tiny red car. Adrian's prior disbelief continued as they proceeded down the gravel path, past various plants, sculptures, and piles of foliage. He ended up so transfixed at the sight that he nearly drove aimlessly into Nicky's car. Slamming the brakes, he parked up,

DEBAUCHERY: PART I

mouth agape as he left.

Steph tore out of the car, vanishing promptly behind the large oak door as Amy shuffled out of the backseat. There was a pause before Steph emerged, proudly gripping Nicky's hand as Amy frowned. Steph threw him towards Adrian, beaming.

"So Nicky, this is Adrian! He's my best friend in the entire world!"

Nicky offered an awkward smile, saluting with his fingers. "Ah yes, the man who screamed at my house. Between the two of you, I would've assumed Steph would be first but sure."

Adrian laughed, declaring, "Christ, mate, how many tombs did you have to raid to get this one?"

"I think it's up to about thirteen, but I'm sure there'll be a fresh one every few years." Nicky grinned. "Did you enjoy Amy? Sorry if she's a bit... intense. You've actually saved me money by appearing in person for her."

Adrian smiled warmly, and the four of them entered the house. As Nicky ushered everyone into the living room, Amy grabbed his arm and with direct eye contact grunted, "He smells like sweat, sex and talent."

With everyone assembled, Nicky sat next to Amy and looked across at Adrian, Steph and a neglected Lily.

"So, shall we go around the room and say something about ourselves? I think that would be fun," said Steph.

"You thought wrong," said Amy flatly.

"Well, I'm in a band for one thing," said Adrian. "I don't really know any of you guys, so yeah. I'm only here because Steph told me to come here."

Amy's eyes narrowed towards Steph, jealousy bursting out of her.

"Well, I'm Steph. I'm a beauty vlogger and I was dumped by

a man. Although, I haven't made a video in a while. I probably should… What do you think, Adrian?"

"Sure, as long as you don't want to do my makeup again."

"Again?" said Amy. "I wish to see this first time!"

"Steph deleted the video because it used copyrighted music."

Amy frowned, as Nicky piped up, "Okay, this is lovely but don't you think you should tell Adrian why he's here, Steph?"

"Would be handy, mate," said Adrian, tying his hair back again.

"Wait, we didn't introduce Lily!" said Steph.

"Oh, it's okay. It's really not important," Lily said, trembling under the pressure of a room full of strangers.

"Oh yeah, do you wanna tell us a bit about yourself? Anything?" said Nicky. "Sorry we didn't include you. You are the free agent of this group."

"Yeah, don't want your greatness bogged down by an idiot, do you?" scoffed Amy.

"Be nice. You're not THAT bad," chided Nicky.

"Fuck off."

"Please don't let our shittiness get in the way. Talk to us," said Nicky, gesturing to Lily to take the floor.

"Umm, I guess… I'm Lily. I work in retail and I like to read books and listen to acoustic music. I came along because, um, Steph said that I could be helpful with the stuff about that man's sign. And I dunno, things were pretty boring. This isn't something I'd normally do, so it's just a big deal to be here, really."

Amy looked at her and offered a rare smile as Nicky said softly, "Well, we're all new to each other in some way, so don't feel intimidated. I'm sure we'll get to know each other over time. There's no rush."

Lily smiled nervously, removed her garish yellow work fleece and sank back into the sofa in an attempt to look as relaxed as possible.

"So when's your next album out?" said Amy, promptly changing the conversation.

"Uhh, dunno to be honest. It's a funding issue, really. Me and the guys have plenty of ideas but it's just time and getting together in a studio to do it."

"Incredible. So where does your inspiration come from? In your song 'Venomous Cumdump 3006' you spoke about the hypocrisy between desensitisation towards overblown violence compared to an honest portrayal of sex. Do you think you could elaborate on where that came from, because that song in particular really spoke to something inside me—"

"Excuse me!" said Nicky. "I don't wanna interrupt your fucking retrospective on music culture, but there's a crazy Satanist stalking us so perhaps we focus on that for now?"

"Well it's not every day that you have one of your idols in the same room as you, dickhead!" spat Amy.

"Wait, a Satanist is after you? All of you? Steph?" said Adrian, turning immediately to his friend.

"Oh yeah! That's why I brought you here. There's this super creepy man who says all these, like, weird things. I thought it might be good if you came with us because I want you to be involved," Steph said with a smile.

"Er, do I want to be?"

"No," said Nicky. "But if he's stalking all of us, it's probably gonna be important cos you're so close to Steph. Perhaps stay for a bit and if it gets too heavy, you can go. There's really no reason to keep you if you're busy or something."

Amy's eyes widened at the prospect of Adrian leaving, but

thankfully he merely smiled, saying, "Well, fuck it. I've been to worse gigs."

"Yay that's the spirit!" beamed Steph, throwing her arms into the air joyfully.

"Okay, so I'll explain this as simply as possible," said Nicky, assuming the role of leader. "Basically, this strange homeless man with a sign has been pestering us and it's just one of a few random bits of bullshit that've been happening. Apparently, we're all connected to this Ol' D guy in some way."

"Er, okay," said Adrian.

"Well, we're together. That part is true at least," said Amy.

"Do you think there is anyone else?" said Lily, bravely speaking up to contribute to the mystery.

"I don't know. I don't really know anything. It's hard to even know how he found us. The main connection is this piece of cardboard, though." Nicky pulled it from the side of the sofa and the group leaned in to look.

The sign had been clumsily made from a cardboard box lid and was adorned with crudely drawn charcoal symbols and the words 'The EnD IS NEEЯ'.

"It's creepy," said Steph.

"It's stupid," said Amy.

"It's Satanic," stated Lily. Everyone turned to her, making her blush. She forced herself to speak up, knowing she probably had more knowledge of this than anyone else. "These symbols all represent a different part of Baphomet, or at least a few examples of mid-nineteenth century drawings."

"Heavy…" said Adrian. "Am I really needed in this conversation?"

Steph took his hand and gripped it. "I need you. I don't know what's going on and I know it's, like, crazy weird at the minute, but I've made some new friends. Since I was dumped things have been, like, impossible. Meeting these new people is so exciting. I just want to have you with me because you're my bestest friend."

Amy rolled her eyes as Adrian smiled. "Sure, Steph. This sounds batshit, but if you need this I'll stay."

The group continued to stare at the sign, then turned back expectantly to Lily. Gaining confidence, she leaned forward and pointed to each symbol as she went along. "Okay, so you see, this symbol on the left is the two-fingered salute. In religion, there are normally two – one pointing up and one pointing down. There's the saying 'as above, so below'. When there are two, it is said to represent opposites connecting and embracing differences."

"That sounds fair," said Nicky, cogs turning in his brain.

Lily continued, "Yes, and this next to it is obviously a pentagram. In Satanism it means re-evaluating viewpoints. Like moving with the times and challenging your perception of things. Many people assume it's evil or demonic, but that's simply not the case when paired with these other symbols. Some dislike or push back change and, especially during LaVeyan Satanism in the sixties, the fear of the pentagram versus what it stood for was quite ironic."

"Re-evaluate viewpoints? Like what?" said Amy.

"I think she means stuff like civil rights. If it all stems from the sixties, it'll mean not to be racist or homophobic or anything like that," replied Nicky.

"Exactly, or simply to challenge tradition if it doesn't benefit people," said Lily. "This third symbol, top middle, is the torch that's normally in between Baphomet's horns. It represents the pursuit of knowledge. Satanists generally believe this is the most important value."

"Okay," said Amy, listening intently.

"Last, there's this middle bottom symbol. The staff with the two serpents wrapped around it. This symbol is called The Caduceus. Satanism aside, it was also used as a medical symbol in Greek mythology. It's called the Staff of Hermes, but I don't think that's relevant in this instance. The symbol, in a Satanic sense, is like the two-fingered salute, as it simply represents friendship between opposites. As in, accept that there are just people who are different to you and live. That's what everything means, or what I've learnt anyway."

The group all sat back and sat in silence, absorbing the information they had just been given.

"So, if there are two salutes, why is there only one on here?" Steph asked, in a strangely lucid moment.

"Actually, that's a great question. I'm not sure," said Lily. "The only salute present is the 'so below' salute. It could symbolise Hell, or it could have a deeper meaning altogether."

"Deeper like what?" said Amy.

"Deeper than in the two-fingered salute symbolises embracing opposites. If there is only one, it could be translated as not embracing them at all."

"Fucking hell, you know your shit! You better have passed this degree!" Nicky said as he got up. "Cuppa, anyone?"

"Yeah please, mate. Coffee, milk, two sugars," said Adrian.

Lily nodded quietly and said, "Can I have a cup of tea, please? Milk, one sugar... and I got a First."

Nicky grinned. "You are an angel. Okay cool, one sec," he said, before heading back to the kettle.

There was another silence as the group contemplated the conversation once more.

DEBAUCHERY: PART I

Adrian eventually broke it.

"This is fucking weird, man. Am I alright to use your bathroom, mate?" said Adrian.

"Upstairs and on your left," Nicky said, as he came back with drinks. Adrian slowly stood up from his seat and left. A moment or so passed before music could be heard blasting from upstairs. Lily jumped with Amy and Nicky, throwing a critical look in the bathroom's direction.

"Oh, he's done that for a while now," said Steph quietly. "Ever since he started being a singer, I guess he just likes to have music around him."

"It covers up the sound of his dumps," said Amy with a smirk.

"For fuck's sake! Be more ladylike!" said Nicky.

"Suck my dick."

Several choruses passed before the music stopped and the toilet could be heard flushing. Adrian seemingly galloped down the stairs before rejoining the group. "What did I miss?"

Nicky broke in. "I was gonna mention the whole removal guy threatening to kill me thing."

"Oh yeah! I forgot about that!" said Amy.

"Thanks, babe. Well, I saw one of my removal men outside Amy's apartment. He grabbed my arm and threatened to kill me. No idea. Has anyone else had anything like that?"

The group shook their heads.

"Oh, okay then. Lucky me!"

"Why would a removal man send you death threats at random? What did you ever do to him?" said Adrian.

Nicky thought back and said, "Nothing, really. Oh, well, I did throw a load of money at them and told them to fuck off."

"As you do," Amy replied flatly. "Anyway, don't you think

it's weird that all this random shit just came out of the blue? I think it's got to the point where we have some questions for this Ol' D. We have to find him."

Lily slumped back in the chair and sighed. "He seems to find us a lot easier than we find him."

"She's right," said Nicky, getting up and walking to the curtains. "The likelihood of finding him again is pretty low."

Nicky threw back the curtains to bathe the room in a picturesque sunset as a muffled scream came from outside.

"THE END IS NEAR!"

Nicky fell backwards as everyone jumped. D's lack of volume control permeated through the triple-glazing, his eyes wide. He smiled and pressed a seemingly mass-produced sign against the window, pointing maniacally at it and nodding, "IT'S HAPPENING! It's all coming together! Two more though! TWO MORE!"

"That little shit! Give me a flamin' 'eart attack, will ya?" shouted Nicky in a strong Yorkshire accent, which seldom appeared unless he was angry or excited. He marched to the front door, with the rest of the group following. D beamed at everyone as they stepped out. They stared for a moment, with D simply pointing and nodding at his sign.

The awkwardness got so intense that Lily chose to speak up. "Why do you have Satanic symbols on a piece of cardboard, and who are these other two people you have mentioned?"

His psychotic grin grew wider as he proclaimed, "There are seven, not five… SEVEN!"

"Okay," said a bewildered Steph, tightening her dressing gown so as to not inadvertently flash her underwear.

"How did you find us, and how the hell did you get onto my property? Am I going to have to call the police?" said Nicky.

DEBAUCHERY: PART I

"No police! It's beyond the police! It's morality!" D shouted before lunging towards Adrian and clasping his arms around him in a bear hug.

Adrian swore and pushed him back, but D simply embraced him again. Lily's eyes widened, and she stood back in the doorway, shaking. It was too much for her to process, while the surroundings were so alien to her that she couldn't find anything to calm her nerves.

"YOU ARE ONE OF SEVEN!" shouted D as he held Adrian's head tightly, staring directly into his eyes. It was then that his voice dropped in tone and became strangely subdued. "The Community dawns. The Seven need to find me at my base so I can relay The Message. Ol' D can't believe it is happening. Ol' D has WAITED!" A single tear fell from wide eyes before he released Adrian from his grip and simply sprinted away.

"Get him!" shouted Amy, on the warpath as she bolted after him by herself, swearing and waving her arms.

"I really need to get that fountain working…" said Nicky to himself.

"Are you gonna fetch your mate?" said Adrian. "She seems pissed."

"She'll tire herself out."

Lily's lips formed into a discrete smile as Adrian grinned.

Nicky turned to everyone and said calmly, "Okay, so we can all admit this is too much and we all need some head space, right? I'll take you all home. We can pick up my maniac on the way out."

As the group watched Amy get smaller and angrier, Steph smiled.

"So, I guess we're all going to be friends now?"

X
JAMES 4:10

Steph woke up at 8 am, laying in a bed of new makeup and a tiara tangled in her hair. Despite this, she felt happy. She wobbled out of bed in pink pyjamas and, throwing the curtains open, felt the warm sun illuminate a gorgeous pink world around her. A sense of inner peace bubbled gently to the surface. She went down to the kitchen, a spring in her step.

"Would you like eggs on toast?" Steph's mum asked with a smile.

"Yes, please!" she beamed in response, sticking her head into the fridge to find juice.

A toilet flush sent her mother rushing away to turn on the television for her husband, shouting, "Stephanie, could you just finish those eggs, please?" behind her.

Steph sighed and shuffled over to the pan. A reluctant spatula in hand, she grudgingly watched the pan, head tilted back and a can't-be-arsed expression on her face. *Demoted to chef.* Toast popped from a toaster behind her and she grabbed the butter. *Four slices, two for me and two for Callum.* She knew her mum would cook for herself as soon as everyone else was sorted, though Steph had never quite grasped this logic.

DEBAUCHERY: PART I

"Thanks, hun," came her mum's voice as she breezed towards a cracked teapot.

Steph took her food and made her way to the sofa where Bruce sat cleaning his groin. A whiff of potential toast hit the pooch's nose and he stopped everything. Frowning, Steph sat next to him as her stepdad strode into view.

"Morning, princess," he said, sinking into his usual sofa groove.

"Morning," said Steph through a mouthful of toast.

He turned to look at her ripped jeans and offered the classic, "Where's the rest of them?" She groaned as his usual honourable mention became a double-whammy of, "So, did yer actually buy 'em like that?" He smirked before turning to light a cigarette and settle into snooker on the TV.

Steph finished her food as her mum entered the room with a plate of her own. The Shaws watched TV as they ate, small talk minimal and crumbs everywhere.

Brushing her pyjamas with her hand, Steph leapt to her feet, declaring, "I'm gonna get dressed and go out for a bit!"

"Tell him I said hi," said her mum with a smile.

A cool breeze blew through Coultas Close as Steph fell into music once more. A fresh journey to Mahmood's began to a soundtrack of 'Girls Just Want To Have Fun' by Cyndi Lauper.

She stepped into the shop, the usual bell sounding her arrival, only to come face to face with her ex-boyfriend.

He was a tall man with short ginger hair and a physique most men would kill for. As she stared into the eyes she once loved, she saw a distinct lack of love for her in them. Every single feeling of safety and security drained from her sanctuary immediately. Her heartbeat quickened as her safe space crumbled before her very eyes.

"Steph," came an Irish accent.

"Noah," she choked, lowering her headphones. She leant to a side, desperate eyes searching for Mahmood.

"He's doing a stock count round back, so we've got some time together," Noah said calmly, a queasy smile forming on his lips. "There's something I need to say. I've needed to say it for a while. I thought that if I distanced myself from you, that if we ended things, I'd be able to save you… but I can't."

"Look, I know we ended badly, but I don't want to argue anymore," said Steph wearily, determined to hold on to her waning positivity.

"Oh Steph, it's beyond that."

She kept quiet, slowly backing away.

"Look Steph, there's no easy way for me to say this, but the Community knows who you are. I prayed to God that breaking up with you would make it easier and that I wouldn't have to complete my mission, but you can't change fate. I'm so glad that we had our time together. It took getting to know you and loving you to realise how truly ugly you are on the inside. You're exactly the person they said you'd be."

Steph stared at him, resisting the urge to laugh. "You're joking, right?"

"Nah, Steph. You've put yourself on a pretty pink pedestal, and it's my job to push you off it. Look, it's beyond us and relationships, and even this city or country. This is about the Community and I can't let them down. It's a gift from God that I have to kill the one I love, so you know… nothing personal."

Steph was flabbergasted.

"W-What do you even mean?" she stammered, a thousand questions quickly dancing around inside her brain.

DEBAUCHERY: PART I

"Wait..." He grinned. "You mean you guys haven't even figured it out? You were never told?"

"Told what?" Steph shouted defensively.

"Fuck!" he laughed. "I knew you were dense, but *fuck!* Do you even know who you are? Do you know how truly dangerous you are?"

Steph wanted to cry from the awful cocktail of fear and confusion. As her back touched the door, she knew she had a choice to make – stay in her tainted sanctuary and risk danger, or simply run. She reached for the door handle and made her choice immediately. She flung it open and ran as if the shop was ablaze, laser-focused on making it back home.

"Oh, you can run. I won't stop you! The Community knows who you are, and we'll hunt you. A reckoning is about to begin! You have no idea what we can unleash!"

Noah laughed malevolently, standing in the doorway and watching Steph stumble away. Eyes watering, she ran faster than she ever knew she could. The sound of Noah's laughter echoed after her.

"Keep wearing that tiara, princess! You'll need to fix more than a pretty face once I'm done with you!"

Every step Steph took made the laughter fade away, but she was still haunted by it. She bolted back down Coultas Court and grabbed her front door handle. It was locked, and she swore. Fumbling in her jeans for a key she prayed was there, she got lucky and crammed it into the lock. As she threw the door open, Bruce burst from the living room barking, only to see Steph, whereupon his angry façade instantly vanished.

Shaking, Steph locked the door and patted the dog's head, safe at last. The one time she wanted to see her stepfather, he wasn't in, and instead a piece of paper took his place in the sofa groove.

Hey princess, hope you have your key. Popped to pub for the afternoon. Be back soon xxx

Still shaken, she opened the back door and sat on the step. Pulling the phone from her pocket, Steph created a group message. She added Adrian, Nicky, Lily and Amy:

Something has happened. Come over ASAP, plz. SOS. Address is 6 Coultas Close. Plz I need u xoxo

Replies rolled in, and after several minutes of trying to convince Amy it was truly urgent, the prospect of company beckoned. Steph sat in silence for half an hour, mulling over everything and stroking Bruce before a knock at the door made her jump. Steph took her dog and stood behind him as she cautiously peered around the door.

"What's up today, then? Did the barista spell your name wrong on your coffee cup?" came the disgruntled charm of Amy's voice. Steph breathed a sigh of relief and ushered both her and Nicky inside as she stared down the street.

As she battled with intrusive thoughts, Lily walked around the corner and eventually looked up from her phone long enough to catch Steph's eye. Timidly smiling, she walked up to Steph, who pulled her into her house and promptly shut the door. She went through into the living room and ushered three very confused people in too, ready to hear what was so important.

Amy stared at the tiara housed in Steph's hair and rolled her eyes.

"It makes me feel good, okay?" protested Steph.

Lily sat in a summery white dress with a baby-blue floral pattern. It was the first time anyone had seen her out of a garish yellow fleece and she looked completely different. Her brown

DEBAUCHERY: PART I

pixie cut was styled, and her lipstick matched a pair of blue flats. Considering her nerves, when the sun poured through the window, Lily radiated a serene aura. Nicky sat in his usual black ensemble, with Amy wearing a leather jacket over a purple dress. The four of them couldn't have looked more different, but a shared curiosity about their increasingly dramatic lives kept bringing them together.

"So, what's wrong?" said Nicky, sparking up the conversation.

"You know you had that guy threaten you? That happened to me today too – except it wasn't a threat for you, it was a threat for me," said Steph, parking herself next to Lily.

Three pairs of eyes widened at this news, and a million silent questions entered the room. A knock at the door made them jump as Steph and Bruce sprang into action once more. Opening it less cautiously, she was greeted by Adrian. He had messy hair and a concerned expression on his face as he locked his car.

"Sorry, I was at the gym. I came as soon as I could."

"It's okay. Well, it's not... I've been threatened!"

"Wait, what?"

"Come through! Everyone's in the living room!"

Adrian hung a zip hoodie on a neglected line of coat hooks and joined the others. He sat between Nicky and Amy while Steph returned to the seat next to Lily.

"So, who threatened you?" said Adrian.

"Noah!"

Adrian's was the lone reaction as everyone else threw clueless glances in Steph's direction.

"Oh no, not Noah!" said Amy sarcastically.

"Noah is her ex-boyfriend," said Adrian, escalating the cluelessness to alarm. Questions poured in, thick and fast.

"Really? This must connect with something!"

"But why are people threatening you?"

"Does that mean there's someone to threaten all of us?"

A contest of voices began battling to make their question the victor amongst the racket.

"Will everyone just shut the hell up for a second!" shouted Amy. The room fell silent and everyone looked at her. "Look, I don't know the answers any more than anyone else, but shouting won't achieve anything. Even if I just shouted then… but that was called for!"

"She's right. We need to do what we did at my house and discuss this," Nicky said in solidarity.

Lily sighed. "So, how do we do this? There are just so many elements to contend with."

"Okay, we can just update everyone and, like, categorise things, maybe? Steph, do you have any paper?" said Amy, gladly taking the leadership position.

"Yeah, I think I do somewhere…" she said before vanishing into a drawer for a moment, returning with a pink notebook and a fluffy pen. Amy grabbed the pen and sighed before springing into action.

"Guys, can we get pizza?" suggested Adrian, which was ignored.

"Right, what are the categories? What has happened to everyone?"

"CATEGORY IS!" bellowed Nicky, abruptly before reverting back to casual chatter. "Well, I've been threatened by my removal guy."

Steph stared blankly at him before continuing the conversation, "I have too, by my ex."

"Right, well, is that all? Adrian, Lily, have you had anything

DEBAUCHERY: PART I

said to you?" said Amy, drawing a box marked THREATENED. They shook their heads as she added Nicky and Steph's names to it.

"Okay, so we can agree that they're people we've seen long enough to remember their faces?"

Steph and Nicky nodded.

"So, if Steph has now been confronted, that potentially means me, Adrian and Lily all have someone coming to us too… and it'll be someone we know or at least vaguely know, right?"

Everyone nodded, a little more anxious.

"Okay, so next would be the weird D guy." Amy continued drawing a second box marked D. "At this point we've all seen him, so this is easy. Third would be that Polly woman. I'll draw a box for her, but only Nicky has seen her, right?"

"Right," Adrian, Lily and Nicky said in unison. Steph's silence cut the flow of the conversation, with everyone turning to look at her.

"I've seen her. It was in the supermarket when I was with you guys. It was the reason I had a… moment."

Amy and Nicky looked at each other. Amy added Steph's name under Nicky's to the POLLY box, with Nicky eagerly asking, "What did she say to you?"

Steph thought back for a second. "Well, she didn't really say anything. She just gave me the creeps. She just told me she was 'a big deal' and that we must all be really, really confused."

They stared at her, yearning for more.

"A big deal…" Adrian said blankly.

"Is that it?" said Nicky. "You'd think after speaking to two of us she'd tell us a little more than *we must be so confused.*"

"Ugh, never mind," interrupted Amy. "So, is there anything

else to add?"

The group shook their heads and stayed silent for a second until Steph whispered, "Isaac…" Everyone turned to her and watched her as she thought back to that day.

"Isaac? Has he done something to you?" asked Amy.

"No. He came up to me in the supermarket before you guys. Well, he came before you guys and before Polly, but there was something off about him. Like, bad vibes…"

"Who's Isaac?" asked Amy.

"I've known him since I was little. We went to school together… but when I saw him in the supermarket, he was different…"

"Different how?" Nicky said.

"He was wearing this, like, sack outfit, and he looked cold. His hair was wet and, I dunno, he just looked weird and cold."

They all stared at her as unanswered questions tormented them, jumping from one brain to another. They sat defeated for a moment, with Amy saying quietly, "Well, your little episode feels a lot less stupid now."

Steph frowned as Amy continued to stare at the sheet of paper.

Adrian suddenly broke the silence. "Wait, do you mean Isaac Morteza? Nerdy guy with a kind of heart-shaped birthmark? I remember him, he was our lead guitar for all of a month – remember, Steph? Before Phillip took over."

"Wait! A heart-shaped birthmark? *That* Isaac? I know him too! I can't believe it's the same guy!" said Nicky. "He was a client years ago. Back when my mum was working in the UK."

"Oh, I remember him!" said Amy. "He was so strange… Do you know him, Lily?"

Arms around herself defensively at the attention, Lily said quietly, "I think he works at my local library. I haven't spoken to

DEBAUCHERY: PART I

him much, but I remember seeing a heart-shaped birthmark on his neck."

Amy smiled and confidently drew a final box, labelling it with his name.

"He must have something to do with all of this! We barely know each other, and now we all have this one friend who randomly connects us all? It can't be a coincidence!"

Everyone nodded in agreement as Amy wrote names in the last box and held the paper up, proudly declaring, "There!"

Nicky looked up at the paper and frowned. "What do you mean? You just drew four boxes and put our confusion into it. That answers nothing!"

"Yeah, knobhead, but it's ordered confusion now! It's all merged into bite-size confusion that we can all slowly lose our minds to."

"I guess..." sighed Nicky, slumping back onto the sofa.

"I'm not sure what to do," said Lily, who had found herself getting progressively more befuzzled. "So, there's a threat, a man and this Polly... and now Isaac has something to do with it? But it's a weird-looking Isaac? I feel like I'm drowning, to be honest, and I don't want to do this."

"Don't be blue!" said Steph at an abrupt and uncomfortably high volume. Springing to her feet and extending her arms, she declared, "Everything will be fine if we all just stick together and figure things out!"

"Oh, fuck off Princess Friendship, this isn't an anime!" shouted Amy.

"Don't speak to her like that!" said Adrian.

"Cram it, Pizzahontas!"

Adrian stood up but Steph immediately pushed him down

to turn towards Amy. Taken aback, he looked up towards Steph, whose fists were clenched.

"I'm sick of your negativity filling up this room like a giant… POO!"

"What. Did. You. Say?" hissed Amy, who struggled to her feet from a sinking sofa cushion. Bruce looked up from his spot under the dining table, assessed the situation, and immediately drifted back off to sleep.

"You heard me! A POO!" Steph shouted.

"I'm very uncomfortable," said Lily, who ended up being the only person to stay seated as everyone else sprang to their feet.

"Not everything is about you and what you want, sweetheart!" shouted Amy.

"Ugh, I'm sick of this! This is all such a mess and you're the one who just wants to bully me!" Steph pointed her finger directly at Amy, who looked as though she could bite it off at any moment. Steph's eyes watered as she dramatically flew over to the back door and left to disperse her drama around the garden. Amy followed immediately, leaving Nicky, Adrian, and Lily together. They swapped glances at each other for a moment before Nicky went to catch up to them. Adrian reluctantly joined as Lily said, "Why me?" under her breath before following suit.

A passing shower revitalised the back gardens of Coultas Court as two furious women entered a damp battlefield. Steph felt this moment was a huge step backwards. She stood once again in the rain, mascara running and feeling stupid and single. She hated it, but this time she would not lose because she was armed with retrospect and a fucking tiara.

"What is your problem with me?" she shouted at Amy, the sound of thunder clapping shortly after.

DEBAUCHERY: PART I

"My problem with you?" shouted a dampening mass of black hair with Amy's voice attached. "My problem with you is that you're thick! I don't like stupid people! I know people like you, and you all think you're the greatest fucking person in the world with a right to bully everyone who doesn't cater to your every ridiculous whim! You have little to no understanding of anything outside of your own immediate bubble! You're vapid, entitled, self-centred and shallow!"

"But if you can't handle her at her worst—" shouted Nicky from the doorway.

"CAN IT! I've had it! There are millions of girls *exactly* like you. You aren't unique! You just float through life wearing that stupid tiara on your head, expecting everyone to bow to you! You have no real problems. You're just… You're fucking basic!"

A flash of lightning filled the world as Steph stood silent. Her eyes watered, but any tears that fell were hidden by the rainfall. As the sky rumbled, she took a deep breath, clenched her fists and said calmly, "You know nothing about me, you bitch."

"What did you just s—"

"I said you know nothing about me, you deaf bitch!"

Amy stood in silence as Steph walked right up to her, squaring up to her despite being several inches smaller. With makeup running and crown askew in a nest of bedraggled hair, she continued, "You think that because I don't know big words or don't know maths and planets that I'm dumb? Well, I'm not! I have things that I like and people I love! I'm just different to you! I have things I want to do! I want to go to Paris and I want to see a whale! I want to see waterfalls and monkeys and I want to go rock climbing! I want ninety-nine luftballons, damn it!"

Her eye contact intensified as she pointed her acrylics towards three dying red balloons hanging limply from a hosepipe tap.

"I'm worth a lot when the world doesn't tell me I'm anything! I know what I like and what I don't like, and that includes people like you! You just judge me because you haven't even known me that long! Who even are you with your… *face?* I'm tired of people not understanding the amount of effort it takes to look like this! The pressure to look perfect constantly. I hate that I feel I have to do it. Everyone in the world judges who I am and what I should be, even when I'm perfect! I haven't judged anyone but so far, you've judged everyone! I might be happy with simple things, but it still makes my life worth something! It's still surviving and moving forward, even if it's just to see moonlight on a pond. Not everybody needs to write a fucking book! LIFE IS HARD, OKAY?"

Amy took a step back as Steph stood out of breath, shaking. The onlookers stood glued to the doorway with bated breath, expecting the worst. It was then that Amy put her arms around Steph. Steph's eyes watered as everyone looked puzzled.

"I get you now," she said quietly to Steph, who squeezed Amy back. A new era dawned as the greyness and rain subsided, replaced by a shy sunlight breaking through the clouds.

The embrace lasted for a moment or so before Amy tried to escape. Steph's unlikely vice-like grip continued the hug, creating a challenge for Amy to remove herself from it. As she struggled, Steph slipped down to her stomach but continued the intense contact, whispering, "Does this mean we'll be friends forever?"

"Oh my Christ!" shouted Amy, throwing a frantic look towards Nicky who simply sighed and walked inside with everyone else.

As the sun bathed the world once more, any negativity between the two faded to nothing. Amy broke free from Steph, who promptly took her hand instead.

"Look Steph, I get that you think we're friends and all, but I like personal space."

Steph beamed before saying cheerily, "There's just one more thing I want to say."

"Okay," said Amy cautiously.

"I just want to say thank you for showing that you care. It can't have been easy. I know things are weird at the moment but we'll solve them together! We're stronger as a team now because, like, all I ever wanted was for people to see how great I am. All these stupid gross things have been happening to me. I only had to turn to myself and say, 'Steph, you are a goddess and you are powerful'."

"Err—"

"I just want you to know that I'll always be there for you… and Adrian and Nicky and Lily! I was so gross and single, but I really just had to see that I was perhaps being too humble!"

"What."

"Yes! I see it now! All this talking and making myself feel like poop has achieved nothing, and I've been too humble about myself. I have to be the amazing woman that I am because I'll just bring out the best in myself and other people! I can't hold in my selflessness anymore."

Amy looked cynical and pulled a face before saying to an elated Steph, "You do you," and rushing inside.

A fully formed Stephanie Shaw threw her arms into the air, twirling around and chuckling to herself. As sunbeams hit her mascara-stained cheeks, she laughed. Digging acrylics into her tiara, forcing it further deeper onto her skull, Steph's lips formed a maniacal smile as she whispered, "Humble…"

ADRIAN HADER tucked into his second pizza of the day. He absolutely adored food. Eating was his lifeblood. It was more than a necessity. It just made him feel right. No matter what emotion event came forth, food made him flourish. Italian, Chinese, Japanese, Indian, French – an entire world of cuisine with one common language, taste. It not only made him full; it made him satisfied. As he finished his final slice of pizza, he sighed. He thought of the seismic new adventure unfolding in front of him. New people, places and events all wrapped up in one tiring stomach ache. He wanted nothing to do with it and only wanted to tour. If he didn't have to keep people grounded, he'd happily retire to a world of eating and singing. Everything else felt so lifeless. He threw his jacket on for another night out with a friend and wondered for a moment if he'd ever truly feel satisfied. As the prospect of pub food came into view, the feeling vanished as quickly as it had appeared and he left, chasing his stomach.

He had always felt this deep within his heart, but never questioned what this feeling actually was.

It had only ever been **GLUTTONY.**

XI
DRUNK

"They're fucking freaks, mate," said Adrian, throwing back his fourth pint. "They're just mental. There's this groupie and this rich guy who you can't understand through all their inside jokes. Then there's this other lass who's basically a dictionary but barely speaks at all. All of that mixed with Steph. It's a lot, man."

Jay Gregorio stared at his best friend through a pair of large, clear-framed glasses; a wavy mop of dark blonde hair half-hiding a vacant expression. Finishing his drink and wiping foam from his stubble he said, "Sounds like it. I don't really know what to say. It sounds fucked up that you've all even bothered to be in the same room together. Why don't you and Steph separate from them? They're obviously bad news. Another round?"

Adrian finished what was left of his pint and said, "Sure mate," adding a newly emptied glass to an ever-increasing stack. As Jay stood up, he knocked the table slightly, panicking as the cluster of glasses wobbled. He wore a blue hoodie to hide a small belly and denim jeans to cover a shit tattoo. Jay sheepishly made his way past fellow pub-goers to the bar as Adrian watched with slightly blurred vision. He sat in their regular booth towards the back of their usual haunt and Adrian's respective place of work, going by the name The Nihilistic Clown.

It was a dimly lit pub which housed the same old conversations: creative musing, genius businessmen on a seemingly endless break, alcoholic sages and alumni from the University of Life all contributed to the chatter that gave this old Tudor building its soul. A hotbed of rumour and gossip emanated from a collection of Jacks-of-all-trades, ready to be hired at any moment. The air was thick with the smell of pub food and stale beer. Adrian came here because he was recognised, but only as the part-time barman. His singing career would never permeate the walls of this baby boomer den.

Adrian sat within his tipsy aura for a moment, thinking purely of kebabs. Another pint was placed in front of him, its foam dripping over the edge as Jay took a seat with arms crossed nervously.

"Are you alright, mate?" said Adrian, pulling himself away from his thoughts.

"Yeah, man, you know what I'm like. It's just… people."

"Well, I'm here, so no one will bother us." The two friends smiled and swigged their drinks. "I dunno what to do," Adrian continued, bringing the previous conversation to the surface. "The whole thing is just a shitstorm, mate. I mean, it's pretty standard that I have Steph breaking down, but with three more people adding to that, it's fucking grim. One thing to be said for that gay guy though – he tolerates Steph's breakdowns. Like they're never over anything important, but he fully commits to what she's feeling. Even if he's a sarcastic twat, it never feels like he's not there for her."

Jay swayed under the soft grip of merriment. He burped before slurring, "Well I dunno, maybe he's good for her?"

"I guess, yeah. Gives me more free time for gigs and the odd

DEBAUCHERY: PART I

gym sesh."

"How is that singing thing coming along anyway, superstar?"

"It's work in progress. Gonna be in the studio soon to record some things and get the creative juices flowing. It'll be good."

"Well, you know I'm your biggest fan, so just keep me updated, okay? I'm happy to draw up any new stuff you need for merch," said Jay.

"Cheers. It feels like I hardly have any time these days. I'm being dragged along to a wedding tomorrow. One of Steph's relatives. I really don't wanna go, but I heard there'll be a buffet and an open bar."

"Sounds good, but more people like Steph? Hard pass."

"I wouldn't even mind, but we all have to wear pink. Steph found me this fucking suit, and it's… it's a lot."

Jay laughed. "I'm sure it'll be very becoming on you." He slammed his glass onto the table, slurring, "Another round?"

"Fucking hell mate, you're a machine tonight, aren't you? Well, sure, I'll get them in this time," said Adrian, springing up too eagerly and nearly falling over.

"You sure?"

"Yeah, man. Mind you, this'll be my last one before I go. Up early tomorrow and I can't afford to miss whatever pink shitshow Steph drags me to."

Jay laughed and watched as his friend meandered through crowds of people, bumping into several as he went.

Adrian rested his arms against the old wooden counter as a woman smiled at him from behind the bar. She was a slightly chubby woman with a tattoo sleeve, a septum piercing and intense eyes that glowed in the warm light. She wore a black apron and looked nervous as she approached him.

"Er, hi, what can I get you?" she said as she moved teal-coloured hair from her face.

"Hey, two pints of lager, a packet of crisps and two packs of nuts, please."

The woman nodded promptly before quickly grabbing the snacks and pouring the drinks with a shaking hand. He watched her and smiled as she caught his kind eyes.

"I haven't seen you here before. Are you new here?" he said, radiating a warm confidence.

"Y-Yes, I'm on my first shift tonight."

"Fair play! I work here too, tonight's my night off. My name's Adrian, by the way. Might be on shift with you sometime."

"It's nice to meet you! I'm Stacy," she said as she handed him his drinks with a smile. He paid up and threw her a grin as he returned to his friend.

"Unbelievable," said Jay.

"What?"

"You're gone for five minutes and manage to drown in pussy and booze."

Adrian snorted into his pint. "Unlucky mate."

Jay frowned. "Jesus, dude, do you ever stop eating?"

"I got you some too, princess, don't worry," replied Adrian, throwing a bag of nuts at Jay's face.

"Prick!"

The two friends sat in silence as they savoured their final drink. Adrian turned to look at Stacy for a moment as Jay interrupted him. "Oi, I am still here, you know!"

"Sorry!"

"Can't believe you'd ruin our romantic night out," Jay said.

"Don't you start too. You're beginning to sound like Steph."

DEBAUCHERY: PART I

Jay grimaced as Adrian burst out laughing.

"Right, I'm off to the bog, be right back!" said Adrian as he stumbled to his feet.

He made his way down a corridor boasting a booze-soaked maroon carpet and claustrophobia-inducing walls. As he walked, Adrian wondered how many times he had staggered down the tiny hallway. The last door on his left housed the men's toilets. Slamming his hand against the door, he pushed and was immediately greeted by the smell of the evening's failed attempts at urination.

Wobbling over to a urinal opposite, he relieved himself, reading a small silver framed advert for a flip phone due to take the third quarter of 2004 by storm.

Adrian's sozzled reflection eventually appeared in a mirror above a sink. It stared back at him with messy hair and a heavy face, making Adrian remark under his brewery breath, "Christ." He pulled out his phone, flicking through music. Resting it on the sink, he sighed, 'The Pretender' by the Foo Fighters echoing around the loo.

Just then, an abrupt and obscenely loud creak of the bathroom cubicle made him jump.

"Always in the bathroom, aren't we, hot stuff?" came an unwelcome voice, and a gloved hand gripping the cubicle wall.

"Not now, Polly," Adrian whispered.

"Well, that's not very nice! I thought you'd be pleased to see me. I'm ALWAYS pleased to see you, handsome!" Her hand mimicked talking as though it were a glove puppet.

"I'm with a friend, so I can't talk. I told him I wouldn't be long," said Adrian, shaking his hands and walking over to the dryer.

"Well, why don't you invite him over—" she shouted as

Adrian abruptly started the hand dryer. Polly huffed from behind the cubicle door, continuing to shout above the noise, "I'M SURE HE'D LOVE TO MEET ME!"

Adrian ignored Polly's hands and continued drying his own. When he finished, there was silence. Adrian went to the mirror and stared at his reflection once more.

"You look good," Polly smirked from inside the cubicle.

"What do you want? Why are you hiding behind there? You know you're in the guy's bathroom, right?"

She then swung whimsically into view, declaring with a grin, "Gender is a social construct."

Adrian groaned, "Well, you are a woman, aren't you?"

"I'm lots of things, darling…"

"Please, just tell me what you want?" Adrian said, exasperated and turning the music off.

Polly's cheerful demeanour fell from her face and she crossed her arms, frowning. "Interrupting, am I? Oh, you're no fun! Okay, well, I'm just here to request… Just to be official… and confirm one hundred percent—"

"—Polly!"

She huffed, putting her hands on her hips, "So rude… Anyway, I wanted to check why, oh why, you had to lie to your new friends about us having our little meetings. I felt very upset that you left your name out of Amy's pretty little diagram. You should know by now how I've longed to be in your box."

Adrian turned to the mirror and stared into the eyes of his blitzed reflection. His hair fell in front of his eyes as though he were a plastered comic book villain.

Polly stepped forward, placing a gloved hand on his arm. "Talk to me, gorgeous."

DEBAUCHERY: PART I

"They can't know. No one can."

"But you really don't believe I would tell them, sweetheart? I've known far worse people…"

The rings on his fingers hit the metal taps as Adrian gripped them. "I… I don't know. You do things; this mad stuff that no one can do and know things no one else would. That's what freaks me out, the not knowing. I-I've gotta go, Jay's waiting." And with that, he left.

Polly smiled and walked back into the cubicle, shrugging and shouting behind her, "Pfft, men!"

Adrian returned to Jay and, with a mastered fake calm in his voice said, "Right, shall we head off?"

"Er sure," said Jay, stumbling to his feet.

Adrian threw his jacket over his shoulders, and they shuffled their way towards the door. They moved past various conversations with varying degrees of intensity. A mix of personalities crammed themselves into the tiny pub, desperate to forget their woes and find all the answers to life's mysteries at the bottom of a glass.

As they got to the exit, Adrian felt a hand grab his arm. He spun around to face his manager, Mike. He was a rough-looking man with a faded neck tattoo and a shiny bald head.

"Look mate, I know yer come in a lot, and I'm glad yer enjoy yourself, but don't yer be callin' up after yer time off expectin' yer shift to be covered 'cos I can't do that again. You know as well as anybody that we're already short-staffed as it is and I got that Stacy lass on training." He had an incredibly gruff voice from years of smoking and, despite being quite a short man, he was still somewhat intimidating.

"That was one time about three months ago, man. I won't let

you down, you know that," said Adrian, impressed he didn't slur his speech.

"Good lad, that's what I wanna hear. Now enjoy the rest of yer night and I'll see you on Friday. Becky's dropping delivery off early so be prepared for some graft."

"Cool, night Mike."

A cool blast of air hit Adrian's face as he walked up to Jay, who was cradling a lighter flame from the wind. Cigarette between his lips, he said, "Mike giving you flack?"

"Yeah, but it's cool. You know how he gets when he's stressed. Anyway, so, Halloween. What are you planning? Who's coming?"

"Not sure, to be fair. I was just gonna invite some mates round and have a few drinks, a few laughs. Wanted to do fancy dress, but no one I know can be arsed."

"Well, here's an idea – why don't I invite my new 'friends'? It could be interesting, and I'm sure they'd dress up. They're all insane."

Jay frowned at the thought, but Adrian pushed for it. "Come on, mate. I know you're anxious, but I'll be there and so will Steph. What's the worst that could happen?"

"Don't say that! Someone will probably die or something! I guess we can invite them, but how many of them are there? I don't know these people."

Adrian scoffed. "That didn't stop you from throwing open house parties in your twenties, did it? Fuck, the amount of people who went through our flat in those days…"

"True, but half of those people now have kids or went to jail," said Jay flatly. There was a short pause, before he continued, "Fuck it, fine. But only 'cos it's you! It can't be any worse than that time Steph danced for four hours straight before throwing up in a laundry basket."

DEBAUCHERY: PART I

"Awesome!" Adrian laughed, smacking his friend on the shoulder enthusiastically. "I'll make the calls... and on that note, I better get going!"

"Cool, I'm getting a lift from my mate so don't worry about me," said Jay, blowing smoke upward.

Adrian waved goodbye, wobbling across a deserted town square and slumped underneath a statue. The air felt good against his face, and he stared up at the bronze figure above him. It depicted a war veteran whose reward for saving the town single-handedly in 1512 was to become a future taxi waypoint and a toilet for pigeons.

"Edward Smith," stated Adrian to himself as he whipped his phone from his pocket and called a cab.

He looked around to see he was completely alone in the square. He clumsily removed a pair of purple earphones from his jeans pocket and did the second-best thing a guy could do when alone, and sang. With the statue of Edward Smith as his audience, he played 'Californication' by the Red Hot Chili Peppers.

Adrian opened his mouth and sang, his gravelly voice pairing with the chorus in joyous harmony. His voice was boozy, but the song burst freely from his lungs, regardless. It felt good to sing, loud and free into the cold air. The moon was on fire and in its light, he pictured himself singing to hundreds of thousands.

This was short-lived as he heard a strange sound coming from behind him. He spun around, tearing the headphones from his ears, and emitted a startled yelp as the bronze statue sizzled. Steam rose from the top of the statue into the cool October air. The statue melted in half down the middle, as Polly burst forth from it with her arms in the air. As the war hero bubbled down to form a blob-like mess, Adrian fell backwards, aghast.

"TAH DAHHH!" declared a joyous Polly over the sizzling of melted metal. Standing on the pedestal, she stared down at Adrian and frowned. "Oh well, that's charming! Here I am creating fabulous visions, and all you can do is shiver on the floor in terror!"

Adrian clambered to his feet, his voice shaking, "Y-Y-Yeah well, it's pretty f-fucking scary! Can't you give me five fucking minutes alone?"

"Actually, I gave you five minutes and twenty-nine seconds if you want to be petty…" Polly smirked. She hopped off the plinth to stand next to him. He walked around the statue and stared at it in total amazement with Polly skipping jovially next to him, her hands behind her back.

"I'm here to help you pass the time, sweetie! Let's play a game! I love games!"

"No games, Polly."

"But it's a game of ask me anything!" she beamed. "It can be anything you want! Will I ever get married, what's my favourite colour, does a mullet really make a man? Y'know, the real burning questions."

Adrian looked toward her, mind ablaze. There were so many things he daren't ask or kept quiet about, but one question leapt forward: "What are you?"

Polly smiled, threw her arms towards the sky and proclaimed brightly, "I'm your intoxication fairy!"

"Seriously though. Do I have schizophrenia or something?"

Polly frowned and her arms fell back to her side as she huffed, "Well, that stinks. Downgrading me to an icky mental illness isn't cool, babe! We're progressive in these parts. I can confirm I'm not in your head! I am real!"

DEBAUCHERY: PART I

"So, if you're real, how come you can do magic?" Adrian slurred.

"Oh my God, Adrian, you can't just ask people why they do magic!"

Polly paused and, smiling, waved a gloved hand at him as a car horn sounded. Adrian swung around to see a taxi driver looking at him through the beam of headlights. Confused, Adrian turned back to Polly, who was nowhere to be seen. He gawped, looking between the taxi driver and the statue, which stood proudly back in one piece.

"66 Walker Road, mate?" said a voice from the car.

"Er yeah, please. Thanks," Adrian said as he walked backwards towards the taxi. He stared, trying to weigh up questions which seemed impossible to answer. Determined to forget about them, he pulled up the group chat Steph had created and sent a message.

HALLOWEEN PARTY, 16 BARTLETT ROAD, 6 pm SATURDAY! FANCY DRESS!

To his surprise, Amy replied almost immediately, saying, "Adventure? I'm there."

Lily and Nicky also confirmed soon after, with Nicky adding, "Well, me and Amy had plans, but sure, we'll drop them for the adventure."

As the confirmations rolled in, his taxi driver turned into his street.

"Anywhere here is fine," Adrian confirmed as he paid up and left.

He wobbled up his front path to be greeted by Sylvester, who brushed up against him. Adrian fussed him and went inside armed with a naïve, drunken feeling that tomorrow would be far less weird than today.

XII
THE SANCTITY OF MARRIAGE

Leanne Shaw put a delicate hand to the window of a lavish Victorian manor house. A lifetime of planning had brought her to this day. Every single thing she had been through was no longer important, as she had arrived at this grand milestone. A well-rehearsed smile formed as she turned to three exhausted women and her maid of honour, all wearing coordinated attire.

A blonde child of five carried a bad attitude and a basket of fuchsia rose petals as a bridesmaid-flower girl hybrid. Bridesmaid number two was thirty-nine-year-old Sharon from the office, hiding an unhealthy weight loss journey in her dress and a very recent divorce in her mind. An eighteen-year-old held a rose-pink veil and a mobile phone packed with dating apps – this was bridesmaid number three.

River was twenty-nine years old with long, dyed grey hair and had the privilege of being Leanne's maid of honour. She had been trained as a paparazzo throughout this journey and snapped photos of the pensive bride continuously through gloved hands.

Turning from the window and lifting the ruffles of a magenta wedding dress from the floor, Leanne said softly, "It's time." She drifted forward and threw an expectant look towards bridesmaid three, who scuttled over obediently to attach the veil over Leanne's bright red hair.

With almost military precision, River assembled the bridesmaids into a line in front of their leader to begin a sombre, funeral-esque march towards the nave of The Church of St. Caesar. An intense, glossed smile formed across Leanne's lips as she was handed the bouquet. Her mind was cast back to the day she met her beloved.

Gareth Atkinson began rising through the ranks of Leanne's heart during a drunken nightclub hook-up. Fortune favoured the pair as they remained attracted to each other without the influence of alcohol. He liked her for her large breasts, and she liked him for his large wallet. It was a match made in Heaven. After several dates, expensive gifts and cheap fumbles, the couple made it official. They moved in together and now, six arguments deep, Leanne walked towards the man and the money she always knew she deserved.

No one could ever know the hardships they had faced, with Gareth wearing every belittling comment, accusation of deceit, and declaration of being unable to handle a real woman, as silent battle scars. After an arduous eight-month trek, Leanne stood here as a curvy boss bitch ready to live, laugh and love her way into a gauche pink future.

Leanne had screamed (adorably) at every living relative to achieve the wedding of her dreams. She had (lovingly) beaten her fiancé over the silly wedding ideas he had selfishly tried to propose for her special day, and her bridesmaids had endured similar. Now mentally neutered, the bridesmaids finally lead their bride into a wedding no one would forget.

Every inch of the church was adorned in pink. Each pew, column and cross bore pink and white flowers with matching tulle blowing around them. 'Air from Orchestral Suite 3' by J. S. Bach danced softly upward as several Saints took a captive seat within stained glass.

Leanne exhaled, impatient for her future, and lunged forward. The youngest bridesmaid was shoved to the floor and became the first casualty of her rampage. The confused child wobbled to her feet as River ushered her back into formation, bridesmaids now behind the bride.

It was then that two people caught Leanne's eye. The smile dropped from her face immediately as she saw Steph staring in the complete opposite direction, and Nicky wearing all black in a sea of pink. Lifting her veil, she hissed through gritted teeth in his direction. Nicky merely fake-smiled and flashed a middle finger featuring a single pink painted nail and a smuggled cigarette between his fingers. Steph turned and noticed the interaction, pushing his hand down with a hushed argument then ensuing. Loud whispers of an angry exchange built up for a moment, with a sudden declaration of the word, "AFTERBIRTH!" obnoxiously exploding around the church.

"Where's Adrian?" whispered Steph as loudly as she could.

"I don't know! Why couldn't you just have brought him here instead of me? I don't know anyone!" hissed Nicky.

"Because you're my boyfriend!"

"What, still?" Nicky said, causing a woman to throw a confused but nonetheless scornful look his way.

"Shut up, we're in love!" Steph retorted.

Nicky groaned, saying flatly, "I want a divorce," as they returned their attention to a flustered groom.

DEBAUCHERY: PART I

Gareth stood in a white suit with a bubble-gum pink flower in his pocket, his shaved head sweating from expectation. A skinny best man stood paralysed with fear as Leanne ascended red carpet steps with her bridesmaids in tow.

The reverend came forward and stood in front of the couple. His calm demeanour was forced and his expression worn as he repressed flashbacks of his own personal Vietnam, which took the form of the wedding rehearsals. The reverend spoke gently to the congregation, "You may be seated," as the sound of one hundred people taking a seat echoed through the hallowed building.

"Dearly beloved, we are gathered together here in the sight of God to join together this man and this woman in holy matrimony."

His voice was pure and reverberated through the church. The audience sat quietly as a collection basket appeared, beckoning a silent obligation as it moved. Eventually it was passed to Steph as the man next to her mumbled, "For the honeymoon."

She stared at the small wicker basket blankly for a moment before taking a ten-pound note from her bra and adding it to the pile. She passed the collection over to Nicky, who simply rolled his eyes and tapped his cigarette ash into it, nonchalantly passing it to a disgusted woman next to him.

"The couple have written their own vows and shall now read them," the reverend declared, as Nicky audibly groaned.

✝

Meanwhile, the wheels of a red car driven by a very hungover passenger crunched over the gravel path outside. The door opened and Adrian stepped out in a pastel-pink suit, feeling impressed he was secure enough to step into anywhere at all. His long hair was tamed and sunglasses covered eye bags from the previous night.

Upon locking his car, Adrian broke into a sprint up a curved path to the church. He approached the giant wooden doors and heard the echoed voice of the reverend. "Shit," he said under his breath, running ringless fingers through his hair.

Pacing as he thought of what to do next, Adrian whipped out his phone. He ignored a slew of angry texts from Steph, opting to call the other best friend.

"H-Hello?" said Jay hoarsely.

An unhealthy coughing spree followed with Adrian walking around the side of the church. "You alright, mate? You sound grim."

"I... I drank so much. Why did I drink so much?"

"Are you asking me that or just yourself?" Adrian grinned.

"I don't even know anymore, man... Anyway, are you outside? I thought you were at a wedding?"

"Yeah, I am, but I'm late. I'm locked out and the ceremony has already started!"

There was a pause on the other end of the line before a prolonged burp echoed into Adrian's ear.

"Do that," said Jay flatly.

"Fuck's sake."

"Well, why are you asking me? Just stay outside and pass the time, I dunno. It's not like you're there for the people, is it?"

"Yeah, I guess you're right."

"Well, I'm glad I could back you up and boost your ego. Now if you're done, I'm fucking dying and I need to get up."

"Cheers babe," said Adrian with a grin.

As his friend hung up, Adrian slumped against the wall, wondering what to do. He was at a loss until his eye caught

DEBAUCHERY: PART I

wayward rose petals blowing from the grounds at the back of the church. They seemed so out of place, yet entirely fitting at the same time. He went with his gut and got up to investigate.

┼

"And the most important thing about us is that we were made to last. Our love is so unique, and I don't know any other love like it. When we met, angels saw us from Heaven and blessed us with a love that's unbreakable. Our hearts are combined—"

"—I'm going to die in this place," Nicky sighed, as the congregation around him felt similarly drained. "I thought it would be at the hands of a mad tramp or a killer removal man but no. It's here at My Big Fat Yorkshire Flower Show." He tilted his head towards Steph, who was sitting forward, resting her chin on her hands.

The reverend suddenly spoke up, making the crowd jump. "If any person can show just cause why this couple may not be joined together, let them speak now or forever hold their peace."

Leanne spun around to narrow her eyes at an audience whose fear of her was greater than that any God could provoke. Steph immediately slammed Nicky's hand down through a deafening silence. Leanne spun back around, the intense smile jumping back onto her face instantly.

Without warning, Gareth raised his hand, and an audible gasp came over the audience. Leanne looked to her fiancé's hand and then at him, her maniacal smile falling to the carpet.

"I-I... have to say something," Gareth said, crippled with fear. The reverend looked at the groom, who continued, "I can't do this. You are everything I wanted but... but I just can't finish what I started, Leanne. I can't lie to you. The truth is… I've been having an affair. An affair with… HER."

Gareth pointed to the audience as everyone gasped a second time and turned to face Steph. Confused for a moment, she sprang upright and smiled vacantly, pointing to herself.

"Er no," said Gareth, "One back… HER."

Steph frowned as the attention of an entire room left her immediately. The woman behind her looked shell-shocked.

Leanne gawked at the woman who sported the exact same hair colour as her, and then back to Gareth. The audience entered the crash position and braced themselves for the oncoming explosion.

Gareth opened his mouth but was immediately interrupted.

"YOU DON'T GET TO SPEAK!" spat Leanne, her voice demonically deep. Her anger suddenly seemed to disappear instantly as she fell to the floor and wailed in a woeful explosion of pink heartbreak. Her mother leapt to console her as incoherent insults erupted between hysterical tears.

Gareth took a step, nervously starting, "Leanne, I—" before being shown a hand by Leanne's mother. The bride descended into despair, ending up on the floor kicking and screaming, fully inconsolable. Her tantrum dissipated as she tumbled down the steps of the altar. Leanne then gracelessly clambered up the steps, resembling a creature from Japanese folklore as she was tangled up in her veil. Seething, she screamed obscenities at her ex-fiancé's feet, hitting his shins with a limp bouquet.

Between bending down to protect his knees and wobbling away from her, Gareth did his best to defuse the situation, using well-worn classics such as "it was a long time ago" and "it didn't mean anything!"

DEBAUCHERY: PART I

To his surprise, this didn't seem to help. A moderately stunned crowd stared in silence at the tragic scene unfolding in front of them. The reverend had quickly backed off into a corner and stood shaking his head.

The father of the bride eventually helped his daughter to her feet. She held her hands up and turned her back to Gareth, freeing the veil from being tangled in her hair.

"I'm fine!" she snapped in her father's direction before turning to look at Gareth and instantaneously changing from woe to rage. She lunged, screaming and throttling him with the exhausted bouquet. Headless stalks hit Gareth's bald head as he stood in a sad pile of petals.

Steph and Nicky sat in silence, watching this circus unfold. Steph piped up saying, "Do you think it's us? Like, do you think we just have this thing that makes drama? Maybe our aura is broken or something?"

"At this point, I have no idea. I guess you just ride the weird wave or drown…" sighed Nicky as they watched the train wreck unfold.

The building froze as Leanne bellowed, "ENOUGH!" She staggered towards a clump of scarred bridesmaids as Gareth attempted to rearrange his suit. He scoured the altar for his best man, who had long since bailed, and looked at Leanne, asking desperately, "Can we please talk about this somewhere else?"

$$\dagger$$

Adrian, meanwhile, stood in the rear grounds of the church, staring at the huge wedding buffet housed under a heated marquee. Eyes wide with excitement at the prospect of a genuine all-he-could-eat meal, Adrian forgot about everything else. A noise came from the church which, for a moment, made him turn away, but mature cheddar and bacon bread scrolls pulled him back.

"Do it!" came Polly's voice abruptly from over his shoulder. Adrian jumped back and spun around to see Polly wearing a grin from ear to ear.

"W-What are you doing here?" Adrian remarked.

"Oh, you know, just sending my love to the happy couple," chuckled Polly, who linked her hands behind herself and started skipping around the table. "Isn't it all tasty? You should definitely try it. It's just so good for you." Polly stopped and pulled out a compact. She reapplied lipstick to already perfectly red lips as Adrian's eyes wandered back to the table. Not even Polly could distract him from the grand display in front of him.

Abruptly clicking the compact shut, Polly leant into his line of view. "It's all just so perfect, isn't it?"

She moved around the table, sliding a finger over it as she moved. "It's such a shame because I can feel your heart racing at the thought of it." Polly smirked as he licked his lips. "I can see you sweating at the thought of running your hands through everything and eating up every. Last. Bite."

"Stop it, I can't," Adrian said, his voice cracking.

Polly merely smiled, putting a confident boot on the table and jumping up. She began joyfully stepping between the buffet, breaking into a dance as she edged towards him. "What if I said that it doesn't even matter if you did it? That anything you did to this little pink tablecloth would be nothing compared to what's about to happen? The unease, you can almost taste it…" she said, dipping her gloved finger into a trifle and licking it. "Besides, isn't it boring to always be the straight character? Imagine how

DEBAUCHERY: PART I

wild it would be if you suspended that pesky moral compass just for a moment!" She crouched in front of him and put a finger to his lips, chuckling, "And what's one more little secret?"

Adrian pushed her away, and she laughed. He turned from the table and said under his breath, "No one can know…"

Polly leapt off the table to embrace him from behind, whispering, "Do you stop yourself because you know you couldn't fix it afterwards? Or is it the irony that really leaves a bad taste?"

Adrian looked to the floor. Pre-emptive regret filled him. He felt weak and ashamed.

"I think you should do it, just once in your life…"

"But—"

"—No one will know, trust me. Do it Adrian. Finally. Feel. Full."

He unbuttoned his blazer to reveal a band vest top. A quick glance was thrown toward the church and as he turned back, Polly was nowhere to be seen. He was alone with the banquet. He swept hair from his face and inhaled, placing his phone gently on the table. 'Danger! High Voltage' by Electric Six started as an intense but familiar feeling of shame filled him.

Then an animal instinct took over as Adrian grabbed every plate he could and pulled it towards him. His tattooed fingers gripped each mound of food, picking up as much as he could and slamming it into his mouth indiscriminately.

But it wasn't enough.

Adrian mounted the table and, on all fours, crawled through the buffet, pulling everything towards his gaping maw. Sandwiches, salads and sausage rolls all fell victim to a black hole of voracious hunger. He choked on the food and even the seconds he took to catch his breath felt too long. His body couldn't keep up with his endless appetite, and all he wanted was to consume the entire table in one impossible bite. He rolled onto his back and lay in the food. Various textures and temperatures touched every inch of his body as he lay smiling in the gluttonous chaos. As he stared toward the roof of the marquee, his thoughts turned to dessert. Crawling over the wreckage he'd created, his hands lunged towards profiteroles just as a noise yanked him back to cruel reality.

"Where are you?" bellowed Leanne from the church's entrance. "You sneak out the door like a rat, but I'll find you! I hope you've found a nice hiding place in this graveyard, because by the time I'm finished with you, you'll be joining the rest of these fuckers!"

Adrian leapt off the table with an intense paranoia that this woman had seen him. He wiped the food from his body and fumbled to turn off the music as Gareth ran into view. Unsure of what to do, Adrian dropped to the floor and hid under the table of the dead buffet. He felt like an idiot, but as Gareth stepped up to the marquee, he knew he'd made the right choice.

"WHERE ARE YOU?" screamed Leanne, still at a considerable distance out front.

Adrian could hear Gareth's panicked breathing and, despite not knowing the man at all, he had never related to someone so much in his life. Voices filtered into the marquee as wedding guests seemed to gravitate towards the groom. Adrian wondered when the best moment was to assimilate into the crowd, just as a familiar voice came into earshot.

"I definitely think it's us, you know…" pondered Steph, disregarding any unease in the room. "I mean, whenever I'm around, stuff just kinda, like, happens."

DEBAUCHERY: PART I

"I know what you mean," came Nicky's voice. "Whenever I'm with Amy, we just end up having these fucking *bizarre* things happen. Maybe we're all like weird magnets or something?"

Gareth had done his best to filter into crowds of friends whilst simultaneously avoiding all conversation. A mysteriously ruined buffet, thankfully, seemed to draw most of the attention from him. Staring at the table and, despite being as confused as everyone else, Gareth felt no need at all to pull focus. He simply stood and prayed that the worst was over. He was quickly proven wrong as Leanne came into view.

Leanne bolted forward, bridesmaids in tow, huffing and pulling clumps of graveyard shrubbery from her hair. Hoisting her now dirty pink dress above her knees, she caught a split-second snapshot of her beloved. Like a lion locking onto a wounded, bald gazelle, Leanne and her bridesmaids sprinted across the lawn with the grace and demeanour of several drunk flamingos.

A tattooed arm extended from under the table to grab a pink blazer and cover Adrian's shame. Taking a deep breath, he rolled out to assimilate into the crowd with near-miraculous timing. With not a single eye on him, Adrian smiled to himself, feeling like the luckiest guy on Earth.

Gareth stood paralysed and, at that moment, felt his soul leave his body. Leanne tore through the marquee as he whimpered, "Babe, I can expl—"

Without pausing, Leanne hoisted up her five-tier wedding cake with one arm and, with almost superhuman strength, launched it at the groom. A faint yelp filled the air as Gareth panicked and grabbed the closest person to him, throwing him into the firing range.

Any luck Adrian had felt was erased as five tiers of karma slammed into his face.

Steph and Nicky bailed from the marquee immediately as slow-motion chaos, reminiscent of a Renaissance painting, unfolded. As Adrian fell back from the force of the cake, his foot caught the ribbon of a large box, releasing four doves.

Doves one and two made a stunned zig-zag ascent to the roof of the marquee, only to bump into each other. Doves three and four leapt upwards, catching their feet within errant pink ribbon, and fell face-first into a bowl of dressing. The buffet table sprang into life as coleslaw-kissed doves flailed helplessly across the blush tablecloth.

An overhead banner declaring *CONGRATULATIONS* for the newlyweds collapsed over startled birds and horrified wedding guests. A fascinated disappointment hit the faces of close family wearing hats and disappointed fascinators as the banner slumped downward. The mother of the bride retired her overused handkerchief and started wailing into a fresh ivory napkin. A silhouette of the groom's parents standing cross-armed and disappointed from under the vinyl banner formed shortly thereafter.

Leanne released a primal scream as a frenzied dove flew into her face. Panicked, all four birds then escaped diagonally out of the marquee, never to be seen again. Wiping potato salad from her eyes, Leanne saw Gareth, who grasped the giant bowl of coleslaw only to hurl it into her face, declaring, "You fucking bitch!"

As the bride ended up with a face full of veg and feathers, a food fight ensued immediately. The mother of the bride fired mini sausage rolls at the mother of the groom, only to have mini quiches thrown back at her. The two fathers threw crisps in the least masculine fight in history as a lone grandma saw this as her one opportunity in life to drop-kick a raspberry pavlova into the face of her least favourite grandson.

DEBAUCHERY: PART I

The three bridesmaids merely screamed from within the crossfire and the best man had just seemingly disassociated altogether.

Adrian stood bewildered. *It was just like Polly said...* He left the marquee covered in piped icing, smiling from ear to ear.

As he made his way across the grass, a voice called his name. He spun around and saw a familiar woman with a septum piercing and teal-coloured hair. As his brain scrambled for her name, she smiled warmly.

"Hi Adrian. Weird seeing you here!"

"Hey, yeah it is uh... Stacy, isn't it?"

"Yeah, I saw you on my shift last night at the pub. You were pretty drunk."

Adrian fell into green eyes and, despite being covered in pasta, she was captivating. From her lips, to body, to her tattoos, she was everything he looked for in a woman. She emanated excitement and was engaging. Better yet, she seemed to be looking at him in the same way. He felt like an idiot, but continued speaking, anyway.

"I'm Adrian," he said with an awkward smile.

"I know, I called your name," Stacy grinned.

Adrian opened his mouth to spark conversation, but was promptly interrupted by a flustered maid of honour, her long grey hair covered in tier three of the wedding cake.

"Come, Stacy. We must leave," said River. Her voice was nasally and seemed soft, despite speaking so firmly. She removed a glove to reveal a bandaged hand, which beckoned Stacy away.

Stacy nodded before quickly searching in her handbag. She walked up to Adrian, took his hand and wrapped his fingers around a small piece of paper, winking. He smiled nervously at her, moving marzipan-covered hair from his face. Stacey giggled and left the grounds with River.

"What do you think that girl gave Adrian?" mused Steph, slightly defensively, as she sat on the thin pathway at the side of the church.

"The riddle of the Sphinx, Steph," said Nicky, deadpan. "He's pulled, obviously!" With that, he yanked Steph from the floor, and together they went to the sunken marquee.

The two friends sat on the grass, with Adrian joining them soon after. Nicky noticed a tray of champagne flutes which had somehow survived the brawl. He reached up and grabbed them, passing them down gently.

It was then that Leanne slumped between Nicky and Steph with her veil torn, her dress covered in everything imaginable, and her face registering pure defeat.

Distraught and drained, Leanne looked at the glasses before leaning over Nicky and grabbing the entire champagne bottle. As the marquee ignited from the heaters underneath, Leanne burst into tears.

Nicky stared behind him and back towards Leanne. With a backdrop of flames, he raised his glass and cheerily declared, "To the sanctity of marriage!"

XIII
A SUBURBIAN FILM

A burning sunset tore across the sky above the unassuming clump of houses forming Bartlett Road. The lines of new-build homes boasting the same white-doored garage and modest gardens sat quiet as darkness beckoned. A stray plastic bag journeyed across the empty road and past the window of number 16, where a flustered Jay could be seen, hanging up fake cobwebs.

"Ugh, just stay on the fucking wall!" he shouted as it insisted on remaining between his fingers. Pushing his glasses up his nose for the fourth time that afternoon, he did as best he could with the flimsy decoration before jumping from a chair.

He slumped onto the leather sofa, twisted strands of webbing trapped within the frame of his glasses. Staring around the room, he felt it was acceptable and relished his vague sense of achievement.

Plastic spiders, pumpkins and dimly lit ghosts were atop every flat surface. Cardboard witches, ghosts and monsters clung hopefully to the wall. Rosy cheeks and overly cheery smiles adorned the monsters' faces, which, when paired with the canary-yellow walls, took away any sense of All Hallows' Eve.

An unused fireplace opposite Jay housed a pumpkin that was smiling away, ready to be lit and evoke some much-needed spookiness. On the mantelpiece above sat a small metal clock with a tiny locked drawer. Jay had gotten it from a cousin who lived in New York many years ago but had never felt so attached as to wonder what tiny secret lived within the small compartment. The antique timepiece ticked away merrily regardless, underneath a gigantic mirror which, for today, was adorned with tiny bat bunting. Similarly, these cardboard creatures had not-so-scary smiles and looked far more likely to omnomnom your blood rather than suck it.

A gigantic glass coffee table was piled with more food than Jay ever expected would fit on it, all of which was Halloween-themed. Purple plastic cups lined the table waiting for a punch that sat in wait within the fridge alongside a 'spooky' trifle, which took the terrifying form of a discounted, regular trifle.

A sigh of relief filled Jay's living room as several small anxieties perished. All was calm. *I've gone over everything*, he thought. *I've done the room, I've done the food, I've got the drink, I've done the cobwebs and the bathroom and the kitchen. Is there anything else?* He looked at the ceiling and closed his eyes. *They're coming at 6 pm, it'll all be fine. It'll all be fine.*

The jarring sound of a dying doorbell echoed loudly through his hallway, making Jay spring up. He wondered who would have the audacity to deviate from the plan that Adrian had so vaguely explained to him earlier.

Turning a stiff lock on the front door, Jay pulled it open to be greeted by an extremely hairy-looking Adrian. Tufts of black fur sprouted from a ripped t-shirt and shorts. His arms and hands were covered in further fur, which only added to his wolf-like façade.

DEBAUCHERY: PART I

"Naow zhen!" he said to Jay through cheap and impractical plastic fangs. "Thuck's zake!" he declared, removing them and stepping through to the living room. Jay shrugged, shutting the door to join him.

Adrian sat back in the chair, arms behind his head, and looked Jay up and down. "You're not ready yet?"

"I had to make sure everything was ready. Getting a house full of Halloween shit ain't that fun on Halloween, you know." Jay frowned. "I'll get ready in a second. Just tell me the plan again, please, to put my mind at ease."

He sat next to his faux canine friend who leaned forward to reach for the crisps, only to have a furry hand smacked away.

"Don't start eating already. You've invited like four people, right? We need as much food as possible!"

"It's a party, don't worry about the food, mate! Oh, and there'll be five, by the way. I may have invited that barmaid from work…"

"Right, so on top of this group of people I haven't met, you just thought to add one more?" said Jay, anxiety washing over his brain.

"Well, I figured one more wouldn't make a difference. Anyway, this will be a great chance for you to get to know them, so I'm sure it'll be fine, mate. Try not to worry."

"Hmm, I guess. Tonight, better be successful. You know we could've just invited our actual mates, right? I guess we have one at least…" Jay said, speaking his thoughts out loud. "Steph is coming, right? I haven't seen her in ages. I'm surprised she didn't cancel because she broke a nail or something."

"Yeah," said Adrian with a smile. "She's been going on about this party all afternoon to me. She told me she had the perfect outfit, so fuck knows what will turn up at your door."

"Right, pizza! Oh, and I got a quiche because you said there was a gay coming. They eat quiche, right? Like, tiny food?"

"Dude, he's not a hamster. You can guarantee I'll eat whatever he doesn't," grinned Adrian.

"You got that right," said Jay as he left for the kitchen. He was gone a second before poking his head back into the living room. "Oi! Leave them!"

Adrian slouched back into the sofa, folding his arms as Jay shouted, "I mean it!" from the kitchen.

"I wasn't even doing anything that time, knobhead!"

Jay threw a quick glance towards a black clock above the kitchen sink, shoving three pizzas onto two baking trays and hurling them into the oven. *Right, pizza done. Quiche…*

He opened a black fridge and grabbed two chilled quiches. He put them onto another baking tray and cast them into the oven.

Quiche done… Trifle… Drinks…

Removing the 'spooky' trifle from its cardboard sleeve, he poked his head into the living room and firmly scorned the hungry werewolf. "Down boy!" Adding a spoon into the trifle, he brought it through, carefully slotting it onto an already-full table.

"Do you want any help?" said Adrian.

"No, I can do it," Jay said, hurrying back to the kitchen and adding under his breath, "You just focus on not fucking eating anything."

Jay looked at the clock and his heartbeat quickened. *Twenty minutes!* Reaching for five chrome pitchers from the fridge, he put them down and threw a handful of ice into them.

As he did so, he noticed car lights through the bay window.

His heart quickened, and he turned to Adrian. "Someone's early!"

Adrian leaned over to look. "Oh yeah."

DEBAUCHERY: PART I

"Can you see who it is?" said Jay, going over to the window and straining his eyes to see. "It looks like… It looks like a cloud?"

Confused, Jay went to the hallway only to see his door ajar. *I'm sure I locked that,* he thought as he opened it, regardless. An explosion of chiffon holding a bouquet of red roses welcomed him.

"Oh, hi Jay! Long time no see!" beamed Steph, lifting a veil. Her face seemed to have a very thin layer of grey cake makeup, which gave her skin a sickly hue. Steph's styled blonde hair sat perfectly, her lips looked luscious and red as always, and she wore thick black mascara which ran down her eyes. She was aiming for spooky, but merely looked unhinged.

She hoisted up her dress and stepped in proudly, revealing red shoes. Jay clicked the door shut and heard Steph squeal, "OH MY GOD THEY HAVE CHEEKS!" He could only assume she'd noticed the bat bunting.

He followed her inside as Adrian caught sight of Steph, shouting, "Bloody hell!"

"You like it?" she said, giving him a twirl. "I'm a zombie bride. I died of a broken heart."

"Standard, well, you're the first one here, technically…"

"Well, you know what they say: the early worm catches the bird!"

Steph grabbed her dress and slid between the table to slump onto the sofa next to Adrian. As she fell back onto the chair, her dress expanded further. Long red acrylics reached out from within the dress, grabbing a handful of crisps between them like some kind of yassified claw machine.

Jay moved to lean against the mantlepiece and feign a relaxed demeanour. "So, what are these other people like?" he asked casually but incredibly seriously.

"Well, there's Lily, she's lovely, and there's Nicky, he's also lovely. Then there's Amy… she wasn't lovely at first, but now she is. I don't know about this other person though, but Adrian likes her, so she has to be lovely, too."

Jay looked at Steph blankly and turned desperately toward Adrian.

Adrian grinned and said, "They're all lovely."

The doorbell made an uncomfortable, battery-deprived noise and everyone looked towards the window.

"I should probably change that…" said Jay.

"Ooh! I'll get it!" said Steph, attempting to stand up. After momentary flailing, she stumbled to her feet and floated out into the hallway. Twiddling the lock for a moment, Steph flung the door open to reveal two piles of living bandages.

"Amy's got the booze and I've brought some vague will to live," came Nicky's voice as he flicked away a cigarette butt and joined the fray, Amy in tow.

"Ooh, lame! I love!" he said, throwing a thumbs-up to a cardboard witch opposite.

"Are you guys naked under those bandages?" Adrian said, staring at Nicky's leg.

"Pfft, like I'd rock out with my cock out for a belated Halloween party with a bunch of randos."

"Are you naked under those clothes? What a daft question," sighed Amy as she slumped on a sofa opposite.

"Touché."

"So, where's our beloved host?" Nicky said, re-wrapping his leg bandage.

"He's getting changed. I did only tell him the specifics this afternoon, so he's a little panicked."

DEBAUCHERY: PART I

"Aww, that's fair. Is he alright?"

"Cool, oh and yeah, he's just got mental health shit, that's all. He thinks too much."

"Relatable," Nicky replied, smiling.

"Except Nicky keeps his disgusting insecurities behind closed doors where they belong," grinned Amy, leaning to grab a drink.

Everyone sat in the embrace of an awkward silence until Jay could be heard nearly falling down the stairs. Everyone turned to the doorway to see him walk in dressed in ripped clothes and painted entirely green. His dark blonde hair was gelled back, and he had two fake bolts sticking out from his neck.

Everyone laughed as Steph declared, "That's amazing!"

"Hey guys, I'm Jay." His voice was shaky, but he fought through his nerves and sat next to Steph, whose outfit was becoming more like fabric quicksand by the minute.

The group chatted for a while, chipping away at a layer of ice that Jay was desperate to break with constant conversation. He felt calmer with every passing minute. *They like me, they like the food, they like my house,* he thought. His party was looking to be a success, so to celebrate, he stood up to play some music via a laptop plugged into the TV.

"This music isn't very scary," Steph said from within her dress.

"It's the Top 40," Jay replied.

"Well then, it's fucking terrifying," said Amy with a grin.

Jay smiled and looked towards the small clock on his mantle. As he did, the doorbell half-chimed once more.

"What in the hell was that?" said Nicky, frowning in the noise's direction.

"It's Jay's doorbell," said Adrian. "The thing's been dying for about six months now but he refuses to replace the fucker. He wants to see how long it'll last."

"C'mon, frugal!" said Nicky, snapping his fingers towards the door.

Adrian stared at him blankly before picking up a plate and saying, "Would you like some quiche?"

"Ooh yeah, I love quiche!" said Nicky. Adrian threw a proud nod in Jay's direction as everyone else tucked in, the stream of chatter continuing.

Another knock at the door made everyone pause for a moment and Jay rushed through to greet the last two guests.

"Hi, I'm really sorry I'm late. The taxi driver put the wrong address in his system and we ended up at The Void Tree pub," came the soft-spoken voice of Lily. She was painted a strange greenish grey, her pixie cut messy, fake blood splattered around with ripped clothes to boot. Jay smiled as Lily added quietly, "Um, I went down your path and this vampire followed me. I assume she's coming in too?"

A woman with gelled teal hair stepped forward from behind Lily with a painted white face, wearing a huge black cape with black gloves and a red dress.

"Hi, I'm Sthathy, Adriahn's friend," she spat through plastic fangs. "Oh, for thuck's zake!"

"Uh hi, come inside! Everyone else is here," Jay said awkwardly as they joined the noise in the living room.

"Hey Lily," said the pile of chiffon masquerading as Steph.

"Hi uh… Steph? What is she meant to be?" Lily whispered to Nicky as she took a seat near him.

"She's a white dwarf sun. She's going to collapse into herself at some point tonight and go supernova."

"Oh…" Lily said blankly, looking at her.

DEBAUCHERY: PART I

"No, she's a sad bitch who died of heart death or some crap like that," Amy said through a mouthful of food.

"Fucking heart death!" laughed Nicky. "Love your outfit, by the way. Zombie, right?"

"Yeah, old-school zombie," Lily said, smiling timidly and revealing some yellowed teeth. "So, you two are mummies and, um, Adrian, was it? You're a scarecrow?"

Jay laughed as Adrian protested, "What the hell? I'm a werewolf!"

"Oh, sorry."

"I'm Stacy!" piped up Stacy. "I work with Adrian at the pub and he said I could pop over before my night out, so…"

"Great. More people to remember," said Amy abruptly.

"Be nice, you twat," hissed Nicky, elbowing her in the side.

"Well, whether we're pre-drinks or a full night out, the more the merrier, I guess!" Jay said, feigning as much enthusiasm for a crowded room as he could. "I'm just glad someone else is painted up, too!"

With all guests present and accounted for, Jay continued, "Uh, I'll just go get some more food, guys," before vanishing into the kitchen.

An orchestra of six different personalities battled it out as Jay opened a multipack of crisps into a skeleton bowl. He blinked several times to adjust a drifting contact lens before continuing. A second 'spooky' trifle was brought from the fridge and gifted to a living room abuzz with chatter.

"What's that?" said Steph.

"Oh, it's a spooky trifle!" Jay replied as he placed it on the coffee table with the skeleton bowl.

"What's spooky about it?" Amy said, digging into the crisps immediately.

"Well… I dunno, to be honest. I mean, it's discounted, I guess."

Nicky and Amy laughed as they started spooning said trifle into small paper bowls with Amy scoffing, "True terror."

"So, what are you guys talking about?" Jay asked over the music, taking a seat on an armrest.

"We're talking about how little we all actually know each other," said Adrian, grinning.

"Oh, okay…"

"Well, it's kinda true, mate. We're all pretty new to each other."

"It is. I mean, don't you guys feel weird being invited to a place where you don't know what'll happen?"

"Not really," said Amy. "Me and Nicky used to go to house parties all the time when we were younger. You just do it less when you're older, so it seems weirder. At least we all have something in common."

"Right, that's the most 'people person' thing Amy will say all night, so if you don't mind, I'm going to have a fag to celebrate!" declared Nicky, grabbing a pitcher as he stood up. "Garden?"

"Yeah dude, just don't go in the last door on the left, please," said Jay nervously.

"Why, what's in the last door on the left?"

"An unnecessary rape scene and death?" said Amy through a mouthful of trifle.

"It's a sex room," grinned Adrian.

"It's not a fucking sex room!" shouted Jay, mortified. Everyone laughed and Nicky proceeded through the kitchen with Jay in tow to open the door.

Stacy moved to sit next to Adrian on the chair arm and whispered, "I'm so glad you invited me. I've wanted to have a proper conversation for a while now."

DEBAUCHERY: PART I

Adrian smiled. "No problem. Texting was getting a little stale."

"Here you go, Stacy, you can sit next to Adrian if you want?" said Steph as she sprang to her feet. Adrian stared at her, shocked at this sudden moment of selflessness.

"We need better music," Steph said to herself, crouching in front of the laptop and revealing her true motive.

Adrian grinned as Stacy sat next to him. She discreetly placed the edge of her cape over his leg and put a hand there too, making his body tense.

"You're really cute," Stacy said just as Steph blasted pop music from the tiny speakers of the laptop. Adrian smiled, happy to finally have a full conversation.

After a suitable amount of time, Lily timidly took the vacant seat next to Amy and looked at her for a moment. Ignoring Steph dancing on her own, she said tactfully, "What do you think of all of this? Do you think we're being too relaxed?"

Amy sat back in the chair with a cup of punch and said quietly, "I think that chart I made is more serious than any of us are taking it, yeah. It's bullshit, but it's also not my fucking job to reel people in. If it's serious and we fuck up, then it's serious and we fuck up."

"Don't you think we should be more proactive, though? What if there's a legitimate danger and we're just sitting here partying?"

"Don't you think I've thought the same? It's weirdly quiet, and no one has seen that Polly woman, or Isaac, or being threatened. My boxes were for nothing," Amy huffed and Lily let out a nervous smile.

"I just studied the things on that card at university. It's not to be ignored," said Lily. "If this is serious, then we need to do something."

"It sounds like you need a new hobby…"

Amy topped up her drink immediately as Lily stared at the floor, quietly saying, "I'm sorry."

Amy caught the tension and sighed. "It's fine. I mean, it's not. I know I come off… how I do. I guess we're just stuck with each other for the time being, so if we get to know a little more about everyone, this might all make sense, right?"

"Right," said Lily with a smile. "So, where do we begin?"

"Well… how is being a retail zombie treating you?" said Amy, as an unlikely conversation formed.

***

"So, what's in the dungeon?" said Nicky bluntly, lighting a cigarette from the darkness.

"Dude! It isn't a dungeon!" said Jay.

"It's okay, I don't kink shame…"

"Ugh, if you want to know, it's kinda a sacred space. I like to draw and I just keep it to myself. I don't even let Adrian in, so I didn't wanna have a party and risk the room turning into a shit-tip."

"That's fair," said Nicky, exhaling and blowing smoke into the crisp Autumn air. Steph's personal playlist could be heard from a party in full swing. They stood on a decked patio with a small metal table and two chairs near them. Jay gestured to Nicky in the chair's direction and they took a seat.

A damp ashtray was the centrepiece of this table and as Jay pulled out a joint, he paused and looked at Nicky for a second. "Sorry dude, do you mind?"

Nicky smiled. "Knock yourself out," he said, putting the pitcher down.

A calm atmosphere filled Jay's garden as it turned into that

DEBAUCHERY: PART I

glorious zone at the edge of the party. People could come and go as they pleased, but a certain intimacy was maintained. Jay liked it and felt far more relaxed out in the cool air than he did inside. *Getting to know one person at a time is easier…*

"So, what do you do for work?"

Nicky took a drag of his cigarette and stared into the distance saying, "I'm a photographer," as he exhaled.

"That's amazing! Is it a full-time thing? Are you popular?"

"Full of questions, aren't you?" said Nicky.

"Sorry. I, uh, ramble… and think too much. Sorry…"

"It's honestly fine, man. Yeah, I do it professionally as a full-time job, so to speak. Following in the family business, I guess. My mum sends me clients and I photograph them. It rarely happens, but I get money for it."

"What's it like?" said Jay sheepishly.

"What's it like to get a fuck-tonne of money?" Nicky laughed, pressing his cigarette butt into a puddle at the base of the ashtray. "It's pretty awesome."

"Nah man, I mean like… What is it like to do something creative for a living? Is it what you always wanted to do?" said Jay.

"That's pretty deep for a first conversation, but yeah, I love it. I like that you can capture a perfect or imperfect snapshot of time. Like, life moves so fast sometimes but, this way, I can grab a moment and so much emotion can come from it. It's just something I was always around. It's easier for me, I guess, because my mum was already well-connected."

"So, do you have a studio? Do you see many famous people? Do you live in an enormous house?" Jay asked eagerly.

Nicky laughed. "Yes, yes and yes. I spend my money creatively. Anyway, why don't you tell me a little about yourself?

At this point I know you less than that Lily."

"Who?"

"Exactly…"

Jay lit another joint, offering Nicky one. Nicky smiled and took it, offering Jay another drink in return. Jay moved hair from his face, saying through his blunt as he lit it, "So, what would you like to know?"

"Anything. What about drawing? What do you like to draw?"

Jay stared up to the night sky, a breeze catching his cheek. "I draw what I like, I guess… Things I see and people I notice. I help with Adrian's band merch too."

"That's nice, man. Similar to me in some ways, I guess. I envy you though…"

Jay turned to Nicky, stammering, "W-What? Why?"

Nicky smiled. "Because you get to record it gradually. You get to savour the process and feel closer to your subjects, right? I don't develop negatives, it's purely all digital. I'm there for a few seconds and rest is in retrospect. You at least get to be present."

"I suppose…" Jay looked to the floor, whispering, "But it's never enough…"

"What?"

"Oh, er, nothing! Shall we have another drink?"

"What kind of music do you like then, because I'm getting pretty dizzy watching Steph spin around at this point?" said Adrian with a smirk, his vision gradually blurring.

Stacy chuckled. "Well, I like rock music more than anything. My tattoos are of my favourite band. I work with a university theatre group."

DEBAUCHERY: PART I

"Seriously?" said Adrian excitedly. "I'm in a band! We're called Acid Lobotomy Demonic Lacerations."

"Oh my God! I think I've seen one of your posters around the university! That's so cool! What do you play?"

"Uh, like… my mouth. I-I sing," stammered Adrian, blushing as Stacy laughed out loud. He looked at her and saw a beautiful woman in front of him. With her hair gelled back, she looked cool, like a model, albeit a model in white cake makeup.

"I play the piano. I've loved it since I was a little girl. There's just something so soothing about it."

"You're amazing…" said Adrian, absently speaking his mind. Stacy laughed again and he became addicted.

"Right," Stacy said, standing up and moving Steph out of the way. "What do you wanna play?"

Steph frowned at her and took a place next to Adrian. He simply ignored her and stood up, too. Steph pouted and slumped back into the endless expanse of her dress.

"That?" suggested Stacy as her face glowed under the harsh light of the laptop.

"Fuck yeah!" said Adrian. "I warn you though, I'm not Steph. I can't dance for shit."

"Oh, same… but that doesn't mean you shouldn't do it anyway!" smiled Stacy as the opening of 'Hit That' by the Offspring played.

Disregarding everyone in the room, Stacy immediately started singing, word for word. He laughed along with Lily and Amy.

Adrian watched her body move, but the only thing he could look at was her face as she was singing every word and living in every second. He was promptly pulled from his infatuation as Stacy said, "C'mon, join in!" over the roar of the music.

Several drinks deep, Adrian mumbled, "Fuck it." Utterly

present and fuckless, Adrian didn't even notice Steph leaving the room.

Lily pulled her eyes away from bizarre scene as Steph vacated and nudged Amy gently.

"Don't care," she said flatly. "Another drink? Surely you wanna live through this horrific singing ritual, too?"

Lily laughed nervously and nodded, preferring to savour Amy's good side.

"I just think that whatever is going on is like… meant to be, y'know?" said Jay, completely baked. "I mean, what if this entire thing is just some story to some people? How crazy would that be?"

"Oh God, she's sentient. Okay, so maybe you've had enough of that," said Nicky, gently taking the blunt. "Why don't you have a drink instead?" Nicky poured him a cup of punch and gave it to Jay, who wrapped his hand around Nicky's as he gripped it. He held it there for a moment before a Steph-shaped clump of fabric tore out into the garden, making them leap out of their skin.

"W-What the fuck was that?" stammered Jay, nearly falling off his seat.

"I think Steph's going supernova…"

"What do you make of her?" said Jay as he stared at yet another breakdown.

Nicky grinned. "I think she's a free spirit."

"Adrian seems to like her too."

As they stared at her having a moment, Nicky turned to Jay and whispered, "Have her and Adrian ever…" He trailed off, waiting for Jay to catch up.

"Wha? Oh! Oh God no! I mean, we all used to, like, live

DEBAUCHERY: PART I

together in student housing way back, but he never mentioned anything like that. Adrian swears they have more in common than I think but... yeah. I've just never seen her that much myself, so I don't really know. We both see Adrian loads but then, like, we barely see each other. Weird..."

Nicky grinned as Steph screamed hysterically from within the darkness. "Well, now's your chance to make a new friend, soldier!"

Jay's eyes widened. "Dude... Pass."

Nicky smiled and fearlessly walked from the safety of the decking into the grassy no-man's-land of another breakdown featuring Stephanie Shaw. She sat on the damp grass in front of a small red shed at the bottom of Jay's garden. As Nicky emerged from within the darkness, Steph immediately ran up to him and latched on tight. Nicky wobbled slightly under the weight of his alcohol consumption and uttered the immortal words, "What's wrong, Steph?"

Steph inhaled and began. "Well, I was sat at the party and I was having a really, really good time and Adrian was with that Stacy girl and I thought she was really nice but then as I was dancing to music that Stacy girl moved me out of the way and put on some of HER music and now, she's dancing with Adrian because she's STEALING HIM AWAY FROM ME!"

Nicky's bandages absorbed most of her tears as she let go and dramatically held her arms out, as though crucified. "I just feel that I'm being left behind. I feel like everything was about me and how much Adrian's my friend, but now it's all just about Adrian and Adrian's life!" She stopped for a moment, flicking frizzy hair back over her shoulder before continuing. "Ugh! It's so fucking unfair because I'M IMPORTANT TOO!"

Nicky smiled softly as she bawled into his chest. "Steph, who the hell could forget you? I doubt you'd let them, you madwoman."

"I'M GOING TO LIVE IN THE SHED!" Steph wailed, makeup running further.

"You're not going to live in the bloody shed! You're far too interesting to be stuck in there."

Steph paused for a moment. "Y-You really think so?" she said, her faux-coy tone out in full force.

"I really think so," smirked Nicky. "You're not being pushed back; you're just adapting and you're part of things that are forever now. Isn't that better? You can get to know so many more people, and they can get to know you too. I have a feeling everyone will love you!"

"I guess," said Steph. "I'm sorry I ruined your bandages."

"You mostly made a mess of your dress, so don't—"

Nicky's reassurance was cut short as 'Coconuts' by Kim Petras came blasting out of the house. In a split second, Steph bolted down the garden path, appearing as a blur to Jay who jumped a second time. Jay threw a confused look towards the outline of Nicky, who merely shrugged from the darkness.

"Well, that was weird," Nicky said, stepping back onto the decking.

Adrian stepped out of the French doors declaring, "Evening gents."

"Well, I stopped Steph from living in a shed for the rest of her life, so I'd say I'm feeling pretty accomplished," said Nicky.

"What happened to her?" asked Jay as Adrian looked expectantly too.

"She was bothered about being forgotten by Adrian or something. It was nothing really."

"I figured that's why she left," grinned Adrian from within his merriment. "I've known her way too long to let her ruin another

DEBAUCHERY: PART I

party. Stacy and I found a song both she and Steph liked so they could have a weird dance moment. You can stop the Grade A chaos that she can cause in a second if you know how."

"Wow," said Jay. "You *really* know her. I'm jealous."

"Course I do, mate! If she ever gets like that, just play a song she likes and she'll calm down in an instant. It sounds really fucking shitty, but she's really a nice lass."

"Well, I asked Jay but I want it from the source. Have you two... y'know?" said Nicky with a devilish grin.

"What? Me and Steph? Nothing like that, no! We just yeah... We just have a lot in common."

"I still don't see it," said Jay.

"It's there... Anyway, shall we go in? The party guests are missing you."

They made their way back to the living room to be greeted by Steph and Stacy dancing terribly and lip-syncing to every word. Most of the food was gone, which Jay could only assume was down to Adrian.

Nicky looked towards Amy and Lily, who sat in drunken stupors together. Lily was swaying along to the music awkwardly and Amy was staring at the ceiling. Nicky took a seat between them and grinned. "Are you okay?"

"I miss people trying to kill us," said Amy blankly. Nicky laughed as Jay and Adrian took a seat opposite.

Everyone watched the girls have their moment and, as the song ended, Stacy looked at her phone, shouting, "Oh God! I'm going to have to go! It was so nice meeting you all, even if it was just for a bit!"

"I'll see you out," said Adrian, springing to his feet immediately.

After several goodbyes and a tight hug from Steph, Adrian and

Stacy walked into the hallway and stood at the door. The party had resumed in the other room immediately, and they smiled.

"I had a really nice night, thank you for inviting me," said Stacy, moving a strand of hair from her face.

"I dunno. I just wanted to see you again." He held her hand. "We didn't speak too much, but at least we had some good times tonight, right?"

They smiled, genuinely and honestly, before hugging. Their embrace lasted for just long enough and although Adrian never wanted to leave it, he did, asking, "So, er… can we meet again?"

"I'd like to get to know you better, so why don't you watch me play at the uni next week and I'll see you after? Deal?" said Stacy.

"Deal."

They faced each other and amongst the quiet, a huge pressure was building. Adrian wanted to stare at Stacy forever, to find every single thing he loved about her and remember it. He wanted to hold her tight and, as she turned to leave, he wanted to kiss her, but all that came out was, "I'll see you soon."

"You will," said Stacy, stepping out into the night. As their hands unlinked, Stacy turned around and, for one glorious moment, they looked into each other's eyes, an eternity of words exchanged in silence.

"See you soon, Adrian! Don't forget the uni! I'll text you the deets!"

"I won't!" Adrian shouted into the night before shutting the door and returning to the party.

"Sooo, did you?" asked Jay immediately as Adrian took a seat.

"Not yet."

Without pausing, Jay probed further. "So, do you think this is definitely something, then? You two really seemed to hit it off tonight."

"Yeah, I think so, but to be honest, I'm a bit wary. She's a good

DEBAUCHERY: PART I

lass, but is this the right time to start dating?"

Jay paused, still high and trying to keep up with the conversation. "I dunno. I think you've gotta grab the good times, right? Like this is probably gonna be a shit show, so if you have something good to come home to at the end... yeah, like, it might be worth it."

"Deep," replied Adrian as they sat back and mused over the bigger narrative.

Lily, Nicky, and Amy sat on the one sofa together. Lily was squashed between two friends, and then Amy stood up, saying a little too loudly, "Fuck this, let's smoke." She ushered Nicky in the door's direction and as the two left Nicky tapped Lily's arm asking, "Care to join us?"

Lily jumped and said quietly, "Oh, no thanks... but don't let me stop you."

"Emo bride, come," said Nicky, beckoning Steph to follow. A distant groan from Amy followed.

Lily sat on her own for a while, listening to the music and feeling increasingly awkward. She didn't know anyone, and she was weighing up whether the night was even productive enough to justify attending. Jay's voice snapped her from the intense thoughts as he moved to sit next to her.

"I don't think we've met yet, right? I'm Jay." He smiled warmly and moved a piece of his curly blonde mop from his face, signalling the demise of his hair gel.

"No, we haven't. My name is Lily. I know – well, I guess I've met everyone except you before. I don't really feel like I know anyone yet."

"It's okay, me neither. To be fair, I was worried about so many new people coming over, but it's actually turned out to be a productive night."

Lily paused for a second before saying quietly, "I don't think I should have come here…"

"What makes you say that?"

"I just don't think I belong here."

"Well, I don't know about that but Adrian will. Why don't we call him over? Maybe he can put your mind at ease."

"No, please don—"

"Adrian! Get here and tell this girl how special she is. She's feeling shitty."

Adrian bounced to his feet and sat on the other side of Lily, the introvert encased by people once more. She sank onto the sofa and the two friends looked at her.

"What's wrong… Lily, was it?" asked Adrian.

"Yeah."

"She was just saying how she doesn't feel she belongs with us."

"Aww, why would you say that?"

Lily shuffled forward from between the two men and put her drink down. "I just don't think that I fit. No one knows me and everyone is connected in some way. I came here looking for answers and I don't feel like anything has happened at all. I'm just on my own in this group and I honestly…" She trailed off and Adrian caught a familiar look in her eye.

"You can say it," he whispered.

"I don't want any part of this. I didn't ask for this and the only reason I'm here at all is because I'm curious about what part I could possibly have to play with a load of strangers. My life is going to work, spending time with my roommate and trying to make the most of the time I have. I wanted excitement in my life but... but not like this. I just feel uncomfortable all the time."

Adrian smiled and put a furry hand to hers. "I'm so fucking happy you said that. Seriously mate, so happy. I feel *exactly* the same way! I just didn't have the balls to say it."

"Really?" Lily said, making timid eye contact.

"Seriously, all I want to do is go to work, come home, sing some shit, have some drinks and have a laugh. Literally only carried on with this stuff because Steph made me. Nicky is nice, but that Amy is just fucking difficult."

"And that's coming from someone who knows Steph," grinned Jay.

"At least with Steph there's some warmth! That Amy is hiding something, I'm sure. I don't trust her."

"She's okay from what I've gathered," said Lily. "She's just a very abrasive person and, to be honest, in a room full of strangers, I don't blame her."

"You're very logical, aren't you?" said Jay.

"I just try to think of things practically. I spent so long in uni and so long self-teaching afterwards that I sometimes feel I can't... function as a true adult."

"Preach," grinned Adrian, grabbing yet another drink from the table opposite. Jay followed suit and Lily grabbed her drink.

"You seem perfectly fine to me," Jay said as he downed a drink.

"You are perfectly fine," started Adrian. "When we were going through all that shit at that Nicky bloke's house, you were the one who stayed grounded with me. You might've carried that conversation, but I was with you the whole time. Oh, and when Steph kicked off at Amy. You were there too! You're awesome and needed in this weird little group because you know shit, and

I need another voice of fucking reason in this madhouse."

Lily looked at him and smiled her first genuine smile of the night. "Thank you. That means a lot."

"Steph, Nicky, and Amy are just chaotic sometimes. I mean, look at them. We can be the quiet ones. I'm fine with that. Deal?" He offered a drunken grin and raised a glass to her hand.

"Deal," Lily said and smiled, clinking her cup to his.

"Wait, what about me?" frowned Jay.

"You're an in-between. God knows what you are, mate," said Adrian with a grin.

"Fuck right off! I can be quiet!" shouted Jay.

"I rest my case!"

"You work better when you have food in your mouth. It's the only thing that can shut you up!" protested Jay.

"Speaking of which, do you have any more food? We're running a little low?"

"You say this like you didn't tell me you ate a whole wedding buffet," said Jay, rolling his eyes. "Luckily for you, I have back-up food because I knew you'd eat most of it." He jumped to his feet and left for the kitchen.

Lily smiled, content within her drunken stupor before realising what was said. She threw a confused glance towards Adrian, slurring, "You ate a whole wedding buffet?"

Amy and Nicky sat on the steps of the decking, staring into the darkness of the garden. Steph was on the grass twirling to music blasting out of a phone, her body and mind cleansing with every turn.

"So how are you and Ethan?" asked Amy.

"We're okay. He's on holiday but we've caught up online.

DEBAUCHERY: PART I

I'm still trying to keep him at a distance from this shit though."

"Alright for some! What does he make of it all?"

Nicky sighed, a layer of cigarette smoke blowing into the cold night air. "He thinks I'm being stupid for hanging around with everyone. Says I should 'spend it with people I know'. Bit hypocritical coming from him, don't you think?"

Amy grinned. "So, the open relationship is going well?"

"It's fine, I think. It's kinda handy he's out getting his end away because we're all so distracted with this. Least I can be as involved as I want. I'm happy to be serious for now. Can't just pack every aspect of my life in for kinky sex now, can I?"

"Dare we dream?"

They watched Steph for a moment as they smoked. They found that watching someone with pale skin, wearing a wedding dress and twirling around the dark, was as hypnotic as it was horrifying.

"She really is fucking insane," said Amy.

"Isn't the saying, 'Hell is empty and all the devils are here'?" smirked Nicky.

It was then that a strange yelp came from inside, making them turn around immediately. The inside of the house was completely dark and burglar alarms could be heard down the street. Steph continued twirling, lost in the music, but Nicky promptly called out and she stopped.

The three of them fumbled their way back into the living room where the silhouettes of Jay, Adrian and Lily were sitting together.

"Watch out, there's chicken!" came Jay's voice from the darkness.

"What, a live chicken?" said Amy, surprised.

"No! I mean a plate of chicken! There's been a power cut, and I dropped it somewhere, so just be careful."

"'Be careful' he says. Like we're out here in the Somme,"

huffed Amy as she, Nicky and Steph clumsily shuffled to the other sofa.

Everyone sat in silence for a moment, the sound of the burglar alarms quickly becoming the only music in the area. The lights suddenly came back and immediately illuminated Polly who stood in the centre of the room and swiftly shouted, "Boo!"

Everyone in the room leapt back on their respective sofa.

"Who the fuck are you?" shouted Jay. "And how did you get into my house? Leave now or I'm calling the police!"

"Oh pish! You're long overdue a locksmith, sweetheart," Polly smirked. "*Anyway*, I just thought I'd make my stunning self known to you and you!" she pointed to Jay and Lily.

"Leave," Amy growled, a red mist ready to descend.

"How very on-brand," said Polly, disregarding her immediately. "Okay, so let's see… Amy, Nicholas, Adrian, Jay, Stephanie and Lilian. Am I right?"

"How do you know our—"

"Oh Lily, my petal! I know oodles of information!" Polly chuckled.

"Well, it'd be great if you could help us out then," shouted Nicky. "When I saw you outside Amy's apartment, you were no help at all."

Polly turned to the mantle and gazed toward the small clock. Stroking the top of the timepiece with a gloved hand, she said solemnly, "Time is just so important… You sweethearts have to spend it ever so fabulously and I couldn't sit back and watch you all waste it! I kinda have a war to win."

"What the fuck are you talking about?" Amy said flatly.

"I'm talking about who you all are, bitch!"

"Don't you fucking DARE—"

Polly squealed and clapped her hands together lightly,

DEBAUCHERY: PART I

declaring, "Eee! You're all coming together!"

The room sat silent, confused and weirdly transfixed by the strange home invader. Lily opened her mouth to speak, but stopped.

"Okay, so you're all very special people, right?" Polly started.

"Definitely," confirmed Steph, with a confident smile.

"Right! So, you need to realise just how special you are. I'm probably the best person to tell you, but you still haven't found that lovely Ol' D yet! You just sit back and party when real life is so much more interesting. Besides," she put a hand at the side of her mouth and pouted, "your Halloween party *really* sucks."

"Sorry, but can you just leave? I don't know how you got here and I don't care if these people know you, but you're in my freaking house!" said Jay, sobering up more with every passing word.

Polly ignored Jay and asked, "Where's the apple-bobbing? Where are the scary movies?" She flicked her jet-black hair over her shoulder and grinned. "Where's the blood?"

"So, you're Polly… Who is D and what exactly are you? I'd like to know why there are people coming out of the woodwork saying they're going to kill us," Lily said suddenly, making everyone throw a surprised glance in her direction.

"See! This is the kind of critical thinking this silly little group needs! Well, my dear, I have all the answers, and all you have to do is sign this contract."

"Contract?" pondered Lily. "Why would a contract release information like that? It sounds like blackmail."

Stunned at Lily's quick thinking, the group looked between her and Polly, who merely smiled.

"Once this contract is signed, I'll supply you with all the help you could ever imagine! Lovely help, courtesy of me, Polly!"

"What help would we ever need from you?" barked Amy.

"Rude much! You never know! When things get dark and the light is lost, I'll be there to pull you back to the glow. Believe me, one of you will need this more than the rest," said Polly as she flicked the small clock and laughed.

"So, if we sign this unknown piece of paper, we'll get your unknown help with some unknown thing? Sounds legit," Adrian scoffed.

"About as legit as Amy drawing boxes," Polly teased.

"IT WAS A GOOD IDEA AT THE TIME!" Amy bellowed.

Everyone immediately stared at Lily, who sank timidly back into the sofa under the immense pressure. "Well, I don't know. Logically speaking, she has a point. If we believe it's pointless, then where is the danger? What can she realistically do?"

"That's the spirit! Now the only teeny tiny condition on the contract is that all you lovely folks sign it, but I can't say what'll happen! It keeps things incredibly interesting, wouldn't you say?"

"Why would we sign a contract without knowing what'll happen?" hissed Amy.

Disregarding this, Polly abruptly slammed a scroll of parchment onto the glass coffee table, knocking several items of food off in the process. Everyone in the room lunged forward to stare as Polly stepped backwards, a grin forming on her red lips.

The aged document was torn yet boasted surprisingly clear handwritten cursive. Seven lines were drawn underneath, all with their names on it, waiting for a signature. As they studied the page, Polly adjusted the barbed wire around her figure.

"What in the hell?" said Amy, turning to Polly and throwing a befuddled look in her direction. Polly winked and blew a kiss in her direction.

"Is this a poem?" said Lily.

DEBAUCHERY: PART I

"What was that, duckling?" Polly said, coming up behind her and placing both hands on her shoulders.

Lily grimaced the sudden invasion of personal space but continued weakly, "Um, is this a poem?"

"It's a poem, spoken word, a sentence, a collection of words, nouns, verbs and a bit of mystery. It's pretty fantastic, to be honest. Do you want me to read it? I have a *wonderful* reading voice, if I do say so myself!"

"Um—"

Polly yanked the paper from them, cleared her throat, then began dramatically.

"Seven under Heaven, seven more above Hell. Discovering truth is the strongest of spells. When over meets under and chaos breaks loose. Choose survival and power, or choose death and the noose."

The entire room sat silent and confused.

Polly beamed. "I know, right? A veritable audiobook! You don't have to say it!"

"You have a lovely voice. I just don't understand anything it said," said Steph flatly as she shuffled back onto the sofa with Adrian, Nicky following her.

"Fuck it! If it'll make you go away, then I'm in," blurted Amy as she stood up and snatched the paper from Polly's hand. "Do you have a pen?"

"I ALWAYS BELIEVED!" Polly beamed as she pulled a pen from her pocket.

As Amy held it in her hand, it was the deepest black she'd ever seen. "What kind of pen is this?"

"Only the greatest pen ever!" shouted Polly, raising her arms in the air dramatically. "I'm actually on this scheme where I receive one every time there's a mass shooting in America, so naturally I'm an entire stationery cupboard!"

Nicky giggled as Adrian and Jay did their best to hold back laughter. Amy said, "You're mad," and signed her name to the paper.

"Eeee!" Polly squealed gleefully.

"Well, if there are more bad-taste jokes to come, I'm definitely in," said Nicky with a sigh.

"Yay, acceptance!" smiled Polly, lightly clapping her hands together.

One by one, peer pressure set in and each person signed on the respective lines. Lily noticed that there was a seventh line which remained nameless.

"What's this line?" asked Lily.

"The last member of your terrible little party," said Polly.

"Who's the last one?" asked Steph, eyes wide with wonder.

"Well, I can't tell you that! I can feel them close though, so it's only a matter of time. Anyway, you're all done signing, so I'll just be taking that! I'll make sure the seventh signs it as well, don't you worry!"

Polly grabbed the paper as everyone stared at her expectantly. She stood perfectly still and smiled vacantly back.

"Well…" said Amy.

"Oh! I thought we were just having a warm moment of looking into each other's eyes!"

"We want answers," said Lily. "Who is D? Who are you exactly and who is trying to kill us?"

"And what about this contract?" added Adrian.

"Oh, this thing?" Polly said, holding up the paper. "Pointless!" She tore it up and threw it upward, jovially declaring, "Woo!" as the parchment became confetti.

"Why you…" shouted Amy, leaping to grab her. Polly laughed and jumped out of the way, moving immediately to the living room door.

DEBAUCHERY: PART I

"Temper, temper! Oh, and before I leave, I have one brilliant plot twist just to keep you on your toes and get that grey matter bulging!"

"Mate, what could you possibly say that would ever surpass the confusion you've already caused?" Adrian said, rubbing his furry temple.

"It's a Halloween gift just for you guys!"

"A party game?" Nicky mused, completely bewildered by everything that had happened so far.

"Yes, for sure! Jay, my love. Why don't you say the word 'Leviathan'?" and with that she left, leaning back into the room for a moment only to shout, "Toodles!"

"Wait, what?" said Jay, running after her, only to be presented with an empty hallway. "How the…" Confused, he turned back and trudged back into the room.

"I'm lost," said Nicky.

"Leviathan?" said Steph thoughtfully. "Why would we say that? What does that mean? I've never even heard that word before." She sent a needy look in Adrian's direction, hoping that her friend could make things less complex, but he merely shrugged.

The room sank into silence for a moment before Amy piped up, "Well, she said Jay specifically. She didn't mention anyone else."

"The only time I've heard that word being used is for a giant sea serpent. Perhaps it's that?"

"Does that word mean anything to you, Jay?" Amy probed.

"No, I've never said it before, when in a sentence would I ever need to use the word Leviathan—"

Jay barely finished the word before he lunged forward and threw up a stream of blood over the coffee table. The night's remaining food became bathed in red, along with everyone sitting in the vicinity. Jay fell to his knees, eyes wide with terror. Steph screamed as Adrian leapt up onto the chair, blurting out, "Jesus Christ!"

Lily wretched as Nicky fought every voice that begged him to stay away to grab his arm in silent solidarity.

Jay's eyes watered, a mixture of tears and blood falling from his eyes. He helplessly grasped Nicky's hand as he vomited a second time. A rising smell of vomit bathed the room, as the group watched in horror. It continued for what seemed like an eternity as the party became a splattered, bloody ooze. He stopped for a moment, gasping for breath and leaning forwards, praying it was over.

With things appearing to subside, Jay brought himself back to everyone's level. The green paint on his face had melted away to reveal ghostly pale shock. "I-I'm so scared."

Lily rushed out of the room with vomiting sounds following from the bathroom shortly after.

"AMBULANCE! AMBULANCE!" Amy bellowed, standing up and flailing in a wild panic. "AMBULANCE!"

Nicky, who realised he was still gripping Jay's hand, quickly released it and yanked some of Amy's bandages. "Saying AMBULANCE doesn't make a fucking ambulance appear!"

Jay's bloody hand cut suddenly gripped Nicky's arm as he shouted, "No hospital!" Everyone stared, and after catching his breath, he reiterated once more, "No hospital! Please! I'm not going to the hospital!"

Concerned looks were thrown around the room as each party guest stared at the sodden table. Blood and bodily fluid oozed to the floor to merge with food and the remnants of a decent party.

"No. Hospital," Jay panted. "I won't go!"

"Okay," said Nicky. "It's your call to make."

Steph lowered her veil and became one with the chiffon as Adrian simply put down the sandwich he'd crushed in his hand

DEBAUCHERY: PART I

during the chaos. Amy sat down, showing a strangely out-of-character expression of panic.

The night officially ended as the power cut off again. A soft moonlight illuminated the horrific scene, with distant sounds of car alarms and Lily throwing up as a soundtrack.

The bat bunting fell limply from the mirror and Amy declared, "Well, this is shit."

XIV
SONDER

Adrian stared upward towards a glowing moon, the sixth car in a traffic jam. He exhaled, a chill coming through a crack in his open window. An accident on the road had sent traffic to a grinding halt and little could be seen through a wall of emergency services and lights.

The opening riff of 'Sick, Sick, Sick' by Queens of the Stone Age burst from the car's speakers as Adrian's mind wandered. Flickering stars in a peaceful night sky were a clear contrast from what was happening on the ground, but Adrian kept his focus on the calm. So many things had happened over the past month, and his mind raced to keep up. He thought back to the people he'd met, Nicky's enormous house and the wedding he'd been locked out of. Front and centre, however, loomed the Halloween party.

A week had passed since the incident and, despite it being a half-pleasant experience for him, Adrian fixated on the misfortune that his best friend had faced. *A party trick?* he thought. *No. You can't fake that kind of fear...* As Adrian rubbed his temple, he glimpsed a memory of Jay's panic-stricken face. A snapshot image of crisps, trifles and coagulating blood dripping over the coffee table. He

DEBAUCHERY: PART I

remembered his heart palpitating, the expletives from the group of friends, but, most of all, he remembered the smell. In that moment, things had gone from confusing to downright terrifying and he felt helpless to stop whatever could happen next. The future had quickly become his enemy.

His attention was pulled back to the present as several people in front had ventured out of their cars. With huddled conversations and morbid curiosity on display, Adrian only wished he had some company beside him to fit in. He unbuckled his seatbelt and pushed his seat back, slumping as best he could. He had no desire to seek out any other prospective difficulty, so instead tied up his hair and put one of his own albums on.

A wave of sound drowned the car and he drifted. Several people had their attention diverted for a moment to this new sound. Adrian stared toward them, catching eyes with an older man and his wife. With his gaze hidden by the glow of his headlights, he looked at their illuminated faces and wondered what they were doing before they set off. He wondered how long they had been married or if they were even a couple at all. *Perhaps brother and sister?*

He cast his eyes to a young woman. She had left her vehicle and had her arms wrapped around herself, exposed to the cold. Her hair was bright purple, and he thought about what her job was. A realisation that everyone, both in front and behind him, was running on their own track only to end up here with him became fascinating.

"It's called 'to sonder' darling."

"W-What?" said Adrian, almost breaking his neck to stare toward his backseat. There was no one there and as he turned down the music, he heard the voice more clearly.

"So polite. So considerate."

He sighed. "What do you want, Polly? Where are you?"

"She's behind you!"

Adrian stared at the back seats of his car with little enthusiasm for any games. "Seriously Polly, not now." He threw a quick glance to his rear-view mirror, only to see Polly laid across all three backseats. Confused, Adrian stared at her in the mirror. "What are you up to?" he probed.

"Oh, I'm just thinking about life. What about you?" she giggled, her black hair shining in the flicker of emergency lights.

"I'm stuck here," Adrian replied flatly.

"Well, I just wanted to show that while you were thinking about the past and the present, I might lay my fabulous self here and be your future." She raised her arms, carefree, and checked her nails. "A little bit of a predicament, eh?"

"Do you just hint at things, or will you ever get to the point?"

"Did you know," began Polly, ignoring him completely, "the couple ahead are married, but the wife has terminal cancer. That poor husband is struggling to care for her and is finding it hard to come to terms with the idea she'll be gone one day soon. Even worse, that he's now hit the point where he can no longer tell her he cheated on her with another man six years ago. It's now a secret he has to take to his grave."

"Jesus Christ! What the fuck is wrong with you?"

"And that lovely lady with the iconic purple hair? She still lives with her parents and she's thirty-seven. It preys on her mind constantly, but she just hasn't had the luck of being able to find an income that will allow her to move out. Everything is just so expensive. She can never quite find her feet enough to be stable. She's incredibly depressed and trying to convince herself

DEBAUCHERY: PART I

right now that it could be so much worse – a mantra she's been telling herself for years. She thinks about suicide but won't ever do it. She'll just hope it gets better because if she doesn't, what's even the point?"

"Polly, stop," said Adrian, looking wearily in the rear-view. "How can you lay there and say those things so... happily?"

"Just thinking about life," she said, eyes ablaze. "You can never really grasp the scope of suffering, can you? Some people choose to think about these things, so their problems don't seem so bad."

"I just..." Adrian said, trailing off. "I don't want to make myself feel better by feeding off other people's suffering."

"A rare empty stomach," came Polly's voice, cynical and warm.

"When Jay said what you told him to say..."

"An eerily familiar scene, isn't it, petal?" Polly said and grinned, sitting up to face him. "Ooh! Alarm call! Beep! Beep!"

Adrian sprung up, disorientated as several car horns sounded from behind. The cars ahead had moved, and an irritated policeman beckoned him on.

He started his car and continued his journey to the university campus. *A little late but it doesn't matter,* he convinced himself. His entire journey was then spent dissecting every little thing Polly had said. He felt horrible by simply driving away from the people he'd seen queuing with him. A weight had been put on him and he just felt low. Darkness engulfed him with intermittent streetlights sending a quick beam of light into the car. He rubbed his eyes through lethargy and drove in silence for twenty minutes.

Passing trees, takeaways and corner shops, Adrian soon found himself back on familiar ground. *It's as though there was never an accident...* he thought, pulling into the university car park.

As Adrian stopped, his leg spasmed, causing a foot to slam onto the brake. His face hit the steering wheel, and he felt a crack from within his mouth. Shaken, he sat back and felt something on his tongue. He removed a shattered piece of tooth. "Shit!"

With little time to find his way inside, Adrian left his car and started his walk to the main entrance of the university.

The site boasted a huge and historic campus dotted with buildings of varying sizes. Adrian was immediately greeted by a long path leading to the reception as he stuffed the tooth into his pocket. He remembered from uni days that you could go anywhere on campus from the end of this road. As he progressed, memories of music theory filled his mind along with many a good vibe.

An impromptu arm linked with his, pulling him back to reality yet again.

"For fuck's sake, Polly. You can't go in with me!" he said sharply, the barbed wire around her dress digging into his side.

With hair blowing in the cold November air, Polly beamed at him. "What if just one of these people, walking this same path, turned around right now to face you? To read your heart? What if they wondered about who you are and learnt about your little secret?"

"Shh!" said Adrian aggressively, spitting through the newfound gap in his teeth.

"Fine, I'll go, but I find it too ironic to not mention…" Polly paused, her lips forming a wicked red smile. "Your foot slamming the brake only sped up that little tooth situation, don't you think? Try honesty, sweetheart…"

Spooked, Adrian called out, "Wait!" as he spun around to face her. She was nowhere to be seen and as two students emerged from the double doors behind him, Adrian jumped.

"Sorry!" he said, hastily stepping into the hallway entrance.

DEBAUCHERY: PART I

The familiar territory looked, sounded, and smelt the same as he remembered. He made his way towards the auditorium, walking through sluggish automatic doors.

Adrian was thrown into a warm pre-show hustle and bustle. A figure emerged from a group of students who Adrian knew from the back of his mind but couldn't quite place it.

The man stood tall and had a defined jawline and an oddly shaped nose, and as he ran towards Adrian, he noticed that his formal appearance had thrown him.

"Frank? Is that really you?" said Adrian, only ever remembering him wearing tracksuits.

"Yeah Adrian, mate! It's me!" bellowed Frank. He moved fast, with every bit of energy compressed into a tailored black suit with a turquoise tie.

"How are you doing? It's been an age!"

"Decent man, yeah! Stacy told me you'd be here, and you've got stonking seats! It'll be awesome views and good vibes all night! I'm singing next to your lass along with some other peeps so it should be a hella good night!"

Frank frantically shoved Adrian towards the auditorium. Guiding him almost at a sprint, he said, "By the way, mate, I'm going out with Stacy's mum. Figured I'd catch you before the show so it wouldn't be crazy daysies if you guys ended up dating. Have to say we've got good taste in chicks but man... Stacy's mum, she's just got it going on!"

"Okay, cool," said Adrian as they abruptly stopped next to a solitary vending machine.

Frank looked around and leaned in, quietly adding, "Oh and there's some... you know, on tab if you want, mate!"

"Er..."

"You know, mate," Frank said quietly, backing away slowly, "some green, reefer, Mary Jane, some grass." He signed a smoking action while winking so fast it looked like a physical tick.

Adrian grinned and threw an 'OK' sign into the fray as the energetic echo from the past promptly dashed off. He continued through towards the auditorium entrance, showing an e-ticket on his phone to an usher with a small scanner. A blast of warm air hit him as he walked to see a huge array of seating stretched before him.

Now incognito within the crowd, Adrian stared toward the stage from his seat. Its wooden floor stretched farther back than he could see, with a lone microphone in the centre. To the left of the stage was a pristine black grand piano, which he assumed would soon give him a view of Stacy. A strange nervousness took hold, despite knowing he'd merely be just another audience member.

A sudden noise from his phone pulled him from his thoughts and as he pulled it from his trousers, he was greeted by a lone text from an unknown caller.

The concert of life is far more colourful than this charade. xoxoxo

Adrian sighed, having very little time to be confused by Polly's riddles. Moments later, the music faded with the lights above him fading as the lights in front brightened. He shuffled into a more comfortable position, ready to eat up the local talent.

A small middle-aged man appeared from stage right. Donning an ill-fitting suit and a kind smile, he stood in front of the microphone and began, "Good evening, everybody and I thank you for attending tonight." He bowed nervously, a mop of grey hair flopping in the air conditioning. Some of the audience clapped but he merely continued, "The talent featured tonight is part of both the university and this wonderful city." He bowed again as confused, disjointed claps could be heard from the darkness.

DEBAUCHERY: PART I

"There will be a diverse range of performances tonight showcasing the best and brightest of the area playing their chosen medium, be it the violin, piano or simply their own instrument. We hope that these amazing artists will transport you to other worlds and prove to be a welcome escape from any trials you face. Thank you, and enjoy!" He bowed a final time to total silence. After a pause containing a single clap, the man smiled. The audience then burst into an abrupt and thunderous applause, causing him to jump and shuffle away.

The lights lowered as two silhouettes ventured onstage. Lights brightened to illuminate two young twins.

"Hey, I'm Jason and this is my friend Matty! We have an original composition, and we hope you enjoy it."

They began and Adrian's attention waned immediately. He felt far more transfixed on the idea of seeing Stacy. Even though he had the perfect distraction from his life, Adrian's mind couldn't help creating intrusive thoughts. *I hope Jay's okay. It can't be real. Are there really people out to get me?* He wanted to leave to check on Jay but knew that he couldn't leave Stacy. *If I don't do this for me, what if I don't get the chance again?*

Adrian jumped as the audience broke into applause, some giving a standing ovation. The men beamed under the heat of the spotlight, bowed and left the stage as it quickly sank into darkness once more.

A second act strolled out, this time from the right of the stage. Adrian sighed quietly as he saw it was another man. The lights went up on a man with pink hair and denim dungarees.

"Hi, I'm Kisu, I'll be playing something I wrote whilst in Tokyo. I hope you enjoy it."

To the audience's surprise, the man pulled the microphone

from the stand and broke into a full J-Rock cover, complete with intricate choreography. Minds were blown by this visionary display of visual kei, and Adrian felt he couldn't look away. It was the single most avant-garde thing he'd ever seen.

The song ended and the audience awkwardly applauded, unable to process the incredible scenes they had just witnessed. Adrian took the risk and stood up, making the man smile and point at him, throwing a rock sign with his hands. Adrian laughed as more people stood, making him jump up and down with excitement. He bounced off the stage and the stage fell to black. *Well, that was distracting at least…*

Music flowed for the next hour with act after act offering the same timid smile before blasting an eclectic display of performance into the crowd. Girls with curls played Vivaldi, guys with crew cuts attempted Beethoven, and one uniquely styled woman with a bridge piercing sang Gary Numan a cappella.

Adrian's phone came to life once more, the screen illuminating disgruntled faces next to him. He stared at it quickly before putting it away.

A constant performance with no intermission. Is it worth it, sweetheart? xoxoxo

Adrian sighed and as the audience sprang to their feet once more, a familiar silhouette rushed onto the stage, followed by a feminine figure. Adrian's heart sprang into action. *This is it!*

The lights came up to reveal both Frank and Stacy. With blood pumping, he stared at her as she sat at the piano. She cast a nervous smile into the darkness of the auditorium, and began.

The opening chords of 'Talking to the Moon' by Bruno Mars danced softly from the piano and Adrian's body relaxed immediately. Poised and perfect, Stacy was a vision in plum

DEBAUCHERY: PART I

purple. The floor-length gown hugged her figure, as her teal hair fell gracefully to rest on her shoulder. A loose friendship bracelet and the occasional shine of her septum piercing made Adrian's heart melt. Beautiful and individual. Stacy turned to the audience as the chorus hit and her beauty was released into the room. Transcendent and mesmerising, all Adrian could do was stare, aching to catch her eye and silently announce himself as her biggest fan.

Frank's voice was strong, but all Adrian heard was the piano. With every passing second, he fell for Stacy more until she turned to the audience. In one glorious moment, their eyes met and his entire being shone.

As the song finished, applause erupted from the audience. They left the stage with the grey-haired man returning to the middle of the stage. He clapped in their direction with a smile as the applause quickly died down.

Bowing once more, he said, "Thank you, everyone, for that marvellous reception. I can't say how happy we have been at the turnout for tonight. It filled our hearts with joy and admiration to host an audience with such passion for the arts. To round off the night, we have an incredible final act. He has taken time off from his tour to grace us with something truly special. So please raise the roof for Kallam."

The room burst into cheers and applause as a figure stepped out, smiling and waving.

The lights faded to a single beam of white light shining on him. He put a hand to the microphone as the first flickering sounds of a piano began. From the moment he opened his mouth to release the high-pitched beginning of 'Bring Him Home' from Les Misérables, the audience sat transported. Adrian had never seen a man sing so powerfully and so from the heart. A moment of silence filled the auditorium as he finished, and the spotlight faded before the room erupted. Adrian got to his feet, surprised at how moved he was by the performance. The silhouette bowed and walked off stage as everyone continued to cheer, the house lights coming up slowly.

A loud mumble spread over the room as everyone rushed to grab their coats and cram out of the exit as fast as possible. Adrian left his seat, passing by praise for the show and light arguments about where cars were parked. He joined the ordered chaos at the exit, passing the grey-haired man who gave thanks, goodbyes and a bow to every person who passed him.

The cold air hit Adrian's face once again as he filtered between people towards the way out. Then, immediately to his left, he saw a plum dress bolting towards him. Stacy came and threw her arms around him. Her embrace ignited his senses and tightened his jeans.

"It was so nice of you to come. I had no idea you knew Frank!" she beamed at him.

"Yeah, we studied here together way back when. He's something…"

"Definitely," Stacy said with a smile. "We should grab a drink sometime soon, yeah?"

"Definitely."

Stacy then walked away, grinning. "Well, you've got my number…"

Adrian floated from the university courtesy of cloud nine. As he walked up the path, he put his hands in his pockets and felt his tooth in there. He smiled, immune to any negativity, bullshit and ominous phone activity. Following a solar-lit path, he gazed to the heavens to see a perfectly peaceful evening.

DEBAUCHERY: PART I

It was then an almost foreign sound echoed through the university. As Adrian stepped through the gates, he recognised a sound he'd only known in movies. It was that of gunfire. A second shot tore through the campus and Adrian's body tensed as screams rose to the clear sky, bringing an instant end to a perfect evening.

XV
NEW TRUTH

Adrian's ears rang amidst the panic of the university campus. *It couldn't have been a gun,* he thought, shaking his head in shock. A distant voice called his name and Adrian instinctively lunged towards the familiarity. He rang towards the darkened silhouette of a Rolls-Royce. Further gunfire struck against concrete, sending everyone around him deeper into a flurry.

The car door opened. "QUICK, GET IN!" Steph screamed from the backseat.

He leapt gracelessly over his friend and face-first into the laps of Lily and Jay. Amy shouted, "Drive!" from the front seat and Nicky floored the accelerator, speeding away into the night.

"Where am I even driving to? There's a fucking gun! I'm pretty sure that it can shoot faster than I can drive!" Nicky shouted as he frantically looked between his rear-view mirror and the road ahead. Without warning, a bullet ricocheted from the roof of the car.

"Fuck!" shouted Amy.

"DRIVE NICKY!" screamed Steph from the back seat, grabbing his shoulders and shaking him.

"What the hell do you think I'm doing?" shouted Nicky.

The car zoomed up blackened concrete, going forty, fifty,

sixty miles per hour. Houses whizzed by in a blur of living room glows and streetlamps as the fancy green car continued its desperate escape. Nicky moved maddening hair from his eyes, mind racing as he darted in between lanes. His palms were sweaty as he gripped the steering wheel tighter than he'd ever gripped anything in his life. He sped past drivers, who blended into a chorus of colour and car horns.

"Ugh, mate, I can't sit up!" shouted Adrian from the back seat, nearly inhaling an errant crisp packet, bouncing frantically around the car.

"Does it look like I'm driving a fucking limousine? Be grateful my priceless baby took a bullet for you!" barked Nicky as he saw a quiet turn-off ahead.

He braked slightly as he came up to the turn and swung the steering wheel round as far as it would go. The car flew to the right, sending everyone flying to the left. Jay hit the window, Lily was thrown into Steph's cleavage, and Adrian inadvertently dry-humped everyone.

Nicky turned the steering wheel back to even it out. Jay, Lily and Steph bumped heads, with Amy emitting a yelp as her seatbelt nearly garrotted her from the front seat.

The car tore down the road for ten minutes in total silence. Every tense second lasted forever and, eventually, a cautious calm filtered into the vehicle. With hearts racing, conversation slowly crept back.

"Do you think it's safe?" Steph whispered. Nobody answered. "Because I think it's safe," she insisted, desperate for agreement.

"It's safe," said Jay quietly as he stared out of the window, a clump of dark blonde hair flopping over his eye.

"Did you know that guy?" Adrian asked, curious for him to

justify his certainty.

"Of course I fucking didn't! If I did, I wouldn't be in the car trying to get away, would I?"

The car was plunged back into silence.

Nicky continued down the road past seemingly endless farmland, darkness encasing the car. Rare glimpses of silhouetted haystacks and farmhouses did nothing to break up a feeling that they may need to drive forever to feel safe again. Nicky had silently decided that the best course of action would be to drive until someone suggested something better.

"How did you know I was in danger?" said Adrian abruptly, breaking the silence.

"We all got the same text about you from an unknown sender," said Jay. "It said to be at that spot at the uni for a set time or we wouldn't see you again. We thought it was a ransom note, but when we all met up, that's when the gunfire happened."

"Do we know who sent it yet?" said Lily, arms around herself defensively.

"Not a fucking clue," said Amy as the car fell back into silence.

As Nicky drove, someone caught his eye. He stared ahead in the darkness as his headlights illuminated a familiar figure waving a piece of even more familiar cardboard. Grabbing Amy's arm immediately and making her jump, he blurted out, "It's that guy! That crazy D! It's that crazy D man... It's that D crazy man!"

Amy squinted, confused, as D came into view. She let out an incoherent noise as the car flew past him with everyone staring back at the source of the excitement.

Nicky flung the car into reverse, three-point turning and declaring, "We're picking him up."

"Aww mate, no," complained Adrian.

DEBAUCHERY: PART I

"Where will he even fit?" asked Jay.

"Can't we just talk to him rather than pick him up? He has a sign, but his sign isn't one I wanna follow, to be honest," said Amy.

"He's on the exact road we are on in the middle of the night! This is a sign in itself! We might be away from danger, but we need answers once and for all! Plus, my car, my rules," said Nicky, signalling to pull over.

As headlights lit up D, the group saw he was wearing the same tattered suit from previous meetings, his face smeared with dirt. Utter joy filled the strange man's eyes as the car pulled into the layby. He raced towards the car, shouting gibberish as crazy, unkempt hair danced in the wind.

"Hey folks… OH FOLKS! I know you folks from before! You folks are the folks who need to find me and LISTEN TO ME, FOLKS!" he shouted through the wind, still seemingly unable to control the volume of his voice. He handed Amy the cardboard sign, still sporting the words 'The EnD IS NEEЯ'.

"Jog on," said Amy, slamming the sign back against his chest.

"Right, everyone out," ordered Nicky. "We're going to talk to D whether you want to or not. I saved your lives back there, so the least you can do is let me pick up this crazy guy. He literally has all the information we need right now, and God knows just getting on with our lives isn't working. We need answers."

The car was filled with a short, silent protest before everyone stepped out of the car.

"THE FOLKS ARE LISTENING!" D declared towards a clear night sky.

Nicky approached him and stared. "Okay, so we have a shit tonne of questions and if you could answer any of them, that'd be just freakin' peachy. Why are people trying to kill us? Who just tried to shoot Adrian? Why can't Jay say the word 'Leviathan'?" Jay shuddered with Steph, offering a silent hand holding for comfort. "Just answer the questions we have, and we'll be on our way."

D smiled, revealing his pearly white teeth.

"Well?" hissed Amy.

D took a deep breath, turned to Steph, and said, "NEW TRUTH IS COMING! Take him to his city house and Ol' D will tell you everything you need to know! OH YES, HE WILL!"

Steph turned to Nicky, who looked towards Amy and Lily, and then Jay and Adrian.

"Yeah, we can take you to your home, but then you answer *everything*, okay? No fucking around!" said Amy.

D smiled and nodded.

Nicky sighed. "I'm watching you, old man!"

D's smile widened as he said, "Ol' D understands, but folks must understand that New Truth is coming!"

"New bloody Truth," Nicky sighed. "Okay, one of you will have to get into the boot. It's the only way I can see us getting anywhere."

He looked at Amy for a second, but she immediately growled, "Fuck off."

Adrian crossed tattooed arms and shook his head. "Nah, mate." Nicky didn't argue.

"So, Jay, Lily, Steph… It's one of you guys."

Steph blurted out, "Well, I'm a lady. You can't make a lady get into a car boot."

"Yeah, but equality and all that. You are a feminist, right?" grinned Amy.

"But Lily is—"

"Steph, feminism states you've gotta get in the boot because you're the most important out of all of us. You'll be better protected

DEBAUCHERY: PART I

from danger in the boot," said Jay with a smirk.

"Really?"

"Sure, whatever…" he continued, ushering her to the back of the car.

"Well, I am a national treasure," said Steph, stepping confidently into the darkness of the boot.

"You're the pride of Britain and we salute you," said Amy quickly, slamming the lid closed.

As everyone returned to the car, Amy looked at Jay and grinned. "That felt so good." She jumped into the front seat alongside Nicky, with Jay and Adrian squashing into one seat. Lily sat in the middle, not comfortable with D next to her, happily grasping his tattered sign.

"Right, everyone comfy?" said Nicky, turning the ignition, any replies irrelevant. "Awesome! Then let's go!"

Nicky pulled out onto the road once again and started a journey to the city centre. Everyone stared out their respective windows, trying their hardest to ignore the fact Nicky had just picked up someone none of them really knew.

After a short stint to keep her scepticism at bay, Amy turned to D and said flatly, "You're not going to blow your brains out, are you?"

Worried glances were thrown towards D, who cheerily replied, "Why no I'm not, young lady."

"Good," said Nicky. "I hoovered my car yesterday."

Thirty minutes passed with D telling stories of how he knew the farmers who had marked the sheep in the fields. Through glazed expressions, the passengers of the fancy green car noticed the countryside taper away and become housing developments and the familiar outskirts of the city. Rows of terraced houses and corner shops passed by as they drove through empty school zones and temporary traffic lights.

The city centre came into view, traffic non-existent because of the late hour. Continued silence sowed the seeds of anticipation of what lay ahead. An ugly multi-storey car park loomed over them as they passed, a gay bar, a small supermarket. Aged public toilets used as a taxi stop and impromptu cruising area signalled a turnoff towards a large car park.

"Are we there yet?" Steph's muffled voice asked from the back of the car.

"We are actually," Nicky replied as he pulled into a car park surrounded by mostly broken wire fencing. All attention was diverted to the car's newest passenger.

"This is the place, folks. Follow me," D said with a grin.

The group continued to stare at him, as he sat completely still. It took a further two minutes for everyone to realise he couldn't move until they left the car.

"This is the place, folks. Follow me."

"Is he an NPC or something?" said Amy, as she released Steph from her prison.

"Wait!" said Nicky, stopping and looking over at a blue 'Pay and Display' sign. He sighed. "Is that valid? What time is it?"

"It's ten o'clock mate, I don't think that's active… right?" said Adrian, looking for further rules to the sign.

"It's a car park. I'm not risking it. God knows the council here are money-grabbing bastards," said Nicky, who had already begun walking towards a pay machine.

Out of nowhere, a hand grasped his shoulder from behind and someone shouted, "Nicky!" He jumped and spun around to see a full suit of armour standing in front of him.

DEBAUCHERY: PART I

"What in the *hell?*" said Nicky, bewildered.

The person walked forward, only to lift the front of their helmet to reveal the widened eyes of Isaac. A flickering streetlight above illuminated his terror. The stoic metal suit, contrasted against the horrified person inside, was jarring. Before anyone could question his ridiculous appearance, Isaac broke into an erratic speech.

"Nicky, Amy, Steph! You won't believe what I-... I-I mean, I've been flushed out of a balloon, a mechanical one! I-I-I can't believe that I saw it! There was a volcano, and I fell from the sky. You must... no! Actually, *please*... Just listen! I was in a city in the mountains and the king there was mad at me! But... But he looked *exactly* like your bloke, Nicky! I was put in prison, but I escaped with a vigilante group! T-There's this city at the foot of the volcano and Nicky... I-I only saw the gate, but it's amazing! You all have to come with me now to see it! You must now!"

Isaac approached three bewildered expressions, grabbing Nicky's arm. A piercing gaze was thrown his way as he whispered, "You have to believe me, Nicky! I mean, out of everyone, you have to!"

Amy and Steph stood in silence as Isaac threw desperate glances their way.

"Well... meth is one hell of a drug. Can I ask? I mean, I really have to ask for the sake of all that is fucking holy, why a full suit of armour? Also, do you have any 10ps? I wanna get rid of some change but I'm short. We're about to hear something amazing from a tramp and we need parking money."

"Y-You don't—"

"Yes, I know, I don't understand," interrupted Nicky, "But some of us have real problems, Isaac. Some of us just don't have the time to dress up in costumes and blitz our minds. Someone tried to kill us. Like someone shot at Adrian. You've been playing too many video games and smoking too much weed. You're probably just on edge."

"But Nicky… someone tried to kill me too! Many have! Hundreds maybe! Listen to me!"

Nicky merely ignored him to face the pay machine. Amy and Steph, who had their faces set to stunned, followed suit in the hope Isaac would vanish. Nicky rummaged through his wallet and said, "Isaac, look, let me just pay the parking so we can join the others. You're connected to us all somehow and it'll be better if we all stay together and go through everythi—"

Nicky stopped. Amy and Steph spun around as he cut off. Isaac had gone, leaving the three friends staring out at the empty car park.

"Maybe he's gone to the other guys?" said Steph. Nicky and Amy shrugged in unison before turning back to the machine as a whirring noise presented them with a ticket.

They returned to the car and saw D sitting on the concrete reciting haiku to a captive audience.

"Winter is like death.
So cold and so unfeeling.
Why so sad, Winter?"

"Thank Christ!" Adrian said as they re-joined him. "This guy is fucking insane. Can we get this over with?"

"Did you guys see Isaac here?" Amy asked.

"Nah mate, we've just been standing here in The Great British Write Off, listening to this bellend."

DEBAUCHERY: PART I

There was a pause.

"But Isaac was here, right?" said Steph.

"Didn't you hear him? See him with us just now? It was literally seconds ago, and he was in a suit of fucking armour!" probed Amy, who received two perplexed stares in return.

"What are you talking about? If we'd have seen Isaac, we'd have brought him to you," said Adrian.

Nicky stared back at the pay machine and frowned. "Er, okay, let's just work on our current maniac for now. Isaac can wait, I'm sure."

Everyone turned to D as he got to his feet and trudged backwards. He then made a gun gesture with his fingers, put it to his head and, with a maniacal smile, declared, "This one's gonna blow your mind, folks!"

Without warning, he turned and sprinted away. The group looked startled as Amy shouted, "Oi! Come back, you twat!" with everyone darting forth after him. D left the car park via a hole in the wire fence before continuing to bolt down a narrow street.

They pursued him down seemingly endless streets. He ran into the city centre, zooming past the City Hall and veering off the path and out of sight down an alleyway. Adrian and Jay were in hot pursuit, followed by Nicky, Amy, Lily and Steph, who focused all her energy on not letting her breasts escape from her low-cut top.

They turned down the alleyway to come face to face with a dead end. Bin bags showed their insides against a wall alongside a tired-looking dumpster.

"What is it with people poofing into thin air?" Amy shouted.

"Maybe it's the dumpster?" said Steph.

"Oh what, is it a magical dumpster?" said Nicky, flatly. "Are we all going to hop in and ride it over a fucking rainbow to find our answers or something?"

"Or maybe she means we could move it to see what's behind it, you melt!" said Adrian, already striding up to it. The group stood back as he pushed the dumpster to a side, its rusty wheels screeching.

"There!" Adrian declared as he stepped back to reveal a large metal door.

"I've got it! We're all going to die!" declared Amy with a sarcastic cheeriness.

"Grim," said Jay as the group walked towards the door, looking between it and each other.

Adrian grabbed the dirty metal handle, and dragged it open.

"Right, if there's some dude chained to the floor waving a hacksaw or his foot around, we're just going to turn the fuck back around, okay?" said Amy as a cautious curiosity swept over the group.

Senses ablaze, they proceeded in single file down a narrow corridor with a white-tiled floor, lit by warm strip lighting. The friends delved deeper and deeper into this unknown building, the sound of the metal door shutting echoing behind them, creating a heightened sense of danger. Overhead pipes, fuse boxes and broken lockers along the walls told a miserable story of a workplace confined to history. The group had their senses primed and ready for something to happen as the end of the corridor came into view.

A second door appeared. This one was a stark contrast to their point of entry, as it stood ornate and proud. A family crest was carved into the mahogany and boasted a bejewelled doorknob. It was a picture of mystery and begged to be opened.

DEBAUCHERY: PART I

"Well, no turning back now…" said Adrian, turning the doorknob and creaking the door open. The group took a deep breath and stepped through. As they filed into this new room, everyone stood in full disbelief at what they were seeing.

A pristine Victorian-era study greeted them. Rows of old oak bookshelves crammed with knowledge and literature encased two of the four walls. Ladders on sliders clipped onto each end of this grand display, inviting anyone and everyone to peruse its wonders. The most elaborate polished marble fireplace any of them had ever seen filled a wall of its own. Its flames crackled, casting the entire room in a mysterious yet inviting glow.

Two antique sofas and a posh padded swivel armchair gathered around the fireplace. Regal and opulent, they beckoned the group to sit down. A coffee table sat in front of the chairs with a Persian rug placed underneath. A globe, housing either alcohol or secrets, was next to an end table sporting Tiffany lamps and expensive-looking ashtrays. The remnants of burnt cigars rested within, leaving a smoky trail up towards a Renaissance-style fresco above.

The group stared, mouths agape. Every corner housed something different, from a coat rack to a small table with handwritten letters on it. A vintage phone looked ready to receive calls from 1920, daring anyone to imagine the conversations which had passed through it. It was a time capsule, a sensory overload, and overpowering intrigue quickly became caution as the swivel armchair turned.

Polly was sitting in a silk dressing gown, smoking a pipe and stroking a white ceramic Persian cat slumped in her lap. She put the pipe to a side for a moment and, with a twirl of a handlebar moustache, declared, "*Aha!* I've been expecting you, old sport!"

"*You?*" shouted Amy. "This whole time we needed to find him just to see you? That's a complete waste of fucking time!"

"Well, when you put it like that, it is!" Polly huffed, placing the ceramic cat on a table and whispering, "Sleep now, my dear Fitzgerald."

Amy paced in front of everyone and seethed. "I don't fucking believe this! I feel like we're just going around in circles! We need to know the answers to our questions NOW!"

A tall figure with a moustache emerged from a door opposite, dressed in a tuxedo and holding a silver tray in white-gloved hands. D followed, wearing an identical silk dressing gown to Polly and smoking the same pipe. He stood in front of them, making a gesture towards the chairs. "And answers, you shall know! Sit folks, please. All will be revealed."

The group shuffled forward and took a seat, silent and confused. Polly stood up and made her way to the corner of the room. Everyone's eyes followed her as she leaned against the wall in the darkest part of the room, waving at them with an unnerving grin.

"Straighten your moustache, sir?" said the butler in an affectedly British accent.

"Later Chigwell," said D, raising a dismissive hand before taking a seat amongst the group. It was unknown whether D wore anything under the dressing gown, and as he crossed his hairy legs, the group did everything possible to not break direct eye contact with him.

"Chigwell?" said Amy, looking towards the tray, which held an intricate silver teapot with matching cups.

"Deontay Octavious Ulrich Cortland Hastings-Emanuel III. I'm simply overcome to form an adequate acquaintance with you all!"

DEBAUCHERY: PART I

"Fucking hell mate, no wonder you just called yourself D!" said Adrian.

"So, I'm assuming you fine folks are pondering what's going on and why Ol' Deontay has brought your cabooses upon these very sofas?"

"You are correct in your thinking, yes," said Nicky, trying in vain to mask his sarcasm with curiosity.

Deontay smiled peacefully before bellowing, "THEN LET US BEGIN!" causing everyone to jump.

"What I am about to word to you has been worded many times before, since time immemorial. This time is special though. This will be the first in history where I know you will have a greater purpose, even in the beyond. You are *the* most important ones yet. There will be doubt as with the ones who came before. You will not believe nor perceive what I have spoken, but alas, it is my duty to speak nonetheless."

"Are you ill?" said Amy, as everyone turned to exchange continued looks of bewilderment.

"This will be hard to fathom, but the informationals your ears will hear rings true. Today you will learn something worse than truth. It is that of New Truth."

"Now wait a minute!" interjected Nicky. "Am I the only one seeing this complete transition? Like you were a tramp in the street to us all less than twenty minutes ago and now you're frickin' Deontay III? Why would we believe anything you say from this point when we're sitting in a… in a…"

"IN A GILDED ROOM OF LIES!" seethed Amy.

The group stared at Deontay for an answer, and he smiled once more before getting to his feet. Pacing the room, he began with everyone's undivided attention.

"The world is simple and cruel. Deontay must wear his disguise as what he preaches is so deeply important. If Chigwell and myself emerged in our silks and fineries, many would listen and hear my mouth words. However, if I am dirty and unclean, ragged and loud, I am ignored and incognito. Even if I leap upon every person on Earth, you folks would always come seek me out as your fate is decided! I am but one of the unholy trinity, THE FIRST MESSENGER OF THE TRUTH!"

"Deep," said Jay as the room stayed silent.

Deontay looked at the knowledge in front of him and towards the six curious faces who sat before him.

"Come closer," he whispered. The group came closer. "And closer still." The group leaned in further. "AND NOW BACK!" Everyone stared before moving back. "Yus, perfect."

Deontay held the parchment in front of his eyes and began. "These scribblings are proof my mouth words are indeed speaking that of New Truth. You folks are in terrible danger and said danger has perhaps already happened. You all must have confusion in such large doses."

"Well, somebody tried to shoot my mate not long ago! Wouldn't you be confused?" said Jay, flustered.

"THEN IT HAS ALREADY BEGUN!" bellowed Deontay, eyes wide, and raising his hands to the fresco above.

"What has already begun?" asked Steph, transfixed.

"The predetermined fate you have all inherited through pure misfortune! Look, I will show you!"

Deontay moved to the bookshelves against the back wall. He rifled through the various tomes and then turned to the group, face hidden behind a pile of books, and strode confidently on.

"Through time, there have been accounts of those who went

DEBAUCHERY: PART I

through the same trouble and strife you folks have had to endure. COMPLETELY UNFAIR, yet but completely justified within the current system!"

He put the leather-bound pile onto the coffee table in front of them. A fresh intrigue took hold as they saw several loose pages, photographs, and other random things from yesteryear poking out from between the pages. As Deontay spoke, he drifted toward the fireplace, his presence only growing greater when stood in front of the flames.

"These books contain the answers you need. They are full of informationals that will push you on in your quest TO DO THE THING and to keep your safety. Times like these have taught folks that the books before your eyeballs will prove invaluable in your hardships. They are priceless and will be the single most important thing you will witness. It is for this reason that I have prepared a DIGITAL PRESENTATION of it all!"

Without warning, Deontay kicked the table, sending the books flying. He threw an arm upward to pull down a projector screen, a beam of light immediately illuminating the whites of his eyes. The group gawked at the abrupt motion as Deontay continued to speak.

"Throughout history there have been seven people who have all become friends through fate." As Deontay spoke, Chigwell stood on the sidelines, a remote in one hand and an elongated pointer to reference his master's words with an expert precision in the other.

"There are people who believe they are goodness." The screen showed a medieval painting of angels and cherubs among the clouds. "It is foretold that every seven generations, THE ALMIGHTY GOD puts seven pieces of purity into a human form known on Earth as the Benevolence. They target you because they have dedicated their whole lives to finding the people who you are presently."

"And who are we presently?" asked Lily, feeling more and more uneasy with each passing second.

Deontay nodded toward Chigwell, who clicked the button of the remote to show a second painting.

"You are all pastly, presently and futurely THIS." Deontay raised his arms dramatically, still standing in the projection's glow as a second painting came into view. Monsters with green skin, split tongues, and horns impaled people with forked weapons. Insidious smiles took sadistic pleasure in tormenting the residents of a hamlet in ruin. Amongst the orange sky, angels wept at the nightmarish scene of tragedy below.

"HIERONYMUS BOSCH!" Deontay yelled abruptly upward, making everyone leap out of their skin.

Between the mysterious setting, the roaring fire and the enthusiasm in their host's eyes, the group felt the grip of a genuine fear.

"It is believed also that every two hundred and eighty-five years, the Devil puts seven pieces of evil into a human form."

He left his presentation and walked toward a small table in front of Polly, who had been standing silently throughout. He opened the drawer and fumbled around inside, oblivious to the woman in the shadows next to him. The group stared at this scene as it played out in front of them. Steph opened her mouth to speak, but Polly put a finger to her own lips, a terrifying smile forming on scarlet lips within the low lighting.

Deontay returned with an all too familiar piece of cardboard which he held up in front of him like a teacher would hold a miniature chalkboard.

"These symbols represent OUR GLORIOUS DEVIL," he said

DEBAUCHERY: PART I

with a warm, albeit inappropriate, look of joy. As he pointed to the symbols, the presentation showed a photograph of Deontay holding the sign exactly as he stood now. With every movement of Deontay's finger over the crude charcoal scribblings, Chigwell used the pointer to echo his movements in the picture behind him.

"So, it is Satanic, then?" probed Lily, substituting all reactive emotions for cold, hard, critical thinking.

Everyone looked towards Deontay for an answer. Smiling, he tossed the cardboard onto the fire before venturing back in front of the projection light.

Pointing towards Steph, he suddenly said, "LUCIFER!"

He moved to Adrian, "BEELZEBUB!"

He turned to Lily, "BELPHEGOR!"

He pointed to Nicky, "MAMMON!"

He paused and stared at Jay, whose face had been drained of all colour. Deontay cast a finger toward him, shouting the all-too-familiar word, "LEVIATHAN!"

Jay's body flooded with fear, but it was Lily who let out a timid cry. She tried to speak, but couldn't form the words.

"You understand, my lady?" said Deontay, his voice taking a solemn tone. Deontay looked toward the final person in the room. Amy stared at him as he opened his mouth only to be interrupted by Lily who, with a single shaken tear falling down her face, whispered, "Satan."

The room fell silent. Steph leant over and held Lily's hand with all attention falling back to Deontay.

"This child knows the horrible truth I must break to you. You are royalty, you are princes and princesses of suffering, you are the Debauchery! These are your hellish titles, and for you to even speak them causes you GREAT PHYSICAL DISCOMFORT!"

"Great physical discomfort? Jay threw up blood!" shouted Adrian, getting flustered from so much unknown. "It wasn't just a little either! It was everywhere! He was fucking scared! We all were!"

"Deontay understands—"

"I don't think Deontay does!" said Adrian, even louder, rising from his seat. "I don't want this! No one does! I'm only here because of Steph and Jay! We don't know these fucking people! We had our own shit going on before this!"

"Adrian, you're scaring me..." whispered Steph, taking her hand from Lily's and placing it softly over his inked fingers.

He glanced around the room and saw everyone looking uncomfortable. He returned to his seat and said weakly, "I-I just... I need to be at the gym. I'm behind a-and I can't let it slip. I need to be at band rehearsals, at work. This isn't a game..."

"I know, man," said Jay. "But we're here now and there's some crazy shit going on. We need to stop these people trying to hurt us so we can return to our old lives."

"If I may..." started Deontay. "You folks are targeted because they have found you. The 7th generation of Benevolence has begun their battle to rid the world of the 7th generation of Debauchery for another ten generations, and thus extend the Earth's life."

"Bullshit," said Amy immediately. "We've never heard of this before, and why are there are only six of us? Shouldn't there be seven if we're sins? Also, how the hell do you know which sin we are before we do?"

"The seventh is out there. One more to join you, going by their true name of ASMODEUS!"

"Asmodeus? What, is he a magician or something?" scoffed Nicky.

Lily, shaken but soldiering on, said, "Okay, so Nicky knows

DEBAUCHERY: PART I

Amy then Adrian, Steph and Jay, all know each other. It would make sense that the seventh person in the group knows me."

"I still call bullshit," said Amy, who joined Jay and leaned back in her chair, arms tightly folded.

"I'm scared," said Steph, gripping Adrian's arm.

Deontay smiled and continued. "I knew you folks would be special. The frustrations and confusions are understandable. My family has been gifted with being the First Messenger for the Benevolence or the Debauchery SINCE RECORDS BEGAN!"

He proudly gestured over to a dimly lit wall which showed a tree of paintings of Deontay's family going up towards the ceiling. Every person within the paintings bore a near identical appearance to Deontay, each adorned in clothing fit for the time. His signature psychotic smile, a seemingly hereditary gift, had been passed down through the ages.

"Wait, so you're saying that we could die?" said Jay, his voice breaking.

"I say that… AND MORE! Find the rest of the Unholy Trinity, for I am but one. Let them teach you to tap into your primal forces and embrace THE DEBAUCHERY!"

Deontay looked around the group, who sat flabbergasted.

"A trinity? So, there are two more messengers, just like you? Is this how we win? Could we actually die?" said Lily, sitting up in a panic.

"I don't want to hurt anyone! This isn't us. This isn't me!" said Steph.

Deontay didn't react. He put his hands together and sat back in the chair, whispering, "It begins… Forget about the world's wars, because once you leave this room, you fine folks have a new battle. It matters not what you believe. How far will you go to survive?

There's evil afoot and you must wipe it all from this Earth."

"No! This. Is. Bullshit!" shouted Amy. "I mean, how come these people know who they are, and we didn't know shit until Little Miss Endtimes here popped up?"

"She has a point," said Nicky.

"GOD TALKS!" replied Deontay enthusiastically. "He most likely spoke a divine plan to the Benevolence from a very young age. Those who work for God know violence from the outset. They believe they are doing it for the lifeblood of the planet. God is cruel to all He deems sinful. He does not speak to them… but the Devil does."

"No one has heard voices," stated Adrian, his tattooed arms firmly folded. "We're hardly keeping up with external voices, mate! Honestly, we're only together because of bad luck."

"Wow," said Amy, shocked that someone said it. With someone on her side, she finally took her moment to speak the cold, hard truth. "To be fair. I agree, this is too much. We have no obligation to keep in touch and every moment we do, we're neglecting our real friends. We have actual friends outside of here, just to remind everyone!"

The group remained silent.

Deontay stood up and ambled towards the presentation once more, declaring, "THIS IS INTELLIGENCE!" causing everyone to jump in their seats. "These informationals Ol' Deontay has gathered about the Benevolence, will help you fine folks out."

He stepped aside as several scanned photographs appeared on the screen. Some had notes written messily in marker pen while others simply had question marks. Notes and personal details were under each person and despite having several gaps, the group pored over this sudden injection of genuinely helpful information.

DEBAUCHERY: PART I

"Hey, that's my removal guy!" said Nicky, pointing at various surveillance photos.

"That's my ex!" Steph shouted at several selfies from social media.

"These are your enemies. The Community contains the most dangerous people in the world to you presently."

"So, if everything you've said is true, that we are human forms of sin, then they are human forms of goodness?" Lily mused, her intrigue overriding any discomfort. "For every Vice there is a Virtue?"

Deontay closed his eyes and agreed with a smile. "This insidious order has a hierarchy, and the subordinates are known as Satellites. Combined, through all the mumbo jumbo, this is nothing but a death cult known as the Community Under New Truth."

Amy and Nicky snickered.

"Deontay has conversed with the Second Messenger and their names ring LOUD IN THE ETHER!"

"Well, we know two of them," stated Nicky. "This Chace guy was my removal man. He just appeared with some other dude to move me into my house. He came up to me one day with an eye patch and said he was going to kill me."

"HE IS PATIENCE! It is known that the Community will commit a large amount of time to their cause and sow the seeds of mistrust. STAY VIGILANT!"

"For, like, a bomb?" Steph said warily.

"Notes, threats, and GENERAL DISCOMFORT!" Deontay bellowed. "Ol' Deontay's ears heard you are aware of Noah?" He looked at Steph, whose eyes widened at the wordplay.

She said earnestly, "I am definitely aware of Noah! He was my ex, and we went out for so long."

"This makes sense. He lives in Temperance and, to him, the informationals he would gather on you would be worth the waitings."

"So, it was all a lie?" Steph whimpered, her eyes ready to flood. Adrian put a comforting arm around her and squeezed tight.

"Can we just move on? Don't upset her mate," said Adrian, quick to jump to his friend's defence. Deontay wasted no time in explaining further.

"August and Nate are enigmas, rarely seen, but with a reputation that makes them known. The whispers tell me that one recruits, the other indoctrinates. They are Chastity and Kindness, the ruthless snakes in the darkest parts of the Community lair. Lost in a love of sadism and CARNAL FLESH!" Deontay's bellowing of the latter words caused everyone to wince, but he merely continued. "The link between all seven of these nemeses is the colour turquoise."

"Turquoise…" mused Adrian.

"Oh yes. This is the colour of the Holy Kingdom of Heaven, and represents purity. They feel if they wear something turquoise, it is a holy armour. It must be said as many times as possible, fine folks, that the Community has resources and informationals. GOD HAS STRUCTURE and they realise their powers early for advantage. You may have known these people for years."

Amy frowned, eager to change the topic. "So anyway, you said there were seven of these arseholes. What about the rest?"

"River and Petra. They are evil and downright psychopathic; they are the demons of surveillance and preaching."

Despite a mass of intel, only one person was photographed.

"Holy shit! That woman was a bridesmaid at Steph's cousin's wedding!" said Adrian, springing forward. "Fuuuck, she knows the lass I'm dating!"

Nodding, Deontay said calmly, "River inhabits the Virtue of Liberality. Some people say she is a witch, others an angel. She is the spectre of the forest, keeping the Community's land in check. Some say that once you enter, you are ensnared by her powers and lost forever."

"Jesus, dude, do you think Stacy's connected to this woman?" said Jay.

"I don't know."

"So, who is the other one? There's barely anything about her," said Amy.

"Petra. Not many informationals on this one, folks. All Deontay knows is that she lives in Diligence and is truly lost to New Truth. She preaches in the glass heart that is the Community chapel and is the most devoted Satellite. She emerges only to 'cleanse' but the whispers still haven't snapped photographs of this RUTHLESS CREATURE!"

"Well, I guess when it comes down to it, we'll see her?" said Jay, speaking up. "I just..." He paused, removing his glasses to clean them on his t-shirt. "I just can't believe we'll have to kill them, y'know? Do we actually have to kill them?"

"Kill or be killed," Deontay said.

"So, what about this last one?" asked Lily, her mind still reeling from the mass of information.

"This is where it gets tricky, my fine folks. He is the Leader of the Community and the most dangerous. He is Humility and Ol' Deontay knows little as he travels silently. Some say he is God himself; others believe he's a mad king."

Everyone sank, deflated, before Deontay continued, "Ol' Deontay can tell you one thing. I know his name. Everyone in the

Community knows it and it is sacred."

They leaned in towards Deontay, who checked to see if the coast was clear. "Magnus," he whispered.

"Jesus wept! Magnus? Is he a wizard or something? Who do these people think they are?" said Nicky. "It just sounds like some idiot did a web search for the most pretentious names in history and made a cult out of it!"

"I CAN NEITHER CONFIRM NOR DENY!" bellowed Deontay, sending the room into confused chaos once more.

"Ugh, there are too many characters," sighed Steph through the noise.

Deontay broke through the scramble of voices, moving the presentation to it's next slide. "THIS is where the Community Under New Truth's base lies!" he said proudly as Chigwell pointed to it.

"Oh! I recognise that building! Isn't it a nursing home?" Lily said, as curiosity took over once more.

"It was a nursing home, but it started life as a sanitorium," Deontay said, sounding impressed with his reconnaissance.

"Of course, it did," said Nicky. "Are we gonna check out any abandoned mines or haunted mills while we're at it?"

"This place is at its worst now."

"Worse than an old-timey insane asylum?" asked Jay.

"Word has it that Magnus bought the care home after all its residents very sadly, accidentally, brutally died in a fire the previous year. The building had been left burnt and broken for a whole year before Magnus remodelled it as a commune for both him and his Satellites. They see hope and ideals that they've written in papers. This is their insignia, and long may you fine folks avoid seeing it in person."

DEBAUCHERY: PART I

The words barely left Deontay's lips before he pulled the first piece of physical intel from under his dressing gown. He slammed a wrinkled piece of paper bearing a symbol which left the friends unsettled.

As the group pondered the image, they felt at a loss and turned to Lily expectantly.

Frowning and with her hand placed thoughtfully over her chin, she spoke up. "Well… It's definitely a take on the Christian crucifix. The 'N' must stand for this 'New Truth'."

Everyone looked towards Deontay, who agreed. "New Truth is a doctrine describing the end of the world. They believe you fine folks represent sin incarnate. It is written that must be purged from this Earth LIKE YOUR BROTHERS AND SISTERS BEFORE YOU! The Community believes that if this is not accomplished, the world will perish!"

Lily stood up and declared, "Okay, I think I'm going to go," as she straightened her dress. "I'm quite overwhelmed. I'm sorry."

"Same. I don't want another Halloween party, cheers," said Jay, making his way back to the ornate door.

"Wait!" Deontay called, as everyone stood up to leave. He ran in front of the group, throwing his body against the door as though a grenade was due to explode on the other side. "You can't leave, fine folks! The end is near!"

"This is dumb!" exclaimed Nicky. "The end isn't near, and anyone who says it is mad! Look at that guy from hundreds of years ago who always seems to predict the end of the world!"

"Nostradamus," Lily whispered.

"Yes, him! He's been dead and we've all long outlived his end-of-world predictions, yet people still give this idiot credibility when a new prediction somehow comes up. If the world didn't end the first few fucking times, then it won't now! Yes, we should protect ourselves if we are in danger, but I don't see how these people are killing us because of some end of days plot! It's ridiculous!"

"Yet none of you opted to leave until you'd heard all of my mouth words!"

"Your mouth words are arse words because they're full of shit!" spat Amy.

The room became silent. Deontay stood planted against the door with everyone else standing firmly planted at an impasse.

"Where's Polly gone?" whispered Steph, but her question was doomed to remain unanswered.

Amy sighed, massaging her temple before breaking the silence. "Okay, so what, we're all meant to believe this? We're really meant to buy into the idea that a nihilistic cult is going to use all their resources to chase us to the end of the world, purely to fulfil some ridiculous good versus evil prophecy, all of which was news to us about until thirty minutes ago? And, on top of all of that, we're the human form of the seven sins and we kill or be killed! Is that seriously the point you're trying to make here?"

The group turned to Deontay, who merely moved from in front of the door, put a hand on her shoulder, and smiled. "That's about the gist of it, yes... Tea?" as Chigwell used the pointer to tap the lid of an ornate silver teapot.

XVI
RIVER

"This has just come out of nowhere. It's stupid and I'm tired of it! I'm done, I can't do this! Sorry, I'm going home." With that, Amy cut herself from the group and stormed off into the familiarity of the city as the group exchanged concerned looks.

Steph whispered, "This is all so creepy."

"It's fucking weird for sure," said Adrian.

"I guess if we're all in danger, the best thing to do is to lie low," said Lily, her level-head rising to the surface once more.

Adrian nodded and stepped to the front of the group, silently asserting himself as leader. "Honestly, let's just grab a bite to eat and go home. Jay? Steph?" He turned to Jay, who appeared to be deep in thought.

Moving the mop of hair from his face, Jay suddenly spoke. "Do you think we're really in danger?"

"Look mate," Adrian said firmly, "let's just eat something and get some headspace as a side. I haven't eaten in ages! Nicky, Lily – detour?"

"Well, this Biblical revelation has made me peckish…" Nicky said, rolling his eyes and buttoning up a black jacket.

Lily looked at them for a moment, before saying timidly, "I

think I'm going to go home. I can still catch the last bus. This is all too much, and I don't feel safe outside right now. I… I just want to go home." Fatigue had hit her and as she left the group, she apologised and took Amy's journey to familiarity.

The remaining friends stared at each other for a moment before continuing to walk back toward the car park.

"And then there were four…" Nicky said, walking next to Jay. "I get their point of view, but let's face it, we need Lily. We could've planned something… anything. Strength in numbers, like."

"Look, I don't like it any more than you, man, but at least we've got Adrian and Steph." Instantly Nicky threw a glance towards Steph who was perkily walking ahead with Adrian and frowned.

"You know what I mean, dickhead," said Jay with a smirk.

They arrived at the car park, which was now shrouded in a thin layer of fog. The heavy air was lit by white-light lampposts, casting an almost otherworldly glow over the few cars that were parked. The group traversed a mass of empty spaces to Nicky's car, which sat poised, ready to gather dew for the evening. Nicky fumbled for his keys and sighed, "What is life?" before unlocking the car.

They drove in silence past modern sculptures and streetlights, all creating the illusion of gentrification without any human activity to back it up. Living within this shell of a city were the homeless who sat in shop doorways; their lives, hopes and dreams shoved tightly into a single torn bin bag. The car eventually happened upon pubs and clubs, avoiding stumbling drunkards starting their hunt for a post-sesh kebab.

As Nicky focused on the journey ahead, his passengers sat deep in thought. Mind racing, he turned the radio on low and hoped it would light a fire for anyone enough to discuss their

DEBAUCHERY: PART I

conversation with Deontay. *Anyone but me,* he thought as he turned out of the city centre and into rainfall.

Nicky turned on the windscreen wipers, creating a systematic squeak. Steph and Adrian stared blankly out of their respective backseat windows, hands still locked together over the middle seat. A distorted view of coloured takeaway signs and pub entrances was shown through drops on the window. Everyone was living their life without a care in the world.

After several moments in silence, mourning their old lives, Nicky took the car along a bypass that ran alongside the city docks. The green car sped on with the eerie silhouettes of fishing boats bobbing up and down on the river nearby. Nicky turned at the first exit and pulled into a retail park.

The fast-food restaurant sat small and proud, a twenty-four-hour bastion of familiar branding that welcomed all into its embrace. Gliding into the drive-thru lane, Nicky lowered the window. The car quickly became chilled, with drizzle falling onto the driver's seat, but it was a welcome sacrifice when the reward was the promise of comfort eating.

"What does everybody want?" Nicky said, stopping in front of the back-lit angel that was the menu. Squinting, Steph made her choice, followed by Adrian. As Jay undid his seatbelt, his hand fell onto the seat between Nicky's legs.

Nicky's body tensed, determined to avoid awkwardness. As Jay made his choice, he realised where his hand was and tore it away, red-faced.

With everyone's orders somewhat memorised, Nicky slowly drove the car to a damp order speaker. He waited for a minute before an abrupt metallic voice said, "Hi can I take your order?"

Nicky sprang into action, reciting everyone's order down to a T.

There was a pause followed by, "Okay, is that everything?"

"Yeah, thanks."

"I'm sorry, what was that?" asked the crackling voice.

"Did you get the order?" Nicky said, raising his voice, with the passengers of the car also taking notice.

It was then that the static twisted into an annoyingly familiar voice. "So are you more up to speed, petal?"

"Polly?" said Nicky. "No, we're bloody not! It feels like a mystery wrapped in an enigma with too many side characters and existential crises."

"Would you like fries with that?" came her gleefully sarcastic tone.

Nicky groaned. "You know Amy and Lily have had it with this shit. We all have!"

"Can you take us to the Community?" Steph asked, possessed by an abrupt yet surprising moment of clarity. Everyone in the car turned expectantly to the speaker.

"Well, aren't you all eager to have unpleasant experiences? There's a phrase for that I'm sure, eh Adrian?" said Polly. "So that's one death cult address, some distracting junk food and a side order of mental health issues, is that all?"

"Ooh and don't forget those fries!" Steph cheerfully called as she leaned forward to rest her chin on Nicky's seat.

A second crackle abruptly cut the conversation short and the voice of a confused employee returned. "Sir, is there a problem? Your order is complete. Please proceed to the payment window!"

"Oh yeah, sorry..." Nicky fumbled, "My friend uh... he shit his pants."

"What the fuck, dude?" Jay shouted as the car started once again.

"It was all I could think of!"

An irritated worker slid the window open and said, "Twenty-

DEBAUCHERY: PART I

six sixty-six."

As the employee brought the card reader closer to Nicky, he caught eyes with Jay and frowned in his direction. Mortified, Jay turned to look out of his window, boasting a stunning panorama of a low-rise concrete wall and marred views of a slip road.

Immediately after the window shut, the car moved forward, and they awaited their precious cargo. The friends stared hopefully at the window as Polly came into view. She stood in full uniform, a headset poking out from shiny black hair. Smiling from behind the window, she took a gloved hand and slowly slid the glass to a side before leaning dreamily against the wall, declaring, "Hey."

"What in the f... frig are you doing here?" Nicky said, the entire car barely reacting at this point.

"It's amazing how far you can get in life just by wearing the right outfit," Polly said with a grin.

Nicky rolled his eyes and said wearily, "Just let us have this one moment."

Polly huffed, "Fiiine. Here you go, butternut, please read the note attached and enjoy your calories, you PIGS!"

"Okay, wait – what?" said Nicky, nearly dropping the drinks over Jay as he passed them back. Polly beamed, waving and slamming the window shut immediately. The car sat in an uneasy quiet until a car horn from behind made Nicky jerk the car forward.

He meandered around the quarter-full car park and found a spot toward the back. Jay removed the food from the bag and passed it to its respective owner. Confused, he pulled the last item, a maroon envelope, from the bag. Everyone gawked as Jay flipped it over to reveal a black wax seal.

Jay whispered, "Do you think we should open it?"

"No, I think we should eat it," said Nicky flatly, tearing into his chicken nuggets.

"I just mean it could be dangerous, like anthrax or something? I can't see the insignia in this light either…"

"But we didn't order any anthrax, did we?" said Steph.

Jay frowned, cautiously breaking the seal to reveal a folded sheet of paper. He removed it to find a postcard holding perfect calligraphy.

Community Under New Truth Agricultural Project
Guyana Lane
Hugs and kisses.
Polly xoxoxo

"Well, there's an address," Jay said through a mouthful of cheeseburger. "It must be where the Community is holed up. If these people are trying to kill us, maybe it's best if we learn about them. What would Lily do?"

Nicky frowned. "Lily isn't even here so with that fact staring us in the face, I can safely say she probably wouldn't go any further down this rabbit hole. It's stupid to be driving up to their headquarters and ringing the doorbell."

"Fair point man, but still… What do you think, Steph?"

Steph, who had been watching a plastic bag drifting through the wind for most of the debate, simply said, "Hm?"

"Do you think we should go to the address?" asked Jay.

"Well… I think that it'd, like, push the story on and stuff so like yeah, why not?"

There was a pause before Adrian said, "Standard."

DEBAUCHERY: PART I

Jay followed up with, "If you guys are down, then I'll stick with you."

They stared at Nicky, who rolled his eyes. "Great, we're all going to die because of peer pressure."

Adrian and Jay laughed as Nicky put the address into his phone. Sticking it in the holder, he started the car and drove off.

Ten minutes passed with the group forming a mental Q&A. Collective thoughts reverberated around the walls of the car. Steph even nodded in agreement with both her questions and answers, which, she knew, were the most helpful.

"We're here. It's just up the road on the right," Nicky said as he pulled into an empty parking spot. Adrian and Steph leant on the front car seats, staring up the road.

"Do you think it's dangerous?" Steph asked directly into Nicky's ear, causing him to shudder and shoo her away.

"We need to just drive past," said Jay. "I mean, what harm could it do?"

Adrian threw a stony look in his direction, choosing to voice what Nicky was thinking. "I mean, we could be bludgeoned on the road by people in light-up masks."

"It sounds like that idea is only good for two films," Jay grinned at Nicky, who genuinely smiled back.

"I love this critical side of you."

"Thanks, babe," Jay smirked, testing the sarcastic waters of their friendship.

Adrian exhaled, "Fuuuck! Fine, let's just drive by quickly and get this whole mess over with."

Nicky started the car once more and proceeded down Guyana Lane. Many of the cars in the surrounding area were parked and the streetlamps showed only normality until they reached a set of tall, white and gold gates about halfway down.

"Holy…" Nicky started.

"Shit-balls" Adrian finished as eyes widened. Nicky stopped in the middle of the road as everyone stared at the Community Under New Truth's base of operations.

Casting their eyes upward, they saw the gates, which kept the enigmatic complex safe. A crest in the centre of this grand entrance depicted angels dramatically fighting off several snakes. Above this Biblical scene were the words Community Under New Truth in cold, hard metal. These ornate gates proudly protected a huge network of buildings which formed a crescent shape. The grounds were huge, with several wooden benches dotted around. A lot of the building lay hidden within the darkness, bar one. A strange egg-shaped building made of stained glass shone far brighter than its dimly lit sister buildings.

Turning their gaze to the grounds, they noticed a single gravel path leading from the gate to a distant sound of water from a fountain deep within the blackness.

The group tried their hardest to absorb every inch of this majestically ominous scene for fear of missing something important. They noticed the cult symbol Deontay had shown them, taking the form of metal works scattered sporadically across the grounds. Each cross bore crudely splattered turquoise paint. Four more of these symbols accompanied the gates, two on each side. The mass of askew crosses around the site gave an off-tangent graveyard effect, and they shuddered to think what secrets the place held.

Nicky eventually broke the stunned silence. "So, thoughts?" before continuing further down the street.

"Umm—" Steph whispered.

DEBAUCHERY: PART I

"—They're definitely a fucking cult mate," interrupted Adrian.

"RIGHT?" shouted Jay, relieved someone thought the same.

Nicky realised he had slowed the car to a snail's pace, so sped up to turn the corner. The group saw that the entire border of the site had a tall white brick wall shrouding everything in further secrecy.

As the car reached the end of the road, Steph screamed, "OH MY GOD, STOP!"

Nicky slammed his foot on the brake as everyone shouted, "What?"

"There's nothing there," said Adrian as he stared into calmness.

"Yes, look!" Steph said, pointing eagerly to the right. They saw that the wall surrounding the site had been cut off, and instead, a small row of trees led to what looked like a forest. "Through there could be our way in!" she said excitedly.

"We don't want a way in," said Adrian.

"Wait…" Jay whispered

"What's up?"

"I think we should check it out. We've discovered the place our enemies stay, and I think we could have so much more of an advantage if we got a little clos—"

"—No."

"But Ade—"

"—No. If these people want to find us and kill us, how about maybe, just maybe, we don't go poking around the back fucking door?"

"Well, we have an expert at poking around the back door right here in this car!" Jay said, turning to look at Nicky whose mouth fell open in shock.

"Mate!" Adrian laughed.

"Oh, it's like that is it?" hissed Nicky.

"Well what do you think, Nicky?" said Jay. "Do you think it's worth checking out?"

"I'd rather have a triage call with Harold Shipman." Nicky replied, flatly.

"Fuck's sake! Fine then, Adrian, come with. Go on. You're the most built out of all of us, so it makes the most sense for you to join me," Jay said, throwing his door open decisively.

"Oh yeah, bring the black guy. I'll make sure to die first so you can all escape!"

As Adrian stepped outside, Nicky called out after him, "Yeah that's right, you two big, strong men go ahead. Woman and gay will hold the fort, we don't mind! We'll just fucking knit!"

Adrian and Jay laughed as Nicky locked the car.

After a momentary silence, Steph squealed, "Oh, I get it! Back door!" and filled the car with overly loud laughter. Nicky pulled a pained expression at her in his rear-view mirror.

✝

The first cautious steps Adrian and Jay took into the darkness of the forest drained away every fraction of life from Earth. Steph's distant laughter promptly faded into silence as they walked past several metal cult insignias dangling from trees. They exchanged cautious glances, evaluating the route ahead. The stillness that engulfed them was stronger than either of them had ever experienced. It felt as though they were in the vacuum of space, as the only sight to be seen was a blanket of stars in the clear night above. The forest was incredibly relaxing, yet simultaneously devoid of life as the skeletal silhouettes of trees lay naked and

DEBAUCHERY: PART I

cold from every direction.

Within the blackened gloom, Adrian reached for his phone torch. Shining a piercing white light towards the ground, he continued on, with Jay following cautiously behind.

"My anxiety is playing up so bad, dude. This is so fucking dumb," Jay whispered, worried that even his faintest breath would be heard.

"You wanted to do this! We've come this far…"

Jay sighed and walked up to Adrian's side, making sure his flicker of familiarity stayed uncomfortably close. As they plunged further into the immeasurable darkness, the treetops rustled in the chilled night air.

The blanket of black deepened so much that anything outside the beam of cold, electronic light remained shrouded. Darkness seemingly ate the fragile light as Jay zipped up his hoodie. Feeling the need to hold his arms out in front of him, he fumbled to familiarise himself with anything. The trees seemed to close in around them as they ventured forward, their sense of direction jarred by the three hundred and sixty degrees of foreign land.

A glow of moonlight ahead seemed to lessen their disorientation, causing Adrian to notice something.

"Look!" he said in a loud whisper, grabbing Jay's arm and pointing.

Adrian's hand couldn't be seen, but as Jay honed in on what he assumed was the same area, he saw some precious light. The friends broke into a jog towards this opening, curiosity ablaze.

They burst from the darkness and stepped onto a worn jetty. The cold wind hit them as they stared ahead at an expansive lake. Moonlight illuminated the water, giving the surrounding area an ethereal glow. Adrian turned off his phone light and breathed a sigh of relief.

Jay's eyes adjusted as he said, "Well, at least we know there's an end somewhere—"

Adrian abruptly nudged his side, pointing to the end of the walkway.

Jay looked ahead to see a woman sat in a large wicker chair at the water's edge, surrounded by animals. A long, flowing wedding dress and veil blew gently to one side. They exchanged confused looks and stepped forward. Further cult insignias dangled from the trees, brushing against each other in the breeze to create a wind chime effect.

"Hello? A-Are you okay?" Adrian called, his voice breaking as they stepped closer.

There was a pause and as they stepped onto the jetty, they stopped in their tracks. The mysterious woman stood up and turned around, her veil dancing in the air.

"Shit," said Jay, recognising her from Deontay's intel. "It's that River lass."

"Hello, River? We met at the wedding, remember?" said Adrian, politely. River stepped out, with the various animals around her following suit. Squirrels, rabbits and deer all formed a gentle parade, which, when lit by moonlight, looked quite magical.

It was then that the woman spoke in a nasally voice that Adrian barely recognised, "Oh! It's ever so nice to see you again! I'm so incredibly glad you came to visit me! It's all just been oh so overdue, don't you think? I see you've brought your friend too, that's lovely! I'm so very excited!"

Her voice emanated a femininity laced with smugness which Jay nor Adrian had ever experienced. With her wedding dress blowing white and graceful, the woman possessed an almost mystical aura.

"Hello, I'm River. It's ever so lovely to officially meet you. What is your name? I hope it's okay that I know it?" River said, a smug smile on pursed lips emerging from behind the veil. She started walking forward, an illusion of weightlessness from the spectacle of her attire.

"Err sure, I'm Jay and this is Adrian."

"How gorgeous," River replied with a sickly sweetness. She extended a bandaged hand before grabbing Jay's and shaking it enthusiastically. "I'm happy to make your acquaintance. I really believe people should just give every ounce of themselves in life, don't you think?"

River moved to Adrian and extended her other hand. Still slightly taken aback, Adrian looked at its wrappings for a moment before shaking it and smiling awkwardly.

Adrian stared at her dyed grey hair and young face. Her eyes were barely visible from beneath the tulle. Now in front of them, he noticed River's breath, heavy and with a hint of rasp. Unnerved, Adrian said, "So what's with the wedding dress?"

"Why not?" River smirked. "So, what brings you to my little piece of Heaven? I'm oh so incredibly grateful!"

"Er... We were just in the area and, well, we didn't really expect to find anyone here," Adrian said honestly as River's constant eager handshake got weirder by the second.

"Well, you found me," River smiled softly.

Adrian stared as the woman seemed so elated at their presence.

"Are you with... the Community?" Jay blurted out so abruptly he was surprised he'd even asked it.

River's smile faded instantly, releasing her grip. The animals behind her dispersed into the darkness as she turned to face the lake. "Always the bridesmaid, never the bride…"

Jay stared as he moved his curly mop from his eyes.

River sent a soft chuckle across the water's surface. "The lake is so peaceful, don't you think? I much prefer it during the night. The world is asleep, and everything just seems… easier. There's no time for pain or hurt because everyone's dreaming of their crushes or that oh-so-wonderful holiday they took last year. I love that. I wish it could always be that way…"

Jay spoke up, his mind desperate for answers. "River? Are you with them? If so, I think we should talk. There must be something we can sort out? An agreement or something?"

River merely stared ahead, her attention focused on the still water of the lake. Seconds passed, with the only movement coming from her dress as a chill blew through the trees. Adrian and Jay backed away with the vast blackness of the forest becoming more appealing by the second.

Suddenly, River broke the silence. "You know, one can have bad thoughts when awake. Oh, to dream forever…" She turned to face them, the veil blowing as the moonlight illuminated her perfect smile. She then extended a bandaged hand towards them, smiling softly, "Don't you think, Beelzebub? Leviathan?"

Both Adrian and Jay knew what a bad sign looked like when it was standing in a wedding dress and beckoning stigmata at them, so turned and ran. Thrown into darkness and uncertainty once again, they tore forward as fast as their legs would allow.

"We know you're here," came River's voice, drifting through the air with a slight echo.

"Is she behind us?" Jay stammered as he felt his chest tightening.

"I hear the water and the water hears me. Now, stop."

Jay slowed, gasping for breath. "Adrian?" The cold air attacked his lungs as his friend was nowhere to be found.

"Adrian?" he called again but the silence continued. Jay's eyes darted in every direction, but all he could see was black. "Adrian, please?"

"Can you feel the silence?" came River's voice from behind. Jay spun around, only to see more darkness. "The peace, the calm, the freedom in this moment? Stop. I come nearer and together, we'll dream into the night."

"Oh my God! I-I... I can't do this!" Jay stammered as anxiety spiked through every fibre of his being. His heart thumped against his chest, fit to burst, as he stood cold and shaking. "Adrian p-please. I-I can't see anything!"

"Close your eyes, Leviathan, it could be oh so easy..."

Eyes watering from sheer fright, Jay breathed in and out as calmly as he could, a fragile attempt at self-care against a torrent of anxiety. An abrupt hand made him yelp as he was pulled forward. Despite the cold, he gripped it hard and felt cold metal rings.

"Adrian?"

"This way!" came Adrian's voice as the fear fell from Jay.

They soon caught a sliver of street light ahead. With their bodies in a blind panic, both Adrian and Jay burst from the unknown and back onto the safety of the pavement. Turning immediately to see Nicky's car parked a short distance away, they forced their aching bodies to sprint on.

"Steph, you can't give up on sleeping because of *one* nightmare about a boiler room. I mean, so what if you pulled a wrench from your dream? Compared to the shit we have now, that's a banal triviality."

Sleep analysis cut short, Nicky and Steph stared through the windscreen to see their friends darting towards them, arms flailing. They got closer and heard Adrian and Jay bellowing, "Start the car! Start the car! Start the car!" in unison. They approached the doors and almost threw them off their hinges, clambering inside.

With such sudden chaos around them, Steph said in a panic, "What's wrong? What happened?"

"NICKY, START THE CAR!" Jay yelled, breathless, as the car sped forward. They left Guyana Lane with bodies running on empty but fear of the Community now river-deep.

XVIII
CORINTHIANS 10:31

"Ade, lad! The pint!" came the gruff voice of Adrian's boss, lunging to grab an overflowing pint glass.

"Shit, sorry!" said Adrian. This marked the fourth time his eyes had glazed over and he promptly grabbed a fresh glass. He pulled a perfect pint and placed it in front of a man with a powerful afro, saying, "This one's on me, sorry."

He turned to Mike, who wore a frown and a black t-shirt bearing the name of the pub. His hairy arms were folded and pub light bounced off his bald head.

"Sorry Mike," said Adrian.

"Your head's not in the game tonight. Is there somethin' up or do I have to tell you to get a grip again? I just need you to be honest. If you're not there, you're not there, but I can't have this shit happen, can I? You've been getting orders wrong all night." Mike cast a stern hand over a batch of failed drinks as Adrian nodded in agreement. "Look, just finish this shift early. Me and Stacy will hold the fort until changeover, okay?"

"Cheers," smiled Adrian weakly.

A quiet Tuesday afternoon had slowly turned into a slightly busier Tuesday evening as regulars finished work and shuffled over to The Nihilistic Clown. Adrian made his way down the familiar maroon carpet and felt happy that he had a manager who saw the people amongst the procedure.

Adrian reached the staff room and as he opened the door, Polly sat perched atop a dated white countertop.

"Hi gorgeous!" she said, swinging her legs playfully.

"Not now Polly," said Adrian, walking to a small table to throw a jacket over his uniform. "I've got a shot at just being fucking normal tonight and I'm gonna grab it."

"BY THE BALLS! Ooh, by the way, don't you wanna know why dear sweet Mike isn't mad at you for not turning up to work for the whooole weekend? I believe this needs to be addressed for the sake of consistency," Polly said with a grin.

"Of course, I do. It's all I've thought about… but for one fucking night, I just wanna chill and have good vibes. I don't want any more fucking riddles!"

"Spoilers, it was aaall me! I twisted a few arms, pulled a few levers," Polly beamed.

Adrian stared at her for a second as she winked and blew a kiss in his direction. He sighed. Too tired for any further conversation, he left the room and made his way outside.

December 1st was glowing on Adrian's phone screen as his body hit the chill of the outside. He couldn't believe where this year had gone, and that it was ending like this. A super-cut of everything prior to his predicament seemed so carefree. All he wanted to do was jump into his memories of good times and minor inconveniences.

Adrian felt weighed down by negativity, and as he stepped into his car, he took his usual nondescript drive through empty streets and past darkened playing fields. After what seemed like

DEBAUCHERY: PART I

no time at all, Adrian cast his eyes over the same old garden path in front of him and relished it. Sylvester jumped up onto a wall, his white winter coat thick and grubby as he brushed up against his owner.

"You couldn't change if you tried," Adrian said as he fussed over him.

His attention was quickly diverted as Harry the housemate, stepped out of the front door.

"Oh, hey, man! I thought you and Stacy were leaving together?"

"Er, yeah, I left work early, feeling a little out of it, to be honest. Stacy's gonna taxi it later."

Harry smiled as he walked down the path. "It's probably just nerves."

"Yeah, I guess."

As he shut the gate, Harry turned to face him, his festival bracelets getting caught for a moment. "Well, you've caught me just in time to see me leave. I'll be back some time tomorrow, okay?" He yanked himself free. "There's a fresh pot of coffee on for you if you want one! I'll see you soon!" he said, rushing away.

"Cheers mate. Enjoy your nerdy shit!"

Adrian stepped inside, so lost in thought that he shut the door on Sylvester. Making his way up to his room, he dumped his coat on the floor and got ready with a little more time than he expected.

He filled this head-start with cleaning his room. Adrian moved empty packets of crisps, bottles and biscuit crumbs from his bed and beanbag, hoping that his quick run with a bin bag would make the room clean enough for a date. *Is this a date?*

As he put the bag in the bin outside, Adrian concluded he should probably shower. His body reeked of spilt pints and sweat. It was an aphrodisiac to some, but perhaps not great for a first date.

Adrian made his way to the shower, stripped, and jumped in. As the water ran down his body, he felt the stress fall off him. Despite everything, the constant water felt as though his sins were draining away. He lathered, rubbed and scrubbed his body as much as possible, the anticipation for his evening growing by the second. *It can't go wrong,* he thought as he dried himself.

Adrian put on a pair of his 'good' boxer shorts and shakily put on a purple shirt, rolling up the sleeves and leaving several buttons open, revealing his tattoos. Adding some faithful rings to his fingers and a thick metal chain around his neck, Adrian stared toward a dirty mirror and saw a reflection of his best self staring back.

Lost in his thoughts, a loud knock tore him from his fantasies. More or less leaping down the stairs, Adrian stopped in front of the door, straightened his shirt, and took a deep breath. He opened the door to see Stacy in her work uniform and Sylvester trying to infiltrate it.

"I'm guessing this little guy is yours?" Stacy said with a friendly smile.

"Sylvester! IN!" said Adrian, firmly pointing inside. "Sorry, he has this weird thing with women."

"I'm flattered," she said with a smirk.

They stood there for a moment, an awkwardness developing until Adrian perked up, saying, "Sorry! Come inside! I hope work was okay?"

He took her coat and led her through to the kitchen, thinking *Fuck, the kitchen!* as they walked into a bombsite.

"Work was fine," said Stacy, seemingly immune to the mess. "I just hoped you were okay. You seemed to have a lot on your mind."

"You could say that, yeah. Anyway, do you want a coffee or anything? There's a fresh pot."

"Oh, I don't really like coffee. Do you have tea?"

"I have plenty of tea, yes!" Adrian declared a little too cheerily.

"Okay, cool."

The kettle seemingly took forever to boil as they stood in silence. Adrian tied his hair, a masculine physique filling his shirt. Quick moments of eye contact caused shy laughter. *I have to say something...*

"Er, so I've lived here for years now. I went to uni to study Music, and I just ended up moving here straight after," said Adrian. "I mean, it's a nice house and I've got my mate Harry living with me. He's okay and so is the house, but we've noticed it's been developing a little damp lately."

Stacy smiled. "Oh yeah, my house had damp a few months back, and it was awful. Thankfully, we didn't need to pull up the floor, but it was still a very stressful time."

"Yeah, it's definitely stressful... the damp..."

The kitchen plunged into a painful silence as Adrian hovered his hand over the kettle, praying it would finish boiling. *Fucking damp.*

Adrian hastily made tea and poured himself a coffee before suggesting they go to the bedroom, only realising what he'd suggested after Stacy nodded. As they made their way down the hallway, Adrian took the lead, punching a light switch to hide further shame of a messy living room.

As Stacy entered Adrian's sanctuary, her eyes widened. She looked around at the celebration of the alternative and smiled.

"Um, sorry, I don't have much seating," said Adrian. "I mean, you can take the beanbag or you can be on the bed… Not that I want you on the bed… Shit, not like that… But yeah… Oh God! Er, sorry," he stammered, flushing red.

Stacy laughed. "It's okay, Adrian. I really enjoyed seeing you at that party, but I'm glad we can finally meet one on one."

Adrian's body shook for a moment. *She said my name!*

They sat on the bed, drinks in hand, in a sober silence.

"Everything seems so hectic at the moment, doesn't it?" Stacy whispered.

"It does," said Adrian, taken aback at the relevance to her words.

"I've been looking forward to meeting because you make me feel happy. What with work being how it is lately… I like to think back to the party with you. You were so funny. I know we barely know each other, but I can't remember the last time I had so much fun." Stacy smiled at him. She looked tired, and her work t-shirt smelt of various drinks, but a warmness still shone through in her smile.

"You make me happy too," said Adrian, gazing towards the floor. "Things are kinda… weird at the minute, but you came along at the right time, I guess. Like, it was random, but good random."

"You're so adorable. Beneath all that hair and tattoos, you're just a teddy bear, aren't you? I love it. I'd love to hear you sing some time."

"I only really sing in gigs these days. Rarely sing outside my own company, to be honest."

"That's sad. Why so private?"

Adrian sighed. "Life… There's not much to sing about at the minute. It's a distraction for me lately. That and the gym, which I'm behind as fuck on. Everything is falling apart at the moment."

Stacy frowned and squeezed his hand. Adrian's body yearned to explore hers. He wanted to show he cared, admired, was inspired by and turned on by her, but in that moment, all he could do was squeeze her hand back.

"Right!" Stacy declared abruptly. "When Christmas is over and the New Year is in, we'll play together, okay? You sing and I'll jump on the piano. I assume you can sing as well as scream?" A cheeky smile formed on her lips.

Adrian looked at her and awkwardly said, "Might be better if you played the piano instead of just jumping on it."

Stacy laughed, pulling him to his feet. "You're such a fucking sweetheart!" Their eyes met, and at that moment, time froze. Every problem Adrian clung to was released and he was weightless. As Adrian pressed a remote to play music, they were drawn closer to each other until their lips finally came together.

They kissed slowly and sensually; every unspoken word finally given form. Stacy moved her body closer as he took her in a tender embrace. An electric emotion burst from them and as Adrian rearranged his trousers, Stacy pulled away and laughed.

"You really know how to kill a moment, don't you? It's so cute."

Adrian blushed, but she moved closer once more, her hands becoming braver. They wanted to learn every single thing about each other, but they knew this was only the beginning. In this moment, they purely yearned to discover each other physically.

Stacy kissed him harder and, in the passion of the moment quickly said, "I want you so bad, Adrian."

Adrian heard his name on her lips and instantly desired to be everywhere else. He took her and slipped her onto the bed. They lay together, and she tugged at his top.

Adrian smiled, unbuttoning his shirt to reveal a broad, masculine frame. Stacy leapt on him as their lips met too hard and they banged heads. They tried again, laughing through breathy, lustful kissing.

Stacy moved down to his neck and then his chest. She kissed every inch of his tatted body before she got to his belt.

"Wait," said Adrian, pulling away slightly.

Stacy stopped, brushing teal hair from her face. He sat up, looked into her eyes and whispered, "I want to eat you."

Stacy's face flushed red, and she said shakily, "Um, are you sure? Usually guys don't—"

"—Please. I can't explain it, but I've always liked it more than anything. I really want to, Stacy."

Adrian's trial of saying his date's name seemed to send Stacy into a flurry. She switched positions and clung to his body. She removed her work top and threw it on the floor. Adrian caressed her, casting inked fingers down her back.

They battled away nervous laughs and several clumsy movements, but the sexual aura between them remained powerful. Adrian removed her work trousers. "Fuck!" he said to himself as he nearly fell from the bed removing his afterwards.

Stacy looked at him and smiled before widening her eyes at his boxer shorts.

"Oh my God!" she said as Adrian laughed awkwardly. He gently laid her down and pressed his lips against hers as their bodies reconnected. It was magnetic and exciting but also felt like the most natural thing. Melanin hands ventured lower; their lips still locked together.

"Do it," Stacy whispered breathily as she removed her underwear.

Adrian pulled her further down the bed and sat between her legs. Hearts racing, he kissed between her breasts and down her stomach, lips worshipping every inch of her body. Caressing her legs, he moved lower. Passion filled the room as Adrian did

DEBAUCHERY: PART I

everything he could to make Stacy feel amazing.

He felt impassioned, and touched himself. An inked hand met Stacy's occasionally in a fiery exchange, and they held each other.

"Keep going," Stacy whimpered, which spurred Adrian on further. Pleasure filled the room, time bleeding into irrelevancy.

Moments later, their bodies exploded with an animalistic ecstasy in all their vocal glory. Adrian and Stacy slumped back on the bed, breathing deeply with Adrian declaring, "Fuck," as he moved. Stacy laughed, relieved to have finally had the moment she craved since they had first met.

Lying next to each other, they stared up at the ceiling.

"I love your room by the way," said Stacy, breaking the silence. "You weren't lying when you said you liked purple!"

Adrian turned to her and smiled. "I dunno why, it just makes me feel chill. Do you want a drink or anything?"

"I'm okay for now."

"Don't leave. Stay over."

Stacy smiled and kissed him. "I'd love to." Adrian sat up abruptly and coughed. She threw a concerned glance his way. "That sounds rough. Are you okay?"

"Yeah, it's nothing," Adrian replied as he jumped up and turned the lights off. After discussing all that they loved and setting the world to rights, they eventually drifted off to sleep.

Adrian woke up at nine o'clock the following morning to see Stacy sleeping soundly. He smiled, unsuccessfully attempting to climb over without disturbing her. As his knee hit her legs, she flew into consciousness, saying, "W-what?" in total confusion.

"Sorry, I slipped. Just need to pee."

Through sleepy eyes she smiled and fumbled around the bed for her phone. She checked her messages for a moment before a toilet flush could be heard. Stacy clambered out of bed with wild hair and recovered her underwear, which had been passionately cast away to the beanbag the previous night.

Adrian entered the room and Stacy immediately perked up. "You know, I really enjoyed last night."

"Same," said Adrian.

"I can't wait to hear you sing, Adrian. The day we play together will be a good one. Promise me?"

"Yeah mate, you'll look great jumping on the piano. Promise."

Stacy laughed, only to have it interrupted by a hoarse cough from Adrian. He coughed again, and nervous glances were sent his way.

"Are you sure you're okay?"

"Yeah, I'm good—" he coughed again, putting his hand over his mouth. As he lowered it, he saw specks of blood in his palm. His throat felt tight, and he coughed once more.

Stacy's eyes widened in terror as Adrian suddenly fell to the floor. She grabbed him, holding his body in her arms, eyes filling with tears. He gasped for breath and grabbed her hand with a panicked expression. Stacy clambered for her phone and dialled for an ambulance, screaming for help against an onslaught of confusion.

With every cough becoming more painful and every breath getting harder, Adrian's vision blurred as he felt light-headed. With fading sight, Adrian lay watching the girl he was falling for cry helplessly over him. In his final moment of consciousness, he struggled to comprehend that this painful snapshot of Stacy may be the last thing he ever saw, as an unwelcome darkness swallowed him up.

JAY GREGORIO stood silent over a hospital bed, unable to process what he saw. His life lay in tatters as the man he had revered for years lay in comatose. His hero, fellow creative and idol was vulnerable and unable to give guidance, selfishly dreaming. Jay's eyelid flickered with a subtle frown forming on his lips, his subconscious rearing its ugly head for a fraction of time. A God had fallen and Jay's mind was sinking under an ocean of disappointment. Adrian was weak, and it disgusted him. Why had Adrian been blinded by someone else instead of being the paragon of virtue Jay craved? His friend was an idiot, and he was done with him. Thankfully, someone else had caught his attention and over time, this person had become a new project. Jay could feel obsession flooding into his mind, and with every waking moment, he would push for something more. Slowly, his frown morphed into a discrete, twisted smile as he contemplated a brighter future with a stronger person.

Jay had always felt this within his heart, but never questioned what this feeling actually was.

It was only ever ENVY.

XVIII
PLUG IN BABY

Drool fell from Jay's mouth as he slept in a visitor's chair, tucked away in the corner of a private hospital room. An eighth missed call flashed over a neglected phone screen.

He changed position in the uncomfortable chair, an ALDL t-shirt twisting as he moved. His navy jacket had been morphed into an impromptu pillow, with Jay's overactive mind whirring away in its folds. A backpack with a sketchbook, doodles and several energy drinks lay at his feet. Jay had spent the evening drawing and listening to the morbid beep of a heart rate monitor plugged into his fallen hero. Adrian's mortality proved a difficult soundtrack to hear, so he had plugged himself into something more light-hearted before drifting off. The two friends lay united in unconsciousness.

On the less fortunate side of things lay Adrian, sound asleep. Life had heard his pleas for mundanity and had granted his wish as he lay in cold, hard, comatose. His brain offered a banal dreamscape of trips to the gym, childhood dental check-ups, and that time a stick insect became entangled within Steph's hair. A ninth call on the phone, however, pulled at least one friend back into reality as Jay sprang up from the chair, an errant pencil entangled in his mop.

"Er h-hello?" he said, squinting under clinical lighting. He reached aimlessly for his glasses on the table next to him as Steph's voice could be heard. Frantic and paranoid, she came in thick and fast with questions. Jay removed the phone from his ear as Steph's electronic anger crackled into the air, demanding why he hadn't answered until now.

"Steph, everything is fine! I'm sorry I haven't called, but nothing has changed since you last checked in." He turned to Adrian and then to a clock which read 7:45 pm. He stood up, if only to move his aching body from the chair, as Steph piled further questions onto his already clogged brain.

Exasperated, he relayed a conversation to her she'd heard hours before. "All the doctors have said is that he's been poisoned by something and they've ran some tests. They're going to keep him in for a while and get the antidote to flush it all out of his system. His body needs to reset. I really don't know anything else, Steph."

He turned to Adrian once more, dismissing Steph for head space and saying flatly, "Look, if anything happens, I'll call you, okay? Okay… Bye."

Placing his phone on the table and returning to the chair, Jay's mind scoured every detail of recent events, trying to figure out how his friend had ended up in such a mess. *Did I miss something? I should've noticed something. There's definitely something we're missing… but what?* Jay was an anxious person and the one guy he looked to for stability lay next to him, unconscious. Jay's mind was drowning in a relentless barrage of questions and worries.

"Fuuuck," he groaned and threw his head back to stare blankly at the ceiling. He saw a smoke alarm flickering and stared at the tiny red light for a moment before noticing a fly. His

DEBAUCHERY: PART I

eyes focused on the tiny insect as it made its rounds across the ceiling before clumsily descending onto Adrian's arm. It sat for a moment, rubbing its legs together, completely oblivious to all the goings on in the human world. Jay frowned, then removed his glasses to rub his eyes again.

"Jealous of a fly," he sighed to himself.

There must've been something we missed. This has to be the Community, but how?

Picking up his phone, Jay's finger hovered over a contact who had stuck in his mind throughout. He wondered if it was weird to make the call. *I can at least fall back on updating him about Adrian,* he thought, pushing the call button over Nicky's contact.

"Hey, what's up?" Nicky said upon answering. The phone was silent for a few seconds as Jay realised he had so much to say and so little order to it all. "Hello? Are you there?"

"Yeah, I'm here. So, Adrian's been poisoned," Jay said quietly, going for a direct approach.

"Jesus! Since when?"

"I don't know. They've induced a coma until his body flushes it out with an antidote or something, but I'm going out of my mind trying to think of how this happened."

There was a slight pause before Nicky replied. "Fuck. Well, thanks for ringing me and letting me know, I guess. How is he holding up?"

Jay looked at Adrian. "Well earlier he was asleep and now... he's still asleep. I'm sorry I called you. I dunno why I did, really. Don't wanna worry you, dude."

"Don't be daft. I'm glad Adrian's okay. How are you holding up? You're the conscious one, after all."

Jay sat in silence, holding the phone to his ear. *He cares.* His lip quivered as he stared at his friend. Adrian lay asleep in his own world, weak and useless to him. Through all the concern and all the worry, Jay felt disappointed. Nicky's voice sent a warm reassurance to him and in that moment, his brain completely abandoned the man he had known for years. This unknown, almost primal feeling had killed any feeling towards Adrian. Despite the overwhelming need to speak his truth, Jay replied with his stock response for whenever his mental health was low: "I'll be fine."

"You sure? I can come over if you want?" The empathy in Nicky's voice sent waves of sincerity to Jay that, somehow, made every wall he had ever built crumble to the ground. Thinking for a moment, he was surprised how natural asking for help was.

"If you're free, I could honestly use the company. I'm at Brook's Haven Hospital."

"Okay cool. Consider it done. Meet me outside, yeah? I'll message you when I'm setting off."

Jay smiled. "Yeah, okay," he said, before hanging up. He sat in silence, time quickly blurring as his mind was still crammed with questions. Opting to ignore them that bit longer, he turned to Adrian and sighed before grabbing his backpack and simply leaving.

The moment he left the room, Jay found that the world started turning again.

He reached the lift and pressed the 'down' button, staring up at a screen above displaying an LED number twelve. He looked to his right at a giant number six and huffed impatiently, moving to the window while he waited.

Darkness had fallen. Car headlights and small windows of light within flats fought back to show that the world wasn't ready to sleep just yet. Tiny figures could be made out from where he stood, but none seemed to do anything interesting. The flicker of

DEBAUCHERY: PART I

home televisions scattered around the city offered a panorama of banality which Jay craved. He wanted his most important thought to be what he was having to eat that night. To relax and remember what it was like to be restless for excitement once more. *But not excitement like this...* he thought, realising the paradox.

A *ping!* pulled Jay from his own personal envy of the world as he turned to enter the lift. As he made it inside, he saw a man in pirate attire standing directly in front of him. Before Jay could double take at the sheer randomness of this encounter, the unknown buccaneer yanked him inside by his hoodie.

"Jay?"

Heart rate instantly doubling, Jay stammered, "Y-Yes? Who are you?"

Lifting a black eyepatch, Isaac's eyes came into full view. His black hair was unkempt underneath a deep blue bandana and he gripped Jay's arm tight, eyes wide as the doors drifted shut.

"Jay, listen to me! No one I've seen has listened to me yet and I need some fucking help! I've been to another world and there are these people who are all of you guys but magical! I tried to say it to Steph, and to Nicky, but they ignored me! Jay, I need you to believe me!"

The lift took forever to descend as Jay stared at Isaac, utterly dumbstruck. His tone sounded so honest, but he looked so ridiculous. Unable to speak, he stuttered, "I-I... Uh, I dunno what to say. Adrian's here, he's really sick—"

"Where even are we, Jay? Ugh, it doesn't matter! I have to take a ship called the Sea Slug up to the Northern Isle of Tsuna. You just need to come back with me and see it for yourself! I need a familiar face on deck with me!"

Jay stood bewildered before cautiously asking, "Are you...

okay? Like, what's with the getup?"

Isaac groaned, slamming Jay against the metal of the lift. Holding both his arms, Isaac lowered his voice and said firmly, "Listen to me. I'm tired of people asking if I'm ill and giving me that same fucking blank stare when I say where I've come from. Please just find some urgency in what I say and come back with me to this goddamn ship! I need a friend on deck just so I know… So, I know I'm not mad."

"Isaac, we're in a lift."

"I know we're in a fucking lift! But these stupid Equinox Blocks don't let me decide where I end up when I come back! Come with me! Just hold my hand when I leave—"

The lift door put the painfully bizarre conversation to an end as it opened two floors early. Jay took no time in pushing Isaac aside and running through a clump of confused paediatricians. He darted towards the stairwell as Isaac gave chase.

"Fuck-FUCK! Jay, wait!" Isaac shouted as he wobbled down each step. "I'm not in the right gear! These boots have shit durability!"

Jay had already leapt halfway down to the lower floor shouting, "W-What the fuck is this?"

"DON'T RUN AWAY FROM ME!" Isaac's voice echoed desperately, but it was all in vain.

Jay tore through the reception, his backpack nearly lost in the process as he ran indiscriminately through the sick and healthy. Disgruntled huffs and the odd obscenity were left in his wake. A December chill hit his face as he burst into the night. It was calming and cool compared to a few moments ago.

Has he gone? Yes? Thank fuck for that! thought Jay as he fumbled in his backpack pocket for a joint and a lighter. Shaking, he held

DEBAUCHERY: PART I

the blunt between his fingers, shielding a tiny flame from the air as he lit it.

"Fuck's sake," he exhaled as smoke blended with the evening air. With his heart still racing, Jay ambled down a small stone path leading to a small walled garden. He took a drag of his cigarette and stuffed a hand in his pocket, only to realise that his phone had been left abandoned in Adrian's hospital room.

Jay eventually found his way to the small, man-made clearing, walking up to a black memorial bench. He cast an eye over a small silver plaque which read, *In memory of Mariella. You may have been silent, but your actions spoke louder than any of us.*

As he took a seat on Mariella's bench, he wondered for a moment what his plaque on a memorial bench would read if he was dead, only to conclude he wouldn't particularly want a plaque on a memorial bench at all.

"You know, we've got to stop meeting up like this…"

Nicky walked into the clearing wearing a black leather jacket zipped up tight. A beanie attempted to tame his wild hair which poked its way out from underneath. As he smiled, his nose ring shone against a flicker of light above.

"You found me," said Jay.

"Well, this ten second walk up a short path threw me but, yeah."

Jay laughed as Nicky extended his arms to hug. Even though Jay wasn't a massively huggy person, this was different. They embraced for a moment, Nicky's jacket creaking as he clung to the attention.

Nicky clocked the extended hug, asking, "Are you alright?"

Jay sprang back, blurting out, "Uh-yeah, no… I think? I dunno…"

Nicky laughed, removing the rogue pencil from Jay's hair. "We love a spectrum. Do you want to stay here or shall we downgrade to visitor status inside?" He turned and started up the path but stopped to throw an expectant expression towards Jay. "Ready?"

Everything in Jay's mind told him they should just return to Adrian, care for him and be at his bedside, but as he looked at Nicky, all he could do was shake his head. At that moment, Jay felt this isolated clearing within a hospital garden held him together. He felt so little towards Adrian now, despite his friend needing him more than ever. He felt bad for not feeling bad, yet his attention settled purely on Nicky. A warmth emanated from him and Jay wanted to soak up every single bit.

Mind untethered and aching for stability, Jay took the chance, turned to Nicky saying, "Can we just stay here for a moment? I really need the head space."

"Sure. So, how are you doing?"

Jay sat up. "I was thinking of the first time I met Adrian."

"Oh?"

"Yeah… It was seven years ago now, maybe eight? I met him in a club and we were both completely wasted. I was with some other people, but Adrian just came from nowhere and started singing at me. It was 'Plug in Baby' by Muse. None of my mates at the time knew that song, so we just stepped onto the dance floor and just shouted it at each other. It was at that point I discovered he could sing really fucking well and I couldn't sing at all."

Jay laughed to himself for a second. "Anyway, I don't really talk to any of my old friends now. Adrian was the only one who stuck around. I mean, it's all just a drunk memory, but it's legit. From that night onward, I always jokingly called him my Plug in Baby. It was just some dumb nickname, but yeah. To think he's… in hospital now because someone's fucked him up. It… It just sucks."

DEBAUCHERY: PART I

Jay turned to face Nicky and, for one brief, electric moment, he saw a new kindness in his eyes as his mask slipped away. He felt a wave of new emotion within him, yet all he could do was stare at this unseen side of this new friend. Jay wanted to see this side of him indefinitely, infinitely, but Nicky caught the intensity, plainly asking, "Yes?"

Realising he was staring, Jay stammered, "Er, nothing."

Nicky laughed, flicking the pencil towards him. "I love this little moment we're having, but we should really see the guy who doesn't have the option to be with us right now."

"You're right," Jay smiled as they stood up, "but I need to ask you something."

"Sure, go on."

"So, you've seen Isaac, haven't you? Like he came to you at some point?"

As they started a slow walk back into the hospital, Nicky stuck his hands in his jacket pockets, saying, "Yeah, he came to me, Amy and Steph in the car park when I had to pay. Didn't you see him?" Jay shook his head as they walked. "Well, he was only dressed in a full suit of armour! It was kinda wild looking back, but he was clearly on something. I know that guys had some decent jobs in the past, so I guess he's just gone off the deep end. He kept rambling on about being flushed out of a balloon or something? That kinda confirmed he was a bit, uh… Tapped."

They walked through the entrance to the hospital, leaving the vague odour of tobacco for the sterile yet old smell unique to certain hospitals. As the two friends moved towards the lift, they became more and more perplexed by Isaac.

"I saw him in the hospital earlier, as I came to meet you. He cornered me in a lift dressed as a pirate."

"A pirate?" Nicky questioned, pushing the call button on the lift.

"Yeah man! He was fully wearing an actual pirate outfit! You wanna know what's even weirder? It didn't seem like a costume. It looked like a legit pirate outfit. He wanted to go to the Northern Isle of somewhere. He also said he was wearing the wrong gear when I ran away from him or some crazy shit."

As the lift opened, they both immediately stared inside for any errant plunderers within. Seeing that it was empty, they walked inside with Jay pushing the button.

The lift ascended, and their conversation died for a few floors. Between forced coughs and a random sensation of claustrophobia, they pondered their situation in silence.

On exiting the lift, Jay walked over to an anti-bac station just before the ward and squidged some onto his hands. Nicky followed suit, and the two proceeded onto the ward, bringing a hundred questions along with them. Passing several rooms, they eventually reached room six and walked quietly inside.

"Don't we have to sign in or anything?" Nicky whispered. "Isn't it weird we can just visit?"

"I thought that too, but I got a text from that Polly woman earlier saying, 'You're welcome', so I figured she'd had words with people or some shit."

Jay walked around the hospital bed, which housed a still sleeping Adrian, and took a seat back on the uncomfortable visitor's chair. He looked over at Nicky, who stared at the bed.

"Nicky?"

"Yeah, I'm fine. It's just… a lot when you see someone hooked up to all that stuff." He walked around to sit near Jay at the foot of the bed, and picked up a piece of paper amongst various sketches of band logos. Nicky threw a concerned expression towards Jay as he held a sketch of an unconscious Adrian.

"Uh, is everything okay?"

Jay fumbled, anxiety coursing through him. "I-I-er… I've just spent a long time here. You don't get how much Adrian means to me, and even though it's weird I just… I-I just draw what's in front of me 'cos it's the only way I can understand it. There are just… so many fucking questions."

He exhaled hopelessly as Nicky gently put the picture aside. "I know how you feel. We all have our ways of coping with life. It'll get better. It has to, right?"

They sat in a strange melancholy for a while. Jay suddenly remembered his phone was sitting on the table. Reaching to grab it, he fiddled with the buttons, Nicky watching him in a patient silence. Jay pushed a button on the side of his phone and placed it back on the table between the three of them.

The opening riff of 'Plug in Baby' blasted around the room as Jay leaned back in the chair, smiling to himself.

If he has to be plugged in, he can at least be plugged into some good times.

XIX
GREEN-EYED MONSTER

"Hi guys! So, I never thought in a million years I'd have to make a video like this. I haven't made a new video in a while now, and I know you've all been wondering where I've been."

Steph's tone veered between vlogger suspense and sombre as she settled on the ledge of Jay's bay window. It was another miserable winter night and the heavy rain made for the perfect soundtrack to an honest life update.

"My best friend in the whole wide world is in hospital, but that's not the worst bit. While he rests, I'm here with no one to comfort me." She exhaled, sweeping voluminous blonde hair from her face. "My friend Claire is not talking to me anymore because I accidentally liked her boyfriend's photo when I was on the toilet, and I want to dye my hair pink and show you the process… but with no one to edit my videos, I don't know what I'm gonna do. Things are very hard for me at the moment and I don't know when I'll have a new video. I can say that I love you all and I'll try to stay safe in these difficult times but, it's touch and go. Keep watching my videos, drop a like and subscribe because I know you'll just be watching the next one! This is A Steph of

DEBAUCHERY: PART I

Fresh Air signing out! MWAH!"

Steph's fake smile fell from her face immediately. She gently placed a hand on the window, wishing she could feel the water to wash away her gloom. This sweeping wave of sadness caused her eyes to well. The sheer difficulty and confusion of where she was in life was represented by the darkness she saw outside. A deep sense of poetry enveloped the room. She wilted. Her life was but one of many stories taking place right now and she could really feel the energy that came from this moment.

"Are you quite finished?" interjected Jay, who'd been given a front seat to her melodrama.

Steph tilted her head from his bay window to gaze wearily across the room. "It's just. So. Difficult," she whispered into the night.

Her body language was fake, her attitude shallow, but Jay couldn't help but wonder if there was really a sadness there. He fell silent, staring at the theatre taking place in front of him.

"Ugh, fine!" exclaimed Steph suddenly. She huffed, wobbling towards the mirror in a pair of unnecessarily high heels.

"You know you can just take your shoes off?" said Jay. "It'd be a lot more comfortable."

She ignored him and stumbled over to grip the mantlepiece. Running fingers through her hair, she declared proudly, "I plan every outfit and today I'm wearing heels! Every time you step outside the house, you're being judged, you know?"

"Yeah, by people who shouldn't be judging in the first place."

"They judge me because I'm pretty and dress to a much higher standard than the average woman. It's completely natural."

Jay turned to look Steph's reflection in the eye and said, "You do know you're not the centre of the universe, right?"

With newly voluminous hair, Steph pulled her attention from

the mirror. "Well duh! That's *obviously* the sun," she said, eyes rolling. Her gaze promptly fell back to the mirror as she applied her makeup.

Jay sat back on the sofa and turned on the TV. He assumed Steph would get ready for her taxi home for a while, so began to channel hop. After several shows failed to pique his interest, he gave up and ended up settling on a seventies music retrospective. An old musician sat in a dimmed studio with his face entirely clouded by cigarette smoke as a hoarse voice spoke about life.

"Well, you see it was the seventies and things were just different back then. You really had to be there – wild nights, son! Nothing like anyone today would understand because it was the seventies. I remember Johnny *'The Brick'* Johnson, God rest his soul, was getting noshed out by Maria in our Ford Pinto. By 'eck, that lass could suck the chrome from a tail pipe! Anyway, guy was off his face on black tar heroin and came up with the riff for 'Jesus is a Beardy Man' in just under five minutes."

The rocker's thick, tattooed fingers then played a fractured riff on a tired guitar.

"You see, the notes speak more than the lyrics. That's something we just came up with because it was the seventies and you really had to be there. Incredible scenes. Now I've told this story approximately ten thousand and sixty-three times, but there's one thing I'll tell yer for free, that's for sure. The greatest musicians in history came from that decade because the seventies were more of a feeling than a decade – a lifestyle, if you will. I mean I lost seventy-five to seventy-seven and part of my left nostril to blow, but it was the seventies and you really just had to be there."

"Ugh, as if you're watching telly!" Steph interjected.

DEBAUCHERY: PART I

Irked, Jay turned off the TV and hissed, "Well what would you rather have me do, Steph? Watch your every movement? Would you like me to be completely addicted to you as well?"

"I want you to listen to what I'm saying!"

"You haven't said anything!" spat Jay as lightning flashed through the window, caused Steph to fall into a defeated silence. Thunder rolled as they desperately avoided eye contact.

This impromptu moment of silence for their fallen friend made Steph sigh. "We need Adrian."

"We do."

Lowering her guard, Steph pulled herself away from the mirror and sat next to Jay. She wore blue denim jeans and a plain white top. Since Adrian had been in hospital, Jay had noticed that Steph wasn't making half as much effort with how she dressed, despite putting on a full face of makeup. Without Adrian to impress, he figured Steph was feeling a little lost and that any effort made was perhaps more for herself.

"It'll be okay..." he said, raising an awkward arm and putting it around Steph's shoulder. She stared straight ahead as they sat completely still and entirely uncomfortable.

"Do we have to have sex now?" said Steph, unprovoked.

"Jesus, what the fuck?" Jay said as his hand recoiled back, mortified. "Why the hell would you think that? I was just hugging you 'cos you hug Adrian all the time!"

"Oh," Steph whispered. "Well, thank you. I think, without Adrian, we're both very different. Do you think Adrian is the only reason we talk at all?"

Jay pondered this thought for a while, surprised at the validity of the question.

"Well," he started, treading carefully so as not to upset her, "I know you like eighties music and chart music. I like rock music and indie music… So, I guess we don't have much in common there. What movies do you like? In fact, I don't really think we've had the chance to get to know each other because Adrian was between us. I guess we just never thought about how much of a distance that was."

Steph smiled. It was the first time he'd seen her show any genuine positive emotion. "I like horror movies and films where the girl gets the guy."

"I love horror movies!" said Jay enthusiastically, the sound of thunder booming after him. "I like the eighties ones the most! You can't beat practical effects. CGI is fine, but even if it looks fake, practical effects prove that horror is all about it being real and acting out real fear."

"Yeah!" Steph said. "I like all the eighties ones because they were the best but I like anything!" She turned to Jay, enthusiasm building by the second as a miserable night turned into a half-decent one.

"Yeah definitely!" Jay smiled as he struggled to match Steph's energy. "Even if some films are ninety percent prosthetics and ten percent actors. I love a bit of gore."

Steph squealed, grabbing his hand and excitedly shaking it. "Maybe we could see a movie together some time? That way, when Adrian wakes up, he can see how much we get on now! Promise?"

Jay smiled. "Sure, let's do it."

"Pinky promise?"

"Er pinky promise!"

"It's settled then!" Steph said, wobbling to her feet to return to the mirror.

"You're fixated on that thing, aren't you?"

DEBAUCHERY: PART I

"If looking good is a crime, then... I'd be a crime or something," she shrugged. After re-volumising her hair for a third time, she looked at the clock on the mantelpiece and grabbed her phone, declaring, "Well, I better call for a taxi! It's getting late and I have stuff to do."

"Okay, cool... well, it was nice—"

"—Hi yeah, can I have a taxi, please? It's from 16 Bartlett Road, going to 6 Coultas Close. Okay, thank you, bye... Sorry, what was that, Jay?"

"Never mind," he said with a knowing smile. "How long will it be?"

"They said there's one about five minutes away..." Steph trailed off as she moved to stare out into the darkness outside.

Jay turned to her. "Are you okay?"

Steph sighed. "Do you really think we're those sins?"

Taken aback by her pensiveness, Jay stood up and joined her at the window. The world seemed a lot darker than it usually was.

Eventually he pushed aside all anxiety, every thought and feeling in his head and simply replied, "I don't know." A million questions ricocheted around the walls of his skull, dying to take form and burst from his lips. He wanted them to bounce around the room and give Steph something that would be helpful, but there was just too much to ask. He knew that even if he figured it all out, there would only be further mysteries. Everything seemed so futile.

Steph turned to him. "I just... I dunno. Like I'm not the best person, but am I, like, *really* that bad? It makes me sad to think I could be..."

Jay turned to her to see teary eyes. He put his arms around her, pulling her into a confident embrace. This time it was natural and as Steph crumbled into a blonde pile of emotion onto his t-shirt, he simply held her. The silent support was stronger than any words he felt he could offer as they stood in front of the window, a picture of strength and defiance against the cold, dark world outside.

The headlights of a taxi quickly tore them apart. Steph wiped her eyes as she wobbled out of the living room in search of her jacket.

"Ugh!" came her voice from the hallway, causing Jay to run through to join her, only to be presented by a wet floor and an open door.

"Oh shit! You know, it's been doing that for a while now. The door just comes unlocked, sorry!"

The sudden overwhelming pressure to not keep the driver waiting consumed Steph as she grabbed her pink puffer jacket and shouted through the rain, "I'll be two minutes!" vaguely in the taxi's direction.

With her hair losing its volume by the second, she turned to Jay. She looked frozen, but her smile was warm as she pulled the hood over her head. She threw her arms around him once more, a muffled "Thank you," coming from under her gigantic coat.

"It's okay. Everything will be fine, promise!" he smiled as Steph ran down the drenched stone path to leap gracelessly into the taxi.

Squinting through the car's headlights as it reversed, Jay raised a hand to wave goodbye. As he shut his front door, he stood alone in the shallow puddle decorating his hallway and sighed.

He went to his kitchen and unenthusiastically grabbed a mop and bucket from a small cupboard. *Bloody door.* After fifteen

DEBAUCHERY: PART I

minutes of half-arsed mopping and wrangling kitchen roll, Jay was rewarded with a clean floor and a door that he at least hoped would stay shut until he could ring to get it fixed the next morning.

Jay looked at the kitchen clock and, knowing he was finally alone, went and grabbed the key to the last door on the left. He put the key in the lock and turned it, taking a deep breath as he stepped inside.

He stepped into a grey room with several desks on the other side. A line of monitors took precedence opposite, their sinister glow flooding his eyes as he entered. He flicked the light on, illuminating a wall of photographs, letters, drawings and personal trophies of his friend Adrian.

Every memory they ever had, every secret they shared and every bit of information on Adrian he could physically get hung on this wall. Clippings of hair, nails, stolen items of clothing and a semen-stained pair of underwear hung there, each in their own individual zip-lock bag. Every social media post Adrian had made on every platform, every drawing Jay had created when Adrian had fallen asleep, was on this wall. A masterclass of brazen obsession towards his best friend in the entire world lay bare and as Jay locked the door, he sighed, allowing the monster inside of him to surface once more.

"You were weak," he said coldly, clenching his fists in frustration. "You were *everything* to me, and now look at you. It isn't easy to do this shit, man! The hardest fucking thing in the world is to just… to fucking function!" Exasperated by how truly lost he felt, Jay punched the wall, shouting, "FUCK!"

Resting his head against an unwashed band t-shirt pinned to the wall, he breathed in deeply. It still smelt of Adrian and his eyes watered. His entire mentality depended on Adrian's existence, but so much rested on uncertainty.

"This fucks up everything! EVERYTHING!" he seethed, tearing the t-shirt from the wall. "All this fucking effort! You should be here, man!" In a rage, Jay started punching the wall. "I get on with Steph now! FUCKING STEPH! I want YOU! This isn't what is supposed to happen! I should be your one! Your only fucking friend because I'm NOTHING and the best I could ever hope to be is YOU!"

Piece by piece, he raged at the past, present and future that were splayed over the wall. "It wasn't meant to be this way! How can you be the one that falls? *You*, for fuck's sake! I've wasted so much fucking time on you and this is how you thank me!"

Jay's fury continued as he clawed at every bit of paper and macabre trophy, throwing it to the floor. Their entire history ended up as ripped, discarded shards – a literal broken friendship.

Resting his twisted mind against a few tattered remains clinging to the wall, a bead of sweat fell from his forehead. Panting, he whispered, "Forget it, man. It doesn't matter. I think I've found someone else. Someone stronger who won't let me down. I deserve better."

His hair over his eyes, he turned to face the wall of monitors on the desk and sat in a swivel chair. Wheeling through the chaos on the floor, Jay rested his elbows on the desk and stared into a live feed of Adrian's entire house. Adrian's housemate, Harry, sat with Sylvester in the living room chair. Jay then moved his attention to a newer screen featuring Adrian's hospital room. A live feed of his unconscious friend glowed before him, mocking him.

With a deep rage through him, Jay's eyelid flickered as he whispered, "I see everything…"

DEBAUCHERY: PART I

He stayed planted in his seat, staring dead-eyed at the monitors, years' worth of loss lying in front of him. As the night progressed, Jay felt himself slipping away. His mind was tired from questions and his body ached for decent company. Jay was tired of sitting alone every night and he felt a new obsession growing. He fell asleep to that thought, the sound of thunderstorms through the blacked-out windows, acting as his own natural ASMR.

Two hours passed and Jay sprang awake as a loud crack of thunder pulled him from his peace. The rain was falling endlessly and as he stumbled to his feet, he breathed in deep. Jay left the destroyed shrine and locked it behind him, sealing away his ugliest trait. His mind slowly sank back into its usual state. The monster had subsided as quickly as it had risen.

Promptly leaving the room, he was greeted by a now-open front door blowing back and forth slightly from the wind.

Frowning and increasingly confused, Jay shuffled towards the open doorway. The rain was falling thick and fast and as he poked his head outside, a cold wind hit his face.

He shut the door and retired upstairs. As he reached the landing, the hall light bulb popped off, making him jump within a fresh darkness.

"Nope, fuck it! I'll do it tomorrow!" he snarled, throwing his bedroom door open and tapping a touch lamp on an end table.

Jay's room was a deep blue colour, as was his double bed's duvet cover, and most of his clothes too. He got undressed and crawled into bed to rest his weary brain, rainfall buffeting against his bedroom window.

Shuffling into a comfy position, Jay breathed a deep sigh of relief. He leant over to pull his mobile phone from within his jeans pocket and stick it on charge next to him. Putting his glasses on the table, he told his tired mind, *If you think about it, not THAT much has happened really…* before soaking up the calm.

No longer had Jay's eyes fully closed before a flash of light burst through the window, illuminating his room a bright green alongside a pulsating electric noise. Jay jerked up, arms flailing in a weird panic exclaiming, "For fuck's sake, what now?"

He looked into the darkness down his nondescript garden at his small red garden shed. It was glowing green from within. The light made a buzzing sound, barely audible over the sound of neighbourhood car alarms. With his own smoke alarm attacking his eardrums, Jay grabbed his glasses, threw on a dressing gown and hurried downstairs with a full frown and a semi-erection mumbling, "I swear to God if it's aliens, just beam me the fuck up." Grabbing a stool from the cupboard under the stairs, he followed the obscene screeching and the panicking red light to yank the alarm squarely from its slot.

With a new appreciation for silence, Jay returned the stool to the cupboard and pulled his falling dressing gown back over his shoulder. He stared through the kitchen to French doors which were inviting the strange green light inside. Cautious but curious, Jay stepped forward.

As he entered the kitchen, his hand searched for the light switch. He flicked it, but it didn't work, and looking between the fitting and the bulb above, Jay frowned. It was then that he heard a click from the hallway behind. His ears pricked up as his front door creaked open, the sound of neighbourhood alarms entering. He spun around and saw the darkness of the front garden. The rain was relentless and as yet another puddle formed, Jay lost his temper.

"Give me a fucking break!" he shouted, striding up the hallway. "Does every second of my life have to have me just

DEBAUCHERY: PART I

trying to keep out the fucking noise?" Enraged, Jay grabbed the door yelling, "Just fucking SHUT!"

The moment the door touched the frame, it filled with rusted iron padlocks. This sudden flash of randomness made Jay's eyes widen. Over a hundred locks, suspended by iron nails, dangled on the door.

"W-What the fuck?" Jay stammered, staring at the strange scene in front of him. He poked a lock, only for it to wobble delicately in front of him. "Impossible…"

He turned to face the kitchen, the pulsating green light still glowing out back. Looking between this and the newly padlocked door, Jay slowly moved towards the back garden.

Unnerved, he slid the French doors open and stepped out onto the sodden decking. He walked through the rain, passing the half-rusted table. He noticed it had the same rusted iron padlocks interlinked through the gaps. This collection of metal bunched up down one leg of the table, leaving a chain of locks leading down the steps, ending on the grass. Jay shook as he followed the chain, his bare feet sinking into the mud.

Driven by a terrified curiosity, Jay ventured on. As he approached the shed, he saw that its intense green light had downgraded to a soft, pulsating glow, as though something nuclear lay in wait within. With every step, Jay noticed he felt warmer. By the time he reached the shed, he was uncomfortably hot. Through the heat, he saw that yet more mysterious iron padlocks adorned the tired wooden door. Further black iron nails hammered into place to support them. He gripped the handle and opened it cautiously, only to see the silhouettes of a broken rake and an old step ladder. Jay sighed, dressing gown damp but quickly drying against the sudden wall of heat. With senses spiked and heart racing, he moved forward. Something quickly caught his eye from the back wall.

A glowing green something hid behind garden shears with a pile of padlocks scattered clumsily around the bench. Jay braved a few steps more and reached to move them. He could hear his heart frantically beating against his ribs, memories of the forest in his head. Extending a shaking hand he slid the shear aside to reveal a strange symbol emitting an almost otherworldly heat.

Illuminated by the radioactive glow, Jay's eyes widened as he removed his glasses to wipe them on a nearby duster. He promptly returned them, staring at the source of the confusing heat.

Jay frowned as he didn't recognise it from any language or any avenue of popular culture. His mind quickly jumped to wondering whether this foreign symbol was Satanic, but had no way of placing it. He continued to stare as rainwater fell from a small hole in the roof, only to turn to steam and hiss the second it touched the mysterious mark.

With heart beating as fast as the rainfall outside, his brain went into overdrive. He moved a clump of drenched curly hair from in

DEBAUCHERY: PART I

front of his eyes and wondered if he should phone someone. *But who would even believe this?*

Jay took a further step, and every primal instinct told him to stop, but he didn't listen. Arm outstretched, Jay reached towards the green light with the hope that this would somehow give him answers to all the questions he craved.

Just before he touched it, Jay heard a voice wheeze from behind him and croakily splutter the words, "Infernum manet."

Jay spun around, startled to face a tall black outline standing at the door of the shed. His heart was beating so rapidly he felt weak, and an intense fear took over him as he stared directly at the wheezing humanoid silhouette.

From what Jay could make out, the figure was at least seven feet tall with nails extending from its face and body. A darkened outline of a crown rested on the figure's head and its clothes were ragged, but Jay couldn't make them out. All that he could see were the figure's glowing green eyes sending a piercing gaze directly towards him.

A sudden mass of sound came from around him, making him yelp. Every padlock on the table clicked open and the locks outside could be heard falling into a pile on the decking.

Jay's way was blocked. The window was too small to jump through, and he wished that he could fit through the tiny leaking hole above him. Panic-stricken, he stammered, "W-what do y-you want?"

The creature didn't answer. It simply stood still, silent and dark as it stared unblinkingly at Jay. He noticed the creature was struggling to breathe, and its deep wheezing only filled Jay with even more horror. Trembling with fear, he attempted to communicate with the figure a second time. "What a-are y-you?

W-What do you w-want?"

The creature remained silent. Its unblinking green eyes felt like they were piercing into Jay's soul. Frozen to the spot in and unable to communicate with this monster, he backed right up to the bench as far as he could go. The heat from the symbol was great, but not as intense as the creature stood before him.

He racked his brain for something he could do, anything he could use. He looked around at all the gardening tools and knew that in every horror movie, none of these things would actually work if this thing attacked. Jay was completely trapped, and it terrified him. His anxious mind couldn't comprehend the situation in front of him and he felt light-headed.

He scoured his brain, and a thought came to mind as he realised that the creature only appeared when he put his hand near the symbol. He figured that his only choice was to touch it again, which he soon realised meant potentially getting either burned to death by the unknown or getting attacked by the creature. The thought that frightened Jay most was that he had to turn his back to this creature. The mere notion of it made him feel sick, but he had no choice.

Jay clambered onto the table slowly, the heat of the symbol almost too much to bear. He took a deep breath and spun around to slam his palm against the symbol.

Immediately, Jay heard an unholy scream burst from the creature's frayed vocal cords. The harrowing sound shattered the shed window as his vision blurred and he fell. Glasses falling to the floor, Jay hit the damp wood floor. His mind begged for clarity as he stared up at the horrific creature, sight fading to black.

I'm going to die.

XX
RED SHED REDEMPTION

"I told you we shouldn't have moved here, George! This area is completely beneath us. It's the day we move in, we have *this* to deal with!"

"Wha?" Jay murmured, squinting to reveal an angry face glaring down at him. He sat up and groaned, noticing that he was in the middle of his front garden. He looked around to see a SOLD sign behind the woman.

Jay wobbled to his feet, holding his head and rubbing his eyes. "What happened? How did I get here?" he said, lightheaded and squinting in the chilled December sunlight.

"See? Drunkards, George! Look at him! He probably listens to the hip-hop!" the woman exclaimed shrilly, turning to face her nearby husband.

Jay focused, locking eyes with her. The pregnant brunette had curly hair and scowled at him with arms folded in judgement. She stood in pink trainers and sky-blue activewear, eyes narrowing further by the second.

"Who the hell are you?" Jay frowned, not in the mood to be judged considering his nightmare the previous night.

"*See?* Rude George! Rude, hip-hop, drunkards!" she barked. He turned to see a long-suffering husband who only seemed present physically.

George was a tall man, donning a navy sports jacket, jeans and a pair of boots. He had short black hair and some designer glasses sat perched above his nose. He looked towards Jay then softly placed a hand against his wife's arm gently saying, "Alice, please, remember what we discussed? First impressions? Think of the baby."

"But look at the first impression he has given us! Hmph!" Alice squawked, her eyes relentlessly shooting daggers at Jay. She promptly unfolded her arms and began her morning jog, taking an angry swig of water from a pink flask as she left.

"Sorry about her, my man, she's very… intense. She never used to be like that, but… yeah," George sighed. He extended a friendly hand to hoist Jay to his feet. "George and Alice Kravitz."

Jay threw an awkward smile into the mix as he shook errant blades of grass from a thankfully closed dressing gown. "Jay… Gregorio. Jay."

"So, why are you in your garden? Partying last night?" George said and grinned, breaking the ice of a freezing morning.

"Er no, I was just by myself, really," Jay said as he stared at the floor, trying desperately to remember the events of the previous night.

"Wow, partying by yourself? It's been years for me… Anyway, best be off. I have a house to unpack, but it was nice meeting you."

George threw a kind nod his way before walking up the path.

"Good luck!" Jay called after him, attempting to forge at least a half-good relationship with his new neighbours.

After searching for his glasses in vain, Jay walked up his path to see the front door wide open. He went inside, checked the hinges and the lock for any sign of a break-in or damage, but there was nothing. He closed it and, with no padlocks to be found, moved to the kitchen for a well-earned cuppa.

His attention waned as he waited for the kettle to boil and a super-cut from the previous night trickled back into memory. *Rain, the shed and a green light.* He threw two tea bags into a teapot and as he poured the boiling water, Jay remembered a vivid flash of the monster that terrorised him. His mind became engulfed with questions as he slammed the kettle on its stand. He ran upstairs to check whether his phone was still in his room.

Relieved to see it lying on his bedside table, he grabbed a spare pair of glasses from a drawer to be greeted by three missed calls and four texts from Steph; the latest one reading, *Why are you so shit at replying?? xxx*

Disregarding this, he got dressed, opting for jeans and a t-shirt. After putting on fresh socks he phoned the only person he felt could cope with the odd news he had to offer. The phone rang and his heartbeat quickened as a familiar voice picked up. Jay smiled, immediately feeling more at ease.

"Hello?"

"Hey Nicky, what are you up to?"

"Well, me and Amy are just at a wine-tasting retreat. What about you?"

"Oh, I've not been up to much... Wait..." Jay paused. "A wine-tasting retreat?"

"Well, wine not? Get it? Soo, what's up?"

"Are you drunk? Anyway, it doesn't matter. I don't even know where to start," said Jay, shuffling back down to the kitchen. "I think there's something wrong with my shed."

"Right, so like woodworm or something?"

Jay stared out towards the small red shed only to see it in a new ominous light, saying, "No, like… aliens."

The line fell silent. Jay desperately waited for a reply, half-expecting Nicky to hang up.

His voice eventually returned. "Sorry I didn't catch that over the sound of… the wine. Run that by me again."

Amy's voice could be heard in the background bellowing, "Why, what a lovely, full-bodied Barolo! Reminds me of our short stint in Montenegrooo!"

"Aliens, Nicky!" shouted Jay, doubling down.

Another pause filled the airwaves before Nicky replied, "Aliens? Like little green men? Or refugees?"

"Like little green men. Well, I think it was an alien, anyway. Oh, it spoke in some weird language… sounded a bit like Latin, to be fair."

"Latin," Nicky said flatly. "Latin aliens…"

"*I swear to God I think it's aliens!* Or something people can't explain! Just come round and see for yourself!"

Jay sighed, ready to accept defeat, and poured himself a cup of tea.

"Are you pouring tea?" came Nicky's voice.

"Er, yes?"

"I'm on my way," and with that, Nicky hung up.

Jay smiled and took his drink out onto the decking, grabbing a hoodie on the way. He pulled up a cold metal chair and fished in his pocket for his 'emergency' joints and a cheap yellow lighter. Disregarding the damp, Jay sparked up and sat back, contemplating the mass of previous events which now seemed so far removed from his insular little life.

He was thankful that he had got to this point, but wondered

DEBAUCHERY: PART I

what it all meant. Everything had been so weird over the past few months, and he felt as though normality had been thrown into the air, only to come down as an entirely new dynamic. It both scared and excited him.

A sudden chill snapped Jay back to reality. He stood up, wondering how long it had been since his phone call with Nicky. *He has to be close by now.* Jay stared at four frazzled joints bobbing in the ashtray's dampened base, which were as good a timepiece as any.

He walked into the hall only to be greeted by Nicky, who stood wearing his usual leather jacket and black jeans. He smiled, striding up to Jay and giving him a confident hug. His body tensed up as he awkwardly hugged back.

"You know, you should really get that door fixed."

"There's something wrong with it! You should've seen it last night! It had padlocks all over it but it just like… changed. It changes!"

"Your door changes? Maybe your house is haunted," Nicky grinned. "Now where are these Latin aliens I've heard so much about? I'd love to meet them!"

Jay shut the door, and the pair made their way through the kitchen. Nicky enthusiastically threw the French doors open and stepped out onto the decking, seemingly unaffected by the early December chill. Jay clambered out after him and they took a moment to stare at the unremarkable wooden shed towards the bottom of the garden.

Nicky turned to Jay, doubtful.

"Well, I don't know if it's specifically aliens or whether it's just… a presence," Jay protested, grabbing some shoes.

"Well, let's check it out then!" said Nicky eagerly, taking a self-assured stride into the wilds of the damp grass, with a nervous but intrigued Jay in tow. They hurried to the shed with Nicky saying, "Oh and by the way, you look like shit mate," as he stepped over a frog.

Nicky grabbed the handle of the shed and swung the door open, the two of them jumping back immediately. Straining their eyes to look for something resembling alien contact, they were quickly let down as a lone rake fell to the floor.

"Not a very advanced civilisation, are they?" said Nicky with a frown.

"Fuck off mate! There was something at the back of the shed! There was this glowing symbol and then I turned around and there was this... thing there! I blacked out after I touched the symbol."

Nicky walked in, casting a cautious eye over every cobweb as he ventured deeper. With a smell of dampened soil in his nostrils, he stepped over the rake to the back of the shed. He stared at the distressed wooden wall before turning to Jay, declaring, "There's nothing here! It's just a wall—"

Without warning, the door slammed shut, causing Nicky to emit something between a yelp and a shout. Jay grabbed the door from the outside and yanked it open with Nicky flying out of it and standing next to him, shivering.

"See!" shouted Jay. "There's something wrong! My fucking shed is magic or something!"

"Let's just go inside and ring some of the other sins," Nicky said hastily, making his way back.

"The other sins? Is that our group's name now?"

"I dunno," Nicky said with a smirk. "Seems like a sinny kinda thing."

After a small journey back to the kitchen, Jay boiled the kettle and showed Nicky through to the living room, before taking a

DEBAUCHERY: PART I

seat next to him. Nicky's eye caught a red stain on the carpet as he sat down. Jay noticed the mask fall from him once more, just for a second. It was a miserable memory which kept anyone who noticed it anchored to a harsh reality.

"We need to chill," Jay said softly as the kettle clicked. He got up and left his friend alone for a moment.

"What were you thinking?" shouted Nicky towards the kitchen.

"Oh, I dunno, just how futile everything seems and how we may actually fucking die before we even get any kind of grasp of what's going on," shouted Jay.

Nicky laughed. "I mean what do you want us to do to relax?"

Having made a fresh pot of tea, Jay went back to join Nicky, who was crouched down near his TV looking at his games collection.

"As if you have *Call of Duty*, are you twelve?"

"Hey! That was a gift!"

"Well, they obviously don't like you that much," Nicky said with a smirk.

Jay stared at Nicky for a moment, mind praying that his movie collection would be approved of. He wanted to leave enough time for him to assess his entire collection so left the room for a moment, blurting out awkwardly, "Er, I just need to get changed."

Jay raced up the stairs and into his room, sliding between his bed and a desk to be greeted by a tired-looking wardrobe with a single broken drawer. Scanning his entire collection of clothes, he looked for the most metal and alternative t-shirt he could find and threw it over his head. He went back downstairs where he found Nicky sitting on the sofa waiting.

"I like your t-shirt, black suits you."

Did he just compliment me? Was it a compliment? Does he approve of me? With his mind in overdrive, Jay turned on the TV and, feigning a chilled mind, asked Nicky, "So what would you like to watch?"

"Well, what kind of movies do you like?"

"I like horrors, action films and animated films."

"I love a cheesy action movie! Let's watch one of those!"

"Sure," said Jay.

Seeing Nicky happy made Jay feel as though he was truly doing something important. He knew Nicky spent so much time around Amy, so impressing him might be a little harder than most. Anxious, Jay flicked through his vast selection of movies, hoping Nicky would pipe up when something appealing came along.

"Ooh wait, stop!" Nicky said as Jay jumped and immediately stopped scrolling. "That! *Mad Max: Fury Road!* It's probably one of my favourite films ever. We have to watch it!"

Jay promptly selected the film and sprang up to pour the tea. Shaking slightly, he mused about everything his new friendship could bring. His world was crumbling around him, yet all he focused on was how to act in front of this new obsession.

He joined Nicky on the sofa and, as they sat tea in hand, the film began. Jay loved the semi-darkness in which they sat, and with each passing second, all negativity was paused. He felt a calm come across him despite being in the presence of someone he didn't know so well.

Nicky asked, "Are you okay?"

"There's just… a lot in my head," Jay said, the white lie feeling heavy as it fell from his lips. "There are so many questions and it's just, well, a lot."

Dying to be honest, he merely ended up blurting out a stream of consciousness. "I just feel so stressed, like every time I do

DEBAUCHERY: PART I

something fun or for myself, it feels like I'm wasting time. It feels like we should do so much more, but we're not because we just don't have enough answers or resources. It's draining, dude."

Nicky stared down at the red patch on the carpet, whispering, "I know. Life was difficult enough before all this…"

"What do you mean?"

"Oh, uh, nothing. Just stuff with me and my bloke. Things haven't been easy. We've been going out for nearly seven years now and… and so much has happened."

Jay's mind perked up and an instant wave of anger came towards this person who was so much closer to Nicky. "Are you two okay?" he asked, despite not caring.

"Honestly? I don't know. We argued about something and then he went on holiday. I said that he should reset and come back with a clear mind. But… With everything that's happening with all of us, I'm kinda scared for him to come back. I screamed at him to calm down and now he'll come back to this? It's not good."

"I'm sorry…" Jay said, hiding a twisted smile.

"It's cool. Is there a bathroom I can use?"

"Oh yeah, just upstairs and on the left."

Jay turned the TV off and brushed his curly mop back with his hand before venturing back into the kitchen. It was half past five and his back garden was already soaked in late autumnal darkness. He stared out of the window, only to be greeted by the same static shock wave from the previous night. The strange green light blasted through the house as he stumbled backwards in shock.

"What in the *fuck* was that?" came Nicky's voice over the sound of a toilet flush.

Various alarms once again filled the street as Jay threw a nervous glance towards his shed, which had become an unexpected lighthouse, proudly signalling its presence.

"Seriously, what was—oh fuck your shed! It's green!" Nicky exclaimed as he joined Jay at the back door. Throwing caution to the wind, he stepped onto the decking, with Jay following somewhat slower. They took a seat on the cold metal chairs, noticing a fresh line of padlocks adorning it. Gawking at the bright light slowly fading to the familiarly ominous, pulsating green glow, Jay wished he could erase the sight from his mind. The deafening sound of various alarms gradually faded as angry residents turned them off.

"Is this what you were talking about? I can't believe you went into that thing! I take back the judgement I put on your shed!" said Nicky, still shocked.

"I can't believe it either, but can we please just go inside? It's dangerous." Jay grabbed Nicky's arm tightly, but he merely stood up and started walking towards the shed.

"Nicky, please!" Jay pleaded, but it was too late. He was possessed by intrigue and stepped into the darkness. Battling between his own fear and his overwhelming need to protect his latest obsession, Jay ran after him, chest tight and brain in overdrive.

As the two of them descended deeper into darkness, the safe glow of Jay's house faded away. The few remaining neighbourhood alarms stopped, and the friends were plunged into a heavy silence. They approached the door of the shed with the pulsating glow, making Jay feel nauseous from anxiety.

"Please…" he whispered. "I've already done this and I can't replay it. That… thing might come back."

Putting his hand to the rusty metal door handle, Nicky

stopped for a moment. "What's with the padlocks?"

"I don't know," Jay whispered. "They were there after the flash yesterday. C-Can we please just go back inside?"

"Look, you said you wanted answers, so the quickest way to get them is to fling this door open, take a photo of this glowing thing you mentioned, and get the fuck back inside. We can ask the others what the mark means and someone will most likely have some ideas, right? We have to do something!"

Jay's anxious mind, struggling to find a flaw in Nicky's logic other than the fact they might die, mumbled, "Fine."

"Right..." said Nicky, sliding his phone from his pocket and taking a breath. "One, two, three!"

The door flew open, and a camera flashed, with the two of them wasting no time bolting through the darkness and back to the safety of Jay's house. The back door was slammed shut, and they leaned with their faces pressed against the cold glass.

"You mentioned the Latin alien. Where is the Latin alien?" Nicky asked impatiently.

"Well, I can't make it appear, can I?"

Jay had barely finished his sentence before the same shadowy figure emerged as a darkened silhouette, right on cue. It staggered out from its wooden confines, before turning to face the house, its bright green eyes glowing directly towards them, unblinking.

Jay's soul shuddered as the figure stood silent and still. It made him feel uneasy, as though it could lunge at him at any moment. The layer of glass in front of him did little to make him feel secure. Grabbing Nicky's arm, he said, "That's it! That's the alien!"

He turned to Nicky, who was speechless. His eyes tried to rationalise the irrational, an echo of Jay's feelings the previous night. All they could do was stare into its luminescent eyes.

"Do you have a floodlight?" Nicky whispered, holding Jay's arm but not breaking eye contact with the figure.

"Y-Yes, I use it to shoo cats away."

"Well, you might wanna turn it on and shoo this guy."

Jay banged his fist against a light switch which bathed his garden in a sudden, intense light. Two cats at the back of the garden scarpered over his fence, leaving Nicky and Jay staring in horror at this now-visible creature.

Long chain-mail armour blew in the evening breeze, a piece of tattered white fabric over the top. The garment was blood-splattered with a red crucifix stitched into its torso. Over its head it wore a coif hood of chainmail, a gold horned crown askew on its misshapen head. Muscle and tissue poked from between the ripped clothes and its legs looked rotten, as though any remaining flesh had consumed itself to keep going. Cast iron nails sat sporadically hammered into its fragile frame. Its face appeared gaunt, with sunken eyes, as though its very body was trying and failing to stay in one piece. It croaked in the night air, every breath a challenge. Between burnt skin and scar tissue, the creature embodied an unimaginable suffering.

Struggling to find words, Jay whispered, "It's smiling…"

His friend merely remained speechless, transfixed by the horror in front of him.

Jay threw a panicked look at Nicky, a sudden wave of adrenaline taking over. Whether it was some primal need to defend his friend or a testosterone-fuelled urgency to protect his land, Jay flung the door open and shouted into the winter air, "Hey you! What do you want? Why are you in my garden dressed like that?"

The figure simply smiled wider, unblinkingly tearing its

DEBAUCHERY: PART I

remaining skin to achieve such a feat. Jay turned to Nicky who merely remained frozen.

"Do you want something? We don't know any more about this sin stuff, if that's why you're here! Do you want to come in and talk over a cup of tea?"

"Jesus fucking wept, did you just invite that thing in for a catch-up?" said Nicky, breaking his stunned silence.

"Well, I don't know! You said we need answers, so maybe this thing has them!" Jay protested. "Oh fuck."

The creature began laughing through torn vocal cords, a rattle emanating from its severely damaged lungs. As the creature laughed, the floodlight shattered, alongside every bulb in the house. The kitchen appliances restarted with a beep as the otherworldly power cut caused a small radio to suddenly play 'Standing in the Way of Control' by The Gossip. The two friends jumped and stared directly into the eyes of a being taking a sadistic glee in the fear pouring out of them.

Jay ran over to the radio, unsuccessfully trying to tinker it to silence. "What's wrong with this stupid thing? It doesn't even hold music!"

"Fuck this, I'm ringing Amy," declared Nicky, reaching into his pocket as the illuminated monster continued to laugh.

"Miss me already—Oh my God, is that The Gossip?" came Amy's voice immediately.

"There's no time to explain!" said Nicky through the noise. "I need you to come—" With that, the phone crackled and Amy's confused replies sank into nothing as an automated but familiar voice spoke into Nicky's ear.

"You have reached the Live, Laugh, Love Latin Alien Agency. Thank you for your call. Calls may be recorded for training purposes. Know that your call is important to us, and a representative will be with you as soon as possible. Please choose from the following options—"

Nicky frowned and stared at Jay, who simply stared back. "My phone's gone weird as fuck. Listen to this!" He put the phone on speaker and they listened to the bizarre transcript.

"If you'd like to enquire about Gender Affirming Surgery, press one. If you know a deeply uninteresting man who describes himself as 'Just Me', press two. Or if you have a rotting Latin monster laughing in your garden, press three."

"Press three!" exclaimed Jay.

Nicky slammed his finger on the keypad and waited. The phone rang a further six times before Polly answered in her usual gleeful tone, "Good evening, and thank you for calling the LLLLAA!" Her jovial singing of the company acronym did little to calm their nerves. "May I take your date of birth and the first line of your address?"

"I knew it was you! Stop fucking around with these cosmic games and help! You clearly know what's going on, so come here and sort this fucking problem out!"

"I'm sorry, I'm going to need your date of birth and the first line of your address to proceed," Polly pushed, a smirk in every word.

Exasperated, Nicky groaned, "Ugh, my date of birth is 17th August and my address is get your fucking arse to Jay's house right now!"

Nicky felt Jay pulling on his jacket. "Oh, what now?" Nicky turned to see Jay drained of colour as he pointed to the monster who had paced slowly towards them.

"NOPE!" Nicky shouted as Polly continued her charade.

"Ah yes, I've got your details up now. It appears you do, in fact, have a rotting Latin monster laughing in your garden. Is this correct?"

"P-Polly! It's coming closer! What do we do?" Nicky stammered as the creature staggered towards them, wheezing under broken laughter and singeing the grass under its feet as it moved. Steam rose to the sky, giving the monster an even more horrific aura of pain.

"That's no problem, my love. I can have someone with you in five to ten seconds. Is that okay?"

"Yes! Yes! Anything!" Jay shouted towards the phone in a panic. The phone merely crackled a second time as Nicky's phone died.

They both exchanged frantic expressions of terror before helplessly watching the monster slowly progress along the damp grass. Every second ate at their brain as the two friends clambered to find some kind of practical solution.

Fifteen seconds passed, and a knock at the door broke them from their trance. They lunged forward, disregarding a mass of unlocked padlocks falling from the door, and threw it open. Polly stood before them, sporting a yellow hard hat and chequered shirt with some very short, very tight dungarees. Striding into the house in a pair of work boots, she lugged a toolbox alongside her. Her jet-black hair was shiny and sleek and as she tipped her hat politely, she declared, "Sorry I'm late, traffic was simply *hellish!*"

"Are you for real?" spat Nicky as she merely ignored them and proceeded to the kitchen. Jay shut the door and the two of them rushed back to the kitchen to stare out of the French doors with Polly.

"Hmm," she said, placing hands on her hips and tilting her head to a side. A few tense seconds passed before Polly turned to loudly slam the metal toolbox on the kitchen table in the middle of the room. She turned to them, finger over her chin thoughtfully, before pointing at Jay and exclaiming, "I see what the problem is! You seem to have a bit of a demon infestation!"

Jay turned to the monster, who staggered up the first step of his decking, then back to Polly to nod frantically. Every bit of faith fell onto her as he asked naïvely, "Can you do anything?"

"Easy peasy, demon, seize me!" Polly chanted, mimicking a cheerleader. "Why don't you sweethearts scamper off and live, laugh, love your night away! I promise, once you come back, it'll be as right as rain!"

They looked at each other, flummoxed but wasted no time retreating to the hallway to deliberate.

"It can't be that easy, can it?" said Nicky.

"I can't do this…"

He turned to Jay who stood drained of all colour from within the darkness of the kitchen. His hands were shaking and Nicky took a moment to stop, despite everything. "It's gonna be alright."

"No, it's not! Dude, I'm fucking scared! This is my fucking house and I'm never gonna feel safe here again! What can she change? I want answers to a hundred different things, I'm going out of my mind with all this shit, let alone all the stuff everyone else has had to deal with. I can't do this anymore! I'm having a panic attack and I feel like I'm gonna break—"

"—Okay, listen!" said Nicky, placing his hands on Jay's shoulders. As their panicked eyes met, Jay's soul cried out for help to quell the raging storm in his head.

"I can't do this anymore…"

"Listen, Jay. I feel everything you do right now. I know everything everyone has dealt with and everything you're dealing with. Even before all this happened, we all probably had

DEBAUCHERY: PART I

so much shit to sort. I know I do. But right now, Polly is defying any kind of logic, so we have to believe that her power can go against whatever the hell is outside, right?

"O-Okay," Jay stammered, eyes watering and body shaking.

"It's okay, Jay. Let's place our faith in her at this moment and remove the problem. We have no choice. Tell me, what do you want to do right now? More than anything else. If everything was just okay."

"Err..." Jay said, slowly feeling the support Nicky was sending. "I-I..."

Nicky's eyes were locked on his, "Name it, Jay. I have the money. Anything."

"I-I-I just wanna get fucking wasted, mate," he said quietly.

"Let's go!" grinned Nicky. "See you later Polly!"

With that, Nicky yanked Jay through the hall as the two friends burst into the night. Polly waved cheerily as they left, the demon directly behind her. The crisp smell of a cold December evening washed over them as every question fell off them. As they ran away from the illogical, an overwhelming sense of freedom warmed them.

Fuck it.

XXI
VIVERE RIDERE, AMARE

The words '*The Brolly Club*' glowed in bright white light. This nightclub was a beacon to those who wanted good vibes and to spill half of every drink they bought. It was past ten, and the street was abuzz with chatter from those queuing to get inside. A black cab pulled up with two more patrons, eager to shake off the negativity of the day.

Both Jay and Nicky had spent the journey in a silence that echoed a sentiment of 'fuck it'. Things had appeared, things had vanished, new people came, old people went, and the only words left were *fuck it.* Blind drunkenness was the logical escape for the evening, and as they emerged into the rain, they joined a long line of people eager to do the same. Music could be heard pounding the walls of the club from inside, sending excited anticipation through the queue.

"It always seems to rain when I come here," Jay shouted over the hustle and bustle of tipsy uni students.

"Is it me, or does everyone look twelve?"

"I think they're mostly in their early twenties, to be honest, dude."

"Oh, I know! Everyone in clubs just stays twenty-one and I

DEBAUCHERY: PART I

keep ageing up. It sucks dick."

Jay looked at Nicky, who stood with arms folded, a light social anxiety bubbling to the surface. He smiled, content that after Nicky saved him, he might support his friend a little in return.

They whittled away time with small talk about games, movies and music. With every step towards the door, they took a step closer to each other, their commonalities coming forth and a friendship strengthening. In what seemed like no time at all, they faced two bouncers asking for ID.

"I'm always so happy when people ask now," said Nicky, whipping out a driver's licence from his pocket. The bouncer laughed as Jay followed suit and waved them through, signalling to a woman with pink hair that two people were coming in.

Thankful to be out of the cold, a damp Nicky interrupted Jay's search for cash and paid for them both. He handed the woman twenty pounds and shouted over the reverb, "Keep the change, I love your hair!" The woman smiled, took their coats and stamped their hands with an umbrella shape.

The music pulled them down the hallway, promising an alcoholic embrace. Jay pushed the doors to the main room, and they were drowned in the sweet sound of good times.

"All of tonight is on me, so don't worry. It's just you, me and the fog now!" Nicky shouted over an onslaught of activity.

There were loud noises, lights, and the air was thick with pheromones and sweat. They had gathered more than enough experience of nights out to find this heavy-aired hustle and bustle a familiar, albeit sticky, safe space.

They turned to the bar, a North Star for alcoholics, and found themselves within a circus of people barging into spaces smaller than any human could fit. After a moment of compromising their personal space, they received their reward in the form of an attractive barman with snakebite piercings, feigning enthusiasm for yet another order. A hearty scream for mass amounts of vodka ensued and moments later, they emerged victorious with three of their chosen poison each.

"Right, so we down these two and nurse the third, okay?" shouted Nicky over the roar of the music. "I don't wanna re-join that fucking queue, so I planned ahead."

Jay threw a thumbs-up as they both downed their first drink. He coughed almost immediately and yelled, "Fuck, did you order a double? What the hell was that?"

"You said vodka and coke, right? I assumed you meant double?"

"Are you trying to kill me?"

"You're definitely not a gay man…" Nicky grinned.

Nicky started on his second drink, which also contained mass amounts of his favourite vodka, while Jay stood staring at his, knowing full well that he was going to get his wish of getting completely wasted.

The night progressed with indie music and dubstep, none of which Nicky liked, but he cured this with further drinking. Jay entered a state of total inebriation quickly as he discovered that every time he reached the bottom of his drink, Nicky returned with two more and a smile.

The odd song that Nicky knew simultaneously brought on a new experience for Jay, which involved being grabbed by the arm by his friend onto the dance floor and being forced to do some of the whitest dancing possible. Everything in Jay's head would normally tell him he couldn't do that, but the bizarre positivity Nicky brought to the night made him feel as though he could be devoid of rhythm without shame. The 'fuck it' mantra seeped

DEBAUCHERY: PART I

into his body as well as his anxious brain.

"I see you can't dance for shit either!" Nicky slurred.

Jay laughed, his vision blurred and his worries all but gone. 'Take Me Out' by Franz Ferdinand abruptly burst from speakers overhead and was greeted by rapturous applause and incoherent drunk noises. Nicky grabbed his arm and pulled him deeper into the mass of strangers.

The song eventually fizzled away into a song less familiar, so Nicky escaped the drunken disarray to attack the bar queue once more. Jay took this moment to retreat to his familiar spot at the back wall of the club. After several minutes of focusing on standing upright, he saw Nicky wobble into his personal space holding two giant glasses with sparklers.

"Holy shit! What is *that?*" said Jay, nearly losing an eyebrow to the shining drink that was thrust upon him.

"It's a cocktail!" declared Nicky cheerily.

"Yeah, but what's in it?"

"You know…You ask all the like… wrong questions. I just asked for two interesting drinks and a beautiful man presented me with these!" Nicky slurred as he raised his drink in both hands as though a gentrified Holy Grail.

"Er, okay… Dude, it's boiling in here. Can we go to the smoking area or something?" Jay said, grabbing Nicky's arm and pulling him in that direction, anyway.

One narrow corridor and three awkward apologies later, the two friends were blasted with cold December air. The small concrete square which formed the smoking area was adorned with the warm glow of fairy lights dangling from tall black fencing. Various heat lamps were dotted around and Nicky immediately honed in on one towards the back, taking sips of his sparky drink as he went.

Jay joined him, only for Nicky to place the drink on a ledge and yank the glasses from his face.

"You're always pushing these up your nose! I wonder what you see like."

Jay grinned. "How do they look?"

"I look… just like Buddy Holly!" slurred Nicky, beaming towards his reflection in the heat lamp. "Also, you're blind as shit!"

Jay laughed and awkwardly removed them from him. A forgotten sensation of being able to hear properly returned, and he took this as a chance to talk.

"I just wanted to say, like, thank you. I get so used to thinking I forget how to have fun. It's nice of you to, you know, stop and have a break."

Nicky swayed, beaming as his increasingly messy hair blew in the wind.

"So have you ever had any girlfriends?" Nicky slurred abruptly, taking a sip from his drink.

"Er, yeah, I have," Jay said, using the conversation as an excuse to nurse his drink for a while. "I've had three, but they all kinda messed me around."

"Messed you around, how?"

"Well, two cheated and one left me. I was always drawn to women who were really independent and I guess I was too intense for them."

"Why intense?"

"Well… wait, why are you digging? What do you want?"

"I dunno. I just wanna get to know you. You said you were friends with Steph, so why not be friends with me, too?"

DEBAUCHERY: PART I

Jay looked at Nicky, who focused on propping himself up against the wall, and smiled with the sparkler in his drink finally fizzling away. Something about this wild pile of brown hair in front of him calmed him, unlike anyone he'd ever known. He felt he could trust him and wanted to tell him everything, so as he leaned against the back wall, drink in hand, he took the leap.

"Well, honestly, I just got jealous, I guess. I wanted to know where they were and I always wanted to be with them. Didn't let them have any male friends, like paranoia and stuff. I dunno, it was just something I've always been unable to control. I try to relax but my mind is so busy and over time it's come up with the most fucked up bullshit. I know I drove them away. I didn't know how toxic I was and yeah... It hurts to be honest, dude."

"Wow," said Nicky, staring at the bubbles in his drink.

"What?"

"You sound... fucking awful! Good job you're cute!"

Jay genuinely laughed for what felt like the first time in ages before realising what was just said. "Wait, what?"

"You heard," Nicky said before wobbling back to the dance floor.

Jay followed and the second his foot touched the sticky black floor of the club, 'When You Were Young' by The Killers blasted out of the speakers. The opening guitar was met with cheers as Jay and Nicky looked at each other and shouted an indescribable drunken noise of approval. They stumbled into the sea of people and happily reunited with fellow music lovers.

"I'm so glad I came out with you, dude!" Jay bellowed over the music. They religiously screamed every single word until their throats were raw. Nicky beamed and finished his drink as he threw his arms around Jay. Shocked, he held his arms out, but slowly closed them over Nicky to form an embrace.

The bridge of the song came on and the two of them stared at each other, swaying and vaguely singing along. Jay looked up at him and something he'd never felt awoke in his soul. A white spotlight shone over Nicky, creating a pleasing glow around him. Jay looked at the light bounce from his nose ring and then up into his eyes. He felt so close to him and in that moment wanted to know every single thing about this human being standing in front of him. He wanted this moment to become endless. He had forgotten about home, his friends, and his life. No problems existed at this moment. His anxiety had died, and it was ethereal. He floated on air within the music, a free man.

Jay had seen Nicky as a new Adrian, but this was different. It felt softer, purer, and natural. There was no sinister undertone, no feelings of inferiority. Jay felt worthy, validated and wanted. His whole being yearned to embrace this completely new something, and then it hit him. A sucker punch of desire to the brain and a wave of emotion coursing through his body.

Jay noticed Nicky's eyes were green, that he had a small birthmark on his neck, the fact that when he properly smiled, it showed in his eyes, and that below all the one-liners and sass, there was a vulnerable human being. Jay's heart skipped a beat as he saw how truly beautiful Nicky was and always had been to him.

The drum build-up finished and an electric guitar tore through the speakers just as Jay gracelessly lunged to kiss Nicky. The speakers vibrated, battling against pure energy bursting from within. An array of spotlights danced around them as a shocked Nicky kissed him back and placed a hand softly on Jay's cheek. They made out in the electric atmosphere with several drunk women cheering them on.

Slightly bashful, they rested their heads together, smiling

DEBAUCHERY: PART I

purely and freely with Jay's hair getting in both of their eyes. They continued the song to its end, with Jay staring at his new crush, his body aching to kiss him again and again. This person who had fascinated him had brought forth a most unexpected sexual awakening, and it was like a drug – a shiny new experience with an exciting, unlimited potential for a hundred more.

The rest of the night took form as a joyous celebration of an unlabelled connection. A taxi back to Jay's was promptly ordered so Nicky could 'get his coat' knowing full well it was sitting pretty in the coat room. The moment Jay received a text to signal the taxi arrival, he grabbed Nicky's arm and pulled him from the dance floor.

He dragged Nicky to the cloakroom attendant and then through to the exit with Nicky singing at varying volumes.

A welcome cold chill hit their faces with Jay saying, "Fuck's saaake dude, shut up!" in Nicky's direction as they entered a taxi, which was thankfully still waiting.

"Shut me up, dickhead!" Nicky beamed as they entered the back seat. Jay took this as another chance to slam his lips against Nicky's. They kissed for a moment, a tatted taxi driver looking in his rear-view mirror and rolling his eyes. Jay stopped to give the driver his address and re-arrange his semi.

The rest of the journey was spent in a comfortable drunkenness. A palette-cleansing mix of pop music bubbled away, with Nicky throwing a few wobbly words into the air. Enamoured, Jay's lips formed a content whisper of, "You look so cool."

"What?"

"You always look so cool…"

Nicky, mesmerised by a blur of takeaway lights outside, simply smiled and interlinked his fingers with Jay's.

Cloud nine came to a halt as the taxi pulled up outside Jay's. Nicky threw fifty pounds at the driver and slurred, "Keep the change, mate, you deserve it for putting up with us."

He then confidently opened the door, only to fall face-first onto the pavement. Jay fell out of the taxi as gracefully as he could and scraped his drunken mess of a friend up from the pavement, placing him on the front lawn.

As the taxi drove away, Nicky lay on the wet grass, looking up at Jay and cheerfully whispered, "You're so prettyyy."

Jay laughed. "Pretty? Okay dude, let's get you inside. You're adorable, but it's bloody freezing!"

The moment the front door clicked shut, Nicky exclaimed, "Fuck it!" and threw Jay against the wall, revealing an unexpected strength. They kissed hard and wobbled halfway up the stairs before Nicky shouted a little too loud, "Wait! Stop! Stop!"

"What? What's up?"

"I need water. I always drink and drunk but no more dying. Water then gay for Jay."

"Er, okay…" replied Jay, raising an eyebrow and leading him back downstairs to the tap. This odd intermission of drinking water inspired Jay to do the same, with a choosy finger hovering over music playlists. They ended up drinking two pints purely because Nicky swore his mum would come over from Italy and slap them if they didn't. As 'Flux' by Bloc Party burst from Jay's phone, he was promptly yanked back into a make-out session.

With the moonlight shining through the glass of the French doors, Nicky slammed Jay against his kitchen table and whispered, "I want you so fucking bad."

Between kissing and heavy breathing, Jay said, "Same, but this is like… *really* new. I don't know what to do…"

DEBAUCHERY: PART I

Nicky hoisted Jay onto the table and unbuckled his belt to reveal a bulge aching for release from a pair of white boxers.

"Fuck… You don't, but I do," Nicky said, removing his t-shirt to reveal a chest tattoo of a skull with wings.

As the t-shirt fell to the floor, Nicky saw from the corner of his eye a seven-foot demon standing immediately behind the glass growling at them, blood dripping from a maw of entirely jagged teeth.

Nicky continued to kiss Jay and said, still lip-locked, "Not now, bitch!" before pulling the blinds down with one hand.

"What was that?"

"Nothing. Fuck it."

Nicky lifted Jay's t-shirt and began kissing his chest. He pushed Jay back down onto the table and opened his legs. He kissed lower and lower on Jay's body as he clunkily removed his jeans, intermittently kissing the bulge in Jay's pants. Mind calm but heart racing, Jay lowered his boxers and let Nicky put his lips against his bare flesh. He then received the best blowjob of his life, all whilst under the hellish scorn of a demon hate-watching them from behind a set of made-to-measure Venetian blinds.

XXII
PETRA

"Where the hell is he?" Amy shouted from across a booth in Ignition gay bar.

"I still don't know, Amy. Just like I didn't know the last two times you asked me," hissed Lily, starting a third pink cocktail.

Amy stared impatiently out into a sea of floral print shirts, septum piercings and tiny black dresses for anyone who looked like Nicky. Lily merely kept drinking, inebriation numbing her social anxiety.

"Why are we here?" Lily said abruptly, swirling the ice around in her drink.

"I told you! Nicky said we all have to meet up again, and it's really important because there are monsters now."

"I'm aware of that! I meant why are we meeting for this discussion in a club? It's so loud!"

"Because," said Amy, sliding around the booth over an abandoned pink handbag to sit next to Lily, "we've got a bunch of mad people after us, a mystery woman who's going to drive us all insane and Isaac who is still an undefinable cluster-fuck, so it'd be nice to get myself some sparkly drinks before we all die horribly. Is that okay?"

DEBAUCHERY: PART I

Lily frowned at Amy, then at her drink before downing what was left and saying, "Fine. Would you like another?"

"Well, aren't you a dark horse? I assumed you wouldn't be able to hold your drink, but sure. Most of it ended up over me, anyway." Amy looked down to mourn what was once a dry black dress.

Wobbling to her feet, Lily fumbled for the arm of her jacket that had somehow become entangled in her white mini-dress. "I have many talents and being able to hold my drink is obviously one of them!" she said before swaying vaguely in the direction of the bar, dragging her coat alongside a pair of white go-go boots.

Amy merely laughed before slumping back in her seat to look at her phone for the seventh time. She saw a new text from Nicky.

On my way, hanging like fuck, don't buy me a drink.

Lily gradually pushed herself forward in a three-person-deep queue. Elbow to elbow against an Asian woman with a buzz-cut, she gave an awkward smile as they stood closer to one another than she ever wanted to. As Lily waited, she looked behind her and towards the dance floor. Wild silhouettes danced in thick fog, illuminated by swirls of colour. She could make out the faint outline of a DJ booth where local drag legend, Tips Fedora, played a carefully organised playlist of chart and mid-noughties dance.

Lily turned back, lost in thought amongst a sea of people, thinking of Amy and the rest of the people she now called friends. They had torn her from her comfort zone so often in the short time she'd known them. She had been to random people's houses, down a darkened alley, and now she stood in the physical embodiment of an anxiety attack. Lily had felt so dull for so long, but now she had new friends and so many random experiences under her belt. A smile formed as she drifted back to reality. Whether it was the music, the atmosphere or the fact she was three cocktails deep for the first time in a while, she felt genuinely happy.

Lily saw an opening to the bar and propelled herself between two bears. A bald barman with a smoky eye, hoop earrings and a Princess Diana memorial t-shirt smiled in her direction. Lily did her best to shout her order over the roar of the music, eventually leaving the chaos four drinks better off. Squeezing past groups of people and wobbling back to the booth, Lily felt a hand touch her shoulder, making her tense up, drinks in hand.

"It's me, don't worry!" shouted Nicky as he swung around a barstool to stand next to her.

"Oh!" she exclaimed cheerily, handing him a drink. "Can you carry these? There are so many people here and I can't see Amy anywhere!"

"Oh, okay sure! By the way, look who else came!" Nicky yelled into her ear, taking the plastic glasses and pointing towards the dance floor.

Steph stood in a cheap angel outfit, absolutely paralytic on the dancefloor. A hopeless stare was sent to the DJ as she stood with wonky wings and a wobbling halo above her head, eternally trapped within the endless key change of 'Love on Top' by Beyoncé. Between her tinsel-lined dress and random strands of hair blowing in the air conditioning above, Steph was a vision. Surrounded by a sea of adoring gay men, she caught Lily's eye for a moment and waved maniacally, beaming and nearly elbowing a twink in the face.

Lily attempted to wave back but, in her half-drunken state, she ended up awkwardly waving her drink up and down. Nicky sighed and guided her through the club, eventually seeing Amy sitting tipsy in the booth.

"Sorry I'm late, I left late," he said nonchalantly as he put the drink down and slid across to sit next to her. "Here, two drinks! Oh, whose bag is this?"

"No idea. It was here when we sat in the booth."

"Have you opened it yet?"

Amy grinned. "Well, I thought I'd wait so we could do it together."

"Babe," said Nicky with a smirk, while he removed his leather jacket to reveal a punkish vest top. Amy grabbed the bag and put it on the table, ready.

"You know that's a total violation of privacy!" protested Lily as she shuffled into the booth. They stopped, stared at her for a moment and continued unzipping it.

"Umm, no wallet," said Amy as she buried her face in it, "Oh wait there's a fiver, some tampons, a keyring and er…" She then pulled a confused expression. "There's hot sauce in this bag!"

"Ooh, swag!" said Nicky.

"Amy, you were going out of your mind wanting to know what Nicky had to tell us and now you're bothered about this handbag!" Lily said, reaching for her new drink. "Don't you want to know why he's brought us together again for the first time in God knows how long!"

Nicky's eyes widened in shock, immediately throwing the bag over his shoulder into a booth behind him.

"Well, don't you have balls?" said Amy. "I'm not sure I like this drunken confidence."

"I'm just being honest! I want answers as much as you do!" said Lily before choosing to retreat into what remained of her drink.

Amy then turned her attention to Nicky and barked, "So why did you drag us together again? Didn't I tell you I want nothing to do with any of that bullshit?"

"Something has happened—" started Nicky.

"Something has always happened. Something will always happen! I'm tired of it, Lily's tired of it, I'm sure Jay is tired of it and Adrian is obviously paying the price for not being tired of it!"

Nicky stared at the floor, whispering, "I know."

"How is Adrian doing, by the way? We tried to ask Steph, but she just ignores us when we mention it," said Lily.

"He's okay. He's stable. You can't really ask for more, I guess."

Amy sank back into her seat. "So, it had to be like food poisoning or something?"

Nicky shook his head. "No, like legit poisoning. From what I was told, he was on a date with that lass Stacy and just collapsed right in front of her."

"Do you think she's with this Community?" Lily mused.

"I don't know. She was the only person with him when he fell. She called him an ambulance, but if these people are after us indefinitely, who knows what's true anymore. It could've all been an act. That's not all, though. I was at Jay's last night after he invited me over."

"Wait, so when you text me, you said you were with Jay this morning?" Amy said with a grin. "Did you get straight dick?"

"I actually did."

Lily choked on her drink, spitting it back into her glass as Amy emitted something akin to a squawk, shouting, "You're shitting me! Jay? Adrian's mate? Specky indie prick?"

"Alright Hemingway! Yeah, I stayed over last night and apparently, he's had some deeply complex sexual awakening in the middle of this shitstorm. But there's something else…"

"You mentioned a demon?" Amy said, starting on her new

DEBAUCHERY: PART I

drink before stopping to exclaim, "Oh, for Christ's sake, no need to explain! We've got Lucifer's fuckwit, inbound!"

"Heyy guys!" Steph beamed as she joined the booth, halo bobbing frantically above a wild head of hair.

"Why are you here?" hissed Amy.

"Be nice, you cunt!" said Nicky, elbowing her.

"For your information, Nicky said he was going to a gay bar tonight to see you guys and I'm *obviously* a gay icon, so I'm obviously here!"

"Obviously," scowled Amy.

"How's your night going so far then, Steph?" slurred Lily.

"Oh em gee it's so amazing! I mean, apart from this one guy I was making out with who didn't even remember my name. Anyway, he's a pig and I'm obviously a star here because of my web show. I've always just felt a connection to gay men. I feel like I am one!"

"She's on PrEP and everything," grinned Nicky, slumping back in the booth.

"Guys, I've been invited to Mykonos! I'm screaming!"

"You're not screaming at all though, are you?" Amy said between drinking. "You're literally not screaming. You're just sitting there like the chocolate teapot you are. Nicky, just tell me about this monster. Now! *Important!*"

"Alright! Calm your tits!" said Nicky. "So Jay called me yesterday and asked me to come over because he thought Latin aliens had taken over his shed."

Latin aliens? Lily mouthed to herself.

"I went over and we had a great time, but then something legit did actually happen. His shed looked like it was some kind of nuclear reactor or something."

"So, his shed is actually a spaceship?" Amy asked flatly, cynicism ablaze amongst the Top 40.

"Well, that's the thing. We went to the shed because Jay told me that inside was some kind of symbol. We opened the door, and I took a quick photo, but there wasn't any pattern at all. When we came back into his house, we saw this thing come out. It was dressed like a Crusader, had burnt skin and glowing eyes! It was fucked up!"

The booth sat stunned, except for Steph, who had lost interest immediately. She instead opted to perform some muscle-memory choreography to the chorus of 'Deeper Shade of Blue' by Steps for a stunned lesbian couple nearby.

This moment was lost to the drama of the conversation as Nicky continued. "Well, Jay and I didn't really know what to do. It just stood smiling at us but saying nothing. It was fucking harrowing! Jay tried to communicate with it, but it laughed at us. It was fucking horrible."

"What did you end up doing?" Lily questioned nervously.

"Well, like I said, I tried to ring you," said Nicky, casting his gaze towards an increasingly drunk Amy, "I rang and spoke for a moment before the phone crackled out and Polly took over."

"Yeah, from my end you just fizzled out, and I tried to call back, but I couldn't get through. I was high as fuck, so I just watched TV instead, to be honest."

"Great sense of urgency there..." said Nicky. "Anyway, Jay said it went away after a while, so we just went out and got smashed. I stayed at his place and I don't remember anything else. It was gone when we woke up today, as was Polly, so we just figured she dealt with it. I just wanted to talk about it, especially with Lily, 'cos you know about otherworldly shit. Maybe you can

DEBAUCHERY: PART I

at least say what we're up against on the off chance—"

"—On the off chance it isn't Latin aliens?" scoffed Amy.

"Yeah... That."

"Hmm..." Lily said aloud. "Dressed like a Crusader?"

"Yeah, with nails in its face and body with bloody, burnt skin and glowing eyes!"

Though slightly disjointed from drink, the cogs in Lily's mind turned. "I mean... it definitely sounds like a demon, but then again, I've never seen one or known anyone who has."

"I think... we should get more drinks!" Steph interjected as she got up and left, anyway.

"Right. So can we pin down which demon it actually is?" Amy asked. "Do we even know if it's a demon? They don't tend to just appear, do they? The more we ask questions, the more bullshit seems to appear."

A defeated silence sat as an extra guest, bringing infectious pop back against their eardrums.

"Wait, do you still have that photo? The one in the shed?" said Lily.

"Yeah, I never deleted it, but there's nothing on it," Nicky said, reaching into his jacket pocket. "Here you go, but like I said... wait a minute! There's a pattern on there! I swear it wasn't there before!"

"Let's see!" Amy said, lunging to grab the phone. "Oh my God! I can see it too and it means absolutely fuck all!" She cynically passed the phone over to Lily, who stared at it for a moment before whipping out her phone.

"See, when I was at uni, I downloaded Spookypedia. It's an app which has all the different, uh... demon sigils in some digital Grimoire alongside everything else in the occult."

"Well, aren't you a walking study in demonology?" grinned Amy.

Lily held the photo on Nicky's phone in front of her screen as Nicky and Amy stared, completely fascinated.

"Errr wait, one sec… I've never done this drunk before… okay I'll just rotate it aaand… there!" She returned Nicky's phone, then turned her phone screen to face both of them, declaring triumphantly, "It's the sigil of Surgat! He's listed as minor daemon Surgat, 'who opens all locks'."

"Oh my God!" said Nicky. "When the light appeared, all these padlocks came from nowhere. Then we saw this demon and they were all unlocked!"

"Incredible!" said Lily, eyes widening with a sozzled excitement. "Let me see if there's anything else… Uhh, useless, useless, useless… hot single ghosts in my area… ah! Here we go! He's been mentioned in *The Secrets of Solomon*, *The Grimoire of Pope Honorius* and *Grimorium Verum*, but apparently appeared around the mid-fifteenth century. It says here that he's one of the lesser demons, but is one of the most frightening because of his deceptive and cunning mind. He can help with medical aid and astral projection, but also opens portals to the Inferno and the anti-Cosmos."

"The anti-cosmos?" said Nicky and Amy in unison.

"I'm baaack and yes, I've bought us all Cosmos, how did you know?" Steph said, carrying a tray of cocktails. She plonked herself next to Lily cheerily, a vision in tinsel as she passed the drinks round. Planting her eyes firmly toward her phone screen, she scrolled through countless social media accounts and said, aloof, "So what did I miss?"

"Jay's shed is maybe haunted by a fifteenth-century demon called Surgat who is going to use cunning to do something that

DEBAUCHERY: PART I

will send us to evil space or somewhere generally shitty," said Amy.

"Oh…" said Steph, looking concerned for a moment before blurting out, "Oh and look! These drinks came with tiny umbrellas, aren't they cute? I'm just gonna pop to the loo," and with that she vanished once more, a tiny umbrella in her increasingly messy blonde mop.

With everyone else's focus back on the conversation at hand, Nicky started with the first wave of questions. "So why has this demon been randomly summoned in Jay's shed and how?"

"Well, uh…" Lily slurred, struggling to keep her factual head on as she poured over her phone notes. "It says here that he can be invoked by a spell called 'For Nailing'. I guess that's why he's covered in them? If he's from like 1450, I suppose he's been summoned a lot."

"Is it really that simple?" Amy asked. "You seem to know more than anyone I've ever met."

"Well, I studied it at uni."

"Even so, Lily…"

"Look, I'm an introvert and I've spent most of my twenties sitting in bed watching occult and serial killer documentaries! I studied it and I just loved it. I won't apologise for my passion because we wouldn't know shit without me coming along! Just because you majored in being a *bitch!*"

Blindsided, Amy opened her mouth to reply, but Nicky merely put a hand up to stop it.

"Okay, so I suggest we all calm down or at least sober up," said Nicky. "Maybe we should leave, seeing as I'm at yet another alcoholic event, hmm? I'm old, gay and fucking tired."

"Look, you wanted answers. I met you and I really didn't

have to or want to… but here I am, and I've given you what you want," said Lily firmly. "What do you think, Amy?"

Arms folded and face like thunder, Amy looked at Nicky, who gestured across the booth. She unfolded her arms and reluctantly spoke up. "Honestly? Bullshit. I haven't seen this thing, and it's probably just some dude in a fancy dress taking the piss."

"It was pretty fucking convincing fancy dress!" Nicky protested.

"I'm just saying! Like why Jay's house and why now? What's the relevance of this to that cult? Surely if we're meant to be made of sinful shit, then this… thing would be on our side, right?"

Unable to answer any of her questions, Nicky looked towards Lily, with Amy following suit.

"I don't have all the answers. Most of what I said was from this app which compiles hundreds of years of obscure occult stuff. I'm not clever, the app is. I'm just drunk and trying to keep it together. Anyway, I'm gonna go to the toilet and see where Steph is so we can go."

"That's the best thing you've said all night," said Amy bluntly.

Lily ignored her and stood up before turning back. "Oh Nicky, by the way. You didn't invite that demon inside, did you?"

"What do you mean?" said Nicky.

"Just like standard demon stuff. If you invite it to your space or give it consent, things become a lot more difficult. You didn't do that, did you?"

He looked to the floor, silent.

"For fuck's sake!" shouted Amy. "What did you do?"

"Jay er, invited it in for a cup of tea," Nicky replied.

"YOU SILLY GAY BASTARDS!" bellowed Amy demonically deep, causing half of the club to turn towards their booth.

Lily sighed. "Okay… I'm just gonna go to the loo and we can

DEBAUCHERY: PART I

work things out from there."

"Take your time," hissed Amy, killing the conversation immediately.

Amy and Nicky sat for a moment, not saying a word. Their booth had existed as something of a haven from eight-minute extended house remixes. The space had become instantly tense and Nicky was thankful no one else was there. He knew Amy like the back of his hand and he knew how to speak her language of abrupt honesty. As she finished her drink, Nicky said calmly, "Why do you have to be so cynical?"

"Nicky! I can't just fall into some occult bullshit that I haven't seen. I need proof and Lily knows too much. It's suspicious as fuck to me! We didn't ask for this and you know how I am with new people. There are *a lot* of new people and we're expected to just have blind faith in them? It's a big ask, mate."

"Why would I lie to you? You're fucking family to me, and no, we didn't ask for this, but neither did anyone else. Especially Lily. If the introvert can pull herself outside, I'm sure you can put your people-person voice on. Surely we're better off together than apart?"

"I… I know. You're right, but it's all just so… dumb. It's hard to believe and there's just so much shit we don't know. I just want an upper hand."

"I know," Nicky sighed. "It's so overwhelming, but we'll get there. I mean, what's the worst that could happen?"

"Well… Do you think Adrian will come out of this? The fact he's in hospital really makes it…"

"Real? It's terrifying, really, isn't it?"

"Yeah. Everything inside me just wants to avoid it, but I guess we can't do that anymore?"

"I doubt it now, to be honest," said Nicky. "We all seem to be clinging to any normality we can, but things are getting worse. I mean, someone is in the hospital and I've seen a legit demon."

"Do you think it's worth taking another look at the Community building?" Amy said, cautiously. "Maybe they know something?"

Nicky frowned. "I'd rather commission a belt from Ed Gein."

Their chat was abruptly cut short as the voice of Tips Fedora spoke over quietened music from the DJ booth. They sat up and looked towards the wide-open space which formed the dance floor.

"And now we have an extra special shout-out to Satan, Lucifer, er Belphegor and… Mammon from Petra, who sends the message, 'Bless those who curse you, pray for those who mistreat you'. Luke 6:28. Phew, what a mouthful! Biblical indeed folks, but at least we know we've got Satan on our side, eh! Here's your song request, Petra, enjoy!"

Nicky grabbed his coat, sprang up and grabbed Amy by the arm. They shuffled through a sea of people, past the bar before reaching the seemingly huge expanse of the dancefloor. Overhead lights faded into a momentary darkness. Spotlights shone downward, casting a bright light over a petite, Jordanian figure.

The mysterious woman stood barefoot in a flowing white kaftan dress with a black embellished collar. Voluminous jet-black hair and intense eyes shone in the crisp white light. As a sudden burst of fog shrouded her into a bizarrely ethereal vision, she threw them a direct and unnerving smile.

The opening to 'Judas' by Lady Gaga reverberated around the club as Petra raised a heavily bangled arm, declaring in a joyfully dramatic voice, "'When you go to war against your enemies and see horses and chariots and an army greater than yours, do not be afraid of them, because the LORD your God, who brought you up out of Egypt, will be with you!' Deuteronomy 20:1."

DEBAUCHERY: PART I

Long black hair fell over deranged eyes as she moved a hand from behind her to drop a large axe to the floor with a loud metal clunk, which appeared to go completely unnoticed by the rest of the crowd.

Nicky and Amy looked at it and saw long turquoise ribbon wrapped clumsily around the weathered wooden handle, as though it were some kind of drunk ballet slipper.

"Shit, the handle! She's in the Community!" shouted Amy as the woman walked slowly towards them, a psychotic smile peeking from her long hair. They threw panicked glances at each other before immediately vanishing into an ever-expanding sea of fog. Nicky ran to the left of the dance floor, Amy to the right, with Petra standing and laughing at the potential of a new hunt.

"Shit, shit, shit!" Nicky said to himself, pushing his way through varying levels of camp. Sweat fell from his forehead as he brushed his increasingly mad hair back. He darted deeper into the crowd, feeling sick from a horrible cocktail of stress, fear, and fatigue.

Nicky zig-zagged around the hordes of people enjoying a mad weekend, jealous of how easy life was for them and how fed up he was with everything. He frantically looked left and saw nothing, then to his right and saw Petra emerging from thick white smoke, smiling and dragging her weapon of choice behind her.

"Fuck!" Nicky shouted as he lunged through two guys, hopelessly in lust. Without warning, he slammed into Lily, who let out a frightened yelp from within the fog.

"Lily! Where's Amy?"

"I-I don't know! I heard the request and came looking for you!"

"There's some mad woman in a kaftan with an axe!" Nicky shouted, pulling her deeper into the blanket of fog.

"An axe? Is she with the Community? Where's Amy?" yelled Lily as she was shoved through a group of leather daddies like an inadvertent wrecking ball.

Amy's incoherent shouting could be heard as a gentle whisper over the music and as Nicky honed in, he saw her on a raised floor pushing her way towards the DJ booth.

Latching onto this idea immediately, Nicky tugged a reluctant Lily towards the stage and up to Amy's position. He touched the back of her right arm, causing her to yelp, fist raised and ready to strike. Upon seeing there was no threat, Amy shouted, "In here!" before throwing a light Perspex door open and shoving her friends inside.

Now behind the roar of the speakers and in the company of iconic drag legend Tips Fedora, things seemed relatively calmer. They stopped for a moment to plan their escape and air their flurry of panicked questions.

"What the fuck was that?"

"I've left my jacket at the booth!"

"Where the fuck is Steph?"

"Who the bloody hell are you people and why are you here?"

They looked at Tips, who stood in a black wig, plum-coloured dress and a face beat for the gods.

"Sorry, we're being stalked by that mad woman who requested the Biblical shout-out," said Amy.

"Ah, okay. Did you break her heart? Does she feel jilted?" Tips pouted, feigning crying with her free hand.

"No!" said Nicky. "She's literally hunting us with an axe!"

"An axe wouldn't make it in here, sweetheart."

"An AxE wOuLdN't MaKe It In HeRe SwEeThEaRt!" Amy spat.

Tips threw an unimpressed look at her. "You're adorable.

DEBAUCHERY: PART I

Look, if you want a way out, there's a back exit left of here," she said pointing to a black door at the end of a sea of people.

"That's perfect!" Nicky said, his eyes filling with hope as he stared at the door. "Thank you, legendary Tips Fedora!"

"No problem, sweetie, now fuck off with you. I'm doing an advert tomorrow morning for some shitty book and I have to prepare." Tips grinned as she went back to her adoring audience, shouting, "Yaass, c'mon queen, hunty, the house down boots!" deadpan down the microphone.

The three friends linked arms, sped off out of the booth and back into the masses.

Lily said, "I guess we're forgetting about Steph, then?"

"Shit! Steph! I'll get her, you guys go!"

Nicky stared towards the tempting glow of the fire exit as Amy and Lily whizzed through in a blur. He took a deep breath as he cautiously re-entered the fog. As the bridge of the song played, Nicky stumbled upon Steph, who stood wingless, talking to a group of tanned men with bleach-blonde hair and barely buttoned-up shirts.

"Steph!" he interjected, making the gaggle of gays cast a stony gaze in his direction. "We have to go. There's someone after us and we just need to leave, okay?"

"Oh Nicky! These are the popular gays! They know me from my cut crease tutorials so they bought me shots and now I can't see!" she said, barely standing.

"Popular with who, exactly?" frowned Nicky. "Anyway, there's no time for tired alcoholics! We need to go, gorgeous. Come on!"

"Okay, Nicky I'll come with you. Bye-bye, popular gays!"

The group looked him up and down with Nicky merely

scoffing at them. He grabbed Steph's arm and yanked her back into the crowd. As the song built up towards the end, Steph felt a sudden and overwhelming need to dance.

"Nickyy, let's dance before we go!"

"Steph, there's literally someone trying to kill y—"

Nicky was interrupted as he ran directly into Petra. His eyes widened as she smiled gleefully and said, "'For like the grass they will soon wither, like green plants they will soon die away'! Psalm 37:2."

"Oh my God!" Steph shrieked, taking Petra's outstretched hand.

"Steph, no!"

"This is the most iconic outfit I've ever seen in my life! Come and dance with me, eeek!"

Blind-sided, Petra threw a flummoxed expression at Nicky, who simply stared as she was transported to the depths of the dancefloor.

Standing on the side-lines and staring out onto the dancefloor, he watched Steph bellow the lyrics, "I CLING TO!" as the gayest armistice in history formed. Breaking into an intricate choreography, Petra, the popular gays, the legendary Tips Fedora and every other patron in the club all danced in unison behind an elated Steph.

As Nicky watched the show of his life as Steph beamed, abruptly yanking the axe from Petra and waving it alongside someone shaking an inflatable flamingo. They spent one final chorus dancing before Steph returned the axe to a speechless Petra. She wobbled back to Nicky smiling from ear-to-ear shouting, "Iconic! Can we please come back here again? I love it so much!"

"Er sure," said Nicky, still unsure of what he had just witnessed. He held her hand and they casually walked towards

DEBAUCHERY: PART I

the back door. As Nicky walked through, he turned to see Petra laughing at them and waving goodbye. It both confused and terrified him, but he was just happy to be in the safety of the outside.

"Oh my God!" said Steph, as Nicky touched the door. "Did I tell you I met the popular gays?"

"Fuck's sake," Nicky mumbled as the two were plunged into the cold winter air. Relieved to be safe, he dragged his musical friend past a line of bins out a small gate which had Amy waiting at the other side.

She said nothing, opting to tap Nicky on his head, making him wince.

"Oi! What happened there?"

"You know, sometimes you can't find the words…" Nicky said as he glanced over to Steph, slumped against the wall.

"How wrecked is she?"

"She's uh, lost her wings, we'll say that." Nicky grinned. "She also has musical superpowers… or at least something close."

"Musical what? Steph, you, okay?"

Steph looked up from under a collapsed halo, raised her arm and proclaimed joyfully, "I… am God's mistake!"

Amy grinned, but it was short-lived as she realised there was someone missing.

"Er… Where's Lily?"

The content smile fell from Nicky's face as he stammered, "I-I thought she was with you?"

"She left and went back in to get you guys! I didn't want her to go back, but she did! That woman has *strength* when she's drunk!"

"*Shit!*" Nicky shouted into the street.

They stood for a moment staring at each other, then at Steph, who swayed gently in the wind. Suddenly, all three of their phones sounded and in unison and they read a horrific shared text message:

The Community Under New Truth has captured one of the seven. She is guilty of the crime of Sloth and shall be punished accordingly. Make no attempt to contact her, as doing so will result in further action.

May my Satellites guide you to the noble path of death and bring New Truth to this world.

Faith without works is dead.

—Magnus.

XXIII
BLIND FAITH

Lily opened her eyes to see nothing but darkness from under a burlap sack. Her senses were heightened, and a panicked deduction of her situation began. An attempt to move her arms and legs became futile as they were bound to an uncomfortable chair.

Looking around desperately, she hoped if she physically moved her head enough, the bag would somehow remove itself, but she quickly found it was tied off loosely around her neck. Breathing heavily, Lily tried to calm herself. She focused on music softly dancing around the room as background. It was 'Für Elise' by Beethoven. A snapshot of her housemate Heather playing it on the apartment's piano centred in her mind. The sound of a safe space was being warped into a sobering tease for an unknown scenario.

Voices could be heard from behind a door, making Lily tug harder at her restraints. Vulnerable and shaking, she heard the door open with grandeur, sound echoing upward. Muffled voices became clear, creating a disorientating furore within a seemingly endless space. Pulling at her restraints, Lily helplessly tried to look around, their chatter everywhere.

"Eeek, this is so cool! Can I play with her yet? I wanna hear the noises that come out of this one!" came a cloying female voice.

A second voice replied, monotone and sombre, "Actually, August, we have to see what our Blessed Magnus says on the matter first. Remember that we were pulled from our valuable work in the Down Below for this female, so it must finally be time."

Lily panicked under the weight of the unknown. She wondered if there had been people with her the whole time. *How did I get here? What are they going to do to me?* Mind ablaze, all she could do was listen as this August addressed her directly, a strawberry scented presence breathing over her.

"Hehe, you're conscious! Super fun! What I'd give to have a look inside!" August placed a hand lightly on Lily's chest. "Oooh! So rapid and warm! Ohoho baby, I can't wait to see what else you do! To tinker with one of the seven, Nate! Wowzers! It makes me feel all squishy inside!"

"You can struggle all you want," said Nate. "We've had this planned for a *very* long time, and we have to stay true to the source material."

Further footsteps could be heard, and every bit of turmoil in Lily's head manifested into soft, nervous whimpers.

A second, gently spoken female came into earshot, her voice echoing as she came closer. "Hello dearest Belphegor. My name is River, and it's oh so nice to meet you! Don't mind August! She gets all hot and bothered when we have new guests. It's oh so rare these days!"

The door could be heard opening and August declared, clapping, "Ooh goodie, a family reunion! You know, Belphegor, me and Nate spend so much time in that icky Down Below we hardly see anyone! It's almost like we're locked away for good reason!"

DEBAUCHERY: PART I

Lily's body tensed as confident chatter began surrounding her, slowly creating a sense of being walled in.

"Mate! I can't believe they actually caught a live one!" came a rough, masculine voice.

"Simply gorgeous, isn't it?" replied River.

Another voice spoke in a Irish accent, "Do you think it's dangerous?"

"'Be on your guard; stand firm in the faith; be courageous; be strong'. Corinthians 16:13."

"What Petra means is that it's all going to be super, Noah! She even came out of that fusty old chapel to spend time with us!" said August happily, as the sound of another door could be heard. Its grand metal frame boomed as it opened. The room immediately broke into a rapturous applause.

Lily couldn't see a thing as a final person walked in and anticipation built. *This is it.*

Straining, she made out the heel of a boot on marble through dwindling applause. A strong cologne hit her nostrils as the figure seemed to stop in front of her. Her hairs stood on end. She felt weak, exposed, and helpless to do anything about her situation.

"My Benevolence," came a calm yet muffled male voice. Lily concluded he was wearing a mask and her skin crawled as he stood towering over her.

"We have a special person with us now. A person who may be wretched, may be cursed to walk the path of the unfaithful, but also, a person who is worthy of repentance." Lily could hear a warmth in his voice, a calm smile commanding the cold room. "One of the Unholy Seven she may be, but God still speaks to those who are lost. Still speaks to those who don't know they are lost. Don't know they have a chance to feel the warm glow of the

Holy Spirit."

Combined with classical music, the words spoken created such presence and theatre. She knew immediately that church was in session.

"Shall we?"

Lily turned as movement could be heard. Several arms raised above her, holding Holy Books as seven people spoke in unison.

"This is New Truth and New Truth speaks to me. New Truth sees my weakness and New Truth sees my strength. On this day, my eyes open, my heart listens, and my soul flows free. We grow today, in New Truth's name. God bless us all."

Lily tensed. *This is a cult…* Every memory of learning and study flashed before her. *Are they violent? Am I truly in danger?*

"Now I want to speak to you today about is change. The Lord gives us change with our thoughts, opinions – heck, even that lady down the street we don't like." The group laughed, as the figure could be heard pacing. "Even God's good green Earth is prone to change. We praise God for these changes and we pray to Him for changes yet to come."

The group clapped with an intense agreement. The music had faded but could still be heard. Lily sat still, picking up every scrap of information she could. She knew she was the focal point of the room, but the longer the man spoke, the more invisible she felt.

"Now we will face the concept of change many times in our lives. It can be scary, it can be alien, but if you open your heart up to New Truth, you arm yourself with a supernatural power!"

The group clapped, sending Lily further into the background. *Have they forgotten I'm here?* came a niggling thought in her mind. She scolded herself immediately for being so naïve. She knew they spoke a language of theatre, anticipation, and ritual. *Context*

DEBAUCHERY: PART I

will come. Breathe, Lily.

"Now if we remember Proverbs 13:9, 'The light of the righteous shines brightly, but the lamp of the wicked is snuffed out'. This is something that speaks to me today through the power of the Lord Jesus Christ. You see, faith is our soul, but New Truth is our armour."

The group cheered, breaking into a thunderous applause as a hand was suddenly placed on Lily's shoulder, making her jump.

"I, Magnus, now address you. One of the Unholy Seven, I speak your name with the knowledge that New Truth can enforce change within you, Belphegor." Lily's soul shuddered as he spoke such a name. A torrent of fear came over her, sweat mixing with the continuous smell of cologne. "We stand here today to remind you, demon, that it is John 1:5 which says, 'The light shines in the darkness, and the darkness has not overcome it'. Do you understand?"

Trembling, Lily stayed silent as small, frightened noises filtered weakly out from the burlap sack.

"The Devil has Belphegor's tongue, it seems," said Magnus in a sinister, mocking tone.

A callous laughter filled the room before immediately stopping again as their Leader raised a hand to silence it.

"Tonight, we disarm the Unholy Seven and render them crawling on the floor like animals. Tonight, we remove the heart of the machine that drives the Unholy Seven forward, for without this, victory is assured!"

Lily's body shook as tangible evil spread around the room. Eyes watering, she felt Magnus near once more.

"Sin lives in the darkness and is therefore blind. Blind to the light, blind to virtue and blind to reason. It is you, Belphegor, who stands most powerful, and if you continue to choose to live in darkness, then it is darkness you shall get. Behold, the power of the Community Under New Truth!"

Suddenly, Lily felt Magnus thrust his palm over her face, several rings pressing into her skin. A thunderous chorus of the Community shouting, "Faith without works is dead!" could be heard as an abrupt gale blew. Whimpering, Lily shook her head in disbelief as she felt the chair sink through the floor.

With her heart in her throat, she fell, the sinister joy fading into a deafening howling wind. The sack clung to her jaw as she flailed in the chair, screaming for help. Despite falling, she still felt the hand of Magnus over her face. It gripped her and as she continued to plummet downward, Lily closed her eyes and prayed.

"How long will you lie there, you sluggard? When will you get up from your sleep?" came Magnus's voice, grand and echoing from within the endless freefall. Lily screamed, her voice vibrating against his palm as the wind blew relentlessly.

It was then that the wind began to lessen. Sweaty and shaking, Lily felt the chair settle softly on solid ground. Her body recalibrated as the warped happiness of the Community returned.

"It is done," said Magnus's voice.

Lily tried to calm her breathing, as her struggles were met with a cruel, mocking laughter and a further eruption of, "Faith without works is dead!" from the entire group. Magnus raised a hand once more and silence fell.

"Do you feel changed? Do you feel weak? Know this. Everyone you love shall perish. Every light in your life will be extinguished and you will live in darkness eternal. Every breath and beat of your rotten heart will become a burden and you will pray for the sweet embrace of death. Why, it was we alone who orchestrated every woe you have faced. Poison, demons, and bullets – it was

DEBAUCHERY: PART I

all the Community. Our Holy work shall continue until the Debauchery is no more. We shall save this rotten Earth and New Truth will reign supreme!"

Lily let out a tearful gasp. It was all their fault. There was never any doubt in her mind, but hearing the confirmation straight from the source made her break down.

"Now go."

Lily felt her hands loosen, then her legs. Magnus then took her shaking hand and pulled her to her feet.

He led Lily on, and they walked hand in hand out of the grand room. The fading cheers from six Satellites made her break down as the doors closed. *It's over...* Her body aching, her mind exhausted, Lily was guided into a colder, quieter hall as she began to cry. They stopped as Magnus turned to place a warm hand on her arm.

"There is much New Truth knows, but I keep certain titbits for my own musings. The Satellites, though passionate, need not know of some things. For example, I know of Leon. Does he still speak to you, perhaps? Do you think he would've faired any better?"

Lily's eyes widened in terror from beneath the burlap. "How…"

"Useless information to my subordinates but really quite fascinating objectively speaking, I assure you," he continued as Lily sobbed helplessly.

"Tell me, do you cry for yourself or for your friends?" His tone was somewhat surprised at such an open display of emotion laid bare before him.

Lily remained silent for a moment before whispering, "I cry for the fact this story ever has to exist."

She would never see the genuinely solemn expression that

filled her captor's face as Magnus stared down to the white marble floor.

"We do not ask to be born, yet here we stand in this moment," he whispered. With that, he untied the chord from around her neck and pushed her outside, saying firmly, "The Satellites will hunt. Five minutes, my sinful one."

Lily stepped into the biting cold, armed with a loose burlap sack and a window of freedom. Through darkness and pain, she inhaled and removed it, making her way forward. Suddenly, she stopped and threw panicked hands over her face. A frantic brain tried to keep up with fingers that clambered over her face for truth. She found her answer, as sharp and cruel as the world around her. A frightened whimper grew to a scream as Lily found that she had fallen blind.

A visceral cry tore through the darkness as she stumbled ahead. Thoughts of every book, person and a piece of art she had connected with became a poison. As her mind raced over all she had lost, Lily's logical brain remembered her whereabouts.

Extending her hands and shuffling along the long gravel path, she rifled through fragmented thoughts of the blueprint in Deontay's hideout. *A fountain, a forest… I'll never see anyone I love again.* Lily wept as she moved forward, her body trying to hold back the crushing weight of emotion.

Her hands felt the stonework of the fountain and she stopped. Through heavy breathing and survival instinct, Lily knew that if she could get to the gate and face the building, she'd be able to see the place as she did the blueprint. With no better plan in place she continued, choking through tears but continuing onward.

Arms still thrown in front of her, her walking turned to a jog. Her foot caught something and she fell. Her skin grazed against

DEBAUCHERY: PART I

the stone and she lay there, defeated.

Staring through sheer darkness, emotion drowned her. She put her hands to her face and cried. She was confused, scared, and alone in a new, unfeeling world. Lily stood, inconsolable under a crushing hopelessness.

The pain seared in the cold night air, yet her anguish proved the stronger pain. Through this intense emotional chokehold, a primal part of Lily spoke up.

Run!

She stumbled to her feet and decided to bolt ahead, the worst-case scenario being simply falling again. Time was her enemy and as she ran into the cold metal bars of the gate, Lily shook them and screamed for help.

Without warning, there was a sound. Unbeknownst to her, the area had filled with a harsh white light taking the form of several spotlights perched on the roof of the building. The bright light shadowed that of the moonlight and pierced every shred of darkness on the grounds. Petrified and exposed, Lily scrambled gracelessly into a bush to her right, muscle memory saving her life. She crouched down, terror filling her eyes and leaves in a bedraggled pixie cut. The crackling of a speaker sounded, filling the site with 'Treasure Waltz' by Strauss.

The abrupt sound of the grand front door being thrown open in the distance caused Lily to jump. A circus of gleefully twisted noise filled a calm night sky as six silhouettes scattered.

"So, what's the tea?" came Polly's voice unprovoked. Lily held back a yelp despite recognising the voice.

"P-Polly? I-I'm blind."

"Well duh! Unlike you, I can see that! I'm here to help, incognito like. Can't have you popping your clogs first now, can I?"

"W-What should I do?" sobbed Lily, desperate to keep her voice to a whisper, despite the noises surrounding her.

"It's dangerous to go alone! Take this."

"O-Okay… What is it? I can't feel anything," said Lily.

"It's my incredible but fleeting support, you silly goose! You can have this nice twig if you want something to hold, however?"

"Polly, I need help!" hissed Lily, cold and frustrated.

"Go left."

Armed with an abrupt but strong command in her ear, Lily wasted no time and veered left. She crawled as the sound of a Satellite came into earshot.

"You better not hope we find you!" he bellowed, terrifyingly close with heavy footsteps on the gravel. "When I find you, I'll break every bone in your fucking body! The last name you'll ever know, is Chace, mate!"

"Straight ahead, darling."

Lily held back emotion and, shaking, she crawled forward. With no rhyme or reason to her movement, Polly was her only hope.

"I'm gonna pull your jaw from your fucking face!" Chace screamed, his voice slightly further from her. "I'll stand on your head 'til your skull breaks! I'M READY!"

"Straight ahead, no left!"

Lily moved only to walk into a shrub. She leapt over it as discretely as she could.

"Hmph! Such a bad egg to hide from me!" came August's strawberry-scented voice. "I just wanna play! Magnus would be so proud! See me senpai, uwu!"

"Left. Ahead. Right. Left."

With every direction ordered, Lily complied immediately.

"Left. Ahead. Right. Ahead. Left. Stop! Stand up!"

DEBAUCHERY: PART I

Lily stopped, jumping to her feet as gravel became hard soil and a voice sounded next to her.

"'The lazy do not roast any game, but the diligent feed on the riches of the hunt'. Proverbs 12:27."

Petra paced at the forest's opening, unaware her adversary stood directly behind an evergreen.

"Did you find her, sweet Petra?" said River, drifting into the conversation. Her long white gown and calm demeanour were illuminated through intermittent spotlight.

"'God is our refuge and strength, a very present help in trouble'. Proverbs 46:1."

"Oh, quite definitely." Their casual attitude to the situation was unnerving but Lily stood steadfast. "I must return to the forest. It calls to me, you see…" River's veil blew in a well-timed breeze as several woodland creatures appeared from the forest to greet her and await instruction.

"'But the Lord is faithful, and he will strengthen you and protect you from the evil one'. Thessalonians 3:3."

"Faithful to the end, my dearest Petra," River smirked, picking up a rabbit. A light-hearted hum accompanied her into the darkness alongside three squirrels sitting pretty on the train of her dress.

A moment or so passed with Lily standing in silence.

"You're safe," came Polly's voice. "Hard part over, kinda easy part left."

"Kinda easy?"

"Well, there are three less psychos to get past now, sweet pea. Anyway, I have urgent business to attend to, toodles!"

"Wait!" said Lily desperately. "I need you next to me. I-I can't do this!"

"Oh sweetheart," Polly said with a smile. "Was I ever even here?"

With that, Lily was left in a solitary chaos once more. Taking the advice given, she stepped out and entered the unknown.

From the moment she stepped onto the frigid ground, the sound of classical music dissipated to deathly silence. She stumbled on, arms extended, aching to see where she was. She walked through myriad trees and dead foliage, every breath escaping into the cold moonlit night. A constant disorientation scrambled Lily's brain as she cupped her hands and blew into them for a sliver of heat, desperate to keep her pace steady towards what she hoped was an exit.

A chuckle from the darkness made Lily stop dead in her tracks. A second laugh made her turn once more.

"W-Who's there?" said Lily, her voice shaking in the bitter cold.

"A beautiful little fool, stumbling through the night…" came the voice.

"Show yourself, River! I know it's you!" said Lily.

Her light chuckle echoed through the trees as Lily thought, 'Is this in my head?' Her mind grasped for any shred of logic from within the blackness.

"I'm paralysed with happiness to experience a one-to-one conversation with Belphegor."

River's voice seemed to be everywhere and nowhere at once, a smug smile floating on the cold winter air. Lily was lost in darkness, confusion and a deafening silence, broken only by occasional influxes of air through the trees.

River continued, "I had the honour of meeting your friends! They were simply delicious. You should be quite envious." A self-satisfied laugh echoed through the forest as she spoke. "Don't be afraid, my love. I wish you no harm, really."

Lily stopped, nervously calling out to the darkness, "Really?"

DEBAUCHERY: PART I

"Really, my love. I don't, however, think the same can be said for the fine young gentleman behind you…"

Lily's heart skipped a beat as a hand grabbed her and threw her to the ground. As she hit frost-bitten soil, she screamed and scrambled ahead. She tore through the darkness, frantic whimpers laced in fatigue.

"Run, bitch, and watch out for renovations!" came Noah's voice from far behind her. She continued to run, mind racing and eyes watering.

Without warning, a shot of pain ran up Lily's leg as metal closed around her ankle. Falling to the ground once more, she screamed as the teeth of a beartrap pressed against her flesh. Shaken she froze under the glare of an ugly new experience. She tried to crawl ahead but the trap pulled against her flesh. Through cries of pain, she shuffled forward, tears falling against cold metal as she clumsily learnt her predicament.

"All you have to do is sit still," came a voice she recognised from inside.

"W-Which one are you?" whispered Lily through the intense pain.

"You'll see… Or maybe you won't"

Lily's attention waned as she barely had the energy to sit, let alone converse. She pulled on the trap, prizing it open slightly before losing grip and having its teeth sink back into her flesh once more. Her defeated cry echoed upward.

Noah's laughter could be heard from the distance as Lily felt her swiftly deadening foot. As his voice got closer, she knew her only route was to force the trap open once more. Taking a deep breath, she put every bit of physical strength she had left into pulling the teeth apart once more. Struggling under the pressure she kept going, unable to see the unknown cultist merely watching her from the darkness.

"It's better to die here," he said. "If you end up in the Down Below with me and August, Hell will be nothing…"

"Fuck you," growled Lily through the pain, clasping at the metal teeth.

In a stroke of good luck, she opened it enough to remove her leg from its cruel grip and rest it gently on the dead ground.

"Caught in a trap?" Noah said with a grin.

Lily stayed silent as a small advantage appeared. She moved her leg next to the trap and looked up at her enemy. *I'll look him in the eye even if I see nothing*, she thought, sitting steadfast.

"Our Leader might've let you go, but there are still so many things that need to be done. I am Noah and I have a divine mission from New Truth. We were always trained to kill just any of you lot, but the fact I've got Petra's anti, that's unreal! I won't kill you, 'cos Magnus's will is absolute, but it's my task to tame the beast that sits in your soul. Our Divine Leader said that we should spread the seeds of our wisdom to the world when the time comes. Well, the time has come, so help me God! I got so tired of wasting my juices railing that dumb bitch so I'll just make do with you instead. Any Sin will do!"

Lily screamed as Noah pushed her backwards, mounting her abruptly and placing a hand over her mouth. His body heat pressed against her cold and fragile frame. It was a cruel warmth she yearned to reject. Lily broke down, hopeless tears falling down her face as her body helplessly flailed.

"You can't spread your seed in the wrong one!" said the mystery cult member, frustrated. "She has to be blonde but she has short hair; this is ridiculous and it's most definitely not New Truth! You have to stick to the source material, Noah! You're

DEBAUCHERY: PART I

ruining our legacy!"

"Shut up!" said Noah, trying to unbutton his jeans with his free hand.

Lily screamed again, dirt from his hand pressing against her lip as she lay defenceless in a hopeless world.

Why me? she thought, defeated. All hope lay in thoughts of warmth and safety in a future far from now. She thought of that time and escaping the darkness and pain of this world to a better reality filled with love and protection. She thought of her housemate Heather, the piano in the apartment, of books waiting to be read. *I should've read them...* she thought, her eyes raw from sadness.

It was then that an unknown voice echoed in her head, the intensity of it making her wince. *Lily! You're so much stronger than you think!* The voice crackled but remained familiar and as it spoke, its words danced around her brain. *Out of the seven, you're the strongest. You have the power to make this stop! All you have to do is will it. Please don't give up!*

With every word spoken, it felt as though her mind was vibrating. The unpleasant mental anguish mixed with the hellish physical suffering was too much for Lily, who clasped her eyes shut. She focused her mind as best she could on the words she had just heard. She felt something in her chest, a delicate feeling of warmth between the violence in front of her. Lily focused on this heat as it grew. Her fear faded away and anger emerged. *Yes, like that! You're doing it! Unlock your power!*

Lily's mind was ablaze, and she felt the warmth become pressure. It grew at such a rate she barely had any time to be afraid of it. Lily suddenly disconnected from the pain and hurt of reality and lost herself to this enigmatic pressure. Her fingers twitched for a moment and then again. Her arm spasmed, causing Noah to pause lowering his boxers to look at her. Lily's eyes became white in a single blink. She inhaled, threw a hand over Noah's face and let out a deep, ungodly scream as the immense pressure ran up her arm to burst out of her hand in a shock wave.

A loud crack and a gushing sound came as Lily regained control. The pressure was gone and she felt Noah fall limply on top of her.

"I-Impossible! Oh my God!" The cracking of twigs was heard as the remaining cultist leapt to his feet shouting, "Magnus!" into the night.

Bloodstained and broken from what had happened, Lily took a moment to stare at the sky above. Even in the unending darkness, she could feel the moonlight somehow. The deathly silence returned and a breeze passed through the canopy above. Lily, though confused, took solace in this once-threatening calm. Noah's weight pressed against her chest and she prayed she could just merely vanish and wake up at home.

Upon taking a deep breath, Lily pulled herself up and threw him off her. Her hands sank into something soft and warm, and as she got on all fours she retched. A smell of damp and a thin layer of smoke filled her nostrils, causing Lily to vomit. Holding her breath and with a racing heart, she rose to her feet as best she could. Unbeknownst to her, Lily's hands were bathed in a twisted mixture of blood, dirt, vomit and moonlight. Her face dripped in glistening red brain matter.

Through the pungent distraction of vomit on her breath, Lily limped on. She stepped over chunks of bone and a vile paste falling into cracks of earth.

Every direction seemingly led to nowhere, and as she shuffled

DEBAUCHERY: PART I

past endless trees and hanging metalwork, all seemed lost. It was then that a car horn sounded in the distance and her body turned quickly to follow the noise. She prayed her ears could keep the direction of the noise long enough for her to follow it to safety. Stumbling on twigs and banging against trees, Lily's pace quickened, fuelled purely by survival instinct.

Through red-raw eyes, Lily heard the sound again. She stumbled but scrambled back to her feet; the light getting ever closer. Exhausted, broken and finally free, Lily burst forth from the forest and into the open air. Stumbling onto solid ground, she called out for help towards the sound she had heard only moments ago. The road stood empty in every direction, and she was alone.

A nightmarish reality descended on Lily's aching body as she collapsed to the floor and into painful freedom. Distraught, she lay under the lamppost, her world upside down and her vision infinite darkness. With so many questions answered, her erratic mind jumped to new problems, which had already begun eating away at her psyche.

For a brief flicker of time, Lily cast her mind back to when Magnus asked why she was crying. She knew that she had truly wept for everything as it was all so wholly unfair, but now she cried for friends; she cried for the world and at this harsh juncture, under the cold metal light, Lily cried for herself.

XXIV
BETWEEN THE DEVIL AND THE DEEP BLUE SEA

"Come on, pick up!" Nicky shouted at his phone as he sat in his car joined by Amy and Steph. As Jay picked up, Nicky put his phone on speaker and threw it into Amy's hand as he drove.

"Hey Nicky, how are—"

"—There's no time! Are you at home?"

"Er yes, why? What's up?" said Jay, switching from pleasantries to high alert immediately.

"The photo we took in the garage ended up catching something! It's the sigil of a demon called Surgat. Lily used a demonology app to identify the symbol. Don't go in your garden, for the love of God!"

"Oh, okay… Well, I'm just going to get a shower. Can I do that, or am I not allowed near water?"

Nicky paused and threw a panicked look at Amy, who just shrugged back at him.

"What are you talking about?"

"Well, sometimes demons have requirements like don't go

outside or don't touch water. Shit like that, I dunno!" said Jay.

"Well, from what Lily told us, it could be why your front door was unlocked. It's the 'One Who Opens All Locks', and apparently it can open portals to Hell and the anti-cosmos…"

"The anti-cosmos?"

"Yeah, we didn't know either, but we've come up with a plan. I'm going to drop Amy off at D's hideout so she can get help and I'm going to leave Steph at the hospital so she can sober the fuck up to be with Adrian. Then I'll grab you so we can figure out this demon problem once and for all. After that, we'll reconvene and work out how we're going to break into the Community – hopefully armed with some kind of power or resources. That sound good?"

"Well, sure. I'll have a shower until you get to me, but what about Lily? I thought you said she'd be with you guys tonight?"

"Lily's been captured by the Community. We've spent twenty minutes driving around the entire complex," Amy explained into the phone. "And we drove past that wood too as slow as possible. We even sounded the horn and put ourselves at risk for her, but she's probably still inside. God knows what's happening to her. She could be dead!"

"Or worse…" slurred Steph.

"What's worse than being dead?" snapped Amy.

"Right, okay, well I'll see you soon, Nicky," said Jay.

"I'll message you when I'm outside. See you soon!" said Nicky as he took the phone off speaker before throwing the car back into silence.

"This is really bad," Steph slurred as she stared out of the window, her head bobbing around in a drunken state.

"It's okay. You've got the easiest job, at least. Nothing can happen while you're at a hospital, so I wouldn't worry!" Amy said in the most reassuring voice she was willing to offer.

"Right, let's split up and look for clues!" said Nicky.

Amy laughed. "Oh yeah, in our fucking Moron Machine we can travel the country solving Biblical Allegories."

"You know what I mean!" said Nicky as he drove through the night toward D's hideout.

☨

Jay removed his glasses and jumped in the shower after a long afternoon of watching TV in bed and feeling sorry for himself. As hot water drenched his hair, the cogs in his anxious brain turned over his conversation with Nicky. He slid fingers through his scalp, hoping every negative thought would be pushed into the water and drift down into the plug, never to be seen again. Unsurprisingly, this wasn't the case, and he thought only of the now-known demon occupying his shed.

"The One Who Opens All Locks…" he said to himself as his mind whirred. He stayed in the shower, continuing to think about how he would banish a demon, what it wanted with him, and whether he would be the top or bottom if he and Nicky ever had sex. These three questions bounced around his brain until he was spent and left the warmth of the shower.

He grabbed a towel, dried himself and wrapped it around his waist. Deciding to let his hair drip dry, he left the bathroom in search of a hand towel to wrap around his head, completely oblivious to a symbol of Surgat which had appeared in the steamed-up mirror. He took a fresh hand towel from a chest of draws in his room and wrapped it around his damp blonde curls.

DEBAUCHERY: PART I

A thought entered his mind as he left the room and smiled, whispering to himself, "I'm bisexual." It was odd saying it out loud, as it was something he never thought he'd say. Grabbing his glasses and phone from the bathroom, he put some music on and proceeded downstairs, thinking of all the new and exciting bisexual adventures that awaited him. Despite everything, he was happy. A new relationship beckoned, and this was also the longest time before he'd need a shower again. He'd always hated the mundanity of getting clean. He'd just have to do it again soon after, anyway.

He shuffled into a darkened kitchen adorned with iron nails and padlocks. Humming to himself, Jay removed his towel wrap and started rubbing his hair as he walked towards the fridge. From below, he noticed the temperature rise, completely missing the seven-foot demon standing smiling at him from a table length away. Its eyes glowed the same eerie green, and its body was still deformed and battered by nails. A cheap wooden table in the middle of the room was the only thing separating him from the twisted entity watching him.

Taking the towel away from his head and throwing it aside, he opened the door to the fridge, a clinical white light shining onto his pale skin. Phone in hand, he peered in to see the few remnants of food left over, honing in on a lone slice of strawberry cheesecake resting on a plate with a chilled fork.

"Oh, go on then. Might as well treat myself, seeing as I am... bisexual," Jay said with a smile, reaching in and picking up the plate with pride. He tucked his phone between his fingers underneath and, with a mouthful of cake, shut the door and exclaimed loud and proud, "I. AM. BISEXUAL."

Surgat stood directly in front of him, smiling and breathing heavily.

"BLERGH!" Jay blurted out in shock, spitting a mouthful of cheesecake at the monster who emitted a banshee-like scream and raised its hand to him. Phone falling from his hand, it cracked and landed on shuffle, 'Laura' by The Scissor Sisters blasting from its speakers. Fear-stricken, Jay fell to the floor, his stubble decorated with strawberry jam and biscuit crumbs. With no time to process things, Jay did the only thing he felt he could do: launch the chilled plate of cake gracelessly towards the demon's face. Unsurprisingly, it shattered, and Jay scurried backwards under the table, pressing his back against the kitchen counters.

He clung to the towel around his body as the demon suddenly fell to the floor and crawled under the table after him, its nails scratching the linoleum as it moved. The sudden rise in heat instantly dried Jay's hair into an insane frizz as he pulled himself to his feet and frantically looked for what was immediately at hand. In a panicked frenzy, he grabbed a colander and a wooden spoon from a draining board full of knives.

A charred hand lashed out at Jay's legs from under a dining chair, causing Jay's body to leap aimlessly onto the tabletop. Clambering over and still carrying his weapons of choice, Jay jumped off the table and into the hallway. His mind raced for places to hide and turned to see Surgat pull itself up onto the table from the floor leg-first. Like a disjointed, burnt spider, the demon contorted its body to rise off the floor to the tabletop. It then dropped its torso onto the table with a *thud* and twisted its head to the side, its green eyes piercing Jay from the darkness of the kitchen.

"W-What... do you want?" shouted Jay as he watched Surgat's arm extend to pick up a chair.

"Shit!" he shouted, sticking the colander on his head and

DEBAUCHERY: PART I

crouching down as Surgat hurled it towards him. The chair hit the colander, shattering and launching Jay backwards to the floor. He scrambled to his feet as the monster suddenly leapt off the table and through the air towards him. Taking a mad dash up the stairs, Jay tried to escape, but Surgat grabbed his leg. The scalding iron nails scratched against his ankle, causing Jay to cry out in pain. Pulling against the red-hot grip holding his ankle, he climbed several stairs, desperate to break free. Without warning, Surgat lifted Jay up by his leg with superhuman strength and slammed him against the wall.

"Fuck!" winced Jay as a stab of pain shot up his arm. The colander cushioned his head, but with no time to recover, Surgat lifted Jay again and flung him through the bannister. Within a pile of splintered wood and unlocked padlocks, he arched his back in pain on the hard hallway floor. He looked at a cut on his arm and groaned. Every inch of him felt bruised, and as he clung to his seemingly indestructible towel, he felt at a loss for what to do.

Weakly rolling to one side, he saw the wooden spoon amongst the dining chair wreckage and grabbed it, hoping that anything was better than nothing. He clambered to his feet once again and reached for the colander as Surgat slid around what remained of the bannister and lunged towards him. Jay veered into his bright yellow living room and slammed the door shut.

Battered and winded, Jay threw the colander and wooden spoon onto the sofa, then yanked the coffee table along the carpet and onto its side to create a light barricade against the door. As he moved round to push the first sofa in front of the door, he stepped over the red stain on the carpet, which served as a gloomy reminder of what his life had become. He pushed the sofa, and his towel fell to the floor. Using every bit of strength left in his body, Jay moved both sofas and stuffed several cushions up against the door, all while completely naked.

He stood out of breath and coughed. A stabbing pain in his ribs made him groan. He fumbled for the towel, wrapped it around his waist, and stared at the makeshift barricade. A loud bang against the door made him jump. A second and more forceful bang made him rush to the bay window. The third time was even harder, and he ducked down and fumbled for a bent colander and spoon.

Suddenly, all went quiet. Jay stood up and moved closer, holding his wooden weapon in front of him cautiously. Without warning, the door broke off its hinges as Surgat slammed its entire body weight into it. Surgat's piercing green gaze went directly towards Jay through the remains of Jay's barricade. The demon barged its way through to the living room, and Jay backed up against the bay window, brandishing the wooden spoon at him, colander firmly on head.

"D-Don't make me use this!" Jay stammered as the demon screeched. "Oh shit!" he said, bracing himself as best he could as Surgat lunged forward.

"Oh George, I had such a wonderful evening. I'm sorry I've been so difficult lately. What with the baby on the way, it's hard when my emotions are so up and down."

"It's okay. I understand that this is a trying time for us both, but know that I'm here, and I love you more than anything."

George placed a loving hand on his wife's pregnant belly, and the two walked hand in hand up their almost new garden path. Alice glowed, excited to have the prospect of a tiny human life

DEBAUCHERY: PART I

almost ready to emerge. It had been the perfect romantic evening, and as they reached the front door, Alice said, "You know, you're probably right. Perhaps I was too hard on that young man next door the other day. I mean, these are difficult times, and we all have our problems. Perhaps I was too quick to judge."

"Oh Alice. Make no mistake, you are the most loving person I've met."

"Oh George. I love you so much."

Bathed in the moonlight and radiating the purest love, the couple kissed long and passionately.

Their intense infatuation was cut short as Jay was thrown naked through his bay window. Alice and George fell to the ground in shock, utterly bewildered. Jay struggled to his feet as he painfully hobbled backwards down his front lawn, hair frizzy under a dented colander. With a blood-splattered face, combined with specks of strawberry jam, he brandished the wooden spoon towards his house, shouting, "BACK DEMON! I KNOW YOUR NAME! YOU ARE SURGAT! THE ONE WHO OPENS ALL THE LOCKS AND YOU WILL NOT TAKE MY SOUL TO THE ANTI-COSMOS!"

"I KNEW IT!" Alice seethed, wide-eyed and brandishing a judgemental finger. "Rude, hip-hop, *delinquent* drunkards!"

"The anti-cosmos?" mused George, pulling his wife to her feet.

"Look at him, George!"

"Babe, let's go inside. We can leave him to it," said George, already mourning a lost evening of festive missionary.

☥

With friends dropped off on quests of their own, Nicky began his one-man rescue mission. From the moment his car pulled up onto the edge of Jay's garden, he saw that something was wrong. Looking at his car clock, which read 3am, he stepped out to see the aftermath of something terrible.

"Jay?" he said nervously. "Jay, where are you? We need to get going." He followed a trail of broken glass, following the wreckage to see a house with no lights and no windows. A half-fallen curtain rail sent fabric billowing under a cool breeze, a colourful distress signal from an already broken home. Nicky knocked softly against the front door.

"Jay?"

He knocked again, only for the door to creak open. Nicky walked into the freezing house and looked at a load of unlocked padlocks at his feet. Reaching into his pocket, he turned on his phone torch, clasping it tightly as he stepped over the wreckage of the bannister. As he peeked cautiously into Jay's living room, he saw overturned sofas and broken furniture, surrounded by a cold wind. It was horrible seeing the house, knowing the warm memories he'd had before all of this.

"Please be okay…" Nicky whispered as his heartbeat doubled.

He proceeded to the kitchen, past a broken wooden table and smashed plates. Walking cautiously around the fragments, he looked towards shattered French door windows to see a trail of blood leading out into the garden.

"Shit."

Avoiding it as best he could, he stepped sideways through the gap in the door and followed a trail he hoped would lead to anyone but Jay. From ever-increasingly ominous surroundings, Nicky noticed that the small metal table and chairs were warped as though they had been melted. With a small sliver of smoke rising from them, they created bizarre silhouettes that emerged from the darkness. He looked ahead and saw that within the small red shed was that same pulsating green light.

"Oh Jay... What happened?" he said to himself as every bone in his body told him to leave. Driven by affection for his new friend, Nicky reluctantly made his way onto the damp grass. He strained his ears for any sound he could make out, but there was only silence. He became enveloped in thick darkness, the light of the phone torch being eaten up by its intensity. With a vigilant expression illuminated, Nicky advanced towards the shed and heard a faint banging sound. He gripped his phone tight, hands shaking under nerves and a winter chill.

A distressed wooden door was the one thing between Nicky and the noise. Bracing himself, he clasped the rusting handle, took a deep breath, and threw it open. He bathed the shed in torchlight to see Jay standing completely naked with his back to him. Straining his eyes, Nicky saw his friend was covered in blood and stared. Nails were sunken in a line up Jay's back to form a horrifying iron spine, with blood pouring down between his legs, sinking into the wood below. Every few seconds, one of his limbs would spasm. Sometimes his arm, other times his head, but Nicky knew his friend had to be in there somewhere, regardless.

"Jay..." he said as his friend's head bumped clumsily against the sigil. Nicky jumped, realising that maybe he wasn't talking to his friend at all. He stepped over a fallen rake as Jay repeatedly banged his head against the sigil. "Please don't be a zombie, please don't be a zombie," said Nicky as a shaking arm extended to offer aid.

"Y-Y-you need to come with me," he stammered, placing a hand on Jay's shoulder. It was then that Jay spun around, his face a painful burnt red with skin falling from his cheeks. Glowing green eyes shone a horrible light on nails that sank into his friend's flesh, protruding painfully near his eyes and neck. Nicky immediately turned and ran, but Jay lifted a hand, causing the door to shut in an act of otherworldly telekinesis.

Nicky froze and slowly turned to look back. "J-Jay, you need to come with me! I'm here to t-take you back to mine. To home!"

"We are home..." Jay said blankly, his voice raspy with a demonic layered echo. Backed against the locked wooden door, Nicky's eyes widened in horror as Jay's mouth pulled itself into the same demonic smile he had seen with Surgat, now illuminated in all its ghastly green glory. His teeth were replaced by disjointed small black nails, a black oily liquid dripped from his mouth, and as he ran a fingernail down the side of his face, tearing at the flesh, he spat out, "Invidia." Pointing to the floor, he tilted his head and smiled. "Infernum." Jay then offered a charred laugh before striding forward and knocking a terrified Nicky out with a single punch.

✝

Nicky's world blurred into focus as he regained consciousness in the passenger seat of his green Rolls-Royce. With head pounding, he tried to speak but quickly found he had duct tape over his mouth. Disoriented, he raised his hands to remove it, but they were bound to each side of his seat. He struggled, tugging at his restraints in vain, shouting obscenities into the tape.

"I wondered when you'd wake up," came a distorted version of Jay's voice. Nicky focused on the driver's seat and saw the same possessed version of his friend looking at him. His voice still had the same deep, layered tone to it, and he still bore the same horrific appearance, albeit hiding under a black hoodie.

"How good it feels to have a tongue sitting in my jaw once more." Surgat smiled, instantly reading Nicky's confused expression.

His friend's voice had become a stranger to Nicky, making him feel sick. He turned to the passenger window to look out and saw that they were in his garden. He sent out desperate shouts, but they stayed muffled. He clawed at his restraints, praying he could just fall out of the car and into his safe zone. *It's so close...*

"Forward," croaked Surgat, spitting black ooze over his new body. His lower eyelid flickered as he threw limp hands one by one onto the steering wheel, learning a new body as he went along.

Nicky's eyes widened, and he desperately tried talking through the tape, hoping his words would be heard.

"Truly joyous to feel myself crawling around under your friend's rotten flesh," spat the demon through ruptured vocal cords. Every sentence seemed thrilling yet exhausting.

Nicky tugged at his restraints, frantically shouting incoherently as Surgat pulled out of the street clunkily. As the car entered a main road, Nicky racked his brain as to where exactly they could possibly go. With every thought, there seemed to be a stab of pain, and as Nicky looked at his hands, there was bruising. His hangover had been replaced with assault. Heart racing, he turned back to Surgat and mumbled something, messy brown hair falling over his face.

"I can hear your boy crying from the dirt," grinned Surgat, black ooze falling from his jaw and over the steering wheel. "His insides were already rotten from envy; I merely feast on the carcass."

Surgat laughed, revelling in every horrible moment he created as Nicky continued to pull frantically against his restraints.

"How does it feel to be the last thing he saw?" Surgat whispered, black ooze dripping from an open jaw.

Nicky huffed from under the tape, eyes watering at both his nemesis and his crush. All he could do was watch and listen.

"The first man he loved is the last love he had," Surgat coughed, the force tearing through his rotting throat. "He didn't love Adrian. He wanted to be Adrian. When Adrian fell, he wanted you. Not envy, though. Love. It was this weakness that made it so easy to climb into his flesh."

A super-cut of their drunken night out played in Nicky's mind. They had felt so alive and so happy at that moment. A flame had been created. Indefinable, fresh, exciting, an adventure, only to be snuffed out.

"Jay may be gone, but he won't be forgotten…"

Nicky's eyes welled at this information, his mind struggling to cope with what was happening as the car sped up. Surgat reached over to remove the tape with a single pull.

"I want to hear your voice scratch your throat from the screaming as we sink into Hell."

Surgat laughed as all Nicky could do was stare, speechless. A tear fell from his eye as his mind cracked trying to process this reality. Surgat looked at him and grinned. With blood oozing from his charred jaw and eyes rolling back in his skull for a moment, he croaked, "Forward…" and increased the car's speed further. "Last words, mortal."

"Why are you doing this? After everything!" Nicky sobbed, defeated. "Is there anything I could've done differently?"

Surgat formed another demented smile and laughed. "Oh Nicholas. If only you'd have used more teeth. Perhaps you'd have

DEBAUCHERY: PART I

been memorable..."

"Fuck!" shouted Nicky desperately, a crack in his voice as he spoke. He looked out the window at a blurred world as the car turned onto a sloped road. He was hit by the realisation that there was a river at the end of this road. Nicky glanced at Surgat, who nodded before slamming his foot on the accelerator.

"FUCK!" Nicky exclaimed again, flailing and banging his head on the window, desperately attempting to attract outside attention. The car went faster and faster, whizzing by a school, through a red light and swerving past random drivers who were up early.

"Don't worry. While unconscious, I put some goods in the trunk. I even emptied your bank account. Your abode is ruined and you're penniles. You are, however, permitted to bring whatever fragmented baggage your mind holds to your grave."

Surgat beamed like a proud parent, blood falling between the gaps of his iron teeth. Nicky felt lightheaded from what he'd just heard and the path ahead. The car tore down the road, racing through a final red light before flying out into an open area.

"N-NO! NO! NO!" Nicky shouted as the car reached the river's edge at break-neck speed. The vintage green car bumped up the curb, onto a small stretch of pavement, then over a small wooden pier.

"AVARITIA! INVIDIA! INFERNUM AETERNUM!" screamed Surgat.

Struggling to breathe through panic and fear, Nicky thought of Ethan, of Jay, Amy, and of his family as the car hurled itself off solid ground. Surgat let go of the steering wheel and grabbed Nicky tight with his left hand as the car hit the river, throwing them against the dashboard and knocking them out instantly.

The car slowly filled with water, an unconscious shadow of Jay holding the arm of the first man he'd ever loved. The boot of the car had warped and fallen open. Nicky's material possessions floated upward through murky water as Nicky's cracked phone screen flickered with a time of 6:66 am.

XXV
DEVIL'S DUE

Amy walked past the neon glow of a takeaway as she inadvertently joined the flap and furore of a Christmas-themed hen party. Hidden amongst the fizz-fuelled pandemonium, Amy scoured the tinsel-strewn path ahead for her exit point.

"Cheer up, love, it might never happen!" slurred a middle-aged woman, slamming fluffy pink devil horns into Amy's hair.

Determined to ignore any and all distractions, she continued on, throwing a fake smile into the small group for extra measure. After a small eternity of listening to them laugh at nothing, Amy disbanded from the group, her eyes casting a wish of divorce proceedings upon the bride. She turned into the dark alley, checking to make sure she wasn't being followed. Her eyes adjusted to the sudden dark and, as all the colour and commotion of the city centre tapered away into stillness, Amy approached a familiar sight.

A skip with an ever-expanding pile of rubbish around it (and newly added furry horns) caused Amy to cast her mind back to her clueless first time here. She still felt so powerless dealing with all that was happening, and she hated it. Clenching her fists at the frustration of being no better off, she pushed the rusting skip aside, creating an unbearable metal scrape. Amy whipped out her phone to text Nicky and Steph.

At D's hideout. I'll be as quick as I can x

She sighed and put her phone away. Rubbing her hands together, Amy then pulled the door open, creating a metal din. She was presented with the same ominous strip lighting as before, only this time she ran forward, armed with the knowledge of what lay ahead. As the door slid shut, she moved black hair from her face.

I'm not leaving without answers.

✝

Steph sat ready to reply to Amy's text, but as she looked at her friend, still mysteriously unconscious, she refrained. Her eyes watered at the sight of Adrian. It was weird, and her heart broke.

"I miss your voice…" she whispered, taking his hand. "That's what makes this so difficult. I can remember all the things we did together, but I haven't heard your voice in so long. It's what I miss most."

Steph held back tears, still in a tired angel fancy dress. "They told me that you might still be able to hear and you might know stuff that's going on. I hope that you can only see what's going on in this room, though. Things are bad outside and… I need you. I need you to tell me things are going to be alright and that all of us will come out of this okay."

Steph wiped her now-runny nose with her arm, bathing in a naïve hope that her bright blue eyes could revive him. Adrian, however, just lay there surrounded by tubes and wires. The only other time she had heard a heartbeat on a machine was when

DEBAUCHERY: PART I

she watched medical dramas with her mother. It had always fascinated her that a machine could read something inside a person and record it.

"I like your heartbeat..." she said with a smile. "It shows me you're still here. I just... need you. There are these really bad people after us, and they're real. It's all real, Adrian! I think they put you in this bed somehow! You need to be in your own bed! You're the only person who's been there for me through thick and thin. I-I can't be alone again..."

Forlorn, Steph reached for a pack of tissues from a table at his side. As she sobbed into it, she prayed that her crying would make him spring up and ask her what was wrong.

"When Noah left me, I was alone. Then when Noah came back like this monster, I felt more alone somehow. But you were always there. You were there before all of this and before we met all of these new people. You're stronger than me and you're the one that's here. It doesn't make any sense because I'm... I'm the weak one."

Sobering up with every passing breath, Steph threw herself over Adrian dramatically, a drunken angel wailing for normality. She wept for the life that had died, unable to imagine what trials lay ahead.

"I just want you to wake up..." she said, blubbing into his chest.

A sudden wave of determination flooded her as she jumped to her feet and pushed back the tears.

"It's okay! I'll be the strong one until you wake up again!" Steph smiled weakly, gripping Adrian's arm. She paced back and forth in the room for a while, staring up at the clinical lighting.

A short, elderly nurse opened the door suddenly, making Steph jump.

"Are you okay, my love?" she asked, a warm expression on her face.

"I-I'm okay, I just... I just wanted to spend some time with him. Is that okay? I know you have visiting hours, but can I have some more time?"

The woman smiled softly. "Take as long as you need, sweetheart," she said, as all the lights in Adrian's room flickered for a moment.

Steph reached down to a bottle of water she'd forgotten about, which had sunk into her chair. She gulped it down, realising how dehydrated she had become.

It was then that the nurse spoke up once more. "Can I ask sweetheart; did you ever notice anything strange about your friend here when you last saw him?"

Steph looked up at the woman before casting her gaze back over Adrian. "Umm, no. I haven't noticed anything. Why, what's wrong?"

The nurse looked tired but her warm smile remained. "We've found that he had a few minor issues upon admission. It's nothing serious, but I have to ask if you or your friends noticed anything untoward about his behaviour before he came here?"

Steph's heartbeat quickened as she whispered, "Is he okay?"

"Of course, sweetheart. We just need to run some more tests. The main thing is that the antidote is working and we can focus on the rest at a later time."

"What do you mean 'the rest'? There's nothing else wrong with him! If there was, I'd know because he wouldn't keep it from me! We had no secrets!" said Steph, frustrated. "What else is wrong?"

The nurse walked to a clipboard at the foot of the bed.

DEBAUCHERY: PART I

Upon flicking through the notes, she said, "I've just doubled-checked but we found that he has hypotension and an electrolyte imbalance. As I said, minor issues, lovely, but they can point to a few things."

Steph stared blankly, racking her brain for a simplified translation of the medical jargon to no avail. "I don't understand…"

"Try not to worry, petal. This is the best place for him right now. I've got to move on but if you need any of us for anything, just let us know."

Slumping back into the chair Steph looked ahead through glazed eyes, whispering, "Okay."

Alone with her friend once more, Steph's booze-fuelled night seemed an age ago. Tilting her head towards him, she saw his heartbeat on the monitor and stared at his face long and hard. With all that had happened, she couldn't believe there was something that pre-dated it all. Even when things were normal, he kept her in the dark. He had a secret and, as the hospital got closer to the answer, he lay powerless to stop them. As Steph looked at Adrian, she concluded her friend lay in a hospital bed, but whoever would wake up after would be someone she didn't know at all.

☩

Amy stood in front of the ornate wooden door to Deontay's hideout and called Steph's number on her phone. She impatiently waited for it to connect from within the miserable corridor, but it went to voicemail.

"Why ignore me at a time like this, you idiot?" Amy said, hanging up and calling Nicky only to be taken straight to a second answer machine. Amy erupted as quietly as possible.

"For Christ's sake, why would you turn your phone off? Where is everyone?" she said angrily before shoving the phone back into her pocket. Staring at a family crest etched into the door, Amy took a deep breath before reaching out to grab the doorknob.

Striding inside, Amy wasn't greeted by the same warmth as before. The room was darkened, and the fireplace housed embers, leaving a slight glow. A small trail of smoke loomed up to the ceiling, drifting away from the scene on the floor.

Amy fumbled to retrieve her phone and flicked the torch light on. The harsh white light illuminated the aftermath of a fight as she panned it around the room.

Four of six gigantic bookcases lay broken over an end table. All the contents they once held were blackened and scattered. The sofas were upside down in the middle of the room with torn fabric and missing legs. A charred Persian rug soaked up the sad remains of vintage whiskeys cast from their cabinet.

Amy stepped forward, only to stand on a painting of a Deontay ancestor. The frame was broken, and the picture torn in half. As Amy stared ahead, a legacy lay in ruin. A noise came from underneath a bookshelf ahead.

"Who's there?" said Amy, now on high alert. A groan came from within a pile of blackened books. She moved over a sofa and crossed a graveyard of shattered glass and fabric to the back of the room. She bathed the bookshelf in torchlight and saw the bloodied body of Deontay lying trapped underneath.

"D!" Amy yelled, lunging forth. She made an attempt to lift the bookshelf, but Deontay cried out in pain. She placed her phone on the floor, the torch illuminating the fresco above, and knelt next to him to hold his hand from within the pocket of light.

DEBAUCHERY: PART I

"Who did this?" she asked, knowing full well what the answer would be.

Wincing in pain, he said wearily, "The Community, the bad folks. They wanted to take all the informationals from Ol' Deontay, but the joke's on them."

Amy felt enraged as every answer she needed lay dying in front of her. "Look, we'll get you out of here and we'll make them all fucking pay!"

"It's too late for Ol' Deontay. It's not too late for Satan and folks, though. Y-You need to stop them. You need to stop them all. Here, take this. She'll know what to do! She'll help all of you folks!"

Deontay coughed as he handed Amy an envelope made from parchment. Amy took it and looked at the words 'DEAREST WARRIORS' in calligraphy. She flipped it over to see a royal green wax seal with a peacock symbol stamped on it.

"What the hell is this?"

Deontay groaned in pain, saying, "Find Lady D. F.! She is two of the three! Ol' Deontay is but one! They looked for the informationals here, but there was never anything! All the books and scribblings here are fakes! I destroyed everything I showed you folks." He chuckled, coughing blood onto a ruined suit. "Lady D. F. has them! Countless informationals! She always did! Find her, find D. F.!"

Exasperated, Amy groaned, "There's more? I don't want any more fucking riddles! None of us do! We didn't ask for this! We don't want any of this! Why does it have to be us?"

"This is only the beginning. We are just pawns in a game larger than we folks can comprehend. It's deeper than all of us!"

Pushing aside her need to scream, Amy squeezed his hand, struggling to say anything caring, but showing she was there, nonetheless. Deontay then abruptly lifted his head and pointed weakly towards the entrance. "Praise be!"

Amy grabbed the phone and squinted to see the figure of Polly skipping jovially into view, arms behind her back.

"And from the darkness there is light," she said cheerily.

"You!" Amy shouted as Polly joyfully walked over a broken family legacy, glass cracking with every step. "Where the fuck have you been all this time?"

Polly chuckled, tossing her hair over her shoulder. "Well I'm a busy bee, to be honest. I always have things to do!"

"Gloriana!" Deontay yelled from under the rubble.

"You knew about Surgat, didn't you? Why didn't you tell us? Why didn't you get rid of it, for Christ's sake!" Amy shouted, springing to her feet.

"Well, where's the fun in that?" grinned Polly, stepping onto the fallen bookcase, making Deontay cry out in pain. "I wonder if he ended up opening *every* lock, hmm?" Her eyes flickered gleefully.

"You fucking bitch!" said Amy, lunging towards Polly who merely laughed and jumped to a different bookshelf. "The amount of pain this has caused us! The nights we've spent awake! When does it end? When do we get the fucking answers we need to stop this?"

"Isn't it all so delicious?" Polly said with a grin, walking up the diagonal bookshelf to sit on top. "Adrian's little secret nearly out in the open, two missing in action, two confused, one broken, and one yet to be found. You complain now but don't you just love the drama?"

"Ugh!" said Amy as a shot of rage flew around her body.

"May she reign forever!" spluttered Deontay through

DEBAUCHERY: PART I

bloodied lips.

"Ah yes, Deontay. You've done amazingly amazing, you absolute gem!" Polly said, playfully swinging her legs from the bookshelf.

"Why aren't you doing anything? He's dying!" Amy shouted.

"Oh, pish, Satan! Do you think I don't already know that? I'm here to say goodbye to him and pay my respects."

Deontay looked upward, straining his eyes through the darkness to see Polly under the harsh white torchlight. Amy looked at him and then to Polly, who simply threw a smile and a wave in their direction.

"Oh my God!" Deontay exclaimed, eyes watering alongside a bloodied smile. "Can it be true? Did Ol' Deontay do his duty? Truly so?"

"What the fuck?" shouted Amy, completely flummoxed. "What duty? You better tell me who you are right now, or so help me God I'll finish you off myself! I'm tired of games, I'm tired of puzzles, cards and letters! Just give me my fucking answers, *now!*"

Polly laughed, gleefully clapping her hands, exclaiming, "And this isn't even her final form!" Her eyes flickered devilishly as Deontay lay crying with happiness.

"Is it really you, my queen?" he sobbed.

Polly pulled out a bright red lipstick and a compact. As she applied it, she pursed her lips and said, "Totes."

Amy looked up to Polly, taking a step towards her, saying, "What... *are* you?"

Polly snapped her compact shut, irked. "As if you haven't figured it out yet, you clueless woman!"

Before Amy could retort, Deontay spoke up, wincing in pain

once more. "She is the all and the everything! THE NIGHT AND BEYOND! She is all that lies below, she is glory, she must be praised and worshipped by all! Ol' Deontay has completed his task! He was the deliverer, and he heard your voice previously, my lady! I am but a peon, chosen to verbalise the message over and over again throughout time immemorial. I am one of the three messengers! In this life, I served the darkness, and YOU ARE MY DARK GODDESS!"

As Deontay's passionate speech drew to a close, every ounce of colour drained from Amy as she stood dumbstruck. "Does what he's saying mean what I think he's saying?"

Polly grinned, tilting her head and slowly raised her arms as though crucified.

"A-Are you the Devil?"

"FOOLISH MORTAL!" Deontay shouted. "Her name transcends language! She is the Deceiver, the Accuser, the Destroyer of Worlds. She is the Angel of the Bottomless Pit, Her Infernal Majesty, she is… APOLLYON!"

Deontay laughed, tears streaming from his eyes as a glowing green pentagram appeared on his forehead. It shone bright, and he yelled in searing pain as blood ran down his face from it.

"What the fuck?" Amy yelped, falling to the floor and clinging to the mysterious letter for dear life.

Polly jumped off the bookcase as Amy scurried backwards, pressing her back up against the wall as hard as she could. Throwing a cheerful smile towards Amy, she moved to stand over her former employee.

"Oh Deontay…" Polly chuckled as the pentagram's glow faded into darkness, "what have I told you about using my Christian name?"

XXVi
PROVERBS 14:30

*I*n a darkened courtyard, 'Moonlight Sonata (1st Movement)' by Beethoven echoed from small overhead speakers. Snow fell over five gravestones sunk into frozen earth. Wax dripped down candlesticks which cast a delicate flicker of light around seven metal thrones forming a circle.

Dressed in white cowls, six members of the Community Under New Truth stared at the huge metalwork of their cult insignia in in the centre of the courtyard. Magnus sat in a chair slightly taller than the rest, a steel crown of thorns resting on his head from under his hood. A metal mask covered his face and his fingers were adorned with various rings. Magnus spoke, his voice masculine yet affirming.

"Shall we begin?"

Six holy books were raised in the air as the group opened their gathering once more.

"This is New Truth, and New Truth speaks to me. New Truth sees my weakness and New Truth sees my strength. On this day, my eyes open, my heart listens, and my soul flows free. We grow today in New Truth's name. God bless us all."

After a small pause, Magnus spoke, his tone sombre and

firm. "We have reached the precipice, and the end is near. The Debauchery has been awakened and we must now use our full force."

The five other figures nodded under their hoods, with twisted smiles forming as their Leader's words echoed towards a dark winter sky.

"First, I want to address my own failure. I was overcome by Sin and countered the very virtues we embody."

The group shook their heads with immediate protests at the thought that their Leader could say such things.

"It is true, my friends. I became overcome with sloth, sitting silent and still as you did our fine work. I should've done more and offer myself to you for judgement."

"We could never judge you, Blessed Magnus!" said River, picking up one of many rabbits that surrounded her. "You are our Father, our teacher. You are Humility itself, and it'd be oh so wrong to judge when we are all guilty of walking in Sin!"

A smile formed from behind the mask. "Thank you, dearest River. Your words are a great boon to me and to New Truth. If I may move forward, I'd like to spend some time giving praise. Firstly, I'd like to congratulate our very own Liberality for poisoning Beelzebub. Who else but River would think to transfer such a pox through something as simple as a handshake? The fool could never have seen it coming."

River smiled weakly, staring at the floor as she whispered, "Thank you, Humility."

"I further want to congratulate Liberality for summoning the demon Surgat through ritualistic intent. Your wounds are an impressive scar towards the greater good and these efforts will not go unnoticed."

DEBAUCHERY: PART I

River stared at her palms, rubbing fresh bandages as she continued to stare towards the floor in silence.

"I congratulate Patience for tearing through the unholy Messenger's hideout within a single hour. This evil Oracle will have passed by now. Chace, your loyalty to New Truth shines bright. I hereby give you permission to complete all further duties however you wish."

"Cheers Humility," said Chace with a smirk, pulling knuckle dusters from his pocket, his eyepatch still firmly in place.

"I congratulate Diligence for being the perfect distraction and allowing us to abduct Belphegor. Long may you alienate these simple souls."

"'Let the peace of Christ rule in your hearts, since as members of one body you were called to peace. And be thankful'. Colossians 3:15."

"Er, yes... I congratulate Kindness for her tireless efforts in the Down Below. The dark web has gifted you the identity of Asmodeus and for that, I applaud you. Amazing work, dear August."

"Eek! Going live real soon!" beamed August, who wore a pair of turquoise cat-eared headphones over the hood of her cowl. As she clapped, pastel pink hair revealed itself from under her hood in the excitement.

"I now wish to address Chastity. Is everything going to plan? Have we identified the remaining Messengers?"

Chastity remained silent, several closed laptops and half a protein shake resting at the side of his cold metal chair.

"Nate, I address you. Is everything going to plan in the Down Below?"

"I found one but not the other." said Nate, swinging a

microphone in front of verified lips. "Actually, hypothetically speaking, I think that it's to our advantage. With the news that Chace gave us, it could be said that the second Messenger would be so hard to find without help that they'll never find them. The third Messenger has no trail. It's dead, Humility. I can't find them anywhere and let's be real, if I can't, they won't!"

Magnus placed his hands together in thought. He took a deep breath and said, "Thank you, Chastity. Despite what could be seen as lacklustre effort, you have done well. Upon destroying the one we know of; it removes any path the Debauchery seeks to create. This is good."

A single tear fell from Nate's face as he whispered, "Thank you, Humility."

"I must now speak of the incident in the forest," said Magnus, renewed grandeur in his tone. Six faces turned to a vacant metal throne as he continued.

"Let this abandoned placement serve as a reminder to all that these sinners cannot be underestimated. They are reckless and cause chaos in their wake. Through Chastity we have known that Temperance's death was but for the greater good. Noah had but a single task and, though he put years of work into said task, it was squandered in the final moments. But yet, we have seen how truly powerful these unholy creatures can be. One spirit is broken because of our dearest Temperance, it's true, but he is not truly gone. His work on the university roof shall not be ignored. A failed attempt but a marksman nontheless, worthy of a chance at redemption. Until that day, we remain blessed by the spirit of the Lord Jesus Christ and await the Decisive Battle!"

The deafening silence was broken as the group broke into rapturous applause.

DEBAUCHERY: PART I

"We cast our minds back to Those Who Came Before." Magnus beckoned to the gravestones they surrounded. "They fought the Unholy Seven, cast out evil and saved the world from annihilation. We say their names so they never die. Ariel, Miranda, Oberon, Titania and Umbriel. These are the five of the Holy Seven who emerged victorious. Remember them always."

The group spoke immediately and in unison: "Ariel, Miranda, Oberon, Titania and Umbriel. Remember them always."

"A war is coming, my Benevolence, and we must win!" said Magnus, raising his arms as his voice echoed into the night. "If we lose, our world shall fall and we simply cannot allow that! We must commit all of our energy and resources to dispatch this filth quickly! No longer shall we work in the shadows, creeping in shame. We shall use every power we have to wipe this menace from the face of the Earth and be proud in our distribution of justice!

"Tonight, is the beginning of the end! Let the Decisive Battle commence! Faith without works is dead!"

"Faith without works is dead!"

"Faith without works is dead!"

"Faith without works is dead!"

"Faith without works is dead!"

"Faith without works is dead!"

IT STARTS WITH:

DEBAUCHERY

PART I

PRIDE

GLUTTONY

ENVY

IT ENDS WITH:

DEBAUCHERY

PART II

GREED

LUST

SLOTH

WRATH

ACKNOWLEDGEMENTS

EVELYN TAYLER – For being my hero and encouraging my creativity since day one. I love you.

WENDY & STEPHEN BRAMLEY – For accepting, supporting and helping me through difficulties both personal and creative. I couldn't have have had better parents. I love you both.

DAVE HINCH – For holding my hand for so many years. You were there when the words 'I am a writer' were scary and you were there when I finished it. I cherish the time I got to spend with your weirdness and warmth. I like to think that there's a universe with a version of us that reached every goal and did all the things. They're badass and I'm happy for them. This wouldn't exist without your support and I'm so excited for people to meet the insane character we made for the sequel. You're every barman bar one. Know your value!

DOMINIC WAKEFORD – For being the best editor I could've asked for! Your patience and knowledge were invaluable. I learnt so much both from you and how you edited my work. I'm a better writer because of you so thank you.

CARLY (JACK) COULTAS – My Busty St. Claire and critique partner. Our friendship can be bizarre and I'm so happy I could use that as the base for Nicky and Amy's. Seeing 'us' in those characters makes them endlessly entertaining to me and a joy to write. Long may we live in that immediate uncomfortable weirdness from that time you booped my dick in Preston (and no, I can't put the part where Adrian becomes curious about eating fucking catfood. It was lost during editing and my editor had to read that, twat!)

AREK POWALISZ – For being font angel. Learning to format the book crucified me but you were there for me, regardless. Our fleeting chats about serifs, aesthetic and spacing were packed with value. So thank you. Big slay bby.

GREG HOWARD JR – For putting up with my bullshit! You're my font of knowledge and podcasting wizard. Your patience with my silly boi questions is so appreciated. Thank you for keeping a watchful eye over me as I made my covers. I bow to your skills king.

SOPH FLETCHER – For being beta reader extraordinaire. You're as obsessive over my writing as me and I love you for it. You were the first one to deep dive into the character's psychology and saw my babies as such. It's so valuable and I adore you! Long may we babble and end up down online Communism rabbitholes.

ROB MAY – For being ultimate hun. Thanks for being long-suffering listener number one. Thank you for being my hype man during marketing. You were as excited as me for its release! I've made you the only 'not Dave' bartender as a reward. Ar Di would be proud. Shantay, you stay xoxo

TOM WALKER – For the nights now antiquity. I spent my twenties rambling on at you about God, the Devil, and plot structure, only to be met with positivity. Honestly, those nights you gave up for me, I could feel the creativity in the room. I'd never felt so energised than when we met to 'talk book'. Those times may be gone but they're not forgotten.

KATIE LIMBRICK – For being beta reader and my first fan! Thank you for loving the story during a time where I wasn't sure if what I'd written was even any good. I'll never forget your sheer fury at the cliffhanger ending haha! Thank you!

IzzyWalsh + NatalieMainprize – Yes, you two! For being the online cheer team! Whenever I reached a milestone with my writing, you both reacted to my Insta and sent comments/DMs. None of this was weird or awkward, you just did to engage, support and be present. Please understand the value that has, when writing can be so solitary so thank you to both of you! Equally!

LEE JAQUES – For being my long term silent support and reluctant ear. You were there for my first step in marketing and it meant the world that I didn't have to do it alone. This information has been acknowledged, Britishly and shall be logged into the system for the next business day (the milk in the staff fridge is out of date btw).
enter Steve Smith 'uHhuNhhH' noise for prosperity

ANDY GREEN – For the support and having the name I want to claim as my own. You can sit next to me back here bbz. You blew air through your nose when you read my shit Chapter 5 in 2014 and probably don't remember… But I do! That was enough to know my humour could translate to my writing so thank you! It was daunting as fuck to start writing comedy as it's so subjective. Thank you for giving this funny guy the confidence to be a funny writer. You're an absolute gem.

ME – We fucking did it!!!!!!!!!

Everyone above is awesomesauce. Anyone below is not mentioned

APPENDIX

Music

pg. 14 - '99 Red Balloons' (1983) - Nena.

pg. 25 - 'Fuck Me Pumps' (2004) - Amy Winehouse.

pg. 58 - 'Have I The Right? (1964) - The Honeycombs.

pg. 88 - 'Without You' (1994) - Mariah Carey.

pg. 91 - 'It's All Coming Back To Me Now (1996) - Céline Dion.

pg.103 - 'Spice Up Your Life' (1997) - The Spice Girls.

pg. 128 - 'Girls Just Want To Have Fun' (1983) - Cyndi Lauper

pg. 148 - 'The Pretender' (2007) - Foo Fighters.

pg. 152 - 'Californication' (2000) - Red Hot Chili Peppers.

pg. 157 - 'Air from Orchestral Suite 3' (1730) - J. S. Bach.

pg. 164 - 'Danger! High Voltage' (2002) - Electric Six.

pg. 184 - 'Hit That' (2003) - The Offspring.

pg. 187 - 'Coconuts' (2021) - Kim Petras.

pg. 203 - 'Sick Sick Sick' (2007) - Queens of the Stone Age.

pg. 210 - 'Talking To The Moon' (2011) - Bruno Mars

pg. 211 - 'Bring Him Home' (1980) - Les Misérables

pg. 280- 'Plug In Baby' (2001) - Muse

pg. 308 - 'Standing In The Way Of Control' (2005) - The Gossip

pg. 316 - 'Take Me Out' (2004) - Franz Ferdinand

pg. 318 - 'When You Were Young' (2006) - The Killers

pg. 321 - 'Flux' (2005) - Bloc Party

pg. 325 - 'Love On Top' (2011) - Beyoncé

pg. 329 - 'Deeper Shade of Blue' (2000) - Steps
pg. 335 - 'Judas' (2011) - Lady Gaga
pg. 342 - 'Für Elise' (1868) - Beethoven
pg. 350 - 'Treasure Waltz' (1885) - Strauss
pg. 363 - 'Laura' (2003) - Scissor Sisters
pg. 384 - 'Moonlight Sonata (1st Movement) (1802) - Beethoven

Song Lyrics

pg. 339 - Judas (2011) - Lady Gaga (Stefani Germanotta, Nadir Khayat

Movies

pg. 92 - The Notebook (2004)
pg. 303 - Mad Max: Fury Road (2015)